The Ghost Stories of
Edith Wharton

The Ghost Stories of Edith Wharton

Illustrated by Laszlo Kubinyi

Charles Scribner's Sons
New York

Contents

The Ghost Stories of Edith Wharton

Preface

"Do you believe in ghosts?" is the pointless question often addressed by those who are incapable of feeling ghostly influences to —I will not say the *ghost-seer*, always a rare bird, but—the *ghost-feeler*, the person sensible of invisible currents of being in certain places and at certain hours.

The celebrated reply (I forget whose): "No, I don't believe in ghosts, but I'm afraid of them," is much more than the cheap paradox it seems to many. To "believe," in that sense, is a conscious act of the intellect, and it is in the warm darkness of the prenatal fluid far below our conscious reason that the faculty dwells with which we apprehend the ghosts we may not be endowed with the gift of seeing. This was oddly demonstrated the other day by the volume of ghost stories collected from the papers of the late Lord Halifax by his son. The test of the value of each tale lay, to the collector's mind, not in the least in its intrinsic interest, but in the fact that someone or other had been willing to vouch for the authenticity of the anecdote. No matter how dull, unoriginal and unimportant the tale—if someone had convinced the late Lord Halifax that it was "true," that it "had really happened," in it went; and can it be only by accident that the one story in this large collection which is even faintly striking and memorable is the one with an apologetic footnote to the effect that the editor had not been able to trace it to its source?

Sources, as a matter of fact, are not what one needs in judging a ghost story. The good ones bring with them the internal proof of their ghostliness; and no other evidence is needed. But since first I dabbled in the creating of ghost stories, I have made the depressing discovery that the faculty required for their enjoyment has become almost atrophied in modern man. No one ever expected a Latin to understand a ghost, or shiver over it; to do that, one must still have in one's ears the hoarse music of the northern Urwald or the churning of dark seas on

1

the outermost shores. But when I first began to read, and then to write, ghost stories, I was conscious of a common medium between myself and my readers, of their meeting me halfway among the primeval shadows, and filling in the gaps in my narrative with sensations and divinations akin to my own.

I had curious evidence of the change when, two or three years ago, one of the tales in the present volume made its first curtsy in an American magazine. I believe most purveyors of fiction will agree with me that the readers who pour out on the author of the published book such floods of interrogatory ink pay little heed to the isolated tale in a magazine. The request to the author to reveal as many particulars as possible of his private life to his eager readers is seldom addressed to him till the scattered products of his pen have been collected in a volume. But when "Pomegranate Seed" (which I hope you presently mean to read) first appeared in a magazine, I was bombarded by a host of inquirers anxious, in the first place, to know the meaning of the story's title (in the dark ages of my childhood an acquaintance with classical fairy lore was as much a part of our stock of knowledge as Grimm and Andersen), and secondly, to be told *how a ghost could write a letter, or put it into a letterbox*. These problems caused sleepless nights to many correspondents whose names seemed to indicate that they were recent arrivals from unhaunted lands. Need I say there was never a Welsh or a Scottish signature among them? But in a few years more perhaps there may be; for, deep within us as the ghost instinct lurks, I seem to see it being gradually atrophied by those two world-wide enemies of the imagination, the wireless and the cinema. To a generation for whom everything which used to nourish the imagination because it had to be won by an effort, and then slowly assimilated, is now served up cooked, seasoned and chopped into little bits, the creative faculty (for reading should be a creative act as well as writing) is rapidly withering, together with the power of sustained attention; and the world which used to be so *grand à la charté des lampes* is diminishing in inverse ratio to the new means of spanning it; so that the more we add to its surface the smaller it becomes.

All this is very depressing to the ghost-story purveyor and his publisher; but in spite of adverse influences and the conflicting attractions of the gangster, the introvert and the habitual drunkard, the ghost may hold his own a little longer in the hands of the experienced chronicler. What is most to be feared is that these seers should fail; for frailer than the ghost is the wand of his evoker, and more easily to be broken in the hard grind of modern speeding-up. Ghosts, to make themselves manifest, require two conditions abhorrent to the modern mind: silence and continuity. Mr. Osbert Sitwell informed us the other day that ghosts went out when electricity came in; but surely this is to misapprehend the nature of the ghostly. What drives ghosts away is not the aspidistra or the electric cooker; I can imagine them more wistfully haunting a mean house in a dull street than the battlemented castle with its boring stage properties. What the ghost really needs is not echoing passages and hidden doors behind tapestry, but only continuity and silence. For where a ghost has once appeared it seems to hanker to appear again; and it obviously prefers the silent hours, when at last the wireless has ceased to jazz. These hours, prophetically called "small," are in fact continually growing smaller; and even if a few diviners keep their wands, the ghost may after all succumb first to the impossibility of finding standing room in a roaring and discontinuous universe.

It would be tempting to dwell on what we shall lose when the wraith and the fetch are no more with us; but my purpose here is rather to celebrate those who have made them visible to us. For the ghost should never be allowed to forget that his only chance of survival is in the tales of those who have encountered him, whether actually or imaginatively—and perhaps preferably the latter. It is luckier for a ghost to be vividly imagined than dully "experienced"; and nobody knows better than a ghost how hard it is to put him or her into words shadowy yet transparent enough.

It is, in fact, not easy to write a ghost story; and in timidly offering these attempts of mine I should like to put them under the protection of those who first stimulated me to make the experiment. The earliest, I believe, was Stevenson, with "Thrawn Janet" and "Markheim"; two remarkable ghost stories, though far from the high level of such wizards as Sheridan Le Fanu and Fitz James O'Brien. I doubt if these have ever been surpassed, though Marion Crawford's isolated effort, "The Upper Berth," comes very near to the crawling horror of O'Brien's "What Is It?"

For imaginative handling of the supernatural no one, to my mind, has touched Henry James in "The Turn of the Screw"; but I suppose a ghost novel can hardly be classed among ghost stories, and that tale in particular is too individual, too utterly different from any other attempt to catch the sense of the supernatural, to be pressed into the current categories.

As for the present day, I have ventured to put my own modest "omnibus" under the special protection of the only modern ghost evoker whom I place in the first rank—and this dispenses with the need of saying why I put him there.* Moreover, the more one thinks the question over, the more one perceives the impossibility of defining the effect of the supernatural. The Bostonian gentleman of the old school who said that his wife always made it a moral issue whether the mutton should be roast or boiled, summed up very happily the relation of Boston to the universe; but the "moral issue" question must not be allowed to enter into the estimating of a ghost story. It must depend for its effect solely on what one might call its thermometrical quality; if it sends a cold shiver down one's spine, it has done its job and done it well. But there is no fixed rule as to the means of producing this shiver, and many a tale that makes others turn cold leaves me at my normal temperature. The doctor who said there were no diseases but only patients would probably agree that there are no ghosts, but only tellers of ghost stories, since what provides a shudder for one leaves another peacefully tepid. Therefore one ought, I am persuaded, simply to tell one's ghostly adventures in the most unadorned language, and "leave the rest to Nature," as the New York alderman said when, many years ago, it was proposed to import "a couple of gondolas" for the lake in the Central Park.

The only suggestion I can make is that the teller of supernatural tales should be well frightened in the telling; for if he is, he may perhaps communicate to his readers the sense of that strange something undreamt of in the philosophy of Horatio.

* *Ghosts* was dedicated as follows: "These ghostly straphangers to Walter de la Mare." De la Mare (1873–1956) was a highly versatile man of letters: poet, novelist, short-story writer, essayist, historian and anthologist. Among his several first-class ghost stories, probably the most famous is "Seaton's Aunt."

The
Lady's Maid's
Bell

*I*t was the autumn after I had the typhoid. I'd been three months in hospital, and when I came out I looked so weak and tottery that the two or three ladies I applied to were afraid to engage me. Most of my money was gone, and after I'd boarded for two months, hanging about the employment agencies, and answering any advertisement that looked any way respectable, I pretty nearly lost heart, for fretting hadn't made me fatter, and I didn't see why my luck should ever turn. It did though—or I thought so at the time. A Mrs. Railton, a friend of the lady that first brought me out to the States, met me one day and stopped to speak to me: she was one that had always a friendly way with her. She asked me what ailed me to look so white, and when I told her, "Why, Hartley," says she, "I believe I've got the very place for you. Come in tomorrow and we'll talk about it."

The next day, when I called, she told me the lady she'd in mind was a niece of hers, a Mrs. Brympton, a youngish lady, but something of an invalid, who lived all the year round at her country place on the Hudson, owing to not being able to stand the fatigue of town life.

"Now, Hartley," Mrs. Railton said, in that cheery way that always made me feel things must be going to take a turn for the better—"now understand me; it's not a cheerful place I'm sending you to. The house is big and gloomy; my niece is nervous, vaporish; her husband—well, he's generally away; and the two children are dead. A year ago I would as soon have thought of shutting a rosy active girl like you into a vault; but you're not particularly brisk yourself just now, are you? and a quiet place, with country air and wholesome food and early hours, ought to be the very thing for you. Don't mistake me," she added, for I suppose I looked a trifle downcast; "you may find it dull but you won't be unhappy. My niece is an angel. Her former maid, who died last spring, had been with her twenty years and worshiped the ground she walked on. She's a kind mistress to all, and where the mistress is kind, as you know, the servants are generally good-humored, so you'll probably get on well enough with the rest of the household. And you're the very woman I want for my niece: quiet, well-mannered, and educated above your station. You read aloud well, I think? That's a good thing; my niece likes to be read to. She wants a maid that can be something of a companion: her last was, and I can't say how she misses her. It's a lonely life. . . . Well, have you decided?"

"Why, ma'am," I said, "I'm not afraid of solitude."

"Well, then, go; my niece will take you on my recommendation. I'll telegraph her at once and you can take the afternoon train. She has no one to wait on her at present, and I don't want you to lose any time."

I was ready enough to start, yet something in me hung back; and to gain time I asked, "And the gentleman, ma'am?"

"The gentleman's almost always away, I tell you," said Mrs. Railton, quicklike—"and when he's there," says she suddenly, "you've only to keep out of his way."

I took the afternoon train and got to the station at about four o'clock. A groom in a dogcart was waiting, and we drove off at a smart pace. It was a dull October day, with rain hanging close overhead, and by the time we turned into Brympton Place woods the daylight was almost gone. The drive wound through the woods for a mile or two, and came out on a gravel court shut in with thickets of tall black-looking shrubs. There were no lights in the windows, and the house *did* look a bit gloomy.

I had asked no questions of the groom, for I never was one to get my notion of new masters from their other servants: I prefer to wait and see for myself. But I could tell by the look of everything that I had got into the right kind of house, and that things were done handsomely. A pleasant-faced cook met me at the back door and called the housemaid to show me up to my room. "You'll see madam later," she said. "Mrs. Brympton has a visitor."

I hadn't fancied Mrs. Brympton was a lady to have many visitors, and somehow the words cheered me. I followed the housemaid upstairs, and saw, through a door on the upper landing, that the main part of the house seemed well furnished, with dark paneling and a number of old portraits. Another flight of stairs led up up to the servants' wing. It was almost dark now, and the housemaid excused herself for not having brought a light. "But there's matches in your room," she said, "and if you go careful you'll be all right. Mind the step at the end of the passage. Your room is just beyond."

I looked ahead as she spoke, and halfway down the passage I saw a woman standing. She drew back into a doorway as we passed and the housemaid didn't appear to notice her. She was a thin woman with a white face, and a dark gown and apron. I took her for the housekeeper and thought it odd that she didn't speak, but just gave me a long look as she went by. My room opened into a square hall at the end of the passage. Facing my door was another which stood open: the housemaid exclaimed when she saw it:

"There—Mrs. Blinder's left that door open again!" said she, closing it.

"Is Mrs. Blinder the housekeeper?"

"There's no housekeeper: Mrs. Blinder's the cook."

"And is that her room?"

"Laws, no," said the housemaid, crosslike. "That's nobody's room. It's empty, I mean, and the door hadn't ought to be open. Mrs. Brympton wants it kept locked."

She opened my door and led me into a neat room, nicely furnished, with a picture or two on the walls; and having lit a candle she took leave, telling me that the servants' hall tea was at six, and that Mrs. Brympton would see me afterward.

I found them a pleasant-spoken set in the servants' hall, and by what they let fall I gathered that, as Mrs. Railton had said, Mrs. Brympton was the kindest of ladies; but I didn't take much notice of their talk, for I was watching to see the pale woman in the dark gown come in. She didn't show herself, however, and I wondered if she ate apart; but if she wasn't the housekeeper, why should she? Suddenly it struck me that she might be a trained nurse, and in that case her meals would of course be served in her room. If Mrs. Brympton was an invalid it was likely enough she had a nurse. The idea annoyed me, I own, for they're not always the easiest to get on with, and if I'd known I shouldn't have taken the place. But there I was and there was no use pulling a long face over it; and not being one to ask questions I waited to see what would turn up.

When tea was over the housemaid said to the footman: "Has Mr. Ranford gone?" and when he said yes, she told me to come up with her to Mrs. Brympton.

Mrs. Brympton was lying down in her bedroom. Her lounge stood near the fire and beside it was a shaded lamp. She was a delicate-looking lady, but when she smiled I felt there was nothing I wouldn't do for her. She spoke very pleasantly, in a low voice, asking me my name and age and so on, and if I had everything I wanted, and if I wasn't afraid of feeling lonely in the country.

"Not with you I wouldn't be, madam," I said, and the words surprised me when I'd spoken them, for I'm not an impulsive person; but it was just as if I'd thought aloud.

She seemed pleased at that, and said she hoped I'd continue in the same mind; then she gave me a few directions about her toilet, and said Agnes the housemaid would show me next morning where things were kept.

"I am tired tonight, and shall dine upstairs," she said. "Agnes will bring me my tray, so that you may have time to unpack and settle yourself; and later you may come and undress me."

"Very well, ma'am," I said. "You'll ring, I suppose?"

I thought she looked odd.

"No—Agnes will fetch you," says she quickly, and took up her book again.

Well—that was certainly strange: a lady's maid having to be fetched by the housemaid whenever her lady wanted her! I wondered if there were no bells in the house; but the next day I satisfied myself that there was one in every room, and a special one ringing from my mistress's room to mine; and after that it did strike me as queer that, whenever Mrs. Brympton wanted anything, she rang for Agnes, who had to walk the whole length of the servants' wing to call me.

But that wasn't the only queer thing in the house. The very next day I found out that Mrs. Brympton had no nurse; and then I asked Agnes about the woman I had seen in the passage the afternoon before. Agnes said she had seen no one, and I saw that she thought I was dreaming. To be sure, it was dusk when we went down the passage, and she had excused herself for not bringing a light; but I had seen the woman plain enough to know her again if we should meet. I decided that she must have been a friend of the cook's, or of one of the other women servants; perhaps she had come down from town for a night's visit, and the servants wanted it kept secret. Some ladies are very stiff about having their servants' friends in the house overnight. At any rate, I made up my mind to ask no more questions.

In a day or two another odd thing happened. I was chatting one afternoon with Mrs. Blinder, who was a friendly-disposed woman, and had been longer in the house than the other servants, and she asked me if I was quite comfortable and had everything I needed. I said I had no fault to find with my place or with my mistress, but I thought it odd that in so large a house there was no sewing room for the lady's maid.

"Why," says she, "there *is* one: the room you're in is the old sewing room."

"Oh," said I; "and where did the other lady's maid sleep?"

At that she grew confused, and said hurriedly that the servants' rooms had all been changed about last year, and she didn't rightly remember.

That struck me as peculiar, but I went on as if I hadn't noticed: "Well, there's a vacant room opposite mine, and I mean to ask Mrs. Brympton if I mayn't use that as a sewing room."

To my astonishment, Mrs. Blinder went white, and gave my hand a kind of squeeze. "Don't do that, my dear," said she, trembling-like. "To tell you the truth, that was Emma Saxon's room, and my mistress has kept it closed ever since her death."

"And who was Emma Saxon?"

"Mrs. Brympton's former maid."

"The one that was with her so many years?" said I, remembering what Mrs. Railton had told me.

Mrs. Blinder nodded.

"What sort of woman was she?"

"No better walked the earth," said Mrs. Blinder. "My mistress loved her like a sister."

"But I mean—what did she look like?"

Mrs. Blinder got up and gave me a kind of angry stare. "I'm no great hand at describing," she said; "and I believe my pastry's rising." And she walked off into the kitchen and shut the door after her.

II

I had been near a week at Brympton before I saw my master. Word came that he was arriving one afternoon, and a change passed over the whole household. It was plain that nobody loved him below stairs. Mrs. Blinder took uncommon care with the dinner that night, but she snapped at the kitchenmaid in a way quite unusual with her; and Mr. Wace, the butler, a serious, slow-spoken man, went about his duties as if he'd been getting ready for a funeral. He was a great Bible reader, Mr. Wace was, and had a beautiful assortment of texts at his command; but that day he used such dreadful language, that I was about to leave the table, when he assured me it was all out of Isaiah; and I noticed that whenever the master came Mr. Wace took to the prophets.

About seven, Agnes called me to my mistress' room; and there I found Mr. Brympton. He was standing on the hearth; a big fair bull-necked man, with a red face and little bad-tempered blue eyes: the kind of man a young simpleton might have thought handsome, and would have been like to pay dear for thinking it.

He swung about when I came in, and looked me over in a trice. I knew what the look meant, from having experienced it once or twice in my former places. Then he turned his back on me, and went on talking to his wife; and I knew what *that* meant, too. I was not the kind of morsel he was after. The typhoid had served me well enough in one way: it kept that kind of gentleman at arm's length.

"This is my new maid, Hartley," says Mrs. Brympton in her kind voice; and he nodded and went on with what he was saying.

In a minute or two he went off, and left my mistress to dress for dinner, and I noticed as I waited on her that she was white, and chill to the touch.

Mr. Brympton took himself off the next morning, and the whole house drew a long breath when he drove away. As for my mistress, she put on her hat and furs (for it was a fine winter morning) and went out for a walk in the gardens, coming back quite fresh and rosy, so that for a minute, before her color faded, I could guess what a pretty young lady she must have been, and not so long ago, either.

She had met Mr. Ranford in the grounds, and the two came back together, I remember, smiling and talking as they walked along the terrace under my window. That was the first time I saw Mr. Ranford, though I had often heard his name mentioned in the hall. He was a neighbor, it appeared, living a mile or two beyond Brympton, at the end of the village; and as he was in the habit of spending his winters in the country he was almost the only company my mistress had at that season. He was a slight tall gentleman of about thirty, and I thought him rather melancholy looking till I saw his smile, which had a kind of surprise in it, like the first warm day in spring. He was a great reader, I heard, like my mistress, and the two were forever borrowing books of one another, and sometimes (Mr. Wace told me) he would read aloud to Mrs. Brympton by the hour, in the big dark library where she sat in the winter afternoons. The servants all liked him, and perhaps that's more of a compliment than the masters suspect. He had a friendly word for every one of us, and we were all glad to think that Mrs. Brympton had a pleasant companionable gentleman like that to keep her company when the master was away. Mr. Ranford seemed on excellent terms with Mr. Brympton too; though I couldn't but wonder that two gentlemen so unlike each other should be so friendly. But then I knew how the real quality can keep their feelings to themselves.

As for Mr. Brympton, he came and went, never staying more than a day or two, cursing the dullness and the solitude, grumbling at everything, and (as I soon found out) drinking a deal more than was good for him. After Mrs. Brympton left the table he would sit half the night over the old Brympton port and madeira, and once, as I was leaving my mistress's room rather later than usual, I met him coming up the stairs in such a state that I turned sick to think of what some ladies have to endure and hold their tongues about.

The servants said very little about their master; but from what they let drop I could see it had been an unhappy match from the beginning. Mr. Brympton was coarse, loud and pleasure-loving; my mistress quiet, retiring, and perhaps a trifle cold. Not that she was not always pleasant-spoken to him: I thought her wonderfully forbearing; but to a gentleman as free as Mr. Brympton I dare say she seemed a little offish.

Well, things went on quietly for several weeks. My mistress was kind, my duties were light, and I got on well with the other servants. In short, I had nothing to complain of; yet there was always a weight on me. I can't say why it was so, but I know it was not the loneliness that I felt. I soon got used to that; and being still languid from the fever, I was thankful for the quiet and the good country air. Nevertheless, I was never quite easy in my mind. My mistress, knowing I had been ill, insisted that I should take my walk regularly, and often invented errands for me: a yard of ribbon to be fetched from the village, a letter posted, or a book returned to Mr. Ranford. As soon as I was out of doors my spirits rose, and I looked forward to my walks through the bare moist-smelling woods; but the moment I caught sight of the house again my heart dropped down like a stone in a well. It was not a gloomy house exactly, yet I never entered it but a feeling of gloom came over me.

Mrs. Brympton seldom went out in winter; only on the finest days did she walk an hour at noon on the south terrace. Excepting Mr. Ranford, we had no visitors but the doctor, who drove over from town about once a week. He sent for me once or twice to give me some trifling direction about my mistress, and though he never told me what her illness was, I thought, from a waxy look she had now and then of a morning, that it might be the heart that ailed her. The season was soft and unwholesome, and in January we had a long spell of rain. That was a sore trial to me, I own, for I couldn't go out, and sitting over my sewing all day, listening to the drip, drip of the eaves, I grew so nervous that the least sound made me jump. Somehow, the thought of that locked room across the passage began to weigh on me. Once or twice, in the long rainy nights, I fancied I heard noises there; but that was nonsense, of course, and the daylight drove such notions out of my head. Well, one morning Mrs. Brympton gave me quite a start of pleasure by telling me she wished me to go to town for some shopping. I hadn't known till then how low my spirits had fallen. I set off in high glee, and my first sight of the crowded streets and the cheerful-looking shops quite took me out of myself. Toward afternoon, however, the noise and confusion began to tire me, and I was actually looking forward to the quiet of Brympton, and thinking how I should enjoy the drive home through the dark woods, when I ran across an old acquaintance, a maid I had once been in service with. We had lost sight of each other for a number of years, and I had to stop and tell her what had happened to me in the interval. When I mentioned where I was living she rolled up her eyes and pulled a long face.

"What! The Mrs. Brympton that lives all the year at her place on the Hudson? My dear, you won't stay there three months."

"Oh, but I don't mind the country," says I, offended somehow at her tone. "Since the fever I'm glad to be quiet."

She shook her head. "It's not the country I'm thinking of. All I know is she's had four maids in the last six months, and the last one, who was a friend of mine, told me nobody could stay in the house."

"Did she say why?" I asked.

"No—she wouldn't give me her reason. But she says to me, 'Mrs. Ansey,' she says, 'if ever a young woman as you know of thinks of going there, you tell her it's not worth-while to unpack her boxes.'"

"Is she young and handsome?" said I, thinking of Mr. Brympton.

"Not her! She's the kind that mothers engage when they've gay young gentlemen at college."

Well, though I knew the woman was an idle gossip, the words stuck in my head, and my heart sank lower than ever as I drove up to Brympton in the dusk. There *was* something about the house—I was sure of it now. . . .

When I went in to tea I heard that Mr. Brympton had arrived, and I saw at a glance that there had been a disturbance of some kind. Mrs. Blinder's hand shook so that she could hardly pour the tea, and Mr. Wace quoted the most dreadful texts full of brimstone. Nobody said a word to me then, but when I went up to my room Mrs. Blinder followed me.

"Oh, my dear," says she, taking my hand, "I'm so glad and thankful you've come back to us!"

That struck me, as you may imagine. "Why," said I, "did you think I was leaving for good?"

"No, no, to be sure," said she, a little confused, "but I can't a-bear to have madam left alone for a day even." She pressed my hand hard, and, "Oh, Miss Hartley," says she, "be good to your mistress, as you're a Christian woman." And with that she hurried away, and left me staring.

A moment later Agnes called me to Mrs. Brympton. Hearing Mr. Brympton's voice in her room, I went round by the dressing room, thinking I would lay out her dinner gown before going in. The dressing room is a large room with a window over the portico that looks toward the gardens. Mr. Brympton's apartments are beyond. When I went in, the door into the bedroom was ajar, and I heard Mr. Brympton saying angrily: "One would suppose he was the only person fit for you to talk to."

"I don't have many visitors in winter," Mrs. Brympton answered quietly.

"You have *me!*" he flung at her, sneeringly.

"You are here so seldom," said she.

"Well—whose fault is that? You make the place about as lively as the family vault."

With that I rattled the toilet things, to give my mistress warning, and she rose and called me in.

The two dined alone, as usual, and I knew by Mr. Wace's manner at supper that things must be going badly. He quoted the prophets something terrible, and worked on the kitchenmaid so that she declared she wouldn't go down alone to put the cold meat in the icebox. I felt nervous myself, and after I had put my mistress to bed I was half tempted to go down again and persuade Mrs. Blinder to sit up awhile over a game of cards. But I heard her door closing for the night and so I went on to my own room. The rain had begun again, and the drip, drip, drip seemed to be dropping into my brain. I lay awake listening to it, and turning over what my friend in town had said. What puzzled me was that it was always the maids who left. . . .

After a while I slept; but suddenly a loud noise wakened me. My bell had rung. I sat up, terrified by the unusual sound, which seemed to go on jangling through the darkness. My hands shook so that I couldn't find the matches. At length I struck a light and jumped out of bed. I began to think I must have been dreaming; but I looked at the bell against the wall, and there was the little hammer still quivering.

I was just beginning to huddle on my clothes when I heard another sound. This time it was the door of the locked room opposite mine softly opening and closing. I heard the sound distinctly, and it frightened me so that I stood stock still. Then I heard a footstep hurrying down the passage toward the main house. The floor being carpeted, the sound was very faint, but I was quite sure it was a woman's step. I turned cold with the thought of it, and for a minute or two I dursn't breathe or move. Then I came to my senses.

"Alice Hartley," says I to myself, "someone left that room just now and ran down the passage ahead of you. The idea isn't pleasant, but you may as well face it. Your mistress has rung for you, and to answer her bell you've got to go the way that other woman has gone."

Well—I did it. I never walked faster in my life, yet I thought I should never get to the end of the passage or reach Mrs. Brympton's room. On the way I heard nothing and saw nothing: all was dark and quiet as the grave. When I reached my mistress' door the silence was so deep that I began to think I must be dreaming, and was half minded to turn back. Then a panic seized me, and I knocked.

There was no answer, and I knocked again, loudly. To my astonishment the door was opened by Mr. Brympton. He started back when he saw me, and in the light of my candle his face looked red and savage.

"*You?*" he said, in a queer voice. "*How many of you are there, in God's name?*"

At that I felt the ground give under me; but I said to myself that he had been drinking, and answered as steadily as I could: "May I go in, sir? Mrs. Brympton has rung for me."

"You may all go in, for what I care," says he, and, pushing by me, walked down the hall to his own bedroom. I looked after him as he went, and to my surprise I saw that he walked as straight as a sober man.

I found my mistress lying very weak and still, but she forced a smile when she saw me, and signed to me to pour out some drops for her. After that she lay without speaking, her breath coming quick, and her eyes closed. Suddenly she groped out with her hand, and "*Emma,*" says she, faintly.

"It's Hartley, madam," I said. "Do you want anything?"

She opened her eyes wide and gave me a startled look.

"I was dreaming," she said. "You may go, now, Hartley, and thank you kindly. I'm quite well again, you see." And she turned her face away from me.

III

There was no more sleep for me that night, and I was thankful when daylight came.

Soon afterward, Agnes called me to Mrs. Brympton. I was afraid she was ill again, for she seldom sent for me before nine, but I found her sitting up in bed, pale and drawn-looking, but quite herself.

"Hartley," says she quickly, "will you put on your things at once and go down to the village for me? I want this prescription made up —" here she hesitated a minute and blushed "—and I should like you to be back again before Mr. Brympton is up."

"Certainly, madam," I said.

"And—stay a moment—" she called me back as if an idea had just struck her "—while you're waiting for the mixture, you'll have time to go on to Mr. Ranford's with this note."

It was a two mile walk to the village, and on my way I had time to turn things over in my mind. It struck me as peculiar that my mistress should wish the prescription made up without Mr. Brympton's knowledge; and, putting this together with the scene of the night before, and with much else that I had noticed and suspected, I began to wonder if the poor lady was weary of her life, and had come to the mad resolve of ending it. The idea took such hold on me that I reached the village on a run, and dropped breathless into a chair before the chemist's counter. The good man, who was just taking down his shutters, stared at me so hard that it brought me to myself.

"Mr. Limmel," I says, trying to speak indifferently, "will you run your eye over this, and tell me if it's quite right?"

He put on his spectacles and studied the prescription.

"Why, it's one of Dr. Walton's," says he. "What should be wrong with it?"

"Well—is it dangerous to take?"

"Dangerous—how do you mean?"

I could have shaken the man for his stupidity.

"I mean—if a person was to take too much of it—by mistake of course—" says I, my heart in my throat.

"Lord bless you, no. It's only lime water. You might feed it to a baby by the bottleful."

I gave a great sigh of relief and hurried on to Mr. Ranford's. But on the way another thought struck me. If there was nothing to conceal about my visit to the chemist's, was it my other errand that Mrs. Brympton wished me to keep private? Somehow, that thought frightened me worse than the other. Yet the two gentlemen seemed fast friends, and I would have staked my head on my mistress' goodness. I felt ashamed of my suspicions, and concluded that I was still disturbed by the strange events of the night. I left the note at Mr. Ranford's, and hurrying back to Brympton, slipped in by a side door without being seen, as I thought.

An hour later, however, as I was carrying in my mistress's breakfast, I was stopped in the hall by Mr. Brympton.

"What were you doing out so early?" he says, looking hard at me.

"Early—me, sir?" I said, in a tremble.

"Come, come," he says, an angry red spot coming out on his forehead, "didn't I see you scuttling home through the shrubbery an hour or more ago?"

I'm a truthful woman by nature, but at that a lie popped out ready-made. "No, sir, you didn't," said I and looked straight back at him.

He shrugged his shoulders and gave a sullen laugh. "I suppose you think I was drunk last night?" he asked suddenly.

"No, sir, I don't," I answered, this time truthfully enough.

He turned away with another shrug. "A pretty notion my servants have of me!" I heard him mutter as he walked off.

Not till I had settled down to my afternoon's sewing did I realize how the events of the night had shaken me. I couldn't pass that locked door without a shiver. I knew I had heard someone come out of it, and walk down the passage ahead of me. I thought of speaking to Mrs. Blinder or to Mr. Wace, the only two in the house who appeared to have an inkling of what was going on, but I had a feeling that if I questioned them they would deny everything, and that I might learn more by holding my tongue and keeping my eyes open. The idea of spending another night opposite the locked room sickened me, and once I was seized with the notion of packing my trunk and taking the first train to town; but it wasn't in me to throw over a kind mistress in that manner, and I tried to go on with my sewing as if nothing had happened. I hadn't worked ten minutes before the sewing machine broke down. It was one I had found in the house, a good machine but a trifle out of order: Mrs. Blinder said it had never been used since Emma Saxon's death. I stopped to see what was wrong, and as I was working at the machine a drawer which I had never been able to open slid forward and a photograph fell out. I picked it up and sat looking at it in a maze. It was a woman's likeness, and I knew I had seen the face somewhere—the eyes had an asking look that I had felt on me before. And suddenly I remembered the pale woman in the passage.

I stood up, cold all over, and ran out of the room. My heart seemed to be thumping in the top of my head, and I felt as if I should never get away from the look in those eyes. I went straight to Mrs. Blinder.

She was taking her afternoon nap, and sat up with a jump when I came in.

"Mrs. Blinder," said I, "who is that?" And I held out the photograph.

She rubbed her eyes and stared.

"Why, Emma Saxon," says she. "Where did you find it?"

I looked hard at her for a minute. "Mrs. Blinder," I said, "I've seen that face before."

Mrs. Blinder got up and walked over to the looking glass. "Dear me! I must have been asleep," she says. "My front is all over one ear. And now do run along, Miss Hartley, dear, for I hear the clock striking four, and I must go down this very minute and put on the Virginia ham for Mr. Brympton's dinner."

IV

To all appearances, things went on as usual for a week or two. The only difference was that Mr. Brympton stayed on, instead of going off as he usually did, and that Mr. Ranford never showed himself. I heard Mr. Brympton remark on this one afternoon when he was sitting in my mistress' room before dinner:

"Where's Ranford?" says he. "He hasn't been near the house for a week. Does he keep away because I'm here?"

Mrs. Brympton spoke so low that I couldn't catch her answer.

"Well," he went on, "two's company and three's trumpery; I'm sorry to be in Ranford's way, and I suppose I shall have to take myself off again in a day or two and give him a show." And he laughed at his own joke.

The very next day, as it happened, Mr. Ranford called. The footman said the three were very merry over their tea in the library, and Mr. Brympton strolled down to the gate with Mr. Ranford when he left.

I have said that things went on as usual; and so they did with the rest of the household; but as for myself, I had never been the same since the night my bell had rung. Night after night I used to lie awake, listening for it to ring again, and for the door of the locked room to open stealthily. But the bell never rang, and I heard no sound across the passage. At last the silence began to be more dreadful to me than the most mysterious sounds. I felt that *someone* was cowering there, behind the locked door, watching and listening as I watched and listened, and I could almost have cried out, "Whoever you are, come out and let me see you face to face, but don't lurk there and spy on me in the darkness!"

Feeling as I did, you may wonder I didn't give warning. Once I very nearly did so; but at the last moment something held me back. Whether it was compassion for my mistress, who had grown more and more dependent on me, or unwillingness to try a new place, or some other feeling that I couldn't put a name to, I lingered on as if spell-bound, though every night was dreadful to me, and the days but little better.

For one thing, I didn't like Mrs. Brympton's looks. She had never been the same since that night, no more than I had. I thought she would brighten up after Mr. Brympton left, but though she seemed easier in her mind, her spirits didn't revive, nor her strength either. She had grown attached to me, and seemed to like to have me about; and Agnes told me one day that, since Emma Saxon's death, I was the only maid her mistress had taken to. This gave me a warm feeling for the poor lady, though after all there was little I could do to help her.

After Mr. Brympton's departure, Mr. Ranford took to coming again, though less often than formerly. I met him once or twice in the grounds, or in the village, and I couldn't but think there was a change in him too; but I set it down to my disordered fancy.

The weeks passed, and Mr. Brympton had now been a month absent. We heard he was cruising with a friend in the West Indies, and Mr. Wace said that was a long way off, but though you had the wings of a dove and went to the uttermost parts of the earth, you couldn't get away from the Almighty. Agnes said that as long as he stayed away from Brympton the Almighty might have him and welcome; and this raised a laugh, though Mrs. Blinder tried to look shocked, and Mr. Wace said the bears would eat us.

We were all glad to hear that the West Indies were a long way off, and I remember that, in spite of Mr. Wace's solemn looks, we had a very merry dinner that day in the hall. I don't know if it was because of my being in better spirits, but I fancied Mrs. Brympton looked better too, and seemed more cheerful in her manner. She had been for a walk in the morning, and after luncheon she lay down in her room, and I read aloud to her. When she dismissed me I went to my own room feeling quite bright and happy, and for the first time in weeks walked past the locked door without thinking of it. As I sat down to my work I looked out and saw a few snowflakes falling. The sight was pleasanter than the eternal rain, and I pictured to myself how pretty the bare gardens would look in their white mantle. It seemed to me as if the snow would cover up all the dreariness, indoors as well as out.

The fancy had hardly crossed my mind when I heard a step at my side. I looked up, thinking it was Agnes.

"Well, Agnes—" said I, and the words froze on my tongue; for there, in the door, stood *Emma Saxon*.

I don't know how long she stood there. I only know I couldn't stir or take my eyes from her. Afterward I was terribly frightened, but at the time it wasn't fear I felt, but something deeper and quieter. She looked at me long and hard, and her face was just one dumb prayer to me—but how in the world was I to help her? Suddenly she turned, and I heard her walk down the passage. This time I wasn't afraid to follow—I felt that I must know what she wanted. I sprang up and ran out. She was at the other end of the passage, and I expected her to take the turn toward my mistress' room; but instead of that she pushed open the door that led to the backstairs. I followed her down the stairs, and across the passageway to the back door. The kitchen and hall were empty at that hour, the servants being off duty, except for the footman, who was in the pantry. At the door she stood still a moment, with another look at me; then she turned the handle, and stepped out. For a minute I hesitated. Where was she leading me to? The door had closed softly after her, and I opened it and looked out, half-expecting to find that she had disappeared. But I saw her a few yards off hurrying across the courtyard to the path through the woods. Her figure looked black and lonely in the snow, and for a second my heart failed me and I thought of turning back. But all the while she was drawing me after her; and catching up an old shawl of Mrs. Blinder's I ran out into the open.

Emma Saxon was in the wood path now. She walked on steadily, and I followed at the same pace, till we passed out of the gates and reached the highroad. Then she struck across the open fields to the

village. By this time the ground was white, and as she climbed the slope of a bare hill ahead of me I noticed that she left no footprints behind her. At sight of that my heart shriveled up within me, and my knees were water. Somehow, it was worse here than indoors. She made the whole countryside seem lonely as the grave, with none but us two in it, and no help in the wide world.

Once I tried to go back; but she turned and looked at me, and it was as if she had dragged me with ropes. After that I followed her like a dog. We came to the village and she led me through it, past the church and the blacksmith's shop, and down the lane to Mr. Ranford's. Mr. Ranford's house stands close to the road: a plain old-fashioned building, with a flagged path leading to the door between box borders. The lane was deserted, and as I turned into it I saw Emma Saxon pause under the old elm by the gate. And now another fear came over me. I saw that we had reached the end of our journey, and that it was my turn to act. All the way from Brympton I had been asking myself what she wanted of me, but I had followed in a trance, as it were, and not till I saw her stop at Mr. Ranford's gate did my brain begin to clear itself. I stood a little way off in the snow, my heart beating fit to strangle me, and my feet frozen to the ground; and she stood under the elm and watched me.

I knew well enough that she hadn't led me there for nothing. I felt there was something I ought to say or do—but how was I to guess what it was? I had never thought harm of my mistress and Mr. Ranford, but I was sure now that, from one cause or another, some dreadful thing hung over them. *She* knew what it was; she would tell me if she could; perhaps she would answer if I questioned her.

It turned me faint to think of speaking to her; but I plucked up heart and dragged myself across the few yards between us. As I did so, I heard the house door open and saw Mr. Ranford approaching. He looked handsome and cheerful, as my mistress had looked that morning, and at sight of him the blood began to flow again in my veins.

"Why, Hartley," said he, "what's the matter? I saw you coming down the lane just now, and came out to see if you had taken root in the snow." He stopped and stared at me. "What are you looking at?" he says.

I turned toward the elm as he spoke, and his ˄es followed me; but there was no one there. The lane was empty as far as the eye could reach.

A sense of helplessness came over me. She was gone, and I had not been able to guess what she wanted. Her last look had pierced me to the marrow; and yet it had not told me! All at once, I felt more desolate than when she had stood there watching me. It seemed as if she had left me all alone to carry the weight of the secret I couldn't guess. The snow went round me in great circles, and the ground fell away from me. . . .

A drop of brandy and the warmth of Mr. Ranford's fire soon brought me to, and I insisted on being driven back at once to Brympton. It was nearly dark, and I was afraid my mistress might be wanting me. I explained to Mr. Ranford that I had been out for a walk and had been taken with a fit of giddiness as I passed his gate. This was true enough; yet I never felt more like a liar than when I said it.

When I dressed Mrs. Brympton for dinner she remarked on my pale looks and asked what ailed me. I told her I had a headache, and she said she would not require me again that evening, and advised me to go to bed.

It was a fact that I could scarcely keep on my feet; yet I had no fancy to spend a solitary evening in my room. I sat downstairs in the hall as long as I could hold my head up; but by nine I crept upstairs, too weary to care what happened if I could but get my head on a pillow. The rest of the household went to bed soon afterward; they kept early hours when the master was away, and before ten I heard Mrs. Blinder's door close, and Mr. Wace's soon after.

It was a very still night, earth and air all muffled in snow. Once in bed I felt easier, and lay quiet, listening to the strange noises that come out in a house after dark. Once I thought I hear a door open and close again below: it might have been the glass door that led to the gardens. I got up and peered out of the window; but it was in the dark of the moon, and nothing visible outside but the streaking of snow against the panes.

I went back to bed and must have dozed, for I jumped awake to the furious ringing of my bell. Before my head was clear I had sprung out of bed, and was dragging on my clothes. *It is going to happen now,* I heard myself saying; but what I meant I had no notion. My hands seemed to be covered with glue—I thought I should never get into my clothes. At last I opened my door and peered down the passage. As far as my candle flame carried, I could see nothing unusual ahead of me. I hurried on, breathless; but as I pushed open the baize door leading to the main hall my heart stood still, for there at the head of the stairs was Emma Saxon, peering dreadfully down into the darkness.

For a second I couldn't stir; but my hand slipped from the door, and as it swung shut the figure vanished. At the same instant there came another sound from below stairs—a stealthy mysterious sound, as of a latchkey turning in the house door. I ran to Mrs. Brympton's room and knocked.

There was no answer, and I knocked again. This time I heard someone moving in the room; the bolt slipped back and my mistress stood before me. To my surprise I saw that she had not undressed for the night. She gave me a startled look.

"What is this, Hartley?" she says in a whisper. "Are you ill? What are you doing here at this hour?"

"I am not ill, madam; but my bell rang."

At that she turned pale, and seemed about to fall.

"You are mistaken," she said harshly; "I didn't ring. You must have been dreaming." I had never heard her speak in such a tone. "Go back to bed," she said, closing the door on me.

But as she spoke I heard sounds again in the hall below: a man's step this time; and the truth leaped out on me.

"Madam," I said, pushing past her, "there is someone in the house—"

"Someone—?"

"Mr. Brympton, I think—I hear his step below—"

A dreadful look came over her, and without a word, she dropped flat at my feet. I fell on my knees and tried to lift her: by the way she breathed I saw it was no common faint. But as I raised her head there came quick steps on the stairs and across the hall: the door was flung open, and there stood Mr. Brympton, in his traveling clothes, the snow dripping from him. He drew back with a start as he saw me kneeling by my mistress.

"What the devil is this?" he shouted. He was less high-colored than usual, and the red spot came out on his forehead.

"Mrs. Brympton has fainted, sir," said I.

He laughed unsteadily and pushed by me. "It's a pity she didn't choose a more convenient moment. I'm sorry to disturb her, but—"

I raised myself up aghast at the man's action.

"Sir," said I, "are you mad? What are you doing?"

"Going to meet a friend," said he, and seemed to make for the dressing room.

At that my heart turned over. I don't know what I thought or feared; but I sprang up and caught him by the sleeve.

"Sir, sir," said I, "for pity's sake look at your wife!"

He shook me off furiously.

"It seems that's done for me," says he, and caught hold of the dressing room door.

At that moment I heard a slight noise inside. Slight as it was, he heard it too, and tore the door open; but as he did so he dropped back. On the threshold stood Emma Saxon. All was dark behind her, but I saw her plainly, and so did he. He threw up his hands as if to hide his face from her; and when I looked again she was gone.

He stood motionless, as if the strength had run out of him; and in the stillness my mistress suddenly raised herself, and opening her eyes fixed a look on him. Then she fell back, and I saw the death flutter pass over her face. . . .

We buried her on the third day, in a driving snowstorm. There were few people in the church, for it was bad weather to come from town, and I've a notion my mistress was one that hadn't many near friends. Mr. Ranford was among the last to come, just before they carried her up the aisle. He was in black, of course, being such a friend of the family, and I never saw a gentleman so pale. As he passed me, I noticed that he leaned a trifle on a stick he carried; and I fancy Mr. Brympton noticed it too, for the red spot came out sharp on his forehead, and all through the service he kept staring across the church at Mr. Ranford, instead of following the prayers as a mourner should.

When it was over and we went out to the graveyard, Mr. Ranford had disappeared, and as soon as my poor mistress's body was underground, Mr. Brympton jumped into the carriage nearest the gate and drove off without a word to any of us. I heard him call out, "To the station," and we servants went back alone to the house.

The Eyes

*W*e had been put in the mood for ghosts, that evening, after an excellent dinner at our old friend Culwin's, by a tale of Fred Murchard's—the narrative of a strange personal visitation.

Seen through the haze of our cigars, and by the drowsy gleam of a coal fire, Culwin's library, with its oak walls and dark old bindings, made a good setting for such evocations; and ghostly experiences at first hand being, after Murchard's opening, the only kind acceptable to us, we proceeded to take stock of our group and tax each member for a contribution. There were eight of us, and seven contrived, in a manner more or less adequate, to fulfill the condition imposed. It surprised us all to find that we could muster such a show of supernatural impressions, for none of us, excepting Murchard himself and young Phil Frenham—whose story was the slightest of the lot—had the habit of sending our souls into the invisible. So that, on the whole, we had every reason to be proud of our seven "exhibits," and none of us would have dreamed of expecting an eighth from our host.

Our old friend, Mr. Andrew Culwin, who had sat back in his armchair, listening and blinking through the smoke circles with the cheerful tolerance of a wise old idol, was not the kind of man likely to be favored with such contacts, though he had imagination enough to enjoy, without envying, the superior privileges of his guests. By age and by education he belonged to the stout Positivist tradition, and his habit of thought had been formed in the days of the epic struggle between physics and metaphysics. But he had been, then and always, essentially a spectator, a humorous detached observer of the immense muddled variety show of life, slipping out of his seat now and then for a brief dip into the convivialities at the back of the house, but never, as far as one knew, showing the least desire to jump on the stage and do a "turn."

Among his contemporaries there lingered a vague tradition of his having, at a remote period, and in a romantic clime, been wounded in a duel; but this legend no more tallied with what we younger men knew of his character than my mother's assertion that he had once been "a charming little man with nice eyes" corresponded to any possible reconstitution of his physiognomy.

"He never can have looked like anything but a bundle of sticks,"

Murchard had once said of him. "Or a phosphorescent log, rather," someone else amended; and we recognized the happiness of this description of his small squat trunk, with the red blink of the eyes in a face like mottled bark. He had always been possessed of a leisure which he had nursed and protected, instead of squandering it in vain activities. His carefully guarded hours had been devoted to the cultivation of a fine intelligence and a few judiciously chosen habits; and none of the disturbances common to human experience seemed to have crossed his sky. Nevertheless, his dispassionate survey of the universe had not raised his opinion of that costly experiment, and his study of the human race seemed to have resulted in the conclusion that all men were superfluous, and women necessary only because someone had to do the cooking. On the importance of this point his convictions were absolute, and gastronomy was the only science which he revered as a dogma. It must be owned that his little dinners were a strong argument in favor of this view, besides being a reason—though not the main one—for the fidelity of his friends.

Mentally he exercised a hospitality less seductive but no less stimulating. His mind was like a forum, or some open meeting place for the exchange of ideas: somewhat cold and drafty, but light, spacious and orderly—a kind of academic grove from which all the leaves have fallen. In this privileged area a dozen of us were wont to stretch our muscles and expand our lungs; and, as if to prolong as much as possible the tradition of what we felt to be a vanishing institution, one or two neophytes were now and then added to our band.

Young Phil Frenham was the last, and the most interesting, of these recruits, and a good example of Murchard's somewhat morbid assertion that our old friend "liked 'em juicy." It was indeed a fact that Culwin, for all his dryness, specially tasted the lyric qualities in youth. As he was far too good an Epicurean to nip the flowers of soul which he gathered for his garden, his friendship was not a disintegrating influence: on the contrary, it forced the young idea to robuster bloom. And in Phil Frenham he had a good subject for experimentation. The boy was really intelligent, and the soundness of his nature was like the pure paste under a fine glaze. Culwin had fished him out of a fog of family dullness, and pulled him up to a peak in Darien; and the adventure hadn't hurt him a bit. Indeed, the skill with which Culwin had contrived to stimulate his curiosities without robbing them of their bloom of awe seemed to me a sufficient answer to Murchard's ogreish metaphor. There was nothing hectic in Frenham's efflorescence, and his old friend had not laid even a finger tip on the sacred stupidities. One wanted no better proof of that than the fact that Frenham still reverenced them in Culwin.

"There's a side of him you fellows don't see. *I* believe that story about the duel!" he declared; and it was of the very essence of this belief that it should impel him—just as our little party was dispersing —to turn back to our host with the joking demand: "And now you've got to tell us about *your* ghost!"

The outer door had closed on Murchard and the others; only Frenham and I remained; and the devoted servant who presided over Culwin's destinies, having brought a fresh supply of soda water, had been laconically ordered to bed.

Culwin's sociability was a night-blooming flower, and we knew that he expected the nucleus of his group to tighten around him after midnight. But Frenham's appeal seemed to disconcert him comically, and he rose from the chair in which he had just reseated himself after his farewells in the hall.

"*My* ghost? Do you suppose I'm fool enough to go to the expense of keeping one of my own, when there are so many charming ones in my friends' closets? Take another cigar," he said, revolving toward me with a laugh.

Frenham laughed too, pulling up his slender height before the chimney piece as he turned to face his short bristling friend.

"Oh," he said, "you'd never be content to share if you met one you really liked."

Culwin had dropped back into his armchair, his shock head embedded in the hollow of worn leather, his little eyes glimmering over a fresh cigar.

"Liked—*liked?* Good Lord!" he growled.

"Ah, you *have,* then!" Frenham pounced on him in the same instant, with a side glance of victory at me; but Culwin cowered gnomelike among his cushions, dissembling himself in a protective cloud of smoke.

"What's the use of denying it? You've seen everything, so of course you've seen a ghost!" his young friend persisted, talking intrepidly into the cloud. "Or, if you haven't seen one, it's only because you've seen two!"

The form of the challenge seemed to strike our host. He shot his head out of the mist with a queer tortoise-like motion he sometimes had, and blinked approvingly at Frenham.

"That's it," he flung at us on a shrill jerk of laughter; "it's only because I've seen two!"

The words were so unexpected that they dropped down and down into a deep silence, while we continued to stare at each other over Culwin's head, and Culwin stared at his ghosts. At length Frenham, without speaking, threw himself into the chair on the other side of the hearth, and leaned forward with his listening smile. . . .

II

"Oh, of course they're not show ghosts—a collector wouldn't think anything of them. . . . Don't let me raise your hopes . . . their one merit is their numerical strength: the exceptional fact of their being *two*. But, as against this, I'm bound to admit that at any moment I could probably have exorcised them both by asking my doctor for a prescription, or my oculist for a pair of spectacles. Only, as I never could make up my mind whether to go to the doctor or the oculist—whether I was afflicted by an optical or a digestive delusion—I left them to pursue their interesting double life, though at times they made mine exceedingly uncomfortable. . . .

"Yes—uncomfortable; and you know how I hate to be uncomfortable! But it was part of my stupid pride, when the thing began, not to admit that I could be disturbed by the trifling matter of seeing two.

"And then I'd no reason, really, to suppose I was ill. As far as I knew I was simply bored—horribly bored. But it was part of my boredom—I remember—that I was feeling so uncommonly well, and didn't know how on earth to work off my surplus energy. I had come back from a long journey—down in South America and Mexico—and had settled down for the winter near New York with an old aunt who had known Washington Irving and corresponded with N. P. Willis. She lived, not far from Irvington, in a damp Gothic villa overhung by

Norway spruces and looking exactly like a memorial emblem done in hair. Her personal appearance was in keeping with this image, and her own hair—of which there was little left—might have been sacrificed to the manufacture of the emblem.

"I had just reached the end of an agitated year, with considerable arrears to make up in money and emotion; and theoretically it seemed as though my aunt's mild hospitality would be as beneficial to my nerves as to my purse. But the deuce of it was that as soon as I felt myself safe and sheltered my energy began to revive; and how was I to work it off inside of a memorial emblem? I had, at that time, the illusion that sustained intellectual effort could engage a man's whole activity; and I decided to write a great book—I forget about what. My aunt, impressed by my plan, gave up to me her Gothic library, filled with classics bound in black cloth and daguerreotypes of faded celebrities; and I sat down at my desk to win myself a place among their number. And to facilitate my task she lent me a cousin to copy my manuscript.

"The cousin was a nice girl, and I had an idea that a nice girl was just what I needed to restore my faith in human nature, and principally in myself. She was neither beautiful nor intelligent—poor Alice Nowell!—but it interested me to see any woman content to be so uninteresting, and I wanted to find out the secret of her content. In doing this I handled it rather rashly, and put it out of joint—oh, just for a moment! There's no fatuity in telling you this, for the poor girl had never seen anyone but cousins. . . .

"Well, I was sorry for what I'd done, of course, and confoundedly bothered as to how I should put it straight. She was staying in the house, and one evening, after my aunt had gone to bed, she came down to the library to fetch a book she'd mislaid, like any artless heroine, on the shelves behind us. She was pink-nosed and flustered, and it suddenly occurred to me that her hair, though it was fairly thick and pretty, would look exactly like my aunt's when she grew older. I was glad I had noticed this, for it made it easier for me to decide to do what was right; and when I had found the book she hadn't lost I told her I was leaving for Europe that week.

"Europe was terribly far off in those days, and Alice knew at once what I meant. She didn't take it in the least as I'd expected—it would have been easier if she had. She held her book very tight, and turned away a moment to wind up the lamp on my desk—it had a ground-glass shade with vine leaves, and glass drops around the edge, I remember. Then she came back, held out her hand, and said: 'Good-bye.' And as she said it she looked straight at me and kissed me. I had never felt anything as fresh and shy and brave as her kiss. It was worse than any reproach, and it made me ashamed to deserve a reproach from her. I said to myself: 'I'll marry her, and when my aunt dies she'll leave us this house, and I'll sit here at the desk and go on with my book; and Alice will sit over there with her embroidery and look at me as she's looking now. And life will go on like that for any number of years.' The prospect frightened me a little, but at the time it didn't frighten me as much as doing anything to hurt her; and ten minutes later she had my seal ring on her finger, and my promise that when I went abroad she should go with me.

"You'll wonder why I'm enlarging on this incident. It's because the evening on which it took place was the very evening on which I first saw the queer sight I've spoken of. Being at that time an ardent believer in a necessary sequence between cause and effect, I naturally tried to trace some kind of link between what had just happened to me in my aunt's library, and what was to happen a few hours later on the same night; and so the coincidence between the two events always remained in my mind.

"I went up to bed with rather a heavy heart, for I was bowed under the weight of the first good action I had ever consciously committed; and young as I was, I saw the gravity of my situation. Don't imagine from this that I had hitherto been an instrument of destruction. I had been merely a harmless young man, who had followed his bent and declined all collaboration with Providence. Now I had suddenly undertaken to promote the moral order of the world, and I felt a good deal like the trustful spectator who has given his gold watch to the conjurer, and doesn't know in what shape he'll get it back when the trick is over. . . . Still, a glow of self-righteousness tempered my fears, and I said to myself as I undressed that when I'd got used to being good it probably wouldn't make me as nervous as it did at the start. And by the time I was in bed, and had blown out my candle, I felt that I really *was* getting used to it, and that, as far as I'd got, it was not unlike sinking down into one of my aunt's very softest wool mattresses.

"I closed my eyes on this image, and when I opened them it must have been a good deal later, for my room had grown cold, and intensely still. I was waked by the queer feeling we all know—the feeling that there was something in the room that hadn't been there when I fell asleep. I sat up and strained my eyes into the darkness. The room was pitch black, and at first I saw nothing; but gradually a vague glimmer at the foot of the bed turned into two eyes staring back at me. I couldn't distinguish the features attached to them, but as I looked the eyes grew more and more distinct: they gave out a light of their own.

"The sensation of being thus gazed at was far from pleasant, and you might suppose that my first impulse would have been to jump out of bed and hurl myself on the invisible figure attached to the eyes. But it wasn't—my impulse was simply to lie still. . . . I can't say whether this was due to an immediate sense of the uncanny nature of the apparition—to the certainty that if I did jump out of bed I should hurl myself on nothing—or merely to the benumbing effect of the eyes themselves. They were the very worst eyes I've ever seen: a man's eyes —but what a man! My first thought was that he must be frightfully old. The orbits were sunk, and the thick red-lined lids hung over the eyeballs like blinds of which the cords are broken. One lid drooped a little lower than the other, with the effect of a crooked leer; and between these folds of flesh, with their scant bristle of lashes, the eyes themselves, small glassy disks with an agate-like rim, looked like sea pebbles in the grip of a starfish.

"But the age of the eyes was not the most unpleasant thing about them. What turned me sick was their expression of vicious security. I don't know how else to describe the fact that they seemed to belong to a man who had done a lot of harm in his life, but had always kept just inside the danger lines. They were not the eyes of a coward, but of someone much too clever to take risks; and my gorge rose at their look of base astuteness. Yet even that wasn't the worst; for as we continued to scan each other I saw in them a tinge of derision, and felt myself to be its object.

"At that I was seized by an impulse of rage that jerked me to my feet and pitched me straight at the unseen figure. But of course there wasn't any figure there, and my fists struck at emptiness. Ashamed and cold, I groped about for a match and lit the candles. The room looked

just as usual—as I had known it would; and I crawled back to bed, and blew out the lights.

"As soon as the room was dark again the eyes reappeared; and I now applied myself to explaining them on scientific principles. At first I thought the illusion might have been caused by the glow of the last embers in the chimney; but the fireplace was on the other side of my bed, and so placed that the fire could not be reflected in my toilet glass, which was the only mirror in the room. Then it struck me that I might have been tricked by the reflection of the embers in some polished bit of wood or metal; and though I couldn't discover any object of the sort in my line of vision, I got up again, groped my way to the hearth, and covered what was left of the fire. But as soon as I was back in bed the eyes were back at its foot.

"They were an hallucination, then: that was plain. But the fact that they were not due to any external dupery didn't make them a bit pleasanter. For if they were a projection of my inner consciousness, what the deuce was the matter with that organ? I had gone deeply enough into the mystery of morbid pathological states to picture the conditions under which an exploring mind might lay itself open to such a midnight admonition; but I couldn't fit it to my present case. I had never felt more normal, mentally and physically; and the only unusual fact in my situation—that of having assured the happiness of an amiable girl—did not seem of a kind to summon unclean spirits about my pillow. But there were the eyes still looking at me.

"I shut mine, and tried to evoke a vision of Alice Nowell's. They were not remarkable eyes, but they were as wholesome as fresh water, and if she had had more imagination—or longer lashes—their expression might have been interesting. As it was, they did not prove very efficacious, and in a few moments I perceived that they had mysteriously changed into the eyes at the foot of the bed. It exasperated me more to feel these glaring at me through my shut lids than to see them, and I opened my eyes again and looked straight into their hateful stare. . . .

"And so it went on all night. I can't tell you what that night was like, nor how long it lasted. Have you ever lain in bed, hopelessly wide awake, and tried to keep your eyes shut, knowing that if you opened 'em you'd see something you dreaded and loathed? It sounds easy, but it's devilishly hard. Those eyes hung there and drew me. I had the *vertige de l'abîme*, and their red lids were the edge of my abyss. . . . I had known nervous hours before: hours when I'd felt the wind of danger on my neck; but never this kind of strain. It wasn't that the eyes were awful; they hadn't the majesty of the powers of darkness. But they had—how shall I say?—a physical effect that was the equivalent of a bad smell: their look left a smear like a snail's. And I didn't see what business they had with me, anyhow—and I stared and stared, trying to find out.

"I don't know what effect they were trying to produce; but the effect they *did* produce was that of making me pack my portmanteau and bolt to town early the next morning. I left a note for my aunt, explaining that I was ill and had gone to see my doctor; and as a matter of fact I did feel uncommonly ill—the night seemed to have pumped all the blood out of me. But when I reached town I didn't go to the doctor's. I went to a friend's rooms, and threw myself on a bed, and slept for ten heavenly hours. When I woke it was the middle of the night, and I turned cold at the thought of what might be waiting for me. I sat up, shaking, and stared into the darkness; but there wasn't a break in its blessed surface, and when I saw that the eyes were not there I dropped back into another long sleep.

"I had left no word for Alice when I fled, because I meant to go back the next morning. But the next morning I was too exhausted to stir. As the day went on the exhaustion increased, instead of wearing off like the fatigue left by an ordinary night of insomnia: the effect of the eyes seemed to be cumulative, and the thought of seeing them again grew intolerable. For two days I fought my dread; and on the third evening I pulled myself together and decided to go back the next morning. I felt a good deal happier as soon as I'd decided, for I knew that my abrupt disappearance, and the strangeness of my not writing, must have been very distressing to poor Alice. I went to bed with an easy mind, and fell asleep at once; but in the middle of the night I woke, and there were the eyes. . . .

"Well, I simply couldn't face them; and instead of going back to my aunt's I bundled a few things into a trunk and jumped aboard the first steamer for England. I was so dead tired when I got on board that I crawled straight into my berth, and slept most of the way over; and I can't tell you the bliss it was to wake from those long dreamless stretches and look fearlessly into the dark, *knowing* that I shouldn't see the eyes. . . .

"I stayed abroad for a year, and then I stayed for another; and during that time I never had a glimpse of them. That was enough reason for prolonging my stay if I'd been on a desert island. Another was, of course, that I had perfectly come to see, on the voyage over, the complete impossibility of my marrying Alice Nowell. The fact that I had been so slow in making this discovery annoyed me, and made me want to avoid explanations. The bliss of escaping at one stroke from the eyes, and from this other embarrassment, gave my freedom an extraordinary zest; and the longer I savored it the better I liked its taste.

"The eyes had burned such a hole in my consciousness that for a long time I went on puzzling over the nature of the apparition, and wondering if it would ever come back. But as time passed I lost this dread, and retained only the precision of the image. Then that faded in its turn.

"The second year found me settled in Rome, where I was planning, I believe, to write another great book—a definitive work on Etruscan influences in Italian art. At any rate, I'd found some pretext of the kind for taking a sunny apartment in the Piazza di Spagna and dabbling about in the Forum; and there, one morning, a charming youth came to me. As he stood there in the warm light, slender and smooth and hyacinthine, he might have stepped from a ruined altar—one to Antinous, say; but he'd come instead from New York, with a letter from (of all people) Alice Nowell. The letter—the first I'd had from her since our break—was simply a line introducing her young cousin, Gilbert Noyes, and appealing to me to befriend him. It appeared, poor lad, that he 'had talent,' and 'wanted to write'; and, an obdurate family having insisted that his calligraphy should take the form of double entry, Alice had intervened to win him six months' respite, during which he was to travel abroad on a meager pittance, and somehow prove his ability to increase it by his pen. The quaint conditions of the test struck me first: it seemed about as conclusive as a medieval 'ordeal.' Then I was touched by her having sent him to me. I had always wanted to do her some service, to justify myself in my own eyes rather than hers; and here was a beautiful occasion.

"I imagine it's safe to lay down the general principle that predestined geniuses don't, as a rule, appear before one in the spring sunshine of the Forum looking like one of its banished gods. At any rate, poor Noyes wasn't a predestined genius. But he *was* beautiful to see, and charming as a comrade. It was only when he began to talk literature that my heart failed me. I knew all the symptoms so well—the things he had 'in him,' and the things outside him that impinged! There's the real test, after all. It was always—punctually, inevitably, with the inexorableness of a mechanical law—it was *always* the wrong thing that struck him. I grew to find a certain fascination in deciding in advance exactly which wrong thing he'd select; and I acquired an astonishing skill at the game. . . .

"The worst of it was that his *bêtise* wasn't of the too obvious sort. Ladies who met him at picnics thought him intellectual; and even at dinners he passed for clever. I, who had him under the microscope, fancied now and then that he might develop some kind of a slim talent, something that he could make 'do' and be happy on; and wasn't that, after all, what I was concerned with? He was so charming—he continued to be so charming—that he called forth all my charity in support of this argument; and for the first few months I really believed there was a chance for him. . . .

"Those months were delightful. Noyes was constantly with me, and the more I saw of him the better I liked him. His stupidity was a natural grace—it was as beautiful, really, as his eyelashes. And he was so gay, so affectionate, and so happy with me, that telling him the truth would have been about as pleasant as slitting the throat of some gentle animal. At first I used to wonder what had put into that radiant head the detestable delusion that it held a brain. Then I began to see that it was simply protective mimicry—an instinctive ruse to get away from family life and an office desk. Not that Gilbert didn't—dear lad! —believe in himself. There wasn't a trace of hypocrisy in him. He was sure that his 'call' was irresistible, while to me it was the saving grace of his situation that it *wasn't*, and that a little money, a little leisure, a little pleasure would have turned him into an inoffensive idler. Un- luckily, however, there was no hope of money, and with the alternative of the office desk before him he couldn't postpone his attempt at literature. The stuff he turned out was deplorable, and I see now that I knew it from the first. Still, the absurdity of deciding a man's whole future on a first trial seemed to justify me in withholding my verdict, and perhaps even in encouraging him a little, on the ground that the human plant generally needs warmth to flower.

"At any rate, I proceeded on that principle, and carried it to the point of getting his term of probation extended. When I left Rome he went with me, and we idled away a delicious summer between Capri and Venice. I said to myself: 'If he has anything in him, it will come out now,' and it *did*. He was never more enchanting and enchanted. There were moments of our pilgrimage when beauty born of murmuring sound seemed actually to pass into his face—but only to issue forth in a flood of the palest ink. . . .

"Well, the time came to turn off the tap; and I knew there was no hand but mine to do it. We were back in Rome, and I had taken him to stay with me, not wanting him to be alone in his *pension* when he had to face the necessity of renouncing his ambition. I hadn't, of course, relied solely on my own judgment in deciding to advise him to drop literature. I had sent his stuff to various people—editors and critics—and they had always sent it back with the same chilling lack of comment. Really there was nothing on earth to say.

"I confess I never felt more shabby than I did on the day when I decided to have it out with Gilbert. It was well enough to tell myself that it was my duty to knock the poor boy's hopes into splinters—but I'd like to know what act of gratuitous cruelty hasn't been justified on that plea? I've always shrunk from usurping the functions of Providence, and when I have to exercise them I decidedly prefer that it shouldn't be on an errand of destruction. Besides, in the last issue, who was I to decide, even after a year's trial, if poor Gilbert had it in him or not?

"The more I looked at the part I'd resolved to play, the less I liked it; and I liked it still less when Gilbert sat opposite me, with his head thrown back in the lamplight, just as Phil's is now. . . . I'd been going over his last manuscript, and he knew it, and he knew that his future hung on my verdict—we'd tacitly agreed to that. The manuscript lay between us, on my table—a novel, his first novel, if you please!—and he reached over and laid his hand on it, and looked up at me with all his life in the look.

"I stood up and cleared my throat, trying to keep my eyes away from his face and on the manuscript.

" 'The fact is, my dear Gilbert,' I began—

"I saw him turn pale, but he was up and facing me in an instant.

" 'Oh, look here, don't take on so, my dear fellow! I'm not so awfully cut up as all that!' His hands were on my shoulders, and he was laughing down on me from his full height, with a kind of mortally stricken gaiety that drove the knife into my side.

"He was too beautifully brave for me to keep up any humbug about my duty. And it came over me suddenly how I should hurt others in hurting him: myself first, since sending him home meant losing him; but more particularly poor Alice Nowell, to whom I had so longed to prove my good faith and my desire to serve her. It really seemed like failing her twice to fail Gilbert.

"But my intuition was like one of those lightning flashes that encircle the whole horizon, and in the same instant I saw what I might be letting myself in for if I didn't tell the truth. I said to myself: 'I shall have him for life'—and I'd never yet seen anyone, man or woman, whom I was quite sure of wanting on those terms. Well, this impulse of egotism decided me. I was ashamed of it, and to get away from it I took a leap that landed me straight in Gilbert's arms.

" 'The thing's all right, and you're all wrong!' I shouted up at him; and as he hugged me, and I laughed and shook in his clutch, I had for a minute the sense of self-complacency that is supposed to attend the footsteps of the just. Hang it all, making people happy *has* its charms.

"Gilbert, of course, was for celebrating his emancipation in some spectacular manner; but I sent him away alone to explode his emotions, and went to bed to sleep off mine. As I undressed I began to wonder what their aftertaste would be—so many of the finest don't keep! Still, I wasn't sorry, and I meant to empty the bottle, even if it *did* turn a trifle flat.

"After I got into bed I lay for a long time smiling at the memory of his eyes—his blissful eyes. . . . Then I fell asleep, and when I woke the room was deathly cold, and I sat up with a jerk—and there were *the other eyes.* . . .

"It was three years since I'd seen them, but I'd thought of them so often that I fancied they could never take me unawares again. Now, with their red sneer on me, I knew that I had never really believed they would come back, and that I was as defenceless as ever against them. . . . As before, it was the insane irrelevance of their coming that made it so horrible. What the deuce were they after, to leap out at me at such a time? I had lived more or less carelessly in the years since I'd seen them, though my worst indiscretions were not dark enough to invite the searchings of their infernal glare; but at this particular moment I was really in what might have been called a state of grace; and I can't tell you how the fact added to their horror. . . .

"But it's not enough to say they were as bad as before: they were worse. Worse by just so much as I'd learned of life in the interval; by all the damnable implications my wider experience read into them. I saw now what I hadn't seen before: that they were eyes which had grown hideous gradually, which had built up their baseness coral-wise, bit by bit, out of a series of small turpitudes slowly accumulated through the industrious years. Yes—it came to me that what made them so bad was that they'd grown bad so slowly. . . .

"There they hung in the darkness, their swollen lids dropped across the little watery bulbs rolling loose in the orbits, and the puff of flesh making a muddy shadow underneath—and as their stare moved with my movements, there came over me a sense of their tacit complicity, of a deep hidden understanding between us that was worse than the first shock of their strangeness. Not that I understood them; but that they made it so clear that someday I should. . . . Yes, that was the worst part of it, decidedly; and it was the feeling that became stronger each time they came back. . . .

"For they got into the damnable habit of coming back. They reminded me of vampires with a taste for young flesh, they seemed so to gloat over the taste of a good conscience. Every night for a month they came to claim their morsel of mine: since I'd made Gilbert happy they simply wouldn't loosen their fangs. The coincidence almost made me hate him, poor lad, fortuitous as I felt it to be. I puzzled over it a good deal, but couldn't find any hint of an explanation except in the chance of his association with Alice Nowell. But then the eyes had let up on me the moment I had abandoned her, so they could hardly be the emissaries of a woman scorned, even if one could have pictured poor Alice charging such spirits to avenge her. That set me thinking, and I began to wonder if they would let up on me if I abandoned Gilbert. The temptation was insidious, and I had to stiffen myself against it; but really, dear boy! he was too charming to be sacrificed to such demons. And so, after all, I never found out what they wanted. . . . "

III

The fire crumbled, sending up a flash which threw into relief the narrator's gnarled face under its grey-black stubble. Pressed into the hollow of the chair back, it stood out an instant like an intaglio of yellowish red-veined stone, with spots of enamel for the eyes; then the fire sank and it became once more a dim Rembrandtish blur.

Phil Frenham, sitting in a low chair on the opposite side of the hearth, one long arm propped on the table behind him, one hand supporting his thrown-back head, and his eyes fixed on his old friend's face, had not moved since the tale began. He continued to maintain his silent immobility after Culwin had ceased to speak, and it was I who, with a vague sense of disappointment at the sudden drop of the story, finally asked: "But how long did you keep on seeing them?"

Culwin, so sunk into his chair that he seemed like a heap of his own empty clothes, stirred a little, as if in surprise at my question. He appeared to have half-forgotten what he had been telling us.

"How long? Oh, off and on all that winter. It was infernal. I never got used to them. I grew really ill."

Frenham shifted his attitude, and as he did so his elbow struck against a small mirror in a bronze frame standing on the table behind him. He turned and changed its angle slightly; then he resumed his former attitude, his dark head thrown back on his lifted palm, his eyes intent on Culwin's face. Something in his silent gaze embarrassed me, and as if to divert attention from it I pressed on with another question:

"And you never tried sacrificing Noyes?"

"Oh, no. The fact is I didn't have to. He did it for me, poor boy!"

"Did it for you? How do you mean?"

"He wore me out—wore everybody out. He kept on pouring out his lamentable twaddle, and hawking it up and down the place till he became a thing of terror. I tried to wean him from writing—oh, ever so gently, you understand, by throwing him with agreeable people, giving him a chance to make himself felt, to come to a sense of what he *really* had to give. I'd foreseen this solution from the beginning— felt sure that, once the first ardor of authorship was quenched, he'd drop into his place as a charming parasitic thing, the kind of chronic Cherubino for whom, in old societies, there's always a seat at table, and a shelter behind the ladies' skirts. I saw him take his place as 'the poet': the poet who doesn't write. One knows the type in every drawing room. Living in that way doesn't cost much—I'd worked it all out in my mind, and felt sure that, with a little help, he could manage it for the next few years; and meanwhile he'd be sure to marry. I saw him married to a widow, rather older, with a good cook and a well-run house. And I actually had my eye on the widow. . . . Meanwhile I did everything to help the transition—lent him money to ease his conscience, introduced him to pretty women to make him forget his vows. But nothing would do him: he had but one idea in his beautiful obstinate head. He wanted the laurel and not the rose, and he kept on repeating Gautier's axiom, and battering and filing at his limp prose till he'd spread it out over Lord knows how many hundred pages. Now and then he would send a barrelful to a publisher, and of course it would always come back.

"At first it didn't matter—he thought he was 'misunderstood.' He took the attitudes of genius, and whenever an opus came home he wrote another to keep it company. Then he had a reaction of despair, and accused me of deceiving him, and Lord knows what. I got angry at that, and told him it was he who had deceived himself. He'd come to me determined to write, and I'd done my best to help him. That was the extent of my offence, and I'd done it for his cousin's sake, not his.

"That seemed to strike home, and he didn't answer for a minute. Then he said: 'My time's up and my money's up. What do you think I'd better do?'

" 'I think you'd better not be an ass,' I said.

" 'What do you mean by being an ass?' he asked.

"I took a letter from my desk and held it out to him.

" 'I mean refusing this offer of Mrs. Ellinger's: to be her secretary at a salary of five thousand dollars. There may be a lot more in it than that.'

"He flung out his hand with a violence that struck the letter from mine. 'Oh, I know well enough what's in it!' he said, red to the roots of his hair.

" 'And what's the answer, if you know?' I asked.

"He made none at the minute, but turned away slowly to the door. There, with his hand on the threshold, he stopped to say, almost under his breath: 'Then you really think my stuff's no good?'

"I was tired and exasperated, and I laughed. I don't defend my laugh—it was in wretched taste. But I must plead in extenuation that the boy was a fool, and that I'd done my best for him—I really had.

"He went out of the room, shutting the door quietly after him. That afternoon I left for Frascati, where I'd promised to spend the Sunday with some friends. I was glad to escape from Gilbert, and by the same token, as I learned that night, I had also escaped from the eyes. I dropped into the same lethargic sleep that had come to me before when I left off seeing them; and when I woke the next morning in my peaceful room above the ilexes, I felt the utter weariness and deep relief that always followed on that sleep. I put in two blessed nights at Frascati, and when I got back to my rooms in Rome I found that Gilbert had gone. . . . Oh, nothing tragic had happened—the episode never rose to *that*. He'd simply packed his manuscripts and left for America—for his family and the Wall Street desk. He left a decent enough note to tell me of his decision, and behaved altogether, in the circumstances, as little like a fool as it's possible for a fool to behave. . . ."

IV

Culwin paused again, and Frenham still sat motionless, the dusky contour of his young head reflected in the mirror at his back.

"And what became of Noyes afterward?" I finally asked, still disquieted by a sense of incompleteness, by the need of some connecting thread between the parallel lines of the tale.

Culwin twitched his shoulders. "Oh, nothing became of him—because he became nothing. There could be no question of 'becoming' about it. He vegetated in an office, I believe, and finally got a clerkship in a consulate, and married drearily in China. I saw him once in Hong Kong, years afterward. He was fat and hadn't shaved. I was told he drank. He didn't recognize me."

"And the eyes?" I asked, after another pause which Frenham's continued silence made oppressive.

Culwin, stroking his chin, blinked at me meditatively through the shadows. "I never saw them after my last talk with Gilbert. Put two and two together if you can. For my part, I haven't found the link."

He rose, his hands in his pockets, and walked stiffly over to the table on which reviving drinks had been set out.

"You must be parched after this dry tale. Here, help yourself, my dear fellow. Here, Phil—" He turned back to the hearth.

Frenham made no response to his host's hospitable summons. He still sat in his low chair without moving, but as Culwin advanced toward him, their eyes met in a long look; after which the young man, turning suddenly, flung his arms across the table behind him, and dropped his face upon them.

Culwin, at the unexpected gesture, stopped short, a flush on his face.

"Phil—what the deuce? Why, have the eyes scared *you?* My dear boy—my dear fellow—I never had such a tribute to my literary ability, never!"

He broke into a chuckle at the thought, and halted on the hearth-rug, his hands still in his pockets, gazing down at the youth's bowed head. Then, as Frenham still made no answer, he moved a step or two nearer.

"Cheer up, my dear Phil! It's years since I've seen them—apparently I've done nothing lately bad enough to call them out of chaos. Unless my present evocation of them has made *you* see them; which would be their worst stroke yet!"

His bantering appeal quivered off into an uneasy laugh, and he moved still nearer, bending over Frenham, and laying his gouty hands on the lad's shoulders.

"Phil, my dear boy, really—what's the matter? Why don't you answer? *Have* you seen the eyes?"

Frenham's face was still hidden, and from where I stood behind Culwin I saw the latter, as if under the rebuff of this unaccountable attitude, draw back slowly from his friend. As he did so, the light of the lamp on the table fell full on his congested face, and I caught its reflection in the mirror behind Frenham's head.

Culwin saw the reflection also. He paused, his face level with the mirror, as if scarcely recognizing the countenance in it as his own. But as he looked his expression gradually changed, and for an appreciable space of time he and the image in the glass confronted each other with a glare of slowly gathering hate. Then Culwin let go of Frenham's shoulders, and drew back a step. . . .

Frenham, his face still hidden, did not stir.

Afterward

"*O*h, there *is* one, of course, but you'll never know it."

The assertion, laughingly flung out six months earlier in a bright June garden, came back to Mary Boyne with a new perception of its significance as she stood, in the December dusk, waiting for the lamps to be brought into the library.

The words had been spoken by their friend Alida Stair, as they sat at tea on her lawn at Pangbourne, in reference to the very house of which the library in question was the central, the pivotal "feature." Mary Boyne and her husband, in quest of a country place in one of the southern or southwestern counties, had, on their arrival in England, carried their problem straight to Alida Stair, who had successfully solved it in her own case; but it was not until they had rejected, almost capriciously, several practical and judicious suggestions that she threw out: "Well, there's Lyng, in Dorsetshire. It belongs to Hugo's cousins, and you can get it for a song."

The reason she gave for its being obtainable on these terms—its remoteness from a station, its lack of electric light, hot water pipes, and other vulgar necessities—were exactly those pleading in its favor with two romantic Americans perversely in search of the economic draw-backs which were associated, in their tradition, with unusual architectural felicities.

"I should never believe I was living in an old house unless I was thoroughly uncomfortable," Ned Boyne, the more extravagant of the two, had jocosely insisted; "the least hint of convenience would make me think it had been bought out of an exhibition, with the pieces numbered, and set up again." And they had proceeded to enumerate, with humorous precision, their various doubts and demands, refusing to believe that the house their cousin recommended was *really* Tudor till they learned it had no heating system, or that the village church was literally in the grounds till she assured them of the deplorable uncertainty of the water supply.

"It's too uncomfortable to be true!" Edward Boyne had continued to exult as the avowal of each disadvantage was successively wrung from her; but he had cut short his rhapsody to ask, with a relapse to distrust: "And the ghost? You've been concealing from us the fact that there is no ghost!"

Mary, at the moment, had laughed with him, yet almost with her laugh, being possessed of several sets of independent perceptions, had been struck by a note of flatness in Alida's answering hilarity.

"Oh, Dorsetshire's full of ghosts, you know."

"Yes, yes; but that won't do. I don't want to have to drive ten miles to see somebody else's ghost. I want one of my own on the premises. *Is* there a ghost at Lyng?"

His rejoinder had made Alida laugh again, and it was then that she had flung back tantalizingly: "Oh, there *is* one, of course, but you'll never know it."

"Never know it?" Boyne pulled her up. "But what in the world constitutes a ghost except the fact of its being known for one?"

"I can't say. But that's the story."

"That there's a ghost, but that nobody knows it's a ghost?"

"Well—not till afterward, at any rate."

"Till afterward?"

"Not till long long afterward."

"But if it's once been identified as an unearthly visitant, why hasn't it *signalement* been handed down in the family? How has it managed to preserve its incognito?"

Alida could only shake her head. "Don't ask me. But it has."

"And then suddenly"—Mary spoke up as if from cavernous depths of divination—"suddenly, long afterward, one says to one's self *'That was it?'* "

She was startled at the sepulchral sound with which her question fell on the banter of the other two, and she saw the shadow of the same surprise flit across Alida's pupils. "I suppose so. One just has to wait."

"Oh, hang waiting!" Ned broke in. "Life's too short for a ghost who can only be enjoyed in retrospect. Can't we do better than that, Mary?"

But it turned out that in the event they were not destined to, for within three months of their conversation with Mrs. Stair they were settled at Lyng, and the life they had yearned for, to the point of planning it in advance in all its daily details, had actually begun for them.

It was to sit, in the thick December dusk, by just such a wide-hooded fireplace, under just such black oak rafters, with the sense that beyond the mullioned panes the downs were darkened to a deeper solitude: it was for the ultimate indulgence of such sensations that Mary Boyne, abruptly exiled from New York by her husband's business, had endured for nearly fourteen years the soul-deadening ugliness of a Middle Western town, and that Boyne had ground on doggedly at his engineering till, with a suddenness that still made her blink, the prodigious windfall of the Blue Star Mine had put them at a stroke in possession of life and the leisure to taste it. They had never for a moment meant their new state to be one of idleness; but they meant to give themselves only to harmonious activities. She had her vision of painting and gardening (against a background of grey walls), he dreamed of the production of his long-planned book on the "Economic Basis of Culture"; and with such absorbing work ahead no existence could be too sequestered: they could not get far enough from the world, or plunge deep enough into the past.

Dorsetshire had attracted them from the first by an air of remoteness out of all proportion to its geographical position. But to the Boynes it was one of the ever-recurring wonders of the whole incredibly compressed island—a nest of counties, as they put it—that for the production of its effects so little of a given quality went so far: that so few miles made a distance, and so short a distance a difference.

"It's that," Ned had once enthusiastically explained, "that gives such depth to their effects, such relief to their contrasts. They've been able to lay the butter so thick on every delicious mouthful."

The butter had certainly been laid on thick at Lyng: the old house hidden under a shoulder of the downs had almost all the finer marks of commerce with a protracted past. The mere fact that it was neither large nor exceptional made it, to the Boynes, abound the more completely in its special charm—the charm of having been for centuries a deep dim reservoir of life. The life had probably not been of the most vivid order: for long periods, no doubt, it had fallen as noiselessly into the past as the quiet drizzle of autumn fell, hour after hour, into the fish pond between the yews; but these backwaters of existence sometimes breed, in their sluggish depths, strange acuities of emotion, and Mary Boyne had felt from the first the mysterious stir of intenser memories.

The feeling had never been stronger than on this particular afternoon when, waiting in the library for the lamps to come, she rose from her seat and stood among the shadows of the hearth. Her husband had gone off, after luncheon, for one of his long tramps on the downs. She had noticed of late that he preferred to go alone; and, in the tried security of their personal relations, had been driven to conclude that his book was bothering him, and that he needed the afternoons to turn over in solitude the problems left from the morning's work. Certainly the book was not going as smoothly as she had thought it would, and there were lines of perplexity between his eyes such as had never been there in his engineering days. He had often, then, looked fagged to the verge of illness, but the native demon of worry had never branded his brow. Yet the few pages he had so far read to her—the introduction, and a summary of the opening chapter—showed a firm hold on his subject, and an increasing confidence in his powers.

The fact threw her into deeper perplexity, since, now that he had done with business and its disturbing contingencies, the one other possible source of anxiety was eliminated. Unless it were his health, then? But physically he had gained since they had come to Dorsetshire, grown robuster, ruddier and fresher eyed. It was only within the last week that she had felt in him the undefinable change which made her restless in his absence, and as tongue-tied in his presence as though it were *she* who had a secret to keep from him!

The thought that there *was* a secret somewhere between them struck her with a sudden rap of wonder, and she looked about her down the long room.

"Can it be the house?" she mused.

The room itself might have been full of secrets. They seemed to be piling themselves up, as evening fell, like the layers and layers of velvet shadow dropping from the low ceiling, the rows of books, the smoke-blurred sculpture of the hearth.

"Why, of course—the house is haunted!" she reflected.

The ghost—Alida's imperceptible ghost—after figuring largely in the banter of their first month or two at Lyng, had been gradually left aside as too ineffectual for imaginative use. Mary had, indeed, as became the tenant of a haunted house, made the customary inquiries among her rural neighbors, but, beyond a vague "They do say so, Ma'am," the villagers had nothing to impart. The elusive specter had apparently never had sufficient identity for a legend to crystallize about it, and after a time the Boynes had set the matter down to their profit-and-loss account, agreeing that Lyng was one of the few houses good enough in itself to dispense with supernatural enhancements.

"And I suppose, poor ineffectual demon, that's why it beats its beautiful wings in vain in the void," Mary had laughingly concluded.

"Or, rather," Ned answered in the same strain, "why, amid so much that's ghostly, it can never affirm its separate existence as *the* ghost." And thereupon their invisible housemate had finally dropped out of their references, which were numerous enough to make them soon unaware of the loss.

Now, as she stood on the hearth, the subject of their earlier curiosity revived in her with a new sense of its meaning—a sense gradually acquired through daily contact with the scene of the lurking mystery. It was the house itself, of course, that possessed the ghost-seeing faculty, that communed visually but secretly with its own past; if one could only get into close enough communion with the house, one might surprise its secret, and acquire the ghost sight on one's own account. Perhaps, in his long hours in this very room, where she never trespassed till the afternoon, her husband *had* acquired it already, and was silently carrying about the weight of whatever it had revealed to him. Mary was too well versed in the code of the spectral world not to know that one could not talk about the ghosts one saw: to do so was almost as great a breach of taste as to name a lady in a club. But this explanation did not really satisfy her. "What, after all, except for the fun of the shudder," she reflected, "would he really care for any of their old ghosts?" And thence she was thrown back once more on the fundamental dilemma: the fact that one's greater or less susceptibility to spectral influences had no particular bearing on the case, since, when one *did* see a ghost at Lyng, one did not know it.

"Not till long afterward," Alida Stair had said. Well, supposing Ned *had* seen one when they first came, and had known only within the last week what had happened to him? More and more under the spell of the hour, she threw back her thoughts to the early days of their tenancy, but at first only to recall a lively confusion of unpacking, settling, arranging of books, and calling to each other from remote corners of the house as, treasure after treasure, it revealed itself to them. It was in this particular connection that she presently recalled a certain soft afternoon of the previous October, when, passing from the first rapturous flurry of exploration to a detailed inspection of the

old house, she had pressed (like a novel heroine) a panel that opened
on a flight of corkscrew stairs leading to a flat ledge of the roof—the
roof which, from below, seemed to slope away on all sides too abruptly
for any but practiced feet to scale.

The view from this hidden coign was enchanting, and she had
flown down to snatch Ned from his papers and give him the freedom
of her discovery. She remembered still how, standing at her side, he
had passed his arm about her while their gaze flew to the long tossed
horizon line of the downs, and then dropped contentedly back to trace
the arabesque of yew hedges about the fish pond, and the shadow of
the cedar on the lawn.

"And now the other way," he had said, turning her about within
his arm; and closely pressed to him, she had absorbed, like some long
satisfying draught, the picture of the grey-walled court, the squat lions
on the gates, and the lime avenue reaching up to the highroad under
the downs.

It was just then, while they gazed and held each other, that she
had felt his arm relax, and heard a sharp "Hullo!" that made her turn
to glance at him.

Distinctly, yes, she now recalled that she had seen, as she glanced,
a shadow of anxiety, of perplexity, rather, fall across his face; and,
following his eyes, had beheld the figure of a man—a man in loose
greyish clothes, as it appeared to her—who was sauntering down the
lime avenue to the court with the doubtful gait of a stranger who seeks
his way. Her shortsighted eyes had given her but a blurred impression
of slightness and greyishness, with something foreign, or at least unlo-
cal, in the cut of the figure or its dress; but her husband had apparently
seen more—seen enough to make him push past her with a hasty
"Wait!" and dash down the stairs without pausing to give her a hand.

A slight tendency to dizziness obliged her, after a provisional
clutch at the chimney against which they had been leaning, to follow
him first more cautiously; and when she had reached the landing she
paused again, for a less definite reason, leaning over the banister to
strain her eyes through the silence of the brown sun-flecked depths.
She lingered there till, somewhere in those depths, she heard the
closing of a door; then, mechanically impelled, she went down the
shallow flights of steps till she reached the lower hall.

The front door stood open on the sunlight of the court, and hall

and court were empty. The library door was open, too, and after listening in vain for any sound of voices within, she crossed the threshold, and found her husband alone, vaguely fingering the papers on his desk.

He looked up, as if surprised at her entrance, but the shadow of anxiety had passed from his face, leaving it even, as she fancied, a little brighter and clearer than usual.

"What was it? Who was it?" she asked.

"Who?" he repeated, with the surprise still all on his side.

"The man we saw coming toward the house."

He seemed to reflect. "The man? Why, I thought I saw Peters; I dashed after him to say a word about the stable drains, but he had disappeared before I could get down."

"Disappeared? But he seemed to be walking so slowly when we saw him."

Boyne shrugged his shoulders. "So I thought; but he must have got up steam in the interval. What do you say to our trying a scramble up Meldon Steep before sunset?"

That was all. At the time the occurrence had been less than nothing, had, indeed, been immediately obliterated by the magic of their first vision from Meldon Steep, a height which they had dreamed of climbing ever since they had first seen its bare spine rising above the roof of Lyng. Doubtless it was the mere fact of the other incident's having occurred on the very day of their ascent to Meldon that had kept it stored away in the fold of memory from which it now emerged; for in itself it had no mark of the portentous. At the moment there could have been nothing more natural than that Ned should dash himself from the roof in the pursuit of dilatory tradesmen. It was the period when they were always on the watch for one or the other of the specialists employed about the place; always lying in wait for them, and rushing out at them with questions, reproaches or reminders. And certainly in the distance the grey figure had looked like Peters.

Yet now, as she reviewed the scene, she felt her husband's explanation of it to have been invalidated by the look of anxiety on his face. Why had the familiar appearance of Peters made him anxious? Why, above all, if it was of such prime necessity to confer with him on the subject of the stable drains, had the failure to find him produced such a look of relief? Mary could not say that any one of these questions had occurred to her at the time, yet, from the promptness with which they now marshalled themselves at her summons, she had a sense that they must all along have been there, waiting their hour.

II

Weary with her thoughts, she moved to the window. The library was now quite dark, and she was surprised to see how much faint light the outer world still held.

As she peered out into it across the court, a figure shaped itself far down the perspective of bare limes: it looked a mere blot of deeper grey in the greyness, and for an instant, as it moved toward her, her heart thumped to the thought "It's the ghost!"

She had time, in that long instant, to feel suddenly that the man of whom, two months earlier, she had had a distant vision from the roof, was now, at his predestined hour, about to reveal himself as *not* having been Peters; and her spirit sank under the impending fear of the disclosure. But almost with the next tick of the clock the figure, gaining substance and character, showed itself even to her weak sight as her husband's; and she turned to meet him, as he entered, with the confession of her folly.

"It's really too absurd," she laughed out, "but I never *can* remember!"

"Remember what?" Boyne questioned as they drew together.

"That when one sees the Lyng ghost one never knows it."

Her hand was on his sleeve, and he kept it there, but with no response in his gesture or in the lines of his preoccupied face.

"Did you think you'd seen it?" he asked, after an appreciable interval.

"Why, I actually took *you* for it, my dear, in my mad determination to spot it!"

"Me—just now?" His arm dropped away, and he turned from her with a faint echo of her laugh. "Really, dearest, you'd better give it up, if that's the best you can do."

"Oh, yes, I give it up. Have *you?*" she asked, turning round on him abruptly.

The parlormaid had entered with letters and a lamp, and the light struck up into Boyne's face as he bent above the tray she presented.

"Have *you?*" Mary perversely insisted, when the servant had disappeared on her errand of illumination.

"Have I what?" he rejoined absently, the light bringing out the sharp stamp of worry between his brows as he turned over the letters.

"Given up trying to see the ghost." Her heart beat a little at the experiment she was making.

Her husband, laying his letters aside, moved away into the shadow of the hearth.

"I never tried," he said, tearing open the wrapper of a newspaper.

"Well, of course," Mary persisted, "the exasperating thing is that there's no use trying, since one can't be sure till so long afterward."

He was unfolding the paper as if he had hardly heard her; but after a pause, during which the sheets rustled spasmodically between his hands, he looked up to ask, "Have you any idea *how long?*"

Mary had sunk into a low chair beside the fireplace. From her seat she glanced over, startled, at her husband's profile, which was projected against the circle of lamplight.

"No; none. Have *you?*" she retorted, repeating her former phrase with an added stress of intention.

Boyne crumpled the paper into a bunch, and then, inconsequently, turned back with it toward the lamp.

"Lord, no! I only meant," he exclaimed, with a faint tinge of impatience, "is there any legend, any tradition, as to that?"

"Not that I know of," she answered; but the impulse to add "What makes you ask?" was checked by the reappearance of the parlormaid, with tea and a second lamp.

With the dispersal of shadows, and the repetition of the daily domestic office, Mary Boyne felt herself less oppressed by that sense of something mutely imminent which had darkened her afternoon. For a few moments she gave herself to the details of her task, and when she looked up from it she was struck to the point of bewilderment by the change in her husband's face. He had seated himself near the farther lamp, and was absorbed in the perusal of his letters; but was it something he had found in them, or merely the shifting of her own point of view, that had restored his features to their normal aspect? The longer she looked the more definitely the change affirmed itself. The lines of tension had vanished, and such traces of fatigue as lingered were of the kind easily attributable to steady mental effort. He glanced up, as if drawn by her gaze, and met her eyes with a smile.

"I'm dying for my tea, you know; and here's a letter for you," he said.

She took the letter he held out in exchange for the cup she proffered him, and, returning to her seat, broke the seal with the languid gesture of the reader whose interests are all enclosed in the circle of one cherished presence.

Her next conscious motion was that of starting to her feet, the letter falling to them as she rose, while she held out to her husband a newspaper clipping.

"Ned! What's this? What does it mean?"

He had risen at the same instant, almost as if hearing her cry before she uttered it; and for a perceptible space of time he and she studied each other, like adversaries watching for an advantage, across the space between her chair and his desk.

"What's what? You fairly made me jump!" Boyne said at length, moving toward her with a sudden half-exasperated laugh. The shadow of apprehension was on his face again, not now a look of fixed foreboding, but a shifting vigilance of lips and eyes that gave her the sense of his feeling himself invisibly surrounded.

Her hand shook so that she could hardly give him the clipping.

"This article—from the *Waukesha Sentinel*—that a man named Elwell has brought suit against you—that there was something wrong about the Blue Star Mine. I can't understand more than half."

They continued to face each other as she spoke, and to her astonishment she saw that her words had the almost immediate effect of dissipating the strained watchfulness of his look.

"Oh, *that!*" He glanced down the printed slip, and then folded it with the gesture of one who handles something harmless and familiar. "What's the matter with you this afternoon, Mary? I thought you'd got bad news."

She stood before him with her undefinable terror subsiding slowly under the reassurance of his tone.

"You knew about this, then—it's all right?"

"Certainly I knew about it; and it's all right."

"But what *is* it? I don't understand. What does this man accuse you of?"

"Pretty nearly every crime in the calendar." Boyne had tossed the clipping down, and thrown himself into an armchair near the fire. "Do you want to hear the story? It's not particularly interesting—just a squabble over interests in the Blue Star."

"But who is this Elwell? I don't know the name."

"Oh, he's a fellow I put into it—gave him a hand up. I told you all about him at the time."

"I dare say. I must have forgotten." Vainly she strained back among her memories. "But if you helped him, why does he make this return?"

"Probably some shyster lawyer got hold of him and talked him over. It's all rather technical and complicated. I thought that kind of thing bored you."

His wife felt a sting of compunction. Theoretically, she deprecated the American wife's detachment from her husband's professional interests, but in practice she had always found it difficult to fix her attention on Boyne's report of the transactions in which his varied interests involved him. Besides, she had felt during their years of exile, that, in a community where the amenities of living could be obtained only at the cost of efforts as arduous as her husband's professional labors, such brief leisure as he and she could command should be used as an escape from immediate preoccupations, a flight to the life they always dreamed of living. Once or twice, now that this new life had actually drawn its magic circle about them, she had asked herself if she had done right; but hitherto such conjectures had been no more than the retrospective excursions of an active fancy. Now, for the first time, it startled her a little to find how little she knew of the material foundation on which her happiness was built.

She glanced at her husband, and was again reassured by the composure of his face; yet she felt the need of more definite grounds for her reassurance.

"But doesn't this suit worry you? Why have you never spoken to me about it?"

He answered both questions at once. "I didn't speak of it at first because it *did* worry me—annoyed me, rather. But it's all ancient history now. Your correspondent must have got hold of a back number of the *Sentinel*."

She felt a quick thrill of relief. "You mean it's over? He's lost his case?"

There was a just perceptible delay in Boyne's reply. "The suit's been withdrawn—that's all."

But she persisted, as if to exonerate herself from the inward charge of being too easily put off. "Withdrawn it because he saw he had no chance?"

"Oh, he had no chance," Boyne answered.

She was still struggling with a dimly felt perplexity at the back of her thoughts.

"How long ago was it withdrawn?"

He paused, as if with a slight return to his former uncertainty. "I've just had the news now; but I've been expecting it."

"Just now—in one of your letters?"

"Yes; in one of my letters."

She made no answer, and was aware only, after a short interval of waiting, that he had risen, and, strolling across the room, had placed himself on the sofa at her side. She felt him, as he did so, pass an arm about her, she felt his hand seek hers and clasp it, and turning slowly, drawn by the warmth of his cheek, she met his smiling eyes.

"It's all right—it's all right?" she questioned, through the flood of her dissolving doubts; and "I give you my word it was never righter!" he laughed back at her, holding her close.

III

One of the strangest things she was afterward to recall out of all the next day's strangeness was the sudden and complete recovery of her sense of security.

It was in the air when she woke in her low-ceiled, dusky room; it went with her downstairs to the breakfast table, flashed out at her from the fire, and reduplicated itself from the flanks of the urn and the sturdy flutings of the Georgian teapot. It was as if in some roundabout way, all her diffused fears of the previous day, with their moment of sharp concentration about the newspaper article—as if this dim questioning of the future, and startled return upon the past, had between them liquidated the arrears of some haunting moral obligation. If she had indeed been careless of her husband's affairs, it was, her new state seemed to prove, because her faith in him instinctively justified such carelessness; and his right to her faith had now affirmed itself in the very face of menace and suspicion. She had never seen him more untroubled, more naturally and unconsciously himself, than after the cross-examination to which she had subjected him: it was almost as if he had been aware of her doubts, and had wanted the air cleared as much as she did.

It was as clear, thank heaven, as the bright outer light that surprised her almost with a touch of summer when she issued from the house for her daily round of the gardens. She had left Boyne at his desk, indulging herself, as she passed the library door, by a last peep at his quiet face, where he bent, pipe in mouth, above his papers; and now she had her own morning's task to perform. The task involved, on such charmed winter days, almost as much happy loitering about the different quarters of her domain as if spring were already at work there. There were such endless possibilities still before her, such opportunities to bring out the latent graces of the old place, without a single irreverent touch of alteration, that the winter was all too short to plan what spring and autumn executed. And her recovered sense of safety gave, on this particular morning, a peculiar zest to her progress through the sweet still place. She went first to the kitchen garden, where the espaliered pear trees drew complicated patterns on the walls, and pigeons were fluttering and preening about the silvery-slated roof of their cot. There was something wrong about the piping of the hothouse, and she was expecting an authority from Dorchester, who was to drive out between trains and make a diagnosis of the boiler. But when she dipped into the damp heat of the greenhouses, among the spiced scents and waxy pinks and reds of old-fashioned exotics—even the flora of Lyng was in the note!—she learned that the great man had not arrived, and, the day being too rare to waste in an artificial atmosphere, she came out again and paced along the springy turf of the bowling green to the gardens behind the house. At their farther end rose a grass terrace, looking across the fish pond and yew hedges to the long house front with its twisted chimney stacks and blue roof angles all drenched in the pale gold moisture of the air.

Seen thus, across the level tracery of the gardens, it sent her, from open windows and hospitably smoking chimneys, the look of some warm human presence, of a mind slowly ripened on a sunny wall of experience. She had never before had such a sense of her intimacy with it, such a conviction that its secrets were all beneficent, kept, as they said to children, "for one's good," such a trust in its power to gather up her life and Ned's into the harmonious pattern of the long long story it sat there weaving in the sun.

She heard steps behind her, and turned, expecting to see the gardener accompanied by the engineer from Dorchester. But only one figure was in sight, that of a youngish slightly built man, who, for reasons she could not on the spot have given, did not remotely resemble her notion of an authority on hothouse boilers. The newcomer, on seeing her, lifted his hat, and paused with the air of a gentleman—perhaps a traveler—who wishes to make it known that his intrusion is involuntary. Lyng occasionally attracted the more cultivated traveler, and Mary half expected to see the stranger dissemble a camera, or justify his presence by producing it. But he made no gesture of any sort, and after a moment she asked, in a tone responding to the courteous hesitation of his attitude: "Is there anyone you wish to see?"

"I came to see Mr. Boyne," he answered. His intonation, rather than his accent, was faintly American, and Mary, at the note, looked at him more closely. The brim of his soft felt hat cast a shade on his face, which, thus obscured, wore to her shortsighted gaze a look of seriousness, as of a person arriving on business, and civilly but firmly aware of his rights.

Past experience had made her equally sensible to such claims; but she was jealous of her husband's morning hours, and doubtful of his having given anyone the right to intrude on them.

"Have you an appointment with my husband?" she asked.

The visitor hesitated, as if unprepared for the question.

"I think he expects me," he replied.

It was Mary's turn to hesitate. "You see this is his time for work: he never sees anyone in the morning."

He looked at her a moment without answering; then, as if accepting her decision, he began to move away. As he turned, Mary saw him pause and glance up at the peaceful house front. Something in his air suggested weariness and disappointment, the dejection of the traveler who has come from far off and whose hours are limited by the timetable. It occurred to her that if this were the case her refusal might have made his errand vain, and a sense of compunction caused her to hasten after him.

"May I ask if you have come a long way?"

He gave her the same grave look. "Yes—I have come a long way."

"Then, if you'll go to the house, no doubt my husband will see you now. You'll find him in the library."

She did not know why she had added the last phrase, except from a vague impulse to atone for her previous inhospitality. The visitor seemed about to express his thanks, but her attention was distracted by the approach of the gardener with a companion who bore all the marks of being the expert from Dorchester.

"This way," she said, waving the stranger to the house; and an instant later she had forgotten him in the absorption of her meeting with the boiler maker.

The encounter led to such far-reaching results that the engineer ended by finding it expedient to ignore his train, and Mary was beguiled into spending the remainder of the morning in absorbed confabulation among the flower pots. When the colloquy ended, she was surprised to find that it was nearly luncheon time, and she half expected, as she hurried back to the house, to see her husband coming out to meet her. But she found no one in the court but an undergardener raking the gravel, and the hall, when she entered it, was so silent that she guessed Boyne to be still at work.

Not wishing to disturb him, she turned into the drawing room, and there, at her writing table, lost herself in renewed calculations of the outlay to which the morning's conference had pledged her. The fact that she could permit herself such follies had not yet lost its novelty; and somehow, in contrast to the vague fears of the previous days, it now seemed an element of her recovered security, of the sense that, as Ned had said, things in general had never been "righter."

She was still luxuriating in a lavish play of figures when the parlormaid, from the threshold, roused her with an inquiry as to the expediency of serving luncheon. It was one of their jokes that Trimmle announced luncheon as if she were divulging a state secret, and Mary, intent upon her papers, merely murmured an absent-minded assent.

She felt Trimmle wavering doubtfully on the threshold, as if in rebuke of such unconsidered assent; then her retreating steps sounded down the passage, and Mary, pushing away her papers, crossed the hall and went to the library door. It was still closed, and she wavered in her turn, disliking to disturb her husband, yet anxious that he should not exceed his usual measure of work. As she stood there, balancing her impulses, Trimmle returned with the announcement of luncheon, and Mary, thus impelled, opened the library door.

Boyne was not at his desk, and she peered about her, expecting to discover him before the bookshelves, somewhere down the length of the room; but her call brought no response, and gradually it became clear to her that he was not there.

She turned back to the parlormaid.

"Mr. Boyne must be upstairs. Please tell him that luncheon is ready."

Trimmle appeared to hesitate between the obvious duty of obedience and an equally obvious conviction of the foolishness of the injunction laid on her. The struggle resulted in her saying: "If you please, Madam, Mr. Boyne's not upstairs."

"Not in his room? Are you sure?"

"I'm sure, Madam."

Mary consulted the clock. "Where is he, then?"

"He's gone out," Trimmle announced, with the superior air of one who has respectfully waited for the question that a well-ordered mind would have put first.

Mary's conjecture had been right, then. Boyne must have gone to the gardens to meet her, and since she had missed him, it was clear that he had taken the shorter way by the south door, instead of going round to the court. She crossed the hall to the French window opening directly on the yew garden, but the parlormaid, after another moment of inner conflict, decided to bring out: "Please, Madam, Mr. Boyne didn't go that way."

Mary turned back. "Where *did* he go? And when?"

"He went out of the front door, up the drive, Madam." It was a matter of principle with Trimmle never to answer more than one question at a time.

"Up the drive? At this hour?" Mary went to the door herself, and glanced across the court through the tunnel of bare limes. But its perspective was as empty as when she had scanned it on entering.

"Did Mr. Boyne leave no message?"

Trimmle seemed to surrender herself to a last struggle with the forces of chaos.

"No, Madam. He just went out with the gentleman."

"The gentleman? What gentleman?" Mary wheeled about, as if to front this new factor.

"The gentleman who called, Madam," said Trimmle resignedly.

"When did a gentleman call? Do explain yourself, Trimmle!"

Only the fact that Mary was very hungry, and that she wanted to consult her husband about the greenhouses, would have caused her to lay so unusual an injunction on her attendant; and even now she was detached enough to note in Trimmle's eye the dawning defiance of the respectful subordinate who has been pressed too hard.

"I couldn't exactly say the hour, Madam, because I didn't let the gentleman in," she replied, with an air of discreetly ignoring the irregularity of her mistress's course.

"You didn't let him in?"

"No, Madam. When the bell rang I was dressing, and Agnes—"

"Go and ask Agnes, then," said Mary.

Trimmle still wore her look of patient magnanimity. "Agnes would not know, Madam, for she had unfortunately burnt her hand in trimming the wick of the new lamp from town"—Trimmle, as Mary was aware, had always been opposed to the new lamp—"and so Mrs. Dockett sent the kitchenmaid instead."

Mary looked again at the clock. "It's after two! Go and ask the kitchenmaid if Mr. Boyne left any word."

She went into luncheon without waiting, and Trimmle presently brought her there the kitchenmaid's statement that the gentleman had called about eleven o'clock, and that Mr. Boyne had gone out with him without leaving any message. The kitchenmaid did not even know the caller's name, for he had written it on a slip of paper, which he had folded and handed to her, with the injunction to deliver it at once to Mr. Boyne.

Mary finished her luncheon, still wondering, and when it was over, and Trimmle had brought the coffee to the drawing room, her wonder had deepened to a first faint tinge of disquietude. It was unlike Boyne to absent himself without explanation at so unwonted an hour, and the difficulty of identifying the visitor whose summons he had apparently obeyed made his disappearance the more unaccountable. Mary Boyne's experience as the wife of a busy engineer, subject to sudden calls and compelled to keep irregular hours, had trained her to the philosophic acceptance of surprises; but since Boyne's withdrawal from business he had adopted a Benedictine regularity of life. As if to make up for the dispersed and agitated years, with their "stand-up" lunches, and dinners rattled down to the joltings of the dining cars, he cultivated the last refinements of punctuality and monotony, discouraging his wife's fancy for the unexpected, and declaring that to a delicate taste there were infinite gradations of pleasure in the recurrences of habit.

Still, since no life can completely defend itself from the unforeseen, it was evident that all Boyne's precautions would sooner or later prove unavailable, and Mary concluded that he had cut short a tiresome visit by walking with his caller to the station, or at least accompanying him for part of the way.

This conclusion relieved her from further preoccupation, and she went out herself to take up her conference with the gardener. Thence she walked to the village post office, a mile or so away; and when she turned toward home the early twilight was setting in.

She had taken a footpath across the downs, and as Boyne, meanwhile, had probably returned from the station by the highroad, there was little likelihood of their meeting. She felt sure, however, of his having reached the house before her; so sure that, when she entered it herself, without even pausing to inquire of Trimmle, she made directly for the library. But the library was still empty, and with an unwonted exactness of visual memory she observed that the papers on her husband's desk lay precisely as they had lain when she had gone in to call him to luncheon.

Then of a sudden she was seized by a vague dread of the unknown. She had closed the door behind her on entering, and as she stood alone in the long silent room, her dread seemed to take shape and sound, to be there breathing and lurking among the shadows. Her shortsighted eyes strained through them, half-discerning an actual presence, something aloof, that watched and knew; and in the recoil from that intangible presence she threw herself on the bell rope and gave it a sharp pull.

The sharp summons brought Trimmle in precipitately with a

lamp, and Mary breathed again at this sobering reappearance of the usual.

"You may bring tea if Mr. Boyne is in," she said, to justify her ring.

"Very well, Madam. But Mr. Boyne is not in," said Trimmle, putting down the lamp.

"Not in? You mean he's come back and gone out again?"

"No, Madam. He's never been back."

The dread stirred again, and Mary knew that now it had her fast.

"Not since he went out with—the gentleman?"

"Not since he went out with the gentleman."

"But who *was* the gentleman?" Mary insisted, with the shrill note of someone trying to be heard through a confusion of noises.

"That I couldn't say, Madam." Trimmle, standing there by the lamp, seemed suddenly to grow less round and rosy, as though eclipsed by the same creeping shade of apprehension.

"But the kitchenmaid knows—wasn't it the kitchenmaid who let him in?"

"She doesn't know either, Madam, for he wrote his name on a folded paper."

Mary, through her agitation, was aware that they were both designating the unknown visitor by a vague pronoun, instead of the conventional formula which, till then, had kept their allusions within the bounds of conformity. And at the same moment her mind caught at the suggestion of the folded paper.

"But he must have a name! Where's the paper?"

She moved to the desk, and began to turn over the documents that littered it. The first that caught her eye was an unfinished letter in her husband's hand, with his pen lying across it, as though dropped there at a sudden summons.

"My dear Parvis"—who was Parvis?—"I have just received your letter announcing Elwell's death, and while I suppose there is now no further risk of trouble, it might be safer—"

She tossed the sheet aside, and continued her search; but no folded paper was discoverable among the letters and pages of manuscript which had been swept together in a heap, as if by a hurried or a startled gesture.

"But the kitchenmaid *saw* him. Send her here," she commanded, wondering at her dullness in not thinking sooner of so simple a solution.

Trimmle vanished in a flash, as if thankful to be out of the room, and when she reappeared, conducting the agitated underling, Mary had regained her self-possession, and had her questions ready.

The gentleman was a stranger, yes—that she understood. But what had he said? And, above all, what had he looked like? The first question was easily enough answered, for the disconcerting reason that he had said so little—had merely asked for Mr. Boyne, and, scribbling something on a bit of paper, had requested that it should at once be carried in to him.

"Then you don't know what he wrote? You're not sure it *was* his name?"

The kitchenmaid was not sure, but supposed it was, since he had written it in answer to her inquiry as to whom she should announce.

"And when you carried the paper in to Mr. Boyne, what did he say?"

The kitchenmaid did not think that Mr. Boyne had said anything, but she could not be sure, for just as she had handed him the paper and he was opening it, she had become aware that the visitor had followed her into the library, and she had slipped out, leaving the two gentlemen together.

"But then, if you left them in the library, how do you know that they went out of the house?"

This question plunged the witness into a momentary inarticulateness, from which she was rescued by Trimmle, who, by means of ingenious circumlocutions, elicited the statement that before she could cross the hall to the back passage she had heard the two gentlemen behind her, and had seen them go out of the front door together.

"Then, if you saw the strange gentleman twice, you must be able to tell me what he looked like."

But with this final challenge to her powers of expression it became clear that the limit of the kitchenmaid's endurance had been reached. The obligation of going to the front door to "show in" a visitor was in itself so subversive of the fundamental order of things that it had thrown her faculties into hopeless disarray, and she could only stammer out, after various panting efforts: "His hat, mum, was different-like, as you might say—"

"Different? How different?" Mary flashed out, her own mind, in the same instant, leaping back to an image left on it that morning, and then lost under layers of subsequent impressions.

"His hat had a wide brim, you mean, and his face was pale—a youngish face?" Mary pressed her, with a white-lipped intensity of interrogation. But if the kitchenmaid found any adequate answer to this challenge, it was swept away for her listener down the rushing current of her own convictions. The stranger—the stranger in the garden! Why had Mary not thought of him before? She needed no one now to tell her that it was he who had called for her husband and gone away with him. But who was he, and why had Boyne obeyed him?

IV

It leaped out at her suddenly, like a grin out of the dark, that they had often called England so little—"such a confoundedly hard place to get lost in."

A confoundedly hard place to get lost in! That had been her husband's phrase. And now, with the whole machinery of official investigation sweeping its flashlights from shore to shore, and across the dividing straits; now, with Boyne's name blazing from the walls of every town and village, his portrait (how that wrung her!) hawked up and down the country like the image of a hunted criminal; now the little compact populous island, so policed, surveyed and administered, revealed itself as a Sphinxlike guardian of abysmal mysteries, staring back into his wife's anguished eyes as if with the wicked joy of knowing something they would never know!

In the fortnight since Boyne's disappearance there had been no word of him, no trace of his movements. Even the usual misleading reports that raise expectancy in tortured bosoms had been few and fleeting. No one but the kitchenmaid had seen Boyne leave the house, and no one else had seen "the gentleman" who accompanied him. All inquiries in the neighborhood failed to elicit the memory of a stranger's presence that day in the neighborhood of Lyng. And no one had met Edward Boyne, either alone or in company, in any of the neighboring villages, or on the road across the downs, or at either of the local railway stations. The sunny English noon had swallowed him as completely as if he had gone out into Cimmerian night.

Mary, while every official means of investigation was working at its highest pressure, had ransacked her husband's papers for any trace of antecedent complications, of entanglements or obligations unknown to her, that might throw a ray into the darkness. But if any such had existed in the background of Boyne's life, they had vanished like the slip of paper on which the visitor had written his name. There remained no possible thread of guidance except—if it were indeed an exception—the letter which Boyne had apparently been in the act of writing when he received his mysterious summons. That letter, read and reread by his wife, and submitted by her to the police, yielded little enough to feed conjecture.

"I have just heard of Elwell's death, and while I suppose there is now no further risk of trouble, it might be safer—" That was all. The "risk of trouble" was easily explained by the newspaper clipping which had apprised Mary of the suit brought against her husband by one of his associates in the Blue Star enterprise. The only new information conveyed by the letter was the fact of its showing Boyne, when he wrote it, to be still apprehensive of the results of the suit, though he had told his wife that it had been withdrawn, and though the letter itself proved that the plaintiff was dead. It took several days of cabling to fix the identity of the "Parvis" to whom the fragment was addressed, but even after these inquiries had shown him to be a Waukesha lawyer, no new facts concerning the Elwell suit were elicited. He appeared to have had no direct concern in it, but to have been conversant with the facts merely as an acquaintance, and possible intermediary; and he declared himself unable to guess with what object Boyne intended to seek his assistance.

This negative information, sole fruit of the first fortnight's search, was not increased by a jot during the slow weeks that followed. Mary knew that the investigations were still being carried on, but she had a vague sense of their gradually slackening, as the actual march of time seemed to slacken. It was as though the days, flying horror-struck from the shrouded image of the one inscrutable day, gained assurance as the distance lengthened, till at last they fell back into their normal gait.

And so with the human imaginations at work on the dark event. No doubt it occupied them still, but week by week and hour by hour it grew less absorbing, took up less space, was slowly but inevitably crowded out of the foreground of consciousness by the new problems perpetually bubbling up from the cloudy caldron of human experience.

Even Mary Boyne's consciousness gradually felt the same lowering of velocity. It still swayed with the incessant oscillations of conjecture; but they were slower, more rhythmical in their beat. There were even moments of weariness when, like the victim of some poison which leaves the brain clear, but holds the body motionless, she saw herself domesticated with the Horror, accepting its perpetual presence as one of the fixed conditions of life.

These moments lengthened into hours and days, till she passed into a phase of stolid acquiescence. She watched the routine of daily life with the incurious eye of a savage on whom the meaningless processes of civilization make but the faintest impression. She had come to regard herself as part of the routine, a spoke of the wheel, revolving with its motion; she felt almost like the furniture of the room in which she sat, an insensate object to be dusted and pushed about with the chairs and tables. And this deepening apathy held her fast at Lyng, in spite of the entreaties of friends and the usual medical recommendation of "change." Her friends supposed that her refusal to move was inspired by the belief that her husband would one day return to the spot from which he had vanished, and a beautiful legend grew up about this imaginary state of waiting. But in reality she had no such belief: the depths of anguish enclosing her were no longer lighted by flashes of hope. She was sure that Boyne would never come back, that he had gone out of her sight as completely as if Death itself had waited that day on the threshold. She had even renounced, one by one, the various theories as to his disappearance which had been advanced by the press, the police, and her own agonized imagination. In sheer lassitude her mind turned from these alternatives of horror, and sank back into the blank fact that he was gone.

No, she would never know what had become of him—no one would ever know. But the house *knew*; the library in which she spent her long lonely evenings knew. For it was here that the last scene had been enacted, here that the stranger had come, and spoken the word which had caused Boyne to rise and follow him. The floor she trod had felt his tread; the books on the shelves had seen his face; and there were moments when the intense consciousness of the old dusky walls seemed about to break out into some audible revelation of their secret. But the revelation never came, and she knew it would never come. Lyng was not one of the garrulous old houses that betray the secrets entrusted to them. Its very legend proved that it had always been the mute accomplice, the incorruptible custodian, of the mysteries it had surprised. And Mary Boyne, sitting face to face with its silence, felt the futility of seeking to break it by any human means.

V

"I don't say it *wasn't* straight, and yet I don't say it *was* straight. It was business."

Mary, at the words, lifted her head with a start, and looked intently at the speaker.

When, half an hour before, a card with "Mr. Parvis" on it had been brought up to her, she had been immediately aware that the name had been a part of her consciousness ever since she had read it at the head of Boyne's unfinished letter. In the library she had found awaiting her a small sallow man with a bald head and gold eyeglasses, and it sent a tremor through her to know that this was the person to whom her husband's last known thought had been directed.

Parvis, civilly, but without vain preamble—in the manner of a man who has his watch in his hand—had set forth the object of his visit. He had "run over" to England on business, and finding himself in the neighborhood of Dorchester, had not wished to leave it without paying his respects to Mrs. Boyne; and without asking her, if the occasion offered, what she meant to do about Bob Elwell's family.

The words touched the spring of some obscure dread in Mary's bosom. Did her visitor, after all, know what Boyne had meant by his unfinished phrase? She asked for an elucidation of his question, and noticed at once that he seemed surprised at her continued ignorance of the subject. Was it possible that she really knew as little as she said?

"I know nothing—you must tell me," she faltered out; and her visitor thereupon proceeded to unfold his story. It threw, even to her confused perceptions, and imperfectly initiated vision, a lurid glare on the whole hazy episode of the Blue Star Mine. Her husband had made his money in that brilliant speculation at the cost of "getting ahead" of someone less alert to seize the chance; and the victim of his ingenuity was young Robert Elwell, who had "put him on" to the Blue Star scheme.

Parvis, at Mary's first cry, had thrown her a sobering glance through his impartial glasses.

"Bob Elwell wasn't smart enough, that's all; if he had been, he might have turned round and served Boyne the same way. It's the kind of thing that happens every day in business. I guess it's what the scientists call the survival of the fittest—see?" said Mr. Parvis, evidently pleased with the aptness of his analogy.

Mary felt a physical shrinking from the next question she tried to frame: it was as though the words on her lips had a taste that nauseated her.

"But then—you accuse my husband of doing something dishonorable?"

Mr. Parvis surveyed the question dispassionately. "Oh, no, I don't. I don't even say it wasn't straight." He glanced up and down the long lines of books, as if one of them might have supplied him with the definition he sought. "I don't say it *wasn't* straight, and yet I don't say it *was* straight. It was business." After all, no definition in his category could be more comprehensive than that.

Mary sat staring at him with a look of terror. He seemed to her like the indifferent emissary of some evil power.

"But Mr. Elwell's lawyers apparently did not take your view, since I suppose the suit was withdrawn by their advice."

"Oh, yes; they knew he hadn't a leg to stand on, technically. It was when they advised him to withdraw the suit that he got desperate. You see, he'd borrowed most of the money he lost in the Blue Star, and he was up a tree. That's why he shot himself when they told him he had no show."

The horror was sweeping over Mary in great deafening waves.

"He shot himself? He killed himself because of *that?*"

"Well, he didn't kill himself, exactly. He dragged on two months before he died." Parvis emitted the statement as unemotionally as a gramophone grinding out its record.

"You mean that he tried to kill himself, and failed? And tried again?"

"Oh, he didn't have to *try* again," said Parvis grimly.

They sat opposite each other in silence, he swinging his eyeglasses thoughtfully about his finger, she, motionless, her arms stretched along her knees in an attitude of rigid tension.

"But if you knew all this," she began at length, hardly able to force her voice above a whisper, "how is it that when I wrote you at the time of my husband's disappearance you said you didn't understand his letter?"

Parvis received this without perceptible embarrassment: "Why, I didn't understand it—strictly speaking. And it wasn't the time to talk about it, if I had. The Elwell business was settled when the suit was withdrawn. Nothing I could have told you would have helped you to find your husband."

Mary continued to scrutinize him. "Then why are you telling me now?"

Still Parvis did not hesitate. "Well, to begin with, I supposed you knew more than you appear to—I mean about the circumstances of Elwell's death. And then people are talking of it now; the whole matter's been raked up again. And I thought if you didn't know you ought to."

She remained silent, and he continued: "You see, it's only come out lately what a bad state Elwell's affairs were in. His wife's a proud woman, and she fought on as long as she could, going out to work, and taking sewing at home when she got too sick—something with the heart, I believe. But she had his mother to look after, and the children, and she broke down under it, and finally had to ask for help. That called attention to the case, and the papers took it up, and a subscription was started. Everybody out there liked Bob Elwell, and most of the prominent names in the place are down on the list, and people began to wonder why—"

Parvis broke off to fumble in an inner pocket. "Here," he continued, "here's an account of the whole thing from the *Sentinel*—a little sensational, of course. But I guess you'd better look it over."

He held out a newspaper to Mary, who unfolded it slowly, remembering, as she did so, the evening when, in that same room, the perusal of a clipping from the *Sentinel* had first shaken the depths of her security.

As she opened the paper, her eyes, shrinking from the glaring headlines, "Widow of Boyne's Victim Forced to Appeal for Aid," ran down the column of text to two portraits inserted in it. The first was her husband's, taken from a photograph made the year they had come to England. It was the picture of him that she liked best, the one that stood on the writing table upstairs in her bedroom. As the eyes in the photograph met hers, she felt it would be impossible to read what was said of him, and closed her lids with the sharpness of the pain.

"I thought if you felt disposed to put your name down—" she heard Parvis continue.

She opened her eyes with an effort, and they fell on the other portrait. It was that of a youngish man, slightly built, with features somewhat blurred by the shadow of a projecting hat brim. Where had she seen that outline before? She stared at it confusedly, her heart hammering in her ears. Then she gave a cry.

"This is the man—the man who came for my husband!"

She heard Parvis start to his feet, and was dimly aware that she had slipped backward into the corner of the sofa, and that he was bending above her in alarm. She straightened herself, and reached out for the paper, which she had dropped.

"It's the man! I should know him anywhere!" she persisted in a voice that sounded to her own ears like a scream.

Parvis's answer seemed to come to her from far off, down endless fog-muffled windings.

"Mrs. Boyne, you're not very well. Shall I call somebody? Shall I get a glass of water?"

"No, no, no!" She threw herself toward him, her hand frantically clutching the newspaper. "I tell you, it's the man! I *know* him! He spoke to me in the garden!"

Parvis took the journal from her, directing his glasses to the portrait. "It can't be, Mrs. Boyne. It's Robert Elwell."

"Robert Elwell?" Her white stare seemed to travel into space. "Then it was Robert Elwell who came for him."

"Came for Boyne? The day he went away from here?" Parvis's voice dropped as hers rose. He bent over, laying a fraternal hand on her, as if to coax her gently back into her seat. "Why, Elwell was dead! Don't you remember?"

Mary sat with her eyes fixed on the picture, unconscious of what he was saying.

"Don't you remember Boyne's unfinished letter to me—the one you found on his desk that day? It was written just after he'd heard of Elwell's death." She noticed an odd shake in Parvis's unemotional voice. "Surely you remember!" he urged her.

Yes, she remembered: that was the profoundest horror of it. Elwell had died the day before her husband's disappearance; and this was Elwell's portrait; and it was the portrait of the man who had spoken to her in the garden. She lifted her head and looked slowly about the library. The library could have borne witness that it was also the portrait of the man who had come in that day to call Boyne from his unfinished letter. Through the misty surgings of her brain she heard the faint boom of half-forgotten words—words spoken by Alida Stair on the lawn at Pangbourne before Boyne and his wife had ever seen the house at Lyng, or had imagined that they might one day live there.

"This was the man who spoke to me," she repeated.

She looked again at Parvis. He was trying to conceal his disturbance under what he probably imagined to be an expression of indulgent commiseration; but the edges of his lips were blue. "He thinks me mad; but I'm not mad," she reflected; and suddenly there flashed upon her a way of justifying her strange affirmation.

She sat quiet, controlling the quiver of her lips, and waiting till she could trust her voice; then she said, looking straight at Parvis: "Will you answer me one question, please? When was it that Robert Elwell tried to kill himself?"

"When—when?" Parvis stammered.

"Yes; the date. Please try to remember."

She saw that he was growing still more afraid of her. "I have a reason," she insisted.

"Yes, yes. Only I can't remember. About two months before, I should say."

"I want the date," she repeated.

Parvis picked up the newspaper. "We might see here," he said, still humoring her. He ran his eyes down the page. "Here it is. Last October—the—"

She caught the words from him. "The 20th, wasn't it?" With a sharp look at her, he verified. "Yes, the 20th. Then you *did* know?"

"I know now." Her gaze continued to travel past him. "Sunday, the 20th—that was the day he came first."

Parvis's voice was almost inaudible. "Came *here* first?"

"Yes."

"You saw him twice, then?"

"Yes, twice." She just breathed it at him. "He came first on the 20th of October. I remember the date because it was the day we went up Meldon Steep for the first time." She felt a faint gasp of inward laughter at the thought that but for that she might have forgotten.

Parvis continued to scrutinize her, as if trying to intercept her gaze.

"We saw him from the roof," she went on. "He came down the lime avenue toward the house. He was dressed just as he is in that picture. My husband saw him first. He was frightened, and ran down ahead of me; but there was no one there. He had vanished."

"Elwell had vanished?" Parvis faltered.

"Yes." Their two whispers seemed to grope for each other. "I couldn't think what had happened. I see now. He *tried* to come then; but he wasn't dead enough—he couldn't reach us. He had to wait for two months to die; and then he came back again—and Ned went with him."

She nodded at Parvis with the look of triumph of a child who has worked out a difficult puzzle. But suddenly she lifted her hands with a desperate gesture, pressing them to her temples.

"Oh, my God! I sent him to Ned—I told him where to go! I sent him to this room!" she screamed.

She felt the walls of books rush toward her, like inward falling ruins; and she heard Parvis, a long way off, through the ruins, crying to her, and struggling to get at her. But she was numb to his touch, she did not know what he was saying. Through the tumult she heard but one clear note, the voice of Alida Stair, speaking on the lawn at Pangbourne.

"You won't know till afterward," it said. "You won't know till long, long afterward."

Kerfol

"You ought to buy it," said my host; "it's just the place for a solitary-minded devil like you. And it would be rather worth-while to own the most romantic house in Brittany. The present people are dead broke, and it's going for a song—you ought to buy it."

It was not with the least idea of living up to the character my friend Lanrivain ascribed to me (as a matter of fact, under my unsociable exterior I have always had secret yearnings for domesticity) that I took his hint one autumn afternoon and went to Kerfol. My friend was motoring over to Quimper on business: he dropped me on the way, at a crossroad on a heath, and said: "First turn to the right and second to the left. Then straight ahead till you see an avenue. If you meet any peasants, don't ask your way. They don't understand French, and they would pretend they did and mix you up. I'll be back for you here by sunset—and don't forget the tombs in the chapel."

I followed Lanrivain's directions with the hesitation occasioned by the usual difficulty of remembering whether he had said the first turn to the right and second to the left, or the contrary. If I had met a peasant I should certainly have asked, and probably been sent astray; but I had the desert landscape to myself, and so stumbled on the right turn and walked across the heath till I came to an avenue. It was so unlike any other avenue I have ever seen that I instantly knew it must be *the* avenue. The grey-trunked trees sprang up straight to a great height and then interwove their pale grey branches in a long tunnel through which the autumn light fell faintly. I know most trees by name, but I haven't to this day been able to decide what those trees were. They had the tall curve of elms, the tenuity of poplars, the ashen color of olives under a rainy sky; and they stretched ahead of me for half a mile or more without a break in their arch. If ever I saw an avenue that unmistakably led to something, it was the avenue at Kerfol. My heart beat a little as I began to walk down it.

Presently the trees ended and I came to a fortified gate in a long wall. Between me and the wall was an open space of grass, with other grey avenues radiating from it. Behind the wall were tall slate roofs mossed with silver, a chapel belfry, the top of a keep. A moat filled with wild shrubs and brambles surrounded the place; the drawbridge had been replaced by a stone arch, and the portcullis by an iron gate. I stood for a long time on the hither side of the moat, gazing about me, and letting the influence of the place sink in. I said to myself: "If I wait long enough, the guardian will turn up and show me the tombs—" and I rather hoped he wouldn't turn up too soon.

I sat down on a stone and lit a cigarette. As soon as I had done it, it struck me as a puerile and portentous thing to do, with that great blind house looking down at me, and all the empty avenues converging on me. It may have been the depth of the silence that made me so conscious of my gesture. The squeak of my match sounded as loud as the scraping of a brake, and I almost fancied I heard it fall when I tossed it onto the grass. But there was more than that: a sense of irrelevance, of littleness, of futile bravado, in sitting there puffing my cigarette smoke into the face of such a past.

I knew nothing of the history of Kerfol—I was new to Brittany, and Lanrivain had never mentioned the name to me till the day before —but one couldn't as much as glance at that pile without feeling in it a long accumulation of history. What kind of history I was not prepared to guess: perhaps only that sheer weight of many associated lives and deaths which gives a majesty to all old houses. But the aspect of Kerfol suggested something more—a perspective of stern and cruel memories stretching away, like its own grey avenues, into a blur of darkness.

Certainly no house had ever more completely and finally broken with the present. As it stood there, lifting its proud roofs and gables to the sky, it might have been its own funeral monument. "Tombs in the chapel? The whole place is a tomb!" I reflected. I hoped more and more that the guardian would not come. The details of the place, however striking, would seem trivial compared with its collective impressiveness; and I wanted only to sit there and be penetrated by the weight of its silence.

"It's the very place for you!" Lanrivain had said; and I was overcome by the almost blasphemous frivolity of suggesting to any living being that Kerfol was the place for him. "Is it possible that anyone could *not* see—?" I wondered. I did not finish the thought: what I meant was undefinable. I stood up and wandered toward the gate. I was beginning to want to know more; not to *see* more—I was by now so sure it was not a question of seeing—but to feel more: feel all the place had to communicate. "But to get in one will have to rout out the keeper," I thought reluctantly, and hesitated. Finally I crossed the bridge and tried the iron gate. It yielded, and I walked through the tunnel formed by the thickness of the *chemin de ronde.* At the farther end, a wooden barricade had been laid across the entrance, and beyond it was a court enclosed in noble architecture. The main building faced me; and I now saw that one-half was a mere ruined front, with gaping windows through which the wild growths of the moat and the trees of the park were visible. The rest of the house was still in its robust beauty. One end abutted on the round tower, the other on the small traceried chapel, and in an angle of the building stood a graceful well-head crowned with mossy urns. A few roses grew against the walls, and on an upper windowsill I remember noticing a pot of fuchsias.

My sense of the pressure of the invisible began to yield to my architectural interest. The building was so fine that I felt a desire to explore it for its own sake. I looked about the court, wondering in which corner the guardian lodged. Then I pushed open the barrier and went in. As I did so, a dog barred my way. He was such a remarkably beautiful little dog that for a moment he made me forget the splendid place he was defending. I was not sure of his breed at the time, but have since learned that it was Chinese, and that he was of a rare variety called the "Sleeve-dog." He was very small and golden brown, with large brown eyes and a ruffled throat: he looked like a large tawny chrysanthemum. I said to myself: "These little beasts always snap and scream, and somebody will be out in a minute."

The little animal stood before me, forbidding, almost menacing: there was anger in his large brown eyes. But he made no sound, he came no nearer. Instead, as I advanced, he gradually fell back, and I noticed that another dog, a vague, rough, brindled thing, had limped up on a lame leg. "There'll be a hubbub now," I thought; for at the same moment a third dog, a long-haired white mongrel, slipped out of a doorway and joined the others. All three stood looking at me with grave eyes; but not a sound came from them. As I advanced they continued to fall back on muffled paws, still watching me. "At a given point, they'll all charge at my ankles: it's one of the jokes that dogs who live together put up on one," I thought. I was not alarmed, for they were neither large nor formidable. But they let me wander about the court as I pleased, following me at a little distance—always the same distance—and always keeping their eyes on me. Presently I looked across at the ruined façade, and saw that in one of its empty window frames another dog stood: a white pointer with one brown ear. He was an old grave dog, much more experienced than the others; and he seemed to be observing me with a deeper intentness.

"I'll hear from *him,*" I said to myself; but he stood in the window frame, against the trees of the park, and continued to watch me without moving. I stared back at him for a time, to see if the sense that he was being watched would not rouse him. Half the width of the court lay between us, and we gazed at each other silently across it. But he did not stir, and at last I turned away. Behind me I found the rest of the pack, with a newcomer added: a small black greyhound with pale agate-colored eyes. He was shivering a little, and his expression was more timid than that of the others. I noticed that he kept a little behind them. And still there was not a sound.

I stood there for fully five minutes, the circle about me—waiting, as they seemed to be waiting. At last I went up to the little golden brown dog and stooped to pat him. As I did so, I heard myself give a nervous laugh. The little dog did not start, or growl, or take his eyes from me—he simple slipped back about a yard, and then paused and continued to look at me. "Oh, hang it!" I exclaimed, and walked across the court toward the well.

As I advanced, the dogs separated and slid away into different corners of the court. I examined the urns on the well, tried a locked door or two, and looked up and down the dumb façade; then I faced about toward the chapel. When I turned I perceived that all the dogs had disappeared except the old pointer, who still watched me from the window. It was rather a relief to be rid of that cloud of witnesses; and I began to look about me for a way to the back of the house. "Perhaps there'll be somebody in the garden," I thought. I found a way across the moat, scrambled over a wall smothered in brambles, and got into the garden. A few lean hydrangeas and geraniums pined in the flower beds, and the ancient house looked down on them indifferently. Its garden side was plainer and severer than the other: the long granite front, with its few windows and steep roof, looked like a fortress prison. I walked around the farther wing, went up some disjointed steps, and entered the deep twilight of a narrow and incredibly old box walk. The walk was just wide enough for one person to slip through, and its branches met overhead. It was like the ghost of a box walk, its lustrous green all turning to the shadowy greyness of the avenues. I walked on and on, the branches hitting me in the face and springing back with a dry rattle; and at length I came out on the grassy top of the *chemin de ronde*. I walked along it to the gate tower, looking down into the court, which was just below me. Not a human being was in sight; and neither were the dogs. I found a flight of steps in the thickness of the wall and went down them; and when I emerged again into the court, there stood the circle of dogs, the golden brown one a little ahead of the others, the black greyhound shivering in the rear.

"Oh, hang it—you uncomfortable beasts, you!" I exclaimed, my voice startling me with a sudden echo. The dogs stood motionless, watching me. I knew by this time that they would not try to prevent my approaching the house, and the knowledge left me free to examine them. I had a feeling that they must be horribly cowed to be so silent and inert. Yet they did not look hungry or ill-treated. Their coats were smooth and they were not thin, except the shivering greyhound. It was more as if they had lived a long time with people who never spoke to them or looked at them: as though the silence of the place had gradually benumbed their busy inquisitive natures. And this strange passivity, this almost human lassitude, seemed to me sadder than the misery of starved and beaten animals. I should have liked to rouse them for a minute, to coax them into a game or a scamper; but the longer I looked into their fixed and weary eyes the more preposterous the idea became. With the windows of that house looking down on us, how could I have imagined such a thing? The dogs knew better: *they* knew what the house would tolerate and what it would not. I even fancied that they knew what was passing through my mind, and pitied me for my frivolity. But even that feeling probably reached them through a thick fog of listlessness. I had an idea that their distance from me was as nothing to my remoteness from them. The impression they produced was that of having in common one memory so deep and dark that nothing that had happened since was worth either a growl or a wag.

"I say," I broke out abruptly, addressing myself to the dumb circle, "do you know what you look like, the whole lot of you? You look as if you'd seen a ghost—that's how you look! I wonder if there *is* a ghost here, and nobody but you left for it to appear to?" The dogs continued to gaze at me without moving. . . .

It was dark when I saw Lanrivain's motor lamps at the crossroads —and I wasn't exactly sorry to see them. I had the sense of having escaped from the loneliest place in the whole world, and of not liking loneliness—to that degree—as much as I had imagined I should. My friend had brought his solicitor back from Quimper for the night, and seated beside a fat and affable stranger I felt no inclination to talk of Kerfol. . . .

But that evening, when Lanrivain and the solicitor were closeted in the study, Madame de Lanrivain began to question me in the drawing room.

"Well—are you going to buy Kerfol?" she asked, tilting up her gay chin from her embroidery.

"I haven't decided yet. The fact is, I couldn't get into the house," I said, as if I had simply postponed my decision, and meant to go back for another look.

"You couldn't get in? Why, what happened? The family are mad to sell the place, and the old guardian has orders—"

"Very likely. But the old guardian wasn't there."

"What a pity! He must have gone to market. But his daughter—?"

"There was nobody about. At least I saw no one."

"How extraordinary! Literally nobody?"

"Nobody but a lot of dogs—a whole pack of them—who seemed to have the place to themselves."

Madame de Lanrivain let the embroidery slip to her knee and folded her hands on it. For several minutes she looked at me thoughtfully.

"A pack of dogs—you *saw* them?"

"Saw them? I saw nothing else!"

"How many?" She dropped her voice a little. "I've always wondered—"

I looked at her with surprise: I had supposed the place to be familiar to her. "Have you never been to Kerfol?" I asked.

"Oh, yes: often. But never on that day."

"What day?"

"I'd quite forgotten—and so had Hervé, I'm sure. If we'd remembered, we never should have sent you today—but then, after all, one doesn't half believe that sort of thing, does one?"

"What sort of thing?" I asked, involuntarily sinking my voice to the level of hers. Inwardly I was thinking: "I *knew* there was something. . . ."

Madame de Lanrivain cleared her throat and produced a reassuring smile. "Didn't Hervé tell you the story of Kerfol? An ancestor of his was mixed up in it. You know every Breton house has its ghost story; and some of them are rather unpleasant."

"Yes—but those dogs?"

"Well, those dogs are the ghosts of Kerfol. At least, the peasants say there's one day in the year when a lot of dogs appear there; and that day the keeper and his daughter go off to Morlaix and get drunk. The women in Brittany drink dreadfully." She stooped to match a silk; then she lifted her charming inquisitive Parisian face. "Did you *really* see a lot of dogs? There isn't one at Kerfol," she said.

II

Lanrivain, the next day, hunted out a shabby calf volume from the back of an upper shelf of his library.

"Yes—here it is. What does it call itself? *A History of the Assizes of the Duchy of Brittany. Quimper,* 1702. The book was written about a hundred years later than the Kerfol affair; but I believe the account is transcribed pretty literally from the judicial records. Anyhow, it's queer reading. And there's a Hervé de Lanrivain mixed up in it—not exactly *my* style, as you'll see. But then he's only a collateral. Here, take the book up to bed with you. I don't exactly remember the details; but after you've read it I'll bet anything you'll leave your light burning all night!"

I left my light burning all night, as he had predicted; but it was chiefly because, till near dawn, I was absorbed in my reading. The account of the trial of Anne de Cornault, wife of the lord of Kerfol, was long and closely printed. It was, as my friend had said, probably an almost literal transcription of what took place in the courtroom;

and the trial lasted nearly a month. Besides, the type of the book was very bad. . . .

At first I thought of translating the old record. But it is full of wearisome repetitions, and the main lines of the story are forever straying off into side issues. So I have tried to disentangle it, and give it here in a simpler form. At times, however, I have reverted to the text because no other words could have conveyed so exactly the sense of what I felt at Kerfol; and nowhere have I added anything of my own.

III

It was in the year 16— that Yves de Cornault, lord of the domain of Kerfol, went to the *pardon* of Locronan to perform his religious duties. He was a rich and powerful noble, then in his sixty-second year, but hale and sturdy, a great horseman and hunter and a pious man. So all his neighbors attested. In appearance he was short and broad, with a swarthy face, legs slightly bowed from the saddle, a hanging nose and broad hands with black hairs on them. He had married young and lost his wife and son soon after, and since then had lived alone at Kerfol. Twice a year he went to Morlaix, where he had a handsome house by the river, and spent a week or ten days there; and occasionally he rode to Rennes on business. Witnesses were found to declare that during these absences he led a life different from the one he was known to lead at Kerfol, where he busied himself with his estate, attended mass daily, and found his only amusement in hunting the wild boar and water-fowl. But these rumors are not particularly relevant, and it is certain that among people of his own class in the neighborhood he passed for a stern and even austere man, observant of his religious obligations, and keeping strictly to himself. There was no talk of any familiarity with the women on his estate, though at that time the nobility were very free with their peasants. Some people said he had never looked at a woman since his wife's death; but such things are hard to prove, and the evidence on this point was not worth much.

Well, in his sixty-second year, Yves de Cornault went to the *pardon* at Locronan, and saw there a young lady of Douarnenez, who had ridden over pillion behind her father to do her duty to the saint. Her name was Anne de Barrigan, and she came of good old Breton stock, but much less great and powerful than that of Yves de Cornault; and her father had squandered his fortune at cards, and lived almost like a peasant in his little granite manor on the moors. . . . I have said I would add nothing of my own to this bald statement of a strange case; but I must interrupt myself here to describe the young lady who rode up to the lych-gate of Locronan at the very moment when the Baron de Cornault was also dismounting there. I take my description from a faded drawing in red crayon, sober and truthful enough to be by a late pupil of the Clouets, which hangs in Lanrivain's study, and is said to be a portrait of Anne de Barrigan. It is unsigned and has no mark of identity but the initials A. B., and the date 16—, the year after her marriage. It represents a young woman with a small oval face, almost pointed, yet wide enough for a full mouth with a tender depression at the corners. The nose is small, and the eyebrows are set rather high, far apart, and as lightly penciled as the eyebrows in a Chinese painting. The forehead is high and serious, and the hair, which one feels to be fine and thick and fair, is drawn off it and lies close like a cap. The eyes are neither large nor small, hazel probably, with a look at once shy and steady. A pair of beautiful long hands are crossed below the lady's breast. . . .

The chaplain of Kerfol, and other witnesses, averred that when the Baron came back from Locronan he jumped from his horse, ordered another to be instantly saddled, called to a young page to come with him, and rode away that same evening to the south. His steward followed the next morning with coffers laden on a pair of pack mules. The following week Yves de Cornault rode back to Kerfol, sent for his vassals and tenants, and told them he was to be married at All Saints to Anne de Barrigan of Douarnenez. And on All Saints' Day the marriage took place.

As to the next few years, the evidence on both sides seems to show that they passed happily for the couple. No one was found to say that Yves de Cornault had been unkind to his wife, and it was plain to all that he was content with his bargain. Indeed, it was admitted by the chaplain and other witnesses for the prosecution that the young lady had a softening influence on her husband, and that he became less exacting with his tenants, less harsh to peasants and dependents, and less subject to the fits of gloomy silence which had darkened his widowhood. As to his wife, the only grievance her champions could call up in her behalf was that Kerfol was a lonely place, and that when her husband was away on business at Rennes or Morlaix—whither she was never taken—she was not allowed so much as to walk in the park unaccompanied. But no one asserted that she was unhappy, though one servant woman said she had surprised her crying, and had heard her say that she was a woman accursed to have no child, and nothing in life to call her own. But that was a natural enough feeling in a wife attached to her husband; and certainly it must have been a great grief to Yves de Cornault that she bore no son. Yet he never made her feel her childlessness as a reproach—she admits this in her evidence—but seemed to try to make her forget it by showering gifts and favors on her. Rich though he was, he had never been openhanded; but nothing was too fine for his wife, in the way of silks or gems or linen, or whatever else she fancied. Every wandering merchant was welcome at Kerfol, and when the master was called away he never came back without bringing his wife a handsome present—something curious and particular—from Morlaix or Rennes or Quimper. One of the waiting women gave, in cross-examination, an interesting list of one year's gifts, which I copy. From Morlaix, a carved ivory junk, with Chinamen at the oars, that a strange sailor had brought back as a votive offering for Notre Dame de la Clarté, above Ploumanac'h; from Quimper, an embroidered gown, worked by the nuns of the Assumption; from Rennes, a silver rose that opened and showed an amber Virgin with a crown of garnets; from Morlaix, again, a length of Damascus velvet shot with gold, bought of a Jew from Syria; and for Michaelmas that same year, from Rennes, a necklet or bracelet of round stones—emeralds and pearls and rubies—strung like beads on a fine gold chain. This was the present that pleased the lady best, the woman said. Later on, as it happened, it was produced at the trial, and appears to have struck the Judges and the public as a curious and valuable jewel.

The very same winter, the baron absented himself again, this time as far as Bordeaux, and on his return he brought his wife something even odder and prettier than the bracelet. It was a winter evening when he rode up to Kerfol and, walking into the hall, found her sitting by the hearth, her chin on her hand, looking into the fire. He carried a velvet box in his hand and, setting it down, lifted the lid and let out a little golden brown dog.

Anne de Cornault exclaimed with pleasure as the little creature bounded toward her. "Oh, it looks like a bird or a butterfly!" she cried as she picked it up; and the dog put its paws on her shoulders and looked at her with eyes "like a Christian's." After that she would never have it out of her sight, and petted and talked to it as if it had been a child—as indeed it was the nearest thing to a child she was to know. Yves de Cornault was much pleased with his purchase. The dog had been brought to him by a sailor from an East India merchantman, and the sailor had bought it of a pilgrim in a bazaar at Jaffa, who had stolen it from a nobleman's wife in China: a perfectly permissible thing to do, since the pilgrim was a Christian and the nobleman a heathen doomed to hell-fire. Yves de Cornault had paid a long price for the dog, for they were beginning to be in demand at the French court, and the sailor knew he had got hold of a good thing; but Anne's pleasure was so great that, to see her laugh and play with the little animal, her husband would doubtless have given twice the sum.

So far, all the evidence is at one, and the narrative plain sailing; but now the steering becomes difficult. I will try to keep as nearly as possible to Anne's own statements, though toward the end, poor thing. . . .

Well, to go back. The very year after the little brown dog was brought to Kerfol, Yves de Cornault, one winter night, was found dead at the head of a narrow flight of stairs leading down from his wife's rooms to a door opening on the court. It was his wife who found him and gave the alarm, so distracted, poor wretch, with fear and horror —for his blood was all over her—that at first the roused household could not make out what she was saying, and thought she had suddenly gone mad. But there, sure enough, at the top of the stairs lay her husband, stone dead, and head foremost, the blood from his wounds dripping down to the steps below him. He had been dreadfully scratched and gashed about the face and throat, as if with curious pointed weapons; and one of his legs had a deep tear in it which had cut an artery, and probably caused his death. But how did he come there, and who had murdered him?

His wife declared that she had been asleep in her bed, and hearing his cry had rushed out to find him lying on the stairs; but this was immediately questioned. In the first place, it was proved that from her

room she could not have heard the struggle on the stairs, owing to the thickness of the walls and the length of the intervening passage; then it was evident that she had not been in bed and asleep, since she was dressed when she roused the house, and her bed had not been slept in. Moreover, the door at the bottom of the stairs was ajar, and it was noticed by the chaplain (an observant man) that the dress she wore was stained with blood about the knees, and that there were traces of small bloodstained hands low down on the staircase walls, so that it was conjectured that she had really been at the postern door when her husband fell and, feeling her way up to him in the darkness on her hands and knees, had been stained by his blood dripping down on her. Of course it was argued on the other side that the blood marks on her dress might have been caused by her kneeling down by her husband when she rushed out of her room; but there was the open door below, and the fact that the finger marks in the staircase all pointed upward.

The accused held to her statement for the first two days, in spite of its improbability; but on the third day word was brought to her that Hervé de Lanrivain, a young nobleman of the neighborhood, had been arrested for complicity in the crime. Two or three witnesses thereupon came forward to say that it was known throughout the country that Lanrivain had formerly been on good terms with the lady of Cornault; but that he had been absent from Brittany for over a year, and people had ceased to associate their names. The witnesses who made this statement were not of a very reputable sort. One was an old herb-gatherer suspected of witchcraft, another a drunken clerk from a neighboring parish, the third a half-witted shepherd who could be made to say anything; and it was clear that the prosecution was not satisfied with its case, and would have liked to find more definite proof of Lanrivain's complicity than the statement of the herb-gatherer, who swore to having seen him climbing the wall of the park on the night of the murder. One way of patching out incomplete proofs in those days was to put some sort of pressure, moral or physical, on the accused person. It is not clear what pressure was put on Anne de Cornault; but on the third day, when she was brought in court, she "appeared weak and wandering," and after being encouraged to collect herself and speak the truth, on her honor and the wounds of her Blessed Redeemer, she confessed that she had in fact gone down the stairs to speak with Hervé de Lanrivain (who denied everything), and had been surprised there by the sound of her husband's fall. That was better; and the prosecution rubbed its hands with satisfaction. The satisfaction increased when various dependents living at Kerfol were induced to say—with apparent sincerity—that during the year or two preceding his death their master had once more grown uncertain and irascible, and subject to the fits of brooding silence which his household had learned to dread before his second marriage. This seemed to show that things had not been going well at Kerfol; though no one could be found to say that there had been any signs of open disagreement between husband and wife.

Anne de Cornault, when questioned as to her reason for going down at night to open the door to Hervé de Lanrivain, made an answer which must have sent a smile around the court. She said it was because she was lonely and wanted to talk with the young man. Was this the only reason? she was asked; and replied: "Yes, by the Cross over your Lordships' heads." "But why at midnight?" the court asked. "Because I could see him in no other way." I can see the exchange of glances across the ermine collars under the Crucifix.

Anne de Cornault, further questioned, said that her married life had been extremely lonely: "desolate" was the word she used. It was true that her husband seldom spoke harshly to her; but there were days when he did not speak at all. It was true that he had never struck or threatened her; but he kept her like a prisoner at Kerfol, and when he rode away to Morlaix or Quimper or Rennes he set so close a watch on her that she could not pick a flower in the garden without having a waiting woman at her heels. "I am no Queen, to need such honors," she once said to him; and he had answered that a man who has a treasure does not leave the key in the lock when he goes out. "Then take me with you," she urged; but to this he said that towns were pernicious places, and young wives better off at their own firesides.

"But what did you want to say to Hervé de Lanrivain?" the court asked; and she answered: "To ask him to take me away."

"Ah—you confess that you went down to him with adulterous thoughts?"

"No."

"Then why did you want him to take you away?"

"Because I was afraid for my life."

"Of whom were you afraid?"

"Of my husband."

"Why were you afraid of your husband?"

"Because he had strangled my little dog."

Another smile must have passed around the courtroom: in days when any nobleman had a right to hang his peasants—and most of them exercised it—pinching a pet animal's windpipe was nothing to make a fuss about.

At this point one of the Judges, who appears to have had a certain sympathy for the accused, suggested that she should be allowed to explain herself in her own way; and she thereupon made the following statement.

The first years of her marriage had been lonely; but her husband had not been unkind to her. If she had had a child she would not have been unhappy; but the days were long, and it rained too much.

It was true that her husband, whenever he went away and left her, brought her a handsome present on his return; but this did not make up for the loneliness. At least nothing had, till he brought her the little brown dog from the East: after that she was much less unhappy. Her husband seemed pleased that she was so fond of the dog; he gave her leave to put her jeweled bracelet around its neck, and to keep it always with her.

One day she had fallen asleep in her room, with the dog at her feet, as his habit was. Her feet were bare and resting on his back. Suddenly she was waked by her husband: he stood beside her, smiling not unkindly.

"You look like my great-grandmother, Juliane de Cornault, lying in the chapel with her feet on a little dog," he said.

The analogy sent a chill through her, but she laughed and answered: "Well, when I am dead you must put me beside her, carved in marble, with my dog at my feet."

"Oho—we'll wait and see," he said, laughing also, but with his black brows close together. "The dog is the emblem of fidelity."

"And do you doubt my right to lie with mine at my feet?"

"When I'm in doubt I find out," he answered. "I am an old man," he added, "and people say I make you lead a lonely life. But I swear you shall have your monument if you earn it."

"And I swear to be faithful," she returned, "if only for the sake of having my little dog at my feet."

Not long afterward he went on business to the Quimper Assizes; and while he was away his aunt, the widow of a great nobleman of the duchy, came to spend a night at Kerfol on her way to the *pardon* of Ste. Barbe. She was a woman of piety and consequence, and much respected by Yves de Cornault, and when she proposed to Anne to go with her to Ste. Barbe no one could object, and even the chaplain declared himself in favor of the pilgrimage. So Anne set out for Ste. Barbe, and there for the first time she talked with Hervé de Lanrivain. He had come once or twice to Kerfol with his father, but she had never before exchanged a dozen words with him. They did not talk for more than five minutes now: it was under the chestnuts, as the procession was coming out of the chapel. He said: "I pity you," and she was surprised, for she had not supposed that anyone thought her an object of pity. He added: "Call for me when you need me," and she smiled a little, but was glad afterward, and thought often of the meeting.

She confessed to having seen him three times afterward: not more. How or where she would not say—one had the impression that she feared to implicate someone. Their meetings had been rare and brief; and at the last he had told her that he was starting the next day for a foreign country, on a mission which was not without peril and might keep him for many months absent. He asked her for a remembrance, and she had none to give him but the collar about the little dog's neck. She was sorry afterward that she had given it, but he was so unhappy at going that she had not had the courage to refuse.

Her husband was away at the time. When he returned a few days later he picked up the animal to pet it, and noticed that its collar was missing. His wife told him that the dog had lost it in the undergrowth of the park, and that she and her maids had hunted a whole day for it. It was true, she explained to the court, that she had made the maids search for the necklet—they all believed the dog had lost it in the park. . . .

Her husband made no comment, and that evening at supper he was in his usual mood, between good and bad: you could never tell which. He talked a good deal, describing what he had seen and done at Rennes; but now and then he stopped and looked hard at her, and when she went to bed she found her little dog strangled on her pillow. The little thing was dead, but still warm; she stooped to lift it, and her distress turned to horror when she discovered that it had been strangled by twisting twice round its throat the necklet she had given to Lanrivain.

The next morning at dawn she buried the dog in the garden, and hid the necklet in her breast. She said nothing to her husband, then or later, and he said nothing to her; but that day he had a peasant hanged for stealing a faggot in the park, and the next day he nearly beat to death a young horse he was breaking.

Winter set in, and the short days passed, and the long nights, one by one; and she heard nothing of Hervé de Lanrivain. It might be that her husband had killed him; or merely that he had been robbed of the necklet. Day after day by the hearth among the spinning maids, night after night alone on her bed, she wondered and trembled. Sometimes at table her husband looked across at her and smiled; and then she felt sure that Lanrivain was dead. She dared not try to get news of him, for she was sure her husband would find out if she did: she had an idea that he could find out anything. Even when a witch woman who was a noted seer, and could show you the whole world in her crystal, came to the castle for a night's shelter, and the maids flocked to her, Anne held back.

The winter was long and black and rainy. One day, in Yves de Cornault's absence, some gypsies came to Kerfol with a troop of performing dogs. Anne bought the smallest and cleverest, a white dog with a feathery coat and one blue and one brown eye. It seemed to have been ill-treated by the gypsies, and clung to her plaintively when she took it from them. That evening her husband came back, and when she went to bed she found the dog strangled on her pillow.

After that she said to herself that she would never have another dog; but one bitter cold evening a poor lean greyhound was found whining at the castle gate, and she took him in and forbade the maids to speak of him to her husband. She hid him in a room that no one went to, smuggled food to him from her own plate, made him a warm bed to lie on and petted him like a child.

Yves de Cornault came home, and the next day she found the greyhound strangled on her pillow. She wept in secret, but said nothing, and resolved that even if she met a dog dying of hunger she would never bring him into the castle; but one day she found a young sheep dog, a brindled puppy with good blue eyes, lying with a broken leg in the snow of the park. Yves de Cornault was at Rennes, and she brought the dog in, warmed and fed it, tied up its leg and hid it in the castle till her husband's return. The day before, she gave it to a peasant woman who lived a long way off, and paid her handsomely to care for it and say nothing; but that night she heard a whining and scratching at her door, and when she opened it the lame puppy, drenched and shivering, jumped up on her with little sobbing barks. She hid him in her bed, and the next morning was about to have him taken back to the peasant woman when she heard her husband ride into the court. She shut the dog in a chest, and went down to receive him. An hour or two later, when she returned to her room, the puppy lay strangled on her pillow. . . .

After that she dared not make a pet of any other dog; and her loneliness became almost unendurable. Sometimes, when she crossed the court of the castle, and thought no one was looking, she stopped to pat the old pointer at the gate. But one day as she was caressing him her husband came out of the chapel; and the next day the old dog was gone. . . .

This curious narrative was not told in one sitting of the court, or received without impatience and incredulous comment. It was plain that the Judges were surprised by its puerility, and that it did not help the accused in the eyes of the public. It was an odd tale, certainly; but what did it prove? That Yves de Cornault disliked dogs, and that his wife, to gratify her own fancy, persistently ignored this dislike. As for pleading this trivial disagreement as an excuse for her relations— whatever their nature—with her supposed accomplice, the argument was so absurd that her own lawyer manifestly regretted having let her make use of it, and tried several times to cut short her story. But she went on to the end, with a kind of hypnotized insistence, as though the scenes she evoked were so real to her that she had forgotten where she was and imagined herself to be reliving them.

At length the Judge who had previously shown a certain kindness to her said (leaning forward a little, one may suppose, from his row of dozing colleagues): "Then you would have us believe that you murdered your husband because he would not let you keep a pet dog?"

"I did not murder my husband."

"Who did, then? Hervé de Lanrivain?"

"No."

"Who then? Can you tell us?"

"Yes, I can tell you. The dogs—" At that point she was carried out of the court in a swoon.

It was evident that her lawyer tried to get her to abandon this line of defense. Possibly her explanation, whatever it was, had seemed convincing when she poured it out to him in the heat of their first private colloquy; but now that it was exposed to the cold daylight of judicial scrutiny, and the banter of the town, he was thoroughly ashamed of it, and would have sacrificed her without a scruple to save his professional reputation. But the obstinate Judge—who perhaps, after all, was more inquisitive than kindly—evidently wanted to hear the story out, and she was ordered, the next day, to continue her deposition.

She said that after the disappearance of the old watchdog nothing particular happened for a month or two. Her husband was much as usual: she did not remember any special incident. But one evening a peddler woman came to the castle and was selling trinkets to the maids. She had no heart for trinkets, but she stood looking on while the women made their choice. And then, she did not know how, but the peddler coaxed her into buying for herself a pear-shaped pomander with a strong scent in it—she had once seen something of the kind on a gypsy woman. She had no desire for the pomander, and did not know why she had bought it. The peddler said that whoever wore it had the power to read the future; but she did not really believe that, or care much either. However, she bought the thing and took it up to her room, where she sat turning it about in her hand. Then the strange scent attracted her and she began to wonder what kind of spice was in the box. She opened it and found a grey bean rolled in a strip of paper; and on the paper she saw a sign she knew, and a message from Hervé de Lanrivain, saying that he was at home again and would be at the door in the court that night after the moon had set. . . .

She burned the paper and sat down to think. It was nightfall, and her husband was at home. . . . She had no way of warning Lanrivain, and there was nothing to do but to wait. . . .

At this point I fancy the drowsy courtroom beginning to wake up. Even to the oldest hand on the bench there must have been a certain relish in picturing the feelings of a woman on receiving such a message at nightfall from a man living twenty miles away, to whom she had no means of sending a warning. . . .

She was not a clever woman, I imagine; and as the first result of her cogitation she appears to have made the mistake of being, that evening, too kind to her husband. She could not ply him with wine, according to the traditional expedient, for though he drank heavily at times he had a strong head; and when he drank beyond its strength it was because he chose to, and not because a woman coaxed him. Not his wife, at any rate—she was an old story by now. As I read the case, I fancy there was no feeling for her left in him but the hatred occasioned by his supposed dishonor.

At any rate, she tried to call up her old graces; but early in the evening he complained of pains and fever, and left the hall to go up to the closet where he sometimes slept. His servant carried him a cup of hot wine, and brought back word that he was sleeping and not to be disturbed; and an hour later, when Anne lifted the tapestry and listened at his door, she heard his loud regular breathing. She thought it might be a feint, and stayed a long time barefooted in the passage, her ear to the crack; but the breathing went on too steadily and naturally to be other than that of a man in a sound sleep. She crept back to her room reassured, and stood in the window watching the moon set through the trees of the park. The sky was misty and starless, and after the moon went down the night was black as pitch. She knew the time had come, and stole along the passage, past her husband's door —where she stopped again to listen to his breathing—to the top of the stairs. There she paused a moment, and assured herself that no one was following her; then she began to go down the stairs in the darkness. They were so steep and winding that she had to go very slowly, for fear of stumbling. Her one thought was to get the door unbolted, tell Lanrivain to make his escape, and hasten back to her room. She had tried the bolt earlier in the evening, and managed to put a little grease on it; but nevertheless, when she drew it, it gave a squeak . . . not loud, but it made her heart stop; and the next minute, overhead, she heard a noise. . . .

"What noise?" the prosecution interposed.

"My husband's voice calling out my name and cursing me."

"What did you hear after that?"

"A terrible scream and a fall."

"Where was Hervé de Lanrivain at this time?"

"He was standing outside in the court. I just made him out in the darkness. I told him for God's sake to go, and then I pushed the door shut."

"What did you do next?"

"I stood at the foot of the stairs and listened."

"What did you hear?"

"I heard dogs snarling and panting." (Visible discouragement of the bench, boredom of the public, and exasperation of the lawyer for the defense. Dogs again—! But the inquisitive Judge insisted.)

"What dogs?"

She bent her head and spoke so low that she had to be told to repeat her answer: "I don't know."

"How do you mean—you don't know?"

"I don't know what dogs. . . ."

The Judge again intervened: "Try to tell us exactly what happened. How long did you remain at the foot of the stairs?"

"Only a few minutes."

"And what was going on meanwhile overhead?"

"The dogs kept on snarling and panting. Once or twice he cried out. I think he moaned once. Then he was quiet."

"Then what happened?"

"Then I heard a sound like the noise of a pack when the wolf is thrown to them—gulping and lapping."

(There was a groan of disgust and repulsion through the court, and another attempted intervention by the distracted lawyer. But the inquisitive Judge was still inquisitive.)

"And all the while you did not go up?"

"Yes—I went up then—to drive them off."

"The dogs?"

"Yes."

"Well—?"

"When I got there it was quite dark. I found my husband's flint and steel and struck a spark. I saw him lying there. He was dead."

"And the dogs?"

"The dogs were gone."

"Gone—where to?"

"I don't know. There was no way out—and there were no dogs at Kerfol."

She straightened herself to her full height, threw her arms above her head, and fell down on the stone floor with a long scream. There was a moment of confusion in the courtroom. Someone on the bench was heard to say: "This is clearly a case for the ecclesiastical authorities"—and the prisoner's lawyer doubtless jumped at the suggestion.

After this, the trial loses itself in a maze of cross-questioning and squabbling. Every witness who was called corroborated Anne de Cornault's statement that there were no dogs at Kerfol: had been none for several months. The master of the house had taken a dislike to dogs, there was no denying it. But, on the other hand, at the inquest, there had been long and bitter discussions as to the nature of the dead man's wounds. One of the surgeons called in had spoken of marks that looked like bites. The suggestion of witchcraft was revived, and the opposing lawyers hurled tomes of necromancy at each other.

At last Anne de Cornault was brought back into court—at the instance of the same Judge—and asked if she knew where the dogs she spoke of could have come from. On the body of her Redeemer she swore that she did not. Then the Judge put his final question: "If the dogs you think you heard had been known to you, do you think you would have recognized them by their barking?"

"Yes."

"Did you recognize them?"

"Yes."

"What dogs do you take them to have been?"

"My dead dogs," she said in a whisper. . . . She was taken out of court, not to reappear there again. There was some kind of ecclesiastical investigation, and the end of the business was that the Judges disagreed with each other, and with the ecclesiastical committee, and that Anne de Cornault was finally handed over to the keeping of her husband's family, who shut her up in the keep of Kerfol, where she is said to have died many years later, a harmless madwoman.

So ends her story. As for that of Hervé de Lanrivain, I had only to apply to his collateral descendant for its subsequent details. The evidence against the young man being insufficient, and his family influence in the duchy considerable, he was set free, and left soon afterward for Paris. He was probably in no mood for a worldly life, and he appears to have come almost immediately under the influence of the famous M. Arnauld d'Andilly and the gentlemen of Port Royal. A year or two later he was received into their Order, and without achieving any particular distinction he followed its good and evil fortunes till his death some twenty years later. Lanrivain showed me a portrait of him by a pupil of Philippe de Champaigne: sad eyes, an impulsive mouth and a narrow brow. Poor Hervé de Lanrivain: it was a grey ending. Yet as I looked at his stiff and sallow effigy, in the dark dress of the Jansenists, I almost found myself envying his fate. After all, in the course of his life two great things had happened to him: he had loved romantically, and he must have talked with Pascal. . . .

The Triumph of
Night

*I*t was clear that the sleigh from Weymore had not come; and the shivering young traveler from Boston, who had counted on jumping into it when he left the train at Northridge Junction, found himself standing alone on the open platform, exposed to the full assault of nightfall and winter.

The blast that swept him came off New Hampshire snowfields and ice-hung forests. It seemed to have traversed interminable leagues of frozen silence, filling them with the same cold roar and sharpening its edge against the same bitter black-and-white landscape. Dark, searching and swordlike, it alternately muffled and harried its victim, like a bullfighter now whirling his cloak and now planting his darts. This analogy brought home to the young man the fact that he himself had no cloak, and that the overcoat in which he had faced the relatively temperate air of Boston seemed no thicker than a sheet of paper on the bleak heights of Northridge. George Faxon said to himself that the place was uncommonly well-named. It clung to an exposed ledge over the valley from which the train had lifted him, and the wind combed it with teeth of steel that he seemed actually to hear scraping against the wooden sides of the station. Other building there was none: the village lay far down the road, and thither—since the Weymore sleigh had not come—Faxon saw himself under the necessity of plodding through several feet of snow.

He understood well enough what had happened: his hostess had forgotten that he was coming. Young as Faxon was, this sad lucidity of soul had been acquired as the result of long experience, and he knew that the visitors who can least afford to hire a carriage are almost always those whom their hosts forget to send for. Yet to say that Mrs. Culme had forgotten him was too crude a way of putting it. Similar incidents led him to think that she had probably told her maid to tell the butler to telephone the coachman to tell one of the grooms (if no one else needed him) to drive over to Northridge to fetch the new secretary; but on a night like this, what groom who respected his rights would fail to forget the order?

Faxon's obvious course was to struggle through the drifts to the village, and there rout out a sleigh to convey him to Weymore; but what if, on his arrival at Mrs. Culme's, no one remembered to ask him what this devotion to duty had cost? That, again, was one of the contingencies he had expensively learned to look out for, and the perspicacity so acquired told him it would be cheaper to spend the night at the Northridge inn, and advise Mrs. Culme of his presence there by telephone. He had reached this decision, and was about to entrust his luggage to a vague man with a lantern, when his hopes were raised by the sound of bells.

Two sleighs were just dashing up to the station, and from the foremost there sprang a young man muffled in furs.

"Weymore? No, these are not the Weymore sleighs."

The voice was that of the youth who had jumped to the platform —a voice so agreeable that, in spite of the words, it fell consolingly on Faxon's ears. At the same moment the wandering station lantern, casting a transient light on the speaker, showed his features to be in the pleasantest harmony with his voice. He was very fair and very young—hardly in the twenties, Faxon thought—but this face, though full of a morning freshness, was a trifle too thin and fine-drawn, as though a vivid spirit contended in him with a strain of physical weakness. Faxon was perhaps the quicker to notice such delicacies of balance because his own temperament hung on lightly quivering nerves, which yet, as he believed, would never quite swing him beyond a normal sensibility.

"You expected a sleigh from Weymore?" the newcomer continued, standing beside Faxon like a slender column of fur.

Mrs. Culme's secretary explained his difficulty, and the other brushed it aside with a contemptuous "Oh, *Mrs. Culme!*" that carried both speakers a long way toward reciprocal understanding.

"But then you must be—" The youth broke off with a smile of interrogation.

"The new secretary? Yes. But apparently there are no notes to be answered this evening." Faxon's laugh deepened the sense of solidarity which had so promptly established itself between the two.

His friend laughed also. "Mrs. Culme," he explained, "was lunching at my uncle's today, and she said you were due this evening. But seven hours is a long time for Mrs. Culme to remember anything."

"Well," said Faxon philosophically, "I suppose that's one of the reasons why she needs a secretary. And I've always the inn at Northridge," he concluded.

"Oh, but you haven't, though! It burned down last week."

"The deuce it did!" said Faxon; but the humor of the situation struck him before its inconvenience. His life, for years past, had been mainly a succession of resigned adaptations, and he had learned, before dealing practically with his embarrassments, to extract from most of them a small tribute of amusement.

"Oh, well, there's sure to be somebody in the place who can put me up."

"No one *you* could put up with. Besides, Northridge is three miles off, and our place—in the opposite direction—is a little nearer." Through the darkness, Faxon saw his friend sketch a gesture of self-introduction. "My name's Frank Rainer, and I'm staying with my uncle at Overdale. I've driven over to meet two friends of his, who are due in a few minutes from New York. If you don't mind waiting till they arrive I'm sure Overdale can do you better than Northridge. We're only down from town for a few days, but the house is always ready for a lot of people."

"But your uncle—?" Faxon could only object, with the odd sense, through his embarrassment, that it would be magically dispelled by his invisible friend's next words.

"Oh, my uncle—you'll see! I answer for *him!* I dare say you've heard of him—John Lavington?"

John Lavington! There was a certain irony in asking if one had heard of John Lavington! Even from a post of observation as obscure as that of Mrs. Culme's secretary the rumor of John Lavington's money, of his pictures, his politics, his charities and his hospitality, was as difficult to escape as the roar of a cataract in a mountain solitude. It might almost have been said that the one place in which one would not have expected to come upon him was in just such a solitude as now surrounded the speakers—at least in this deepest hour of its desertedness. But it was just like Lavington's brilliant ubiquity to put one in the wrong even there.

"Oh, yes, I've heard of your uncle."

"Then you *will* come, won't you? We've only five minutes to wait," young Rainer urged, in the tone that dispels scruples by ignoring them; and Faxon found himself accepting the invitation as simply as it was offered.

A delay in the arrival of the New York train lengthened their five minutes to fifteen; and as they paced the icy platform Faxon began to see why it had seemed the most natural thing in the world to accede to his new acquaintance's suggestion. It was because Frank Rainer was one of the privileged beings who simplify human intercourse by the atmosphere of confidence and good humor they diffuse. He produced this effect, Faxon noted, by the exercise of no gift but his youth, and of no art but his sincerity; and these qualities were revealed in a smile of such sweetness that Faxon felt, as never before, what Nature can achieve when she deigns to match the face with the mind.

He learned that the young man was the ward, and the only nephew, of John Lavington, with whom he had made his home since the death of his mother, the great man's sister. Mr. Lavington, Rainer said, had been "a regular brick" to him—"But then he is to everyone, you know"—and the young fellow's situation seemed in fact to be perfectly in keeping with his person. Apparently the only shade that had ever rested on him was cast by the physical weakness which Faxon had already detected. Young Rainer had been threatened with tuberculosis, and the disease was so far advanced that, according to the highest authorities, banishment to Arizona or New Mexico was inevitable. "But luckily my uncle didn't pack me off, as most people would have done, without getting another opinion. Whose? Oh, an awfully clever chap, a young doctor with a lot of new ideas, who simply laughed at my being sent away, and said I'd do perfectly well in New York if I didn't dine out too much, and if I dashed off occasionally to Northridge for a little fresh air. So it's really my uncle's doing that I'm not in exile—and I feel no end better since the new chap told me I needn't bother." Young Rainer went on to confess that he was extremely fond of dining out, dancing and similar distractions; and Faxon, listening to him, was inclined to think that the physician who had refused to cut him off altogether from these pleasures was probably a better psychologist than his seniors.

"All the same you ought to be careful, you know." The sense of elder-brotherly concern that forced the words from Faxon made him, as he spoke, slip his arm through Frank Rainer's.

The latter met the movement with a responsive pressure. "Oh, I *am:* awfully, awfully. And then my uncle has such an eye on me!"

"But if your uncle has such an eye on you, what does he say to your swallowing knives out here in this Siberian wild?"

Rainer raised his fur collar with a careless gesture. "It's not that that does it—the cold's good for me."

"And it's not the dinners and dances? What is it, then?" Faxon good-humoredly insisted; to which his companion answered with a laugh: "Well, my uncle says it's being bored; and I rather think he's right!"

His laugh ended in a spasm of coughing and a struggle for breath that made Faxon, still holding his arm, guide him hastily into the shelter of the fireless waiting room.

Young Rainer had dropped down on the bench against the wall and pulled off one of his fur gloves to grope for a handkerchief. He tossed aside his cap and drew the handkerchief across his forehead, which was intensely white, and beaded with moisture, though his face retained a healthy glow. But Faxon's gaze remained fastened to the hand he had uncovered: it was so long, so colorless, so wasted, so much older than the brow he passed it over.

"It's queer—a healthy face but dying hands," the secretary mused: he somehow wished young Rainer had kept on his glove.

The whistle of the express drew the young men to their feet, and the next moment two heavily-furred gentlemen had descended to the platform and were breasting the rigor of the night. Frank Rainer introduced them as Mr. Grisben and Mr. Balch, and Faxon, while their luggage was being lifted into the second sleigh, discerned them, by the roving lantern gleam, to be an elderly grey-headed pair, of the average prosperous business cut.

They saluted their host's nephew with friendly familiarity, and Mr. Grisben, who seemed the spokesman of the two, ended his greeting with a genial—"and many many more of them, dear boy!" which suggested to Faxon that their arrival coincided with an anniversary. But he could not press the inquiry, for the seat allotted him was at the coachman's side, while Frank Rainer joined his uncle's guests inside the sleigh.

A swift flight (behind such horses as one could be sure of John Lavington's having) brought them to tall gateposts, an illuminated lodge, and an avenue on which the snow had been leveled to the smoothness of marble. At the end of the avenue the long house loomed up, its principal bulk dark, but one wing sending out a ray of welcome; and the next moment Faxon was receiving a violent impression of warmth and light, of hothouse plants, hurrying servants, a vast spectacular oak hall like a stage setting, and, in its unreal middle distance, a small figure, correctly dressed, conventionally featured, and utterly unlike his rather florid conception of the great John Lavington.

The surprise of the contrast remained with him through his hurried dressing in the large luxurious bedroom to which he had been shown. "I don't see where he comes in," was the only way he could put it, so difficult was it to fit the exuberance of Lavington's public personality into his host's contracted frame and manner. Mr. Lavington, to whom Faxon's case had been rapidly explained by young Rainer, had welcomed him with a sort of dry and stilted cordiality that exactly matched his narrow face, his stiff hand, and the whiff of scent on his evening handkerchief. "Make yourself at home—at home!" he had repeated, in a tone that suggested, on his own part, a complete inability to perform the feat he urged on his visitor. "Any friend of Frank's . . . delighted . . . make yourself thoroughly at home!"

II

In spite of the balmy temperature and complicated conveniences of Faxon's bedroom, the injunction was not easy to obey. It was wonderful luck to have found a night's shelter under the opulent roof of Overdale, and he tasted the physical satisfaction to the full. But the place, for all its ingenuities of comfort, was oddly cold and unwelcoming. He couldn't have said why, and could only suppose that Mr. Lavington's intense personality—intensely negative, but intense all the same—must, in some occult way, have penetrated every corner of his dwelling. Perhaps, though, it was merely that Faxon himself was tired and hungry, more deeply chilled than he had known till he came in from the cold, and unutterably sick of all strange houses, and of the prospect of perpetually treading other people's stairs.

"I hope you're not famished?" Rainer's slim figure was in the doorway. "My uncle has a little business to attend to with Mr. Grisben, and we don't dine for half an hour. Shall I fetch you, or can you find your way down? Come straight to the dining room—the second door on the left of the long gallery."

He disappeared, leaving a ray of warmth behind him, and Faxon, relieved, lit a cigarette and sat down by the fire.

Looking about with less haste, he was struck by a detail that had escaped him. The room was full of flowers—a mere "bachelor's room," in the wing of a house opened only for a few days, in the dead middle of a New Hampshire winter! Flowers were everywhere, not in senseless profusion, but placed with the same conscious art that he had remarked in the grouping of the blossoming shrubs in the hall. A vase of arums stood on the writing table, a cluster of strange-hued carnations on the stand at his elbow, and from bowls of glass and porcelain clumps of freesia bulbs diffused their melting fragrance. The fact implied acres of glass—but that was the least interesting part of it. The flowers themselves, their quality, selection and arrangement, attested on someone's part—and on whose but John Lavington's?—a solicitous and sensitive passion for that particular form of beauty. Well, it simply made the man, as he had appeared to Faxon, all the harder to understand!

The half hour elapsed, and Faxon, rejoicing at the prospect of food, set out to make his way to the dining room. He had not noticed the direction he had followed in going to his room, and was puzzled, when he left it, to find that two staircases, of apparently equal importance, invited him. He chose the one to his right, and reached, at its foot, a long gallery such as Rainer had described. The gallery was empty, the doors down its length were closed; but Rainer had said: "The second to the left," and Faxon, after pausing for some chance enlightenment which did not come, laid his hand on the second knob to the left.

The room he entered was square, with dusky picture-hung walls. In its center, about a table lit by veiled lamps, he fancied Mr. Lavington and his guests to be already seated at dinner; then he perceived that the table was covered not with viands but with papers, and that he had blundered into what seemed to be his host's study. As he paused Frank Rainer looked up.

"Oh, here's Mr. Faxon. Why not ask him—?"

Mr. Lavington, from the end of the table, reflected his nephew's smile in a glance of impartial benevolence.

"Certainly. Come in, Mr. Faxon. If you won't think it a liberty—"

Mr. Grisben, who sat opposite his host, turned his head toward the door. "Of course Mr. Faxon's an American citizen?"

Frank Rainer laughed. "That's all right! . . . Oh, no, not one of your pin-pointed pens, Uncle Jack! Haven't you got a quill somewhere?"

Mr. Balch, spoke slowly and as if reluctantly, in a muffled voice of which there seemed to be very little left, raised his hand to say: "One moment: you acknowledge this to be—?"

"My last will and testament?" Rainer's laugh redoubled. "Well, I won't answer for the 'last.' It's the first, anyway."

"It's a mere formula," Mr. Balch explained.

"Well, here goes." Rainer dipped his quill in the inkstand his uncle had pushed in his direction, and dashed a gallant signature across the document.

Faxon, understanding what was expected of him, and conjecturing that the young man was signing his will on the attainment of his majority, had placed himself behind Mr. Grisben, and stood awaiting his turn to affix his name to the instrument. Rainer, having signed, was about to push the paper across the table to Mr. Balch; but the latter, again raising his hand, said in his sad imprisoned voice: "The seal—?"

"Oh, does there have to be a seal?"

Faxon, looking over Mr. Grisben at John Lavington, saw a faint frown between his impassive eyes. "Really, Frank!" He seemed, Faxon thought, slightly irritated by his nephew's frivolity.

"Who's got a seal?" Frank Rainer continued, glancing about the table. "There doesn't seem to be one here."

Mr. Grisben interposed. "A wafer will do. Lavington, you have a wafer?"

Mr. Lavington had recovered his serenity. "There must be some in one of the drawers. But I'm ashamed to say I don't know where my secretary keeps these things. He ought to have seen to it that a wafer was sent with the document."

"Oh, hang it—" Frank Rainer pushed the paper aside: "It's the hand of God—and I'm as hungry as a wolf. Let's dine first, Uncle Jack."

"I think I've a seal upstairs," said Faxon.

Mr. Lavington sent him a barely perceptible smile. "So sorry to give you the trouble—"

"Oh, I say, don't send him after it now. Let's wait till after dinner!"

Mr. Lavington continued to smile on his guest, and the latter, as if under the faint coercion of the smile, turned from the room and ran upstairs. Having taken the seal from his writing case he came down again, and once more opened the door of the study. No one was speaking when he entered—they were evidently awaiting his return with the mute impatience of hunger, and he put the seal in Rainer's reach, and stood watching while Mr. Grisben struck a match and held it to one of the candles flanking the inkstand. As the wax descended on the paper Faxon remarked again the strange emaciation, the premature physical weariness, of the hand that held it: he wondered if Mr. Lavington had ever noticed his nephew's hand, and if it were not poignantly visible to him now.

With this thought in mind, Faxon raised his eyes to look at Mr. Lavington. The great man's gaze rested on Frank Rainer with an expression of untroubled benevolence; and at the same instant Faxon's attention was attracted by the presence in the room of another person, who must have joined the group while he was upstairs searching for the seal. The newcomer was a man of about Mr. Lavington's age and figure, who stood just behind his chair, and who, at the moment when Faxon first saw him, was gazing at young Rainer with an equal intensity of attention. The likeness between the two men—perhaps increased by the fact that the hooded lamps on the table left the figure behind the chair in shadow—struck Faxon the more because of the contrast in their expression. John Lavington, during his nephew's clumsy attempt to drop the wax and apply the seal, continued to fasten on him a look of half-amused affection; while the man behind the chair, so oddly reduplicating the lines of his features and figure, turned on the boy a face of pale hostility.

The impression was so startling that Faxon forgot what was going on about him. He was just dimly aware of young Rainer's exclaiming: "Your turn, Mr. Grisben!" of Mr. Grisben's protesting: "No—no; Mr. Faxon first," and of the pen's being thereupon transferred to his own hand. He received it with a deadly sense of being unable to move, or even to understand what was expected of him, till he became conscious of Mr. Grisben's paternally pointing out the precise spot on which he was to leave his autograph. The effort to fix his attention and steady his hand prolonged the process of signing, and when he stood up—a strange weight of fatigue on all his limbs—the figure behind Mr. Lavington's chair was gone.

Faxon felt an immediate sense of relief. It was puzzling that the man's exit should have been so rapid and noiseless, but the door behind Mr. Lavington was screened by a tapestry hanging, and Faxon concluded that the unknown looker-on had merely had to raise it to pass out. At any rate he was gone, and with his withdrawal the strange weight was lifted. Young Rainer was lighting a cigarette, Mr. Balch inscribing his name at the foot of the document, Mr. Lavington—his eyes no longer on his nephew—examining a strange white-winged orchid in the vase at his elbow. Everything suddenly seemed to have grown natural and simple again, and Faxon found himself responding with a smile to the affable gesture with which his host declared: "And now, Mr. Faxon, we'll dine."

III

"I wonder how I blundered into the wrong room just now; I thought you told me to take the second door to the left," Faxon said to Frank Rainer as they followed the older men down the gallery.

"So I did; but I probably forgot to tell you which staircase to take. Coming from your bedroom, I ought to have said the fourth door to the right. It's a puzzling house, because my uncle keeps adding to it from year to year. He built this room last summer for his modern pictures."

Young Rainer, pausing to open another door, touched an electric button which sent a circle of light about the walls of a long room hung with canvases of the French Impressionist school.

Faxon advanced, attracted by a shimmering Monet, but Rainer laid a hand on his arm.

"He bought that last week. But come along—I'll show you all this after dinner. Or *he* will, rather—he loves it."

"Does he really love things?"

Rainer stared, clearly perplexed at the question. "Rather! Flowers and pictures especially! Haven't you noticed the flowers? I suppose you think his manner's cold; it seems so at first; but he's really awfully keen about things."

Faxon looked quickly at the speaker. "Has your uncle a brother?"

"Brother? No—never had. He and my mother were the only ones."

"Or any relation who—who looks like him? Who might be mistaken for him?"

"Not that I ever heard of. Does he remind you of someone?"

"Yes."

"That's queer. We'll ask him if he's got a double. Come on!"

But another picture had arrested Faxon, and some minutes elapsed before he and his young host reached the dining room. It was a large room, with the same conventionally handsome furniture and delicately grouped flowers; and Faxon's first glance showed him that only three men were seated about the dining table. The man who had stood behind Mr. Lavington's chair was not present, and no seat awaited him.

When the young men entered, Mr. Grisben was speaking, and his host, who faced the door, sat looking down at his untouched soup plate and turning the spoon about in his small dry hand.

"It's pretty late to call them rumors—they were devilish close to facts when we left town this morning," Mr. Grisben was saying, with an unexpected incisiveness of tone.

Mr. Lavington laid down his spoon and smiled interrogatively. "Oh, facts—what *are* facts? Just the way a thing happens to look at a given minute. . . ."

"You haven't heard anything from town?" Mr. Grisben persisted.

"Not a syllable. So you see. . . . Balch, a little more of that *petite marmite*. Mr. Faxon . . . between Frank and Mr. Grisben, please."

The dinner progressed through a series of complicated courses, ceremoniously dispensed by a prelatical butler attended by three tall footmen, and it was evident that Mr. Lavington took a certain satisfaction in the pageant. That, Faxon reflected, was probably the joint in his armor—that and the flowers. He had changed the subject—not abruptly but firmly—when the young men entered, but Faxon perceived that it still possessed the thoughts of the two elderly visitors, and Mr. Balch presently observed, in a voice that seemed to come from the last survivor down a mine shaft: "If it *does* come, it will be the biggest crash since '93."

Mr. Lavington looked bored but polite. "Wall Street can stand crashes better than it could then. It's got a robuster constitution."

"Yes; but—"

"Speaking of constitutions," Mr. Grisben intervened: "Frank, are you taking care of yourself?"

A flush rose to young Rainer's cheeks.

"Why, of course! Isn't that what I'm here for?"

"You're here about three days in the month, aren't you? And the rest of the time it's crowded restaurants and hot ballrooms in town. I thought you were to be shipped off to New Mexico?"

"Oh, I've got a new man who says that's rot."

"Well, you don't look as if your new man were right," said Mr. Grisben bluntly.

Faxon saw the lad's color fade, and the rings of shadow deepen under his gay eyes. At the same moment his uncle turned to him with a renewed intensity of attention. There was such solicitude in Mr. Lavington's gaze that it seemed almost to fling a shield between his nephew and Mr. Grisben's tactless scrutiny.

"We think Frank's a good deal better," he began; "this new doctor—"

The butler, coming up, bent to whisper a word in his ear, and the communication caused a sudden change in Mr. Lavington's expression. His face was naturally so colorless that it seemed not so much to pale as to fade, to dwindle and recede into something blurred and blotted out. He half rose, sat down again and sent a rigid smile about the table.

"Will you excuse me? The telephone. Peters, go on with the dinner." With small precise steps he walked out of the door which one of the footmen had thrown open.

A momentary silence fell on the group; then Mr. Grisben once more addressed himself to Rainer. "You ought to have gone, my boy; you ought to have gone."

The anxious look returned to the youth's eyes. "My uncle doesn't think so, really."

"You're not a baby, to be always governed by your uncle's opinion. You came of age today, didn't you? Your uncle spoils you . . . that's what's the matter. . . ."

The thrust evidently went home, for Rainer laughed and looked down with a slight accession of color.

"But the doctor—"

"Use your common sense, Frank! You had to try twenty doctors to find one to tell you what you wanted to be told."

A look of apprehension overshadowed Rainer's gaiety. "Oh, come —I say! . . . What would *you* do?" he stammered.

"Pack up and jump on the first train." Mr. Grisben leaned forward and laid his hand kindly on the young man's arm. "Look here: my nephew Jim Grisben is out there ranching on a big scale. He'll take you in and be glad to have you. You say your new doctor thinks it won't do you any good; but he doesn't pretend to say it will do you harm, does he? Well, then—give it a trial. It'll take you out of hot theaters and night restaurants, anyhow. . . . And all the rest of it. . . . Eh, Balch?"

"Go!" said Mr. Balch hollowly. "Go *at once*," he added, as if a closer look at the youth's face had impressed on him the need of backing up his friend.

Young Rainer had turned ashy pale. He tried to stiffen his mouth into a smile. "Do I look as bad as all that?"

Mr. Grisben was helping himself to terrapin. "You look like the day after an earthquake," he said.

The terrapin had encircled the table, and been deliberately enjoyed by Mr. Lavington's three visitors (Rainer, Faxon noticed, left his plate untouched) before the door was thrown open to readmit their host.

Mr. Lavington advanced with an air of recovered composure. He seated himself, picked up his napkin and consulted the gold-monogrammed menu. "No, don't bring back the filet. . . . Some terrapin; yes. . . ." He looked affably about the table. "Sorry to have deserted you, but the storm has played the deuce with the wires, and I had to wait a long time before I could get a good connection. It must be blowing up a blizzard."

"Uncle Jack," young Rainer broke out, "Mr. Grisben's been lecturing me."

Mr. Lavington was helping himself to terrapin. "Ah—what about?"

"He thinks I ought to have given New Mexico a show."

"I want him to go straight out to my nephew at Santa Paz and stay there till his next birthday." Mr. Lavington signed to the butler to hand the terrapin to Mr. Grisben, who, as he took a second helping, addressed himself again to Rainer. "Jim's in New York now, and going back the day after tomorrow in Olyphant's private car. I'll ask Olyphant to squeeze you in if you'll go. And when you've been out there a week or two, in the saddle all day and sleeping nine hours a night, I suspect you won't think much of the doctor who prescribed New York."

Faxon spoke up, he knew not why. "I was out there once: it's a splendid life. I saw a fellow—oh, a really *bad* case—who'd been simply made over by it."

"It *does* sound jolly," Rainer laughed, a sudden eagerness in his tone.

His uncle looked at him gently. "Perhaps Grisben's right. It's an opportunity—"

Faxon glanced up with a start: the figure dimly perceived in the study was now more visibly and tangibly planted behind Mr. Lavington's chair.

"That's right, Frank: you see your uncle approves. And the trip out there with Olyphant isn't a thing to be missed. So drop a few dozen dinners and be at the Grand Central the day after tomorrow at five."

Mr. Grisben's pleasant grey eye sought corroboration of his host, and Faxon, in a cold anguish of suspense, continued to watch him as he turned his glance on Mr. Lavington. One could not look at Lavington without seeing the presence at his back, and it was clear that, the next minute, some change in Mr. Grisben's expression must give his watcher a clue.

But Mr. Grisben's expression did not change: the gaze he fixed on his host remained unperturbed, and the clue he gave was the startling one of not seeming to see the other figure.

Faxon's first impulse was to look away, to look anywhere else, to resort again to the champagne glass the watchful butler had already brimmed; but some fatal attraction, at war in him with an overwhelming physical resistance, held his eyes upon the spot they feared.

The figure was still standing, more distinctly, and therefore more resemblingly, at Mr. Lavington's back; and while the latter continued to gaze affectionately at his nephew, his counterpart, as before, fixed young Rainer with eyes of deadly menace.

Faxon, with what felt like an actual wrench of the muscles, dragged his own eyes from the sight to scan the other countenances about the table; but not one revealed the least consciousness of what he saw, and a sense of mortal isolation sank upon him.

"It's worth considering, certainly—" he heard Mr. Lavington continue; and as Rainer's face lit up, the face behind his uncle's chair seemed to gather into its look all the fierce weariness of old unsatisfied hates. That was the thing that, as the minutes labored by, Faxon was becoming most conscious of. The watcher behind the chair was no longer merely malevolent: he had grown suddenly, unutterably tired. His hatred seemed to well up out of the very depths of balked effort and thwarted hopes, and the fact made him more pitiable, and yet more dire.

Faxon's look reverted to Mr. Lavington, as if to surprise in him a corresponding change. At first none was visible: his pinched smile was screwed to his blank face like a gaslight to a whitewashed wall. Then the fixity of the smile became ominous: Faxon saw that its wearer was afraid to let it go. It was evident that Mr. Lavington was unutterably tired too, and the discovery sent a colder current through Faxon's veins. Looking down at his untouched plate, he caught the soliciting twinkle of the champagne glass; but the sight of the wine turned him sick.

"Well, we'll go into the details presently," he heard Mr. Lavington say, still on the question of his nephew's future. "Let's have a cigar first. No—not here, Peters." He turned his smile on Faxon. "When we've had coffee I want to show you my pictures."

"Oh, by the way, Uncle Jack—Mr. Faxon wants to know if you've got a double?"

"A double?" Mr. Lavington, still smiling, continued to address himself to his guest. "Not that I know of. Have you seen one, Mr. Faxon?"

Faxon thought: "My God, if I look up now they'll *both* be looking at me!" To avoid raising his eyes he made as though to lift the glass to his lips; but his hand sank inert, and he looked up. Mr. Lavington's glance was politely bent on him, but with a loosening of the strain about his heart he saw that the figure behind the chair still kept its gaze on Rainer.

"Do you think you've seen my double, Mr. Faxon?"

Would the other face turn if he said yes? Faxon felt a dryness in his throat. "No," he answered.

"Ah? It's possible I've a dozen. I believe I'm extremely usual-looking," Mr. Lavington went on conversationally; and still the other face watched Rainer.

"It was . . . a mistake . . . a confusion of memory. . . ." Faxon heard himself stammer. Mr. Lavington pushed back his chair, and as he did so Mr. Grisben suddenly leaned forward.

"Lavington! What have we been thinking of? We haven't drunk Frank's health!"

Mr. Lavington reseated himself. "My dear boy! . . . Peters, another bottle. . . ." He turned to his nephew. "After such a sin of omission I don't presume to propose the toast myself . . . but Frank knows. . . . Go ahead, Grisben!"

The boy shone on his uncle. "No, no. Uncle Jack! Mr. Grisben won't mind. Nobody but *you*—today!"

The butler was replenishing the glasses. He filled Mr. Lavington's last, and Mr. Lavington put out his small hand to raise it. . . . As he did so, Faxon looked away.

"Well, then—All the good I've wished you in all the past years. . . . I put it into the prayer that the coming ones may be healthy and happy and many . . . and *many*, dear boy!"

Faxon saw the hands about him reach out for their glasses. Automatically, he reached for his. His eyes were still on the table, and he repeated to himself with a trembling vehemence: "I won't look up! I won't. . . . I won't. . . ."

His fingers clasped the glass and raised it to the level of his lips. He saw the other hands making the same motion. He heard Mr. Grisben's genial "Hear! Hear!" and Mr. Balch's hollow echo. He said to himself, as the rim of the glass touched his lips: "I won't look up! I swear I won't!—" and he looked.

The glass was so full that it required an extraordinary effort to hold it there, brimming and suspended, during the awful interval before he could trust his hand to lower it again, untouched, to the table. It was this merciful preoccupation which saved him, kept him from crying out, from losing his hold, from slipping down into the bottomless blackness that gaped for him. As long as the problem of the glass engaged him he felt able to keep his seat, manage his muscles, fit unnoticeably into the group; but as the glass touched the table his last link with safety snapped. He stood up and dashed out of the room.

IV

In the gallery, the instinct of self-preservation helped him to turn back and sign to young Rainer not to follow. He stammered out something about a touch of dizziness, and joining them presently; and the boy nodded sympathetically and drew back.

At the foot of the stairs Faxon ran against a servant. "I should like to telephone to Weymore," he said with dry lips.

"Sorry, sir; wires all down. We've been trying the last hour to get New York again for Mr. Lavington."

Faxon shot on to his room, burst into it, and bolted the door. The lamplight lay on furniture, flowers, books; in the ashes a log still glimmered. He dropped down on the sofa and hid his face. The room was profoundly silent, the whole house was still: nothing about him gave a hint of what was going on, darkly and dumbly, in the room he had flown from, and with the covering of his eyes oblivion and reassurance seemed to fall on him. But they fell for a moment only; then his lids opened again to the monstrous vision. There it was, stamped on his pupils, a part of him forever, an indelible horror burnt into his body and brain. But why into his—just his? Why had he alone been chosen to see what he had seen? What business was it of *his*, in God's name? Any one of the others, thus enlightened, might have exposed the horror and defeated it; but *he*, the one weaponless and defenceless spectator, the one whom none of the others would believe or understand if he attempted to reveal what he knew—*he* alone had been singled out as the victim of this dreadful initiation!

Suddenly he sat up, listening: he had heard a step on the stairs. Someone, no doubt, was coming to see how he was—to urge him, if he felt better, to go down and join the smokers. Cautiously he opened his door; yes, it was young Rainer's step. Faxon looked down the passage, remembered the other stairway and darted to it. All he wanted was to get out of the house. Not another instant would he breathe its abominable air! What business was it of *his*, in God's name?

He reached the opposite end of the lower gallery, and beyond it saw the hall by which he had entered. It was empty, and on a long table he recognized his coat and cap. He got into his coat, unbolted the door, and plunged into the purifying night.

The darkness was deep, and the cold so intense that for an instant it stopped his breathing. Then he perceived that only a thin snow was falling, and resolutely he set his face for flight. The trees along the avenue marked his way as he hastened with long strides over the beaten snow. Gradually, while he walked, the tumult in his brain subsided. The impulse to fly still drove him forward, but he began to feel that he was flying from a terror of his own creating, and that the most urgent reason for escape was the need of hiding his state, of shunning other eyes till he should regain his balance.

He had spent the long hours in the train in fruitless broodings on a discouraging situation, and he remembered how his bitterness had turned to exasperation when he found that the Weymore sleigh was not awaiting him. It was absurd, of course; but, though he had joked with Rainer over Mrs. Culme's forgetfulness, to confess it had cost a pang. That was what his rootless life had brought him to: for lack of a personal stake in things his sensibility was at the mercy of such trifles. . . . Yes; that, and the cold and fatigue, the absence of hope and the haunting sense of starved aptitudes, all these had brought him to the perilous verge over which, once or twice before, his terrified brain had hung.

Why else, in the name of any imaginable logic, human or devilish, should he, a stranger, be singled out for this experience? What could it mean to him, how was he related to it, what bearing had it on his case? . . . Unless, indeed, it was just because he was a stranger—a stranger everywhere—because he had no personal life, no warm screen of private egotisms to shield him from exposure, that he had developed this abnormal sensitiveness to the vicissitudes of others. The thought pulled him up with a shudder. No! Such a fate was too

abominable; all that was strong and sound in him rejected it. A thousand times better regard himself as ill, disorganized, deluded, than as the predestined victim of such warnings!

He reached the gates and paused before the darkened lodge. The wind had risen and was sweeping the snow into his face. The cold had him in its grasp again, and he stood uncertain. Should he put his sanity to the test and go back? He turned and looked down the dark drive to the house. A single ray shone through the trees, evoking a picture of the lights, the flowers, the faces grouped about that fatal room. He turned and plunged out into the road. . . .

He remembered that, about a mile from Overdale, the coachman had pointed out the road to Northridge; and he began to walk in that direction. Once in the road he had the gale in his face, and the wet snow on his moustache and eyelashes instantly hardened to ice. The same ice seemed to be driving a million blades into his throat and lungs, but he pushed on, the vision of the warm room pursuing him.

The snow in the road was deep and uneven. He stumbled across ruts and sank into drifts, and the wind drove against him like a granite cliff. Now and then he stopped, gasping, as if an invisible hand had tightened an iron band about his body; then he started again, stiffening himself against the stealthy penetration of the cold. The snow continued to descend out of a pall of inscrutable darkness, and once or twice he paused, fearing he had missed the road to Northridge; but, seeing no sign of a turn, he ploughed on.

At last, feeling sure that he had walked for more than a mile, he halted and looked back. The act of turning brought immediate relief, first because it put his back to the wind, and then because, far down the road, it showed him the gleam of a lantern. A sleigh was coming —a sleigh that might perhaps give him a lift to the village! Fortified by the hope, he began to walk back toward the light. It came forward very slowly, with unaccountable zigzags and waverings; and even when he was within a few yards of it he could catch no sound of sleigh bells. Then it paused and became stationary by the roadside, as though carried by a pedestrian who had stopped, exhausted by the cold. The thought made Faxon hasten on, and a moment later he was stooping over a motionless figure huddled against the snowbank. The lantern had dropped from its bearer's hand, and Faxon, fearfully raising it, threw its light into the face of Frank Rainer.

"Rainer! What on earth are you doing here?"

The boy smiled back through his pallor. "What are *you*, I'd like to know?" he retorted; and, scrambling to his feet with a clutch on Faxon's arm, he added gaily: "Well, I've run you down!"

Faxon stood confounded, his heart sinking. The lad's face was grey.

"What madness—" he began.

"Yes, it *is*. What on earth did you do it for?"

"I? Do what? . . . Why I. . . . I was just taking a walk. . . . I often walk at night. . . ."

Frank Rainer burst into a laugh. "On such nights? Then you hadn't bolted?"

"Bolted?"

"Because I'd done something to offend you? My uncle thought you had."

Faxon grasped his arm. "Did your uncle send you after me?"

"Well, he gave me an awful rowing for not going up to your room with you when you said you were ill. And when we found you'd gone we were frightened—and he was awfully upset—so I said I'd catch you. . . . You're *not* ill, are you?"

"Ill? No. Never better." Faxon picked up the lantern. "Come; let's go back. It was awfully hot in that dining room."

"Yes; I hoped it was only that."

They trudged on in silence for a few minutes; then Faxon questioned: "You're not too done up?"

"Oh, no. It's a lot easier with the wind behind us."

"All right. Don't talk any more."

They pushed ahead, walking, in spite of the light that guided them, more slowly than Faxon had walked alone into the gale. The fact of his companion's stumbling against a drift gave Faxon a pretext for saying: "Take hold of my arm," and Rainer obeying, gasped out: "I'm blown!"

"So am I. Who wouldn't be?"

"What a dance you led me! If it hadn't been for one of the servants happening to see you—"

"Yes; all right. And now, won't you kindly shut up?"

Rainer laughed and hung on him. "Oh, the cold doesn't hurt me. . . ."

For the first few minutes after Rainer had overtaken him, anxiety for the lad had been Faxon's only thought. But as each laboring step carried them nearer to the spot he had been fleeing, the reasons for his flight grew more ominous and more insistent. No, he was not ill, he was not distraught and deluded—he was the instrument singled out to warn and save; and here he was, irresistibly driven, dragging the victim back to his doom!

The intensity of the conviction had almost checked his steps. But what could he do or say? At all costs he must get Rainer out of the cold, into the house and into his bed. After that he would act.

The snowfall was thickening, and as they reached a stretch of the road between open fields the wind took them at an angle, lashing their faces with barbed thongs. Rainer stopped to take breath, and Faxon felt the heavier pressure of his arm.

"When we get to the lodge, can't we telephone to the stable for a sleigh?"

"If they're not all asleep at the lodge."

"Oh, I'll manage. Don't talk!" Faxon ordered; and they plodded on. . . .

At length the lantern ray showed ruts that curved away from the road under tree darkness.

Faxon's spirits rose. "There's the gate! We'll be there in five minutes."

As he spoke he caught, above the boundary hedge, the gleam of a light at the farther end of the dark avenue. It was the same light that had shone on the scene of which every detail was burnt into his brain; and he felt again its overpowering reality. No—he couldn't let the boy go back!

They were at the lodge at last, and Faxon was hammering on the door. He said to himself: "I'll get him inside first, and make them give him a hot drink. Then I'll see—I'll find an argument. . . ."

There was no answer to his knocking, and after an interval Rainer said: "Look here—we'd better go on."

"No!"

"I can, perfectly—"

"You shan't go to the house, I say!" Faxon redoubled his blows, and at length steps sounded on the stairs. Rainer was leaning against the lintel, and as the door opened the light from the hall flashed on his pale face and fixed eyes. Faxon caught him by the arm and drew him in.

"It *was* cold out there," he sighed; and then, abruptly, as if invisible shears at a single stroke had cut every muscle in his body, he swerved, drooped on Faxon's arm, and seemed to sink into nothing at his feet.

The lodgekeeper and Faxon bent over him, and somehow, between them, lifted him into the kitchen and laid him on a sofa by the stove.

The lodgekeeper, stammering: "I'll ring up the house," dashed out of the room. But Faxon heard the words without heeding them: omens mattered nothing now, beside this woe fulfilled. He knelt down to undo the fur collar about Rainer's throat, and as he did so he felt a warm moisture on his hands. He held them up, and they were red. . . .

V

The palms threaded their endless line along the yellow river. The little steamer lay at the wharf, and George Faxon, sitting in the verandah of the wooden hotel, idly watched the coolies carrying the freight across the gangplank.

He had been looking at such scenes for two months. Nearly five had elapsed since he had descended from the train at Northridge and strained his eyes for the sleigh that was to take him to Weymore: Weymore, which he was never to behold! . . . Part of the interval—the first part—was still a great grey blur. Even now he could not be quite sure how he had got back to Boston, reached the house of a cousin, and been thence transferred to a quiet room looking out on snow under bare trees. He looked out a long time at the same scene, and finally one day a man he had known at Harvard came to see him and invited him to go out on a business trip to the Malay Peninsula.

"You've had a bad shake-up, and it'll do you no end of good to get away from things."

When the doctor came the next day it turned out that he knew of the plan and approved it. "You ought to be quiet for a year. Just loaf and look at the landscape," he advised.

Faxon felt the first faint stirrings of curiosity.

"What's been the matter with me, anyway?"

"Well, overwork, I suppose. You must have been bottling up for a bad breakdown before you started for New Hampshire last December. And the shock of that poor boy's death did the rest."

Ah, yes—Rainer had died. He remembered. . . .

He started for the East, and gradually, by imperceptible degrees, life crept back into his weary bones and leaden brain. His friend was patient and considerate, and they traveled slowly and talked little. At first Faxon had felt a great shrinking from whatever touched on familiar things. He seldom looked at a newspaper and he never opened a letter without a contraction of the heart. It was not that he had any special cause for apprehension, but merely that a great trail of darkness lay on everything. He had looked too deep down into the abyss. . . . But little by little health and energy returned to him, and with them the common promptings of curiosity. He was beginning to wonder how the world was going, and when, presently, the hotelkeeper told him there were no letters for him in the steamer's mailbag, he felt a distinct sense of disappointment. His friend had gone into the jungle on a long excursion, and he was lonely, unoccupied and wholesomely bored. He got up and strolled into the stuffy reading room.

There he found a game of dominoes, a mutilated picture puzzle, some copies of *Zion's Herald* and a pile of New York and London newspapers.

He began to glance through the papers, and was disappointed to find that they were less recent than he had hoped. Evidently the last numbers had been carried off by luckier travelers. He continued to turn them over, picking out the American ones first. These, as it happened, were the oldest; they dated back to December and January. To Faxon, however, they had all the flavor of novelty, since they covered the precise period during which he had virtually ceased to exist. It had never before occurred to him to wonder what had happened in the world during that interval of obliteration; but now he felt a sudden desire to know.

To prolong the pleasure, he began by sorting the papers chronologically, and as he found and spread out the earliest number, the date at the top of the page entered into his consciousness like a key slipping into a lock. It was the seventeenth of December: the date of the day after his arrival at Northridge. He glanced at the first page and read in blazing characters: "Reported Failure of Opal Cement Company. Lavington's name involved. Gigantic Exposure of Corruption Shakes Wall Street to Its Foundations."

He read on; when he had finished the first paper he turned to the next. There was a gap of three days, but the Opal Cement "Investigation" still held the center of the stage. From its complex revelations of greed and ruin his eye wandered to the death notices, and he read: "Rainer. Suddenly, at Northridge, New Hampshire, Francis John, only son of the late . . ."

His eyes clouded, and he dropped the newspaper and sat for a long time with his face in his hands. When he looked up again he noticed that his gesture had pushed the other papers from the table and scattered them at his feet. The uppermost lay spread out before him, and heavily his eyes began their search again. "John Lavington comes forward with plan for reconstructing company. Offers to put in ten millions of his own—The proposal under consideration by the District Attorney."

Ten millions . . . ten millions of his own. But if John Lavington was ruined? . . . Faxon stood up with a cry. That was it, then—that was what the warning meant! And if he had not fled from it, dashed wildly away from it into the night, he might have broken the spell of iniquity, the powers of darkness might not have prevailed! He caught up the pile of newspapers and began to glance through each in turn for the headline: "Wills Admitted to Probate." In the last of all he found the paragraph he sought, and it stared up at him as if with Rainer's dying eyes.

T hat—*that* was what he had done! The powers of pity had singled him out to warn and save, and he had closed his ears to their call, and washed his hands of it, and fled. Washed his hands of it! That was the word. It caught him back to the dreadful moment in the lodge when, raising himself up from Rainer's side, he had looked at his hands and seen that they were red . . .

Miss Mary Pask

*I*t was not till the following spring that I plucked up courage to tell Mrs. Bridgeworth what had happened to me that night at Morgat.

In the first place, Mrs. Bridgeworth was in America; and after the night in question I lingered on abroad for several months—not for pleasure, God knows, but because of a nervous collapse supposed to be the result of having taken up my work again too soon after my touch of fever in Egypt. But, in any case, if I had been door to door with Grace Bridgeworth I could not have spoken of the affair before, to her or to anyone else; not till I had been rest-cured and built up again at one of those wonderful Swiss sanatoria where they clean the cobwebs out of you. I could not even have written to her—not to save my life. The happenings of that night had to be overlaid with layer upon layer of time and forgetfulness before I could tolerate any return to them.

The beginning was idiotically simple; just the sudden reflex of a New England conscience acting on an enfeebled constitution. I had been painting in Brittany, in lovely but uncertain autumn weather, one day all blue and silver, the next shrieking gales or driving fog. There is a rough little whitewashed inn out on the Pointe du Raz, swarmed over by tourists in summer but a sea-washed solitude in autumn; and there I was staying and trying to do waves, when someone said: "You ought to go over to Cape something else, beyond Morgat."

I went, and had a silver-and-blue day there; and on the way back the name of Morgat set up an unexpected association of ideas: Morgat —Grace Bridgeworth—Grace's sister, Mary Pask—"You know my darling Mary has a little place now near Morgat; if you ever go to Brittany do go to see her. She lives such a lonely life—it makes me so unhappy."

That was the way it came about. I had known Mrs. Bridgeworth well for years, but had only a hazy intermittent acquaintance with Mary Pask, her older and unmarried sister. Grace and she were greatly attached to each other, I knew; it had been Grace's chief sorrow, when she married my old friend Horace Bridgeworth, and went to live in New York, that Mary, from whom she had never before been separated, obstinately lingered on in Europe, where the two sisters had been traveling since their mother's death. I never quite understood why Mary Pask refused to join Grace in America. Grace said it was because she was "too artistic"—but, knowing the elder Miss Pask, and the extremely elementary nature of her interest in art, I wondered whether it were not rather because she disliked Horace Bridgeworth. There was a third alternative—more conceivable if one knew Horace —and that was that she may have liked him too much. But that again became untenable (at least I supposed it did) when one knew Miss Pask: Miss Pask with her round flushed face, her innocent bulging eyes, her old-maidish flat decorated with art-tidies, and her vague and timid philanthropy. Aspire to Horace—!

Well, it was all rather puzzling, or would have been if it had been interesting enough to be worth puzzling over. But it was not. Mary Pask was like hundreds of other dowdy old maids, cheerful derelicts content with their innumerable little substitutes for living. Even Grace would not have interested me particularly if she hadn't happened to marry one of my oldest friends, and to be kind to his friends. She was a handsome, capable and rather dull woman, absorbed in her husband and children, and without an ounce of imagination; and between her attachment to her sister and Mary Pask's worship of her there lay the inevitable gulf between the feelings of the sentimentally unemployed and those whose affections are satisfied. But a close intimacy had linked the two sisters before Grace's marriage, and Grace was one of the sweet conscientious women who go on using the language of devotion about people whom they live happily without seeing; so that when she said: "You know it's years since Mary and I have been together—not since little Molly was born. If only she'd come to America! Just think . . . Molly is six, and has never seen her darling auntie. . . ." When she said this, and added: "If you go to Brittany promise me you'll look up my Mary," I was moved in that dim depth of one where unnecessary obligations are contracted.

And so it came about that, on that silver-and-blue afternoon, the idea "Morgat—Mary Pask—to please Grace" suddenly unlocked the sense of duty in me. Very well: I would chuck a few things into my bag, do my day's painting, go to see Miss Pask when the light faded, and spend the night at the inn at Morgat. To this end I ordered a rickety one-horse vehicle to await me at the inn when I got back from my painting, and in it I started out toward sunset to hunt for Mary Pask. . . .

As suddenly as a pair of hands clapped over one's eyes, the sea fog shut down on us. A minute before we had been driving over a wide bare upland, our backs turned to a sunset that crimsoned the road ahead; now the densest night enveloped us. No one had been able to tell me exactly where Miss Pask lived; but I thought it likely that I should find out at the fishers' hamlet toward which we were trying to make our way. And I was right . . . an old man in a doorway said: Yes —over the next rise, and then down a lane to the left that led to the sea; the American lady who always used to dress in white. Oh, *he* knew . . . near the *Baie des Trépassés*.

"Yes; but how can we see to find it? I don't know the place," grumbled the reluctant boy who was driving me.

"You will when we get there," I remarked.

"Yes—and the horse foundered meantime! I can't risk it, sir; I'll get into trouble with the *patron*."

Finally an opportune argument induced him to get out and lead the stumbling horse, and we continued on our way. We seemed to crawl on for a long time through a wet blackness impenetrable to the glimmer of our only lamp. But now and then the pall lifted or its folds divided; and then our feeble light would drag out of the night some perfectly commonplace object—a white gate, a cow's staring face, a heap of roadside stones—made portentous and incredible by being thus detached from its setting, capriciously thrust at us, and as suddenly withdrawn. After each of these projections the darkness grew three times as thick; and the sense I had had for some time of descending a gradual slope now became that of scrambling down a precipice. I jumped out hurriedly and joined my young driver at the horse's head.

"I can't go on—I won't, sir!" he whimpered.

"Why, see, there's a light over there—just ahead!"

The veil swayed aside, and we beheld two faintly illuminated squares in a low mass that was surely the front of a house.

"Get me as far as that—then you can go back if you like."

The veil dropped again; but the boy had seen the lights and took heart. Certainly there was a house ahead of us; and certainly it must be Miss Pask's, since there could hardly be two in such a desert. Besides, the old man in the hamlet had said: "Near the sea"; and those endless modulations of the ocean's voice, so familiar in every corner of the Breton land that one gets to measure distances by them rather than by visual means, had told me for some time past that we must be making for the shore. The boy continued to lead the horse on without making any answer. The fog had shut in more closely than ever, and our lamp merely showed us the big round drops of wet on the horse's shaggy quarters.

The boy stopped with a jerk. "There's no house—we're going straight down to the sea."

"But you saw those lights, didn't you?"

"I thought I did. But where are they now? The fog's thinner again. Look—I can make out trees ahead. But there are no lights any more."

"Perhaps the people have gone to bed," I suggested jocosely.

"Then hadn't we better turn back, sir?"

"What—two yards from the gate?"

The boy was silent: certainly there was a gate ahead, and presumably, behind the dripping trees, some sort of dwelling. Unless there was just a field and the sea . . . the sea whose hungry voice I heard asking and asking, close below us. No wonder the place was called the Bay of the Dead! But what could have induced the rosy benevolent Mary Pask to come and bury herself there? Of course the boy wouldn't wait for me . . . I knew that . . . the *Baie des Trépassés* indeed! The sea whined down there as if it were feeding time, and the Furies, its keepers, had forgotten it. . . .

There *was* the gate! My hand had struck against it. I felt along to the latch, undid it, and brushed between wet bushes to the house front. Not a candle glint anywhere. If the house were indeed Miss Pask's, she certainly kept early hours. . . .

II

Night and fog were now one, and the darkness as thick as a blanket. I felt vainly about for a bell. At last my hand came in contact with a knocker and I lifted it. The clatter with which it fell sent a prolonged echo through the silence; but for a minute or two nothing else happened.

"There's no one there, I tell you!" the boy called impatiently from the gate.

But there was. I had heard no steps inside, but presently a bolt shot back, and an old woman in a peasant's cap pushed her head out. She had set her candle down on a table behind her, so that her face, aureoled with lacy wings, was in obscurity; but I knew she was old by the stoop of her shoulders and her fumbling movements. The candle-light, which made her invisible, fell full on my face, and she looked at me.

"This is Miss Mary Pask's house?"

"Yes, sir." Her voice—a very old voice—was pleasant enough, unsurprised and even friendly.

"I'll tell her," she added, shuffling off.

"Do you think she'll see me?" I threw after her.

"Oh, why not? The idea!" she almost chuckled. As she retreated I saw that she was wrapped in a shawl and had a cotton umbrella under her arm. Obviously she was going out—perhaps going home for the night. I wondered if Mary Pask lived all alone in her hermitage.

The old woman disappeared with the candle and I was left in total darkness. After an interval I heard a door shut at the back of the house and then a slow clumping of aged *sabots* along the flags outside. The old woman had evidently picked up her *sabots* in the kitchen and left the house. I wondered if she had told Miss Pask of my presence before going, or whether she had just left me there, the butt of some grim practical joke of her own. Certainly there was no sound within doors. The footsteps died out, I heard a gate click—then complete silence closed in again like the fog.

"I wonder—" I began within myself; and at that moment a smoth-ered memory struggled abruptly to the surface of my languid mind.

"But she's *dead*—Mary Pask is *dead*!" I almost screamed it aloud in my amazement.

It was incredible, the tricks my memory had played on me since my fever! I had known for nearly a year that Mary Pask was dead—had died suddenly the previous autumn—and though I had been think-ing of her almost continuously for the last two or three days it was only now that the forgotten fact of her death suddenly burst up again to consciousness.

Dead! But hadn't I found Grace Bridgeworth in tears and crepe the very day I had gone to bid her good-bye before sailing for Egypt? Hadn't she laid the cable before my eyes, her own streaming with tears while I read: "Sister died suddenly this morning requested burial in garden of house particulars by letter"—with the signature of the American Consul at Brest, a friend of Bridgeworth's I seemed to recall? I could see the very words of the message printed on the darkness before me.

As I stood there I was a good deal more disturbed by the discovery of the gap in my memory than by the fact of being alone in a pitch-dark house, either empty or else inhabited by strangers. Once before of late I had noted this queer temporary blotting-out of some well-known fact; and here was a second instance of it. Decidedly, I wasn't as well over my illness as the doctors had told me. . . . Well, I would get back to Morgat and lie up there for a day or two, doing nothing, just eating and sleeping. . . .

In my self-absorption I had lost my bearings, and no longer remembered where the door was. I felt in every pocket in turn for a match—but since the doctors had made me give up smoking, why should I have found one?

The failure to find a match increased my sense of irritated helplessness, and I was groping clumsily about the hall among the angles of unseen furniture when a light slanted along the rough-cast wall of the stairs. I followed its direction, and on the landing above me I saw a figure in white shading a candle with one hand and looking down. A chill ran along my spine, for the figure bore a strange resemblance to that of Mary Pask as I used to know her.

"Oh, it's *you!*" she exclaimed in the cracked twittering voice which was at one moment like an old woman's quaver, at another like a boy's falsetto. She came shuffling down in her baggy white garments, with her usual clumsy swaying movements; but I noticed that her steps on the wooden stairs were soundless. Well—they would be, naturally!

I stood without a word, gazing up at the strange vision above me, and saying to myself: "There's nothing there, nothing whatever. It's your digestion, or your eyes, or some damned thing wrong with you somewhere—"

But there was the candle, at any rate; and as it drew nearer, and lit up the place about me, I turned and caught hold of the doorlatch. For, remember, I had seen the cable, and Grace in crepe. . . .

"Why, what's the matter? I assure you, you don't disturb me!" the white figure twittered; adding, with a faint laugh: "I don't have so many visitors nowadays—"

She had reached the hall, and stood before me, lifting her candle shakily and peering up into my face. "You haven't changed—not as much as I should have thought. But I have, haven't I?" She appealed to me with another laugh; and abruptly she laid her hand on my arm. I looked down at the hand, and thought to myself: "*That* can't deceive me."

I have always been a noticer of hands. The key to character that other people seek in the eyes, the mouth, the modeling of the skull, I find in the curve of the nails, the cut of the finger tips, the way the palm, rosy or sallow, smooth or seamed, swells up from its base. I remembered Mary Pask's hand vividly because it was so like a carica-ture of herself; round, puffy, pink, yet prematurely old and useless. And there, unmistakably, it lay on my sleeve: but changed and shriv-eled—somehow like one of those pale freckled toadstools that the least touch resolves to dust . . . Well—to dust? Of course . . .

I looked at the soft wrinkled fingers, with their foolish little oval finger tips that used to be so innocently and naturally pink, and now were blue under the yellowing nails—and my flesh rose in ridges of fear.

"Come in, come in," she fluted, cocking her white untidy head on one side and rolling her bulging blue eyes at me. The horrible thing was that she still practiced the same arts, all the childish wiles of a clumsy capering coquetry. I felt her pull on my sleeve and it drew me in her wake like a steel cable.

The room she led me into was—well, "unchanged" is the term generally used in such cases. For as a rule, after people die, things are tidied up, furniture is sold, remembrances are dispatched to the family. But some morbid piety (or Grace's instructions, perhaps) had kept this room looking exactly as I supposed it had in Miss Pask's lifetime. I wasn't in the mood for noting details; but in the faint dabble of moving candlelight I was half aware of bedraggled cushions, odds and ends of copper pots, and a jar holding a faded branch of some late-flowering shrub. A real Mary Pask "interior"!

The white figure flitted spectrally to the chimney piece, lit two more candles, and set down the third on a table. I hadn't supposed I was superstitious—but those three candles! Hardly knowing what I did, I hurriedly bent and blew one out. Her laugh sounded behind me.

"Three candles—you still mind that sort of thing? I've got beyond all that, you know," she chuckled. "Such a comfort . . . such a sense of freedom. . . ." A fresh shiver joined the others already coursing over me.

"Come and sit down by me," she entreated, sinking to a sofa. "It's such an age since I've seen a living being!"

Her choice of terms was certainly strange, and as she leaned back on the white slippery sofa and beckoned me with one of those unburied hands my impulse was to turn and run. But her old face, hovering there in the candlelight, with the unnaturally red cheeks like varnished apples and the blue eyes swimming in vague kindliness, seemed to appeal to me against my cowardice, to remind me that, dead or alive, Mary Pask would never harm a fly.

"Do sit down!" she repeated, and I took the other corner of the sofa.

"It's so wonderfully good of you—I suppose Grace asked you to come?" She laughed again—her conversation had always been punctuated by rambling laughter. "It's an event—quite an event! I've had so few visitors since my death, you see."

Another bucketful of cold water ran over me; but I looked at her resolutely, and again the innocence of her face disarmed me.

I cleared my throat and spoke—with a huge panting effort, as if I had been heaving up a gravestone. "You live here alone?" I brought out.

"Ah, I'm glad to hear your voice—I still remember voices, though I hear so few," she murmured dreamily. "Yes—I live here alone. The old woman you saw goes away at night. She won't stay after dark . . . she says she can't. Isn't it funny? But it doesn't matter; I like the darkness." She leaned to me with one of her irrelevant smiles. "The dead," she said, "naturally get used to it."

Once more I cleared my throat; but nothing followed.

She continued to gaze at me with confidential blinks. "And Grace? Tell me all about my darling. I wish I could have seen her again

. . . just once." Her laugh came out grotesquely. "When she got the news of my death—were you with her? Was she terribly upset?"

I stumbled to my feet with a meaningless stammer. I couldn't answer—I couldn't go on looking at her.

"Ah, I see . . . it's too painful," she acquiesced, her eyes brimming, and she turned her shaking head away.

"But after all . . . I'm glad she was so sorry. . . . It's what I've been longing to be told, and hardly hoped for. Grace forgets. . . ." She stood up too and flitted across the room, wavering nearer and nearer to the door.

"Thank God," I thought, "she's going."

"Do you know this place by daylight?" she asked abruptly.

I shook my head.

"It's very beautiful. But you wouldn't have seen *me* then. You'd have had to take your choice between me and the landscape. I hate the light—it makes my head ache. And so I sleep all day. I was just waking up when you came." She smiled at me with an increasing air of confidence. "Do you know where I usually sleep? Down below there—in the garden!" Her laugh shrilled out again. "There's a shady corner down at the bottom where the sun never bothers one. Sometimes I sleep there till the stars come out."

The phrase about the garden, in the consul's cable, came back to me and I thought: "After all, it's not such an unhappy state. I wonder if she isn't better off than when she was alive?"

Perhaps she was—but I was sure I wasn't, in her company. And her way of sidling nearer to the door made me distinctly want to reach it before she did. In a rush of cowardice I strode ahead of her—but a second later she had the latch in her hand and was leaning against the panels, her long white raiment hanging about her like graveclothes. She drooped her head a little sideways and peered at me under her lashless lids.

"You're not going?" she reproached me.

I dived down in vain for my missing voice, and silently signed that I was.

"Going—going away? Altogether?" Her eyes were still fixed on me, and I saw two tears gather in their corners and run down over the red glistening circles on her cheeks. "Oh, but you mustn't," she said gently. "I'm too lonely. . . ."

I stammered something inarticulate, my eyes on the blue-nailed hand that grasped the latch. Suddenly the window behind us crashed open, and a gust of wind, surging in out of the blackness, extinguished the candle on the nearest chimney corner. I glanced back nervously to see if the other candle were going out too.

"You don't like the noise of the wind? I do. It's all I have to talk to. People don't like me much since I've been dead. Queer, isn't it? The peasants are so superstitious. At times I'm really lonely. . . ." Her voice cracked in a last effort at laughter, and she swayed toward me, one hand still on the latch.

"Lonely, lonely! If you *knew* how lonely! It was a lie when I told you I wasn't! And now you come, and your face looks friendly . . . and you say you're going to leave me! No—no—no—you shan't! Or else, why did you come? It's cruel . . . I used to think I knew what loneliness was . . . after Grace married, you know. Grace thought she was always thinking of me, but she wasn't. She called me 'darling,' but she was thinking of her husband and children. I said to myself then: 'You couldn't be lonelier if you were dead.' But I know better now. . . . There's been no loneliness like this last year's . . . none! And sometimes I sit here and think: 'If a man came along someday and took a fancy to you?'" She gave another wavering cackle. "Well, such things *have* happened, you know, even after youth's gone . . . a man who'd had his troubles too. But no one came till tonight . . . and now you say you're going!" Suddenly she flung herself toward me. "Oh, stay with me, stay with me . . . just tonight. . . . It's so sweet and quiet here. . . . No one need know . . . no one will ever come and trouble us."

I ought to have shut the window when the first gust came. I might have known there would soon be another, fiercer one. It came now, slamming back the loose-hinged lattice, filling the room with the noise of the sea and with wet swirls of fog, and dashing the other candle to the floor. The light went out, and I stood there—we stood there—lost to each other in the roaring coiling darkness. My heart seemed to stop beating; I had to fetch up my breath with great heaves that covered me with sweat. The door—the door—well, I knew I had been facing it when the candle went. Something white and wraithlike seemed to melt and crumple up before me in the night, and avoiding the spot where it had sunk away I stumbled around it in a wide circle, got the latch in my hand, caught my foot in a scarf or sleeve, trailing loose and invisible, and freed myself with a jerk from this last obstacle. I had the door open now. As I got into the hall I heard a whimper from the blackness behind me; but I scrambled on to the hall door, dragged it open and bolted out into the night. I slammed the door on that pitiful low whimper, and the fog and wind enveloped me in healing arms.

III

When I was well enough to trust myself to think about it all again I found that a very little thinking got my temperature up, and my heart hammering in my throat. No use . . . I simply couldn't stand it . . . for I'd seen Grace Bridgeworth in crepe, weeping over the cable, and yet I'd sat and talked with her sister, on the same sofa—her sister who'd been dead a year!

The circle was a vicious one; I couldn't break through it. The fact that I was down with fever the next morning might have explained it; yet I couldn't get away from the clinging reality of the vision. Supposing it *was* a ghost I had been talking to, and not a mere projection of my fever? Supposing something survived of Mary Pask—enough to cry out to me the unuttered loneliness of a lifetime, to express at last what the living woman had always had to keep dumb and hidden? The thought moved me curiously—in my weakness I lay and wept over it. No end of women were like that, I supposed, and perhaps, after death, if they got their chance they tried to use it. . . . Old tales and legends floated through my mind; the bride of Corinth, the medieval vampire —but what names to attach to the plaintive image of Mary Pask!

My weak mind wandered in and out among these visions and conjectures, and the longer I lived with them the more convinced I became that something *which had been Mary Pask* had talked with me that night. . . . I made up my mind, when I was up again, to drive back to the place (in broad daylight, this time), to hunt out the grave in the garden—that "shady corner where the sun never bothers one"—and appease the poor ghost with a few flowers. But the doctors decided otherwise; and perhaps my weak will unknowingly abetted them. At any rate, I yielded to their insistence that I should be driven straight from my hotel to the train for Paris, and thence shipped, like a piece of luggage, to the Swiss sanatorium they had in view for me. Of course I meant to come back when I was patched up again . . . and meanwhile, more and more tenderly, but more intermittently, my thoughts went back from my snow mountain to that wailing autumn night above the *Baie des Trépassés*, and the revelation of the dead Mary Pask who was so much more real to me than ever the living one had been.

IV

After all, why should I tell Grace Bridgeworth—ever? I had had a glimpse of things that were really no business of hers. If the revelation had been vouchsafed to me, ought I not to bury it in those deepest depths where the inexplicable and the unforgettable sleep together? And besides, what interest could there be to a woman like Grace in a tale she could neither understand nor believe in? She would just set me down as "queer"—and enough people had done that already. My first object, when I finally did get back to New York, was to convince everybody of my complete return to mental and physical soundness; and into this scheme of evidence my experience with Mary Pask did not seem to fit. All things considered, I would hold my tongue.

But after a while the thought of the grave began to trouble me. I wondered if Grace had ever had a proper gravestone put on it. The queer neglected look of the house gave me the idea that perhaps she had done nothing—had brushed the whole matter aside, to be attended to when she next went abroad. "Grace forgets," I heard the poor ghost quaver. . . . No, decidedly, there could be no harm in putting (tactfully) just that one question about the care of the grave; the more so as I was beginning to reproach myself for not having gone back to see with my own eyes how it was kept. . . .

Grace and Horace welcomed me with all their old friendliness, and I soon slipped into the habit of dropping in on them for a meal when I thought they were likely to be alone. Nevertheless my opportunity didn't come at once—I had to wait for some weeks. And then one evening, when Horace was dining out and I sat alone with Grace, my glance lit on a photograph of her sister—an old faded photograph which seemed to meet my eyes reproachfully.

"By the way, Grace," I began with a jerk, "I don't believe I ever told you: I went down to that little place of . . . of your sister's the day before I had that bad relapse."

At once her face lit up emotionally. "No, you never told me. How sweet of you to go!" The ready tears overbrimmed her eyes. "I'm *so* glad you did." She lowered her voice and added softly: "And did you see her?"

The question sent one of my old shudders over me. I looked with amazement at Mrs. Bridgeworth's plump face, smiling at me through a veil of painless tears. "I do reproach myself more and more about darling Mary," she added tremulously. "But tell me—tell me everything."

There was a knot in my throat; I felt almost as comfortable as I had in Mary Pask's own presence. Yet I had never before noticed anything uncanny about Grace Bridgeworth. I forced my voice up to my lips.

"Everything? Oh, I can't—" I tried to smile.

"But you did see her?"

I managed to nod, still smiling.

Her face grew suddenly haggard—yes, haggard! "And the change was so dreadful that you can't speak of it? Tell me—was that it?"

I shook my head. After all, what had shocked me was that the change was so slight—that between being dead and alive there seemed after all to be so little difference, except that of a mysterious increase in reality. But Grace's eyes were still searching me insistently. "You must tell me," she reiterated. "I know I ought to have gone there long ago—"

"Yes; perhaps you ought." I hesitated. "To see about the grave, at least. . . ."

She sat silent, her eyes still on my face. Her tears had stopped, but her look of solicitude slowly grew into a stare of something like terror. Hesitatingly, almost reluctantly, she stretched out her hand and laid it on mine for an instant. "Dear old friend—" she began.

"Unfortunately," I interrupted, "I couldn't get back myself to see the grave . . . because I was taken ill the next day."

"Yes, yes; of course. I know." She paused. "Are you *sure* you went there at all?" she asked abruptly.

"Sure? Good Lord—" It was my turn to stare. "Do you suspect

me of not being quite right yet?" I suggested with an uneasy laugh.

"No—no . . . of course not . . . but I don't understand."

"Understand what? I went into the house . . . I saw everything, in fact, *but* her grave. . . ."

"Her grave?" Grace jumped up, clasping her hands on her breast and darting away from me. At the other end of the room she stood and gazed, and then moved slowly back.

"Then, after all—I wonder?" She held her eyes on me, half fearful and half reassured. "Could it be simply that you never heard?"

"Never heard?"

"But it was in all the papers! Don't you ever read them? I meant to write . . . I thought I *had* written . . . but I said: 'At any rate he'll see it in the papers.' . . . You know I'm always lazy about letters. . . ."

"See what in the papers?"

"Why, that she *didn't* die. . . . She isn't dead! There isn't any grave, my dear man! It was only a cataleptic trance . . . an extraordinary case, the doctors say. . . . But didn't she tell you all about it—if you say you saw her?" She burst into half-hysterical laughter: "Surely she must have told you that she wasn't dead?"

"No," I said slowly, "she didn't tell me that."

We talked about it together for a long time after that—talked on till Horace came back from his men's dinner, after midnight. Grace insisted on going in and out of the whole subject, over and over again. As she kept repeating, it was certainly the only time that poor Mary had ever been in the papers. But though I sat and listened patiently I couldn't get up any real interest in what she said. I felt I should never again be interested in Mary Pask, or in anything concerning her.

Bewitched

*T*he snow was still falling thickly when Orrin Bosworth, who farmed the land south of Lonetop, drove up in his cutter to Saul Rutledge's gate. He was surprised to see two other cutters ahead of him. From them descended two muffled figures. Bosworth, with increasing surprise, recognized Deacon Hibben, from North Ashmore, and Sylvester Brand, the widower, from the old Bearcliff farm on the way to Lonetop.

It was not often that anybody in Hemlock County entered Saul Rutledge's gate; least of all in the dead of winter, and summoned (as Bosworth, at any rate, had been) by Mrs. Rutledge, who passed, even in that unsocial region, for a woman of cold manners and solitary character. The situation was enough to excite the curiosity of a less imaginative man than Orrin Bosworth.

As he drove in between the broken-down white gateposts topped by fluted urns the two men ahead of him were leading their horses to the adjoining shed. Bosworth followed, and hitched his horse to a post. Then the three tossed off the snow from their shoulders, clapped their numb hands together, and greeted each other.

"Hallo, Deacon."

"Well, well, Orrin—" They shook hands.

" 'Day, Bosworth," said Sylvester Brand, with a brief nod. He seldom put any cordiality into his manner, and on this occasion he was still busy about his horse's bridle and blanket.

Orrin Bosworth, the youngest and most communicative of the three, turned back to Deacon Hibben, whose long face, queerly blotched and moldy-looking, with blinking peering eyes, was yet less forbidding than Brand's heavily-hewn countenance.

"Queer, our all meeting here this way. Mrs. Rutledge sent me a message to come," Bosworth volunteered.

The Deacon nodded. "I got a word from her too—Andy Pond come with it yesterday noon. I hope there's no trouble here—"

He glanced through the thickening fall of snow at the desolate front of the Rutledge house, the more melancholy in its present neglected state because, like the gateposts, it kept traces of former elegance. Bosworth had often wondered how such a house had come to be built in that lonely stretch between North Ashmore and Cold

Corners. People said there had once been other houses like it, forming a little township called Ashmore, a sort of mountain colony created by the caprice of an English Royalist officer, one Colonel Ashmore, who had been murdered by the Indians, with all his family, long before the Revolution. This tale was confirmed by the fact that the ruined cellars of several smaller houses were still to be discovered under the wild growth of the adjoining slopes, and that the Communion plate of the moribund Episcopal church of Cold Corners was engraved with the name of Colonel Ashmore, who had given it to the church of Ashmore in the year 1723. Of the church itself no traces remained. Doubtless it had been a modest wooden edifice, built on piles, and the conflagration which had burnt the other houses to the ground's edge had reduced it utterly to ashes. The whole place, even in summer, wore a mournful solitary air, and people wondered why Saul Rutledge's father had gone there to settle.

"I never knew a place," Deacon Hibben said, "as seemed as far away from humanity. And yet it ain't so in miles."

"Miles ain't the only distance," Orrin Bosworth answered; and the two men, followed by Sylvester Brand, walked across the drive to the front door. People in Hemlock County did not usually come and go by their front doors, but all three men seemed to feel that, on an occasion which appeared to be so exceptional, the usual and more familiar approach by the kitchen would not be suitable.

They had judged rightly; the Deacon had hardly lifted the knocker when the door opened and Mrs. Rutledge stood before them.

"Walk right in," she said in her usual dead-level tone; and Bosworth, as he followed the others, thought to himself: "Whatever's happened, she's not going to let it show in her face."

It was doubtful, indeed, if anything unwonted could be made to show in Prudence Rutledge's face, so limited was its scope, so fixed were its features. She was dressed for the occasion in a black calico with white spots, a collar or crochet lace fastened by a gold brooch, and a gray woolen shawl, crossed under her arms and tied at the back. In her small narrow head the only marked prominence was that of the brow projecting roundly over pale spectacled eyes. Her dark hair, parted above this prominence, passed tight and flat over the tips of her ears into a small braided coil at the nape; and her contracted head looked still narrower from being perched on a long hollow neck with cord-like throat muscles. Her eyes were of a pale cold gray, her complexion was an even white. Her age might have been anywhere from thirty-five to sixty.

The room into which she led the three men had probably been the dining room of the Ashmore house. It was now used as a front parlor, and a black stove planted on a sheet of zinc stuck out from the delicately fluted panels of an old wooden mantel. A newly-lit fire smoldered reluctantly, and the room was at once close and bitterly cold.

"Andy Pond," Mrs. Rutledge cried out to some one at the back of the house, "Step out and call Mr. Rutledge. You'll likely find him in the woodshed, or round the barn somewheres." She rejoined her visitors. "Please suit yourselves to seats," she said.

The three men, with an increasing air of constraint, took the chairs she pointed out, and Mrs. Rutledge sat stiffly down upon a fourth, behind a rickety beadwork table. She glanced from one to the other of her visitors.

"I presume you folks are wondering what it is I asked you to come here for," she said in her dead-level voice. Orrin Bosworth and Deacon Hibben murmured an assent; Sylvester Brand sat silent, his eyes, under their great thicket of eyebrows, fixed on the huge boot tip swinging before him.

"Well, I allow you didn't expect it was for a party," continued Mrs. Rutledge.

No one ventured to respond to this chill pleasantry, and she continued: "We're in trouble here, and that's the fact. And we need advice—Mr. Rutledge and myself do." She cleared her throat, and added in a lower tone, her pitilessly clear eyes looking straight before her: "There's a spell been cast over Mr. Rutledge."

The Deacon looked up sharply, an incredulous smile pinching his thin lips. "A spell?"

"That's what I said: he's bewitched."

Again the three visitors were silent; then Bosworth, more at ease or less tongue-tied than the others, asked with an attempt at humor: "Do you use the word in the strict Scripture sense, Mrs. Rutledge?"

She glanced at him before replying: "That's how *he* uses it."

The Deacon coughed and cleared his long rattling throat. "Do you care to give us more particulars before your husband joins us?"

Mrs. Rutledge looked down at her clasped hands, as if considering the question. Bosworth noticed that the inner fold of her lids was of the same uniform white as the rest of her skin, so that when she drooped them her rather prominent eyes looked like the sightless orbs of a marble statue. The impression was unpleasing, and he glanced away at the text over the mantelpiece, which read:

The Soul That Sinneth It Shall Die.

"No," she said at length, "I'll wait."

At this moment Sylvester Brand suddenly stood up and pushed back his chair. "I don't know," he said, in his rough bass voice, "as I've got any particular lights on Bible mysteries; and this happens to be the day I was to go down to Starkfield to close a deal with a man."

Mrs. Rutledge lifted one of her long thin hands. Withered and wrinkled by hard work and cold, it was nevertheless of the same leaden white as her face. "You won't be kept long," she said. "Won't you be seated?"

Farmer Brand stood irresolute, his purplish underlip twitching. "The Deacon here—such things is more in his line. . . ."

"I want you should stay," said Mrs. Rutledge quietly; and Brand sat down again.

A silence fell, during which the four persons present seemed all to be listening for the sound of a step; but none was heard, and after a minute or two Mrs. Rutledge began to speak again.

"It's down by that old shack on Lamer's pond; that's where they meet," she said suddenly.

Bosworth, whose eyes were on Sylvester Brand's face, fancied he saw a sort of inner flush darken the farmer's heavy leathern skin. Deacon Hibben leaned forward, a glitter of curiosity in his eyes.

"They—*who*, Mrs. Rutledge?"

"My husband, Saul Rutledge . . . and her. . . ."

Sylvester Brand again stirred in his seat. "Who do you mean by *her?*" he asked abruptly, as if roused out of some far-off musing.

Mrs. Rutledge's body did not move; she simply revolved her head on her long neck and looked at him.

"Your daughter, Sylvester Brand."

The man staggered to his feet with an explosion of inarticulate sounds. "My—my daughter? What the hell are you talking about? My daughter? It's a damned lie . . . it's . . . it's. . . ."

"Your daughter *Ora*, Mr. Brand," said Mrs. Rutledge slowly.

Bosworth felt an icy chill down his spine. Instinctively he turned his eyes away from Brand, and they rested on the mildewed countenance of Deacon Hibben. Between the blotches it had become as white as Mrs. Rutledge's, and the Deacon's eyes burned in the whiteness like live embers among ashes.

Brand gave a laugh: the rusty creaking laugh of one whose springs of mirth are never moved by gaiety. "My daughter *Ora?*" he repeated.

"Yes."

"My *dead* daughter?"

"That's what he says."

"Your husband?"

"That's what Mr. Rutledge says."

Orrin Bosworth listened with a sense of suffocation; he felt as if he were wrestling with long-armed horrors in a dream. He could no longer resist letting his eyes turn to Sylvester Brand's face. To his surprise it had resumed a natural imperturbable expression. Brand rose to his feet. "Is that all?" he queried contemptuously.

"All? Ain't it enough? How long is it since you folks seen Saul Rutledge, any of you?" Mrs. Rutledge flew out at them.

Bosworth, it appeared, had not seen him for nearly a year; the Deacon had only run across him once, for a minute, at the North Ashmore post office, the previous autumn, and acknowledged that he wasn't looking any too good then. Brand said nothing, but stood irresolute.

"Well, if you wait a minute you'll see with your own eyes; and he'll tell you with his own words. That's what I've got you here for —to see for yourselves what's come over him. Then you'll talk different," she added, twisting her head abruptly toward Sylvester Brand.

The Deacon raised a lean hand of interrogation.

"Does your husband know we've been sent for on this business, Mrs. Rutledge?"

Mrs. Rutledge signed assent.

"It was with his consent, then—?"

She looked coldly at her questioner. "I guess it had to be," she said. Again Bosworth felt the chill down his spine. He tried to dissipate the sensation by speaking with an affectation of energy.

"Can you tell us, Mrs. Rutledge, how this trouble you speak of shows itself . . . what makes you think . . . ?"

She looked at him for a moment; then she leaned forward across the rickety beadwork table. A thin smile of disdain narrowed her colorless lips. "I don't think—I know."

"Well—but how?"

She leaned closer, both elbows on the table, her voice dropping. "I seen 'em."

In the ashen light from the veiling of snow beyond the windows the Deacon's little screwed-up eyes seemed to give out red sparks. "Him and the dead?"

"Him and the dead."

"Saul Rutledge and—and Ora Brand?"

"That's so."

Sylvester Brand's chair fell backward with a crash. He was on his feet again, crimson and cursing. "It's a God-damned fiend-begotten lie. . . ."

"Friend Brand . . . friend Brand . . ." the Deacon protested.

"Here, let me get out of this. I want to see Saul Rutledge himself, and tell him—"

"Well, here he is," said Mrs. Rutledge.

The outer door had opened; they heard the familiar stamping and shaking of a man who rids his garments of their last snowflakes before penetrating to the sacred precincts of the best parlor. Then Saul Rutledge entered.

II

As he came in he faced the light from the north window, and Bosworth's first thought was that he looked like a drowned man fished out from under the ice—"self-drowned," he added. But the snow light plays cruel tricks with a man's color, and even with the shape of his features; it must have been partly that, Bosworth reflected, which transformed Saul Rutledge from the straight muscular fellow he had been a year before into the haggard wretch now before them.

The Deacon sought for a word to ease the horror. "Well, now,

Saul—you look's if you'd ought to set right up to the stove. Had a touch of ague, maybe?"

The feeble attempt was unavailing. Rutledge neither moved nor answered. He stood among them silent, incommunicable, like one risen from the dead.

Brand grasped him roughly by the shoulder. "See here, Saul Rutledge, what's this dirty lie your wife tells us you've been putting about?"

Still Rutledge did not move. "It's no lie," he said.

Brand's hand dropped from his shoulder. In spite of the man's rough bullying power he seemed to be undefinably awed by Rutledge's look and tone.

"No lie? You've gone plumb crazy, then, have you?"

Mrs. Rutledge spoke. "My husband's not lying, nor he ain't gone crazy. Don't I tell you I seen 'em?"

Brand laughed again. "Him and the dead?"

"Yes."

"Down by the Lamer pond, you say?"

"Yes."

"And when was that, if I might ask?"

"Day before yesterday."

A silence fell on the strangely assembled group. The Deacon at length broke it to say to Mr. Brand: "Brand, in my opinion we've got to see this thing through."

Brand stood for a moment in speechless contemplation: there was something animal and primitive about him, Bosworth thought, as he hung thus, lowering and dumb, a little foam beading the corners of that heavy purplish underlip. He let himself slowly down into his chair. "I'll see it through."

The two other men and Mrs. Rutledge had remained seated. Saul Rutledge stood before them, like a prisoner at the bar, or rather like a sick man before the physicians who were to heal him. As Bosworth scrutinized that hollow face, so wan under the dark sunburn, so sucked inward and consumed by some hidden fever, there stole over the sound healthy man the thought that perhaps, after all, husband and wife spoke the truth, and that they were all at that moment really standing on the edge of some forbidden mystery. Things that the rational mind would reject without a thought seemed no longer so easy to dispose of as one looked at the actual Saul Rutledge and remembered the man he had been a year before. Yes; as the Deacon said, they would have to see it through. . . .

"Sit down then, Saul; draw up to us, won't you?" the Deacon suggested, trying again for a natural tone.

Mrs. Rutledge pushed a chair forward, and her husband sat down on it. He stretched out his arms and grasped his knees in his brown bony fingers; in that attitude he remained, turning neither his head nor his eyes.

"Well, Saul," the Deacon continued, "your wife says you thought mebbe we could do something to help you through this trouble, whatever it is."

Rutledge's gray eyes widened a little. "No; I didn't think that. It was her idea to try what could be done."

"I presume, though, since you've agreed to our coming, that you don't object to our putting a few questions?"

Rutledge was silent for a moment; then he said with a visible effort: "No; I don't object."

"Well—you've heard what your wife says?"

Rutledge made a slight motion of assent.

"And—what have you got to answer? How do you explain . . . ?"

Mrs. Rutledge intervened. "How can he explain? I seen 'em."

There was a silence; then Bosworth, trying to speak in an easy reassuring tone, queried: "That so, Saul?"

"That's so."

Brand lifted up his brooding head. "You mean to say you . . . you sit here before us all and say. . . ."

The Deacon's hand again checked him. "Hold on, friend Brand. We're all of us trying for the facts, ain't we?" He turned to Rutledge. "We've heard what Mrs. Rutledge says. What's your answer?"

"I don't know as there's any answer. She found us."

"And you mean to tell me the person with you was . . . was what you took to be . . ." the Deacon's thin voice grew thinner, "Ora Brand?"

Saul Rutledge nodded.

"You knew . . . or thought you knew . . . you were meeting with the dead?"

Rutledge bent his head again. The snow continued to fall in a steady unwavering sheet against the window, and Bosworth felt as if a winding sheet were descending from the sky to envelop them all in a common grave.

"Think what you're saying! It's against our religion! Ora . . . poor child! . . . died over a year ago. I saw you at her funeral, Saul. How can you make such a statement?"

"What else can he do?" thrust in Mrs. Rutledge.

There was another pause. Bosworth's resources had failed him, and Brand once more sat plunged in dark meditation. The Deacon laid his quivering finger tips together, and moistened his lips.

"Was the day before yesterday the first time?" he asked.

The movement of Rutledge's head was negative.

"Not the first? Then when . . . ?"

"Nigh on a year ago, I reckon."

"God! And you mean to tell us that ever since—?"

"Well . . . look at him," said his wife. The three men lowered their eyes.

After a moment Bosworth, trying to collect himself, glanced at the Deacon. "Why not ask Saul to make his own statement, if that's what we're here for?"

"That's so," the Deacon assented. He turned to Rutledge. "Will you try and give us your idea . . . of . . . of how it began?"

There was another silence. Then Rutledge tightened his grasp on his gaunt knees, and still looking straight ahead, with his curiously clear, unseeing gaze: "Well," he said, "I guess it begun away back, afore even I was married to Mrs. Rutledge. . . ." He spoke in a low automatic tone, as if some invisible agent were dictating his words, or even uttering them for him. "You know," he added, "Ora and me was to have been married."

Sylvester Brand lifted his head. "Straighten that statement out first, please," he interjected.

"What I mean is, we kept company. But Ora she was very young. Mr. Brand here he sent her away. She was gone nigh to three years, I guess. When she come back I was married."

"That's right," Brand said, relapsing once more into his sunken attitude.

"And after she came back did you meet her again?" the Deacon continued.

"Alive?" Rutledge questioned.

A perceptible shudder ran through the room.

"Well—of course," said the Deacon nervously.

Rutledge seemed to consider. "Once I did—only once. There was a lot of other people round. At Cold Corners Fair it was."

"Did you talk with her then?"

"Only a minute."

"What did she say?"

His voice dropped. "She said she was sick and knew she was going to die, and when she was dead she'd come back to me."

"And what did you answer?"

"Nothing."

"Did you think anything of it at the time?"

"Well, no. Not till I heard she was dead I didn't. After that I thought of it—and I guess she drew me." He moistened his lips.

"Drew you down to that abandoned house by the pond?"

Rutledge made a faint motion of assent, and the Deacon added: "How did you know it was there she wanted you to come?"

"She . . . just drew me. . . ."

There was a long pause. Bosworth felt, on himself and the other two men, the oppressive weight of the next question to be asked. Mrs. Rutledge opened and closed her narrow lips once or twice, like some beached shellfish gasping for the tide. Rutledge waited.

"Well, now, Saul, won't you go on with what you was telling us?" the Deacon at length suggested.

"That's all. There's nothing else."

The Deacon lowered his voice. "She just draws you?"

"Yes."

"Often?"

"That's as it happens. . . ."

"But if it's always there she draws you, man, haven't you the strength to keep away from the place?"

For the first time, Rutledge wearily turned his head toward his questioner. A spectral smile narrowed his colorless lips. "Ain't any use. She follers after me. . . ."

There was another silence. What more could they ask, then and there? Mrs. Rutledge's presence checked the next question. The Deacon seemed hopelessly to revolve the matter. At length he spoke in a more authoritative tone. "These are forbidden things. You know that, Saul. Have you tried prayer?"

Rutledge shook his head.

"Will you pray with us now?"

Rutledge cast a glance of freezing indifference on his spiritual adviser. "If you folks want to pray, I'm agreeable," he said. But Mrs. Rutledge intervened.

"Prayer ain't any good. In this kind of thing it ain't no manner of use; you know it ain't. I called you here, Deacon, because you remember the last case in this parish. Thirty years ago it was, I guess; but you remember. Lefferts Nash—did praying help *him?* I was a little girl then, but I used to hear my folks talk of it winter nights. Lefferts Nash and Hannah Cory. They drove a stake through her breast. That's what cured him."

"Oh—" Orrin Bosworth exclaimed.

Sylvester Brand raised his head. "You've speaking of that old story as if this was the same sort of thing?"

"Ain't it? Ain't my husband pining away the same as Lefferts Nash did? The Deacon here knows—"

The Deacon stirred anxiously in his chair. "These are forbidden things," he repeated. "Supposing your husband is quite sincere in thinking himself haunted, as you might say. Well, even then, what proof have we that the . . . the dead woman . . . is the specter of that poor girl?"

"Proof? Don't he say so? Didn't she tell him? Ain't I seen 'em?" Mrs. Rutledge almost screamed.

The three men sat silent, and suddenly the wife burst out: "A stake through the breast! That's the old way; and it's the only way. The Deacon knows it!"

"It's against our religion to disturb the dead."

"Ain't it against your religion to let the living perish as my husband is perishing?" She sprang up with one of her abrupt movements and took the family Bible from the whatnot in a corner of the parlor. Putting the book on the table, and moistening a livid fingertip, she turned the pages rapidly, till she came to one on which she laid her hand like a stony paperweight. "See here," she said, and read out in her level chanting voice:

" '*Thou shalt not suffer a witch to live.*'

"That's in Exodus, that's where it is," she added, leaving the book open as if to confirm the statement.

Bosworth continued to glance anxiously from one to the other of the four people about the table. He was younger than any of them, and had had more contact with the modern world; down in Starkfield, in the bar of the Fielding House, he could hear himself laughing with the rest of the men at such old wives' tales. But it was not for nothing that he had been born under the icy shadow of Lonetop, and had shivered and hungered as a lad through the bitter Hemlock County winters. After his parents died, and he had taken hold of the farm himself, he had got more out of it by using improved methods, and by supplying the increasing throng of summer boarders over Stotesbury way with milk and vegetables. He had been made a Selectman of North Ashmore; for so young a man he had a standing in the county. But the roots of the old life were still in him. He could remember, as a little boy, going twice a year with his mother to that bleak hill farm out beyond Sylvester Brand's, where Mrs. Bosworth's aunt, Cressidora Cheney, had been shut up for years in a cold clean room with iron bars to the windows. When little Orrin first saw Aunt Cressidora she was a small white old woman, whom her sisters use to "make decent" for visitors the day that Orrin and his mother were expected. The child wondered why there were bars on the window. "Like a canary bird," he said to his mother. The phrase made Mrs. Bosworth reflect. "I do believe they keep Aunt Cressidora too lonesome," she said; and the next time she went up the mountain with the little boy she carried to his great-aunt a canary in a little wooden cage. It was a great excitement; he knew it would make her happy.

The old woman's motionless face lit up.when she saw the bird, and her eyes began to glitter. "It belongs to me," she said instantly, stretching her soft bony hand over the cage.

"Of course it does, Aunt Cressy," said Mrs. Bosworth, her eyes filling.

But the bird, startled by the shadow of the old woman's hand, began to flutter and beat its wings distractedly. At the sight, Aunt Cressidora's calm face suddenly became a coil of twitching features. "You she-devil, you!" she cried in a high squealing voice; and thrusting her hand into the cage she dragged out the terrified bird and wrung its neck. She was plucking the hot body, and squealing "she-devil, she-devil!" as they drew little Orrin from the room. On the way down the mountain his mother wept a great deal, and said: "You must never tell anybody that poor Auntie's crazy, or the men would come and take her down to the asylum at Starkfield, and the shame of it would kill us all. Now promise." The child promised.

He remembered the scene now, with its deep fringe of mystery, secrecy and rumor. It seemed related to a great many other things below the surface of his thoughts, things which stole up anew, making him feel that all the old people he had known, and who "believed in these things," might after all be right. Hadn't a witch been burned at North Ashmore? Didn't the summer folk still drive over in jolly buckboard loads to see the meetinghouse where the trial had been held, the pond where they had ducked her and she had floated? . . . Deacon Hibben believed; Bosworth was sure of it. If he didn't, why did people from all over the place come to him when their animals had queer sicknesses, or when there was a child in the family that had to be kept shut up because it fell down flat and foamed? Yes, in spite of his religion, Deacon Hibben *knew.* . . .

And Brand? Well, it came to Bosworth in a flash: that North Ashmore woman who was burned had the name of Brand. The same stock, no doubt; there had been Brands in Hemlock County ever since the white men had come there. And Orrin, when he was a child, remembered hearing his parents say that Sylvester Brand hadn't ever oughter married his own cousin, because of the blood. Yet the couple had had two healthy girls, and when Mrs. Brand pined away and died nobody suggested that anything had been wrong with her mind. And Vanessa and Ora were the handsomest girls anywhere round. Brand knew it, and scrimped and saved all he could to send Ora, the eldest, down to Starkfield to learn bookkeeping. "When she's married I'll send you," he used to say to little Venny, who was his favorite. But Ora never married. She was away three years, during which Venny ran wild on the slopes of Lonetop; and when Ora came back she sickened and died—poor girl! Since then Brand had grown more savage and morose. He was a hard-working farmer, but there wasn't much to be got out of those barren Bearcliff acres. He was said to have taken to drink since his wife's death; now and then men ran across him in the "dives" of Stotesbury. But not often. And between times he labored hard on his stony acres and did his best for his daughters. In the neglected graveyard of Cold Corners there was a slanting headstone marked with his wife's name; near it, a year since, he had laid his eldest daughter. And sometimes, at dusk, in the autumn, the village people saw him walk slowly by, turn in between the graves, and stand looking down on the two stones. But he never brought a flower there, or planted a bush; nor Venny either. She was too wild and ignorant. . . .

Mrs. Rutledge repeated: "That's in Exodus."

The three visitors remained silent, turning about their hats in reluctant hands. Rutledge faced them, still with that empty pellucid gaze which frightened Bosworth. What was he seeing?

"Ain't any of you folks got the grit—?" his wife burst out again, half hysterically.

Deacon Hibben held up his hand. "That's no way, Mrs. Rutledge. This ain't a question of having grit. What we want first of all is . . . proof . . ."

"That's so," said Bosworth, with an explosion of relief, as if the words had lifted something black and crouching from his breast. Involuntarily the eyes of both men had turned to Brand. He stood there smiling grimly, but did not speak.

"Ain't it so, Brand?" the Deacon prompted him.

"Proof that spooks walk?" the other sneered.

"Well—I presume you want this business settled too?"

The old farmer squared his shoulders. "Yes—I do. But I ain't a sperritualist. How the hell are you going to settle it?"

Deacon Hibben hesitated; then he said, in a low incisive tone: "I don't see but one way—Mrs. Rutledge's."

There was a silence.

"What?" Brand sneered again. "Spying?"

The Deacon's voice sank lower. "If the poor girl *does* walk . . . her that's your child . . . wouldn't you be the first to want her laid quiet? We all know there've been such cases . . . mysterious visitations. . . . Can any one of us here deny it?"

"I seen 'em," Mrs. Rutledge interjected.

There was another heavy pause. Suddenly Brand fixed his gaze on Rutledge. "See here, Saul Rutledge, you've got to clear up this damned calumny, or I'll know why. You say my dead girl comes to you." He labored with his breath, and then jerked out: "When? You tell me that, and I'll be there."

Rutledge's head drooped a little, and his eyes wandered to the window. "Round about sunset, mostly."

"You know beforehand?"

Rutledge made a sign of assent.

"Well, then—tomorrow, will it be?"

Rutledge made the same sign.

Brand turned to the door. "I'll be there." That was all he said. He strode out between them without another glance or word. Deacon Hibben looked at Mrs. Rutledge. "We'll be there too," he said, as if she had asked him; but she had not spoken, and Bosworth saw that her thin body was trembling all over. He was glad when he and Hibben were out again in the snow.

III

They thought that Brand wanted to be left to himself, and to give him time to unhitch his horse they made a pretense of hanging about in the doorway while Bosworth searched his pockets for a pipe he had no mind to light.

But Brand turned back to them as they lingered. "You'll meet me down by Lamer's pond tomorrow?" he suggested. "I want witnesses. Round about sunset."

They nodded their acquiescence, and he got into his sleigh, gave the horse a cut across the flanks, and drove off under the snow-smothered hemlocks. The other two men went to the shed.

"What do you make of this business, Deacon?" Bosworth asked, to break the silence.

The Deacon shook his head. "The man's a sick man—that's sure. Something's sucking the life clean out of him."

But already, in the biting outer air, Bosworth was getting himself under better control. "Looks to me like a bad case of the ague, as you said."

"Well—ague of the mind, then. It's his brain that's sick."

Bosworth shrugged. "He ain't the first in Hemlock County."

"That's so," the Deacon agreed. "It's a worm in the brain, solitude is."

"Well, we'll know this time tomorrow, maybe," said Bosworth. He scrambled into his sleigh, and was driving off in his turn when he heard his companion calling after him. The Deacon explained that his horse had cast a shoe; would Bosworth drive him down to the forge near North Ashmore, if it wasn't too much out of his way? He didn't want the mare slipping about on the freezing snow, and he could probably get the blacksmith to drive him back and shoe her in Rutledge's shed. Bosworth made room for him under the bearskin, and the two men drove off, pursued by a puzzled whinny from the Deacon's old mare.

The road they took was not the one that Bosworth would have followed to reach his own home. But he did not mind that. The shortest way to the forge passed close by Lamer's pond, and Bosworth, since he was in for the business, was not sorry to look the ground over. They drove on in silence.

The snow had ceased, and a green sunset was spreading upward into the crystal sky. A stinging wind barbed with ice flakes caught them in the face on the open ridges, but when they dropped down into the hollow by Lamer's pond the air was as soundless and empty as an unswung bell. They jogged along slowly, each thinking his own thoughts.

"That's the house . . . that tumble-down shack over there, I suppose?" the Deacon said, as the road drew near the edge of the frozen pond.

"Yes: that's the house. A queer hermit fellow built it years ago, my father used to tell me. Since then I don't believe it's ever been used but by the gypsies."

Bosworth had reined in his horse, and sat looking through pine trunks purpled by the sunset at the crumbling structure. Twilight already lay under the trees, though day lingered in the open. Between two sharply-patterned pine boughs he saw the evening star, like a white boat in a sea of green.

His gaze dropped from that fathomless sky and followed the blue-white undulations of the snow. It gave him a curious agitated feeling to think that here, in this icy solitude, in the tumble-down house he had so often passed without heeding it, a dark mystery, too deep for thought, was being enacted. Down that very slope, coming from the graveyard at Cold Corners, the being they called "Ora" must pass toward the pond. His heart began to beat stiflingly. Suddenly he gave an exclamation: "Look!"

He had jumped out of the cutter and was stumbling up the bank toward the slope of snow. On it, turned in the direction of the house by the pond, he had detected a woman's footprints; two; then three; then more. The Deacon scrambled out after him, and they stood and stared.

"God—barefoot!" Hibben gasped. "Then it *is* . . . the dead. . . ."

Bosworth said nothing. But he knew that no live woman would travel with naked feet across that freezing wilderness. Here, then, was the proof the Deacon had asked for—they held it. What should they do with it?

"Supposing we was to drive up nearer—round the turn of the pond, till we get close to the house," the Deacon proposed in a colorless voice. "Mebbe then. . . ."

Postponement was a relief. They got into the sleigh and drove on. Two or three hundred yards farther the road, a mere lane under steep bushy banks, turned sharply to the right, following the bend of the pond. As they rounded the turn they saw Brand's cutter ahead of them. It was empty, the horse tied to a treetrunk. The two men looked at each other again. This was not Brand's nearest way home.

Evidently he had been actuated by the same impulse which had made them rein in their horse by the pondside, and then hasten on to the deserted hovel. Had he too discovered those spectral footprints? Perhaps it was for that very reason that he had left his cutter and vanished in the direction of the house. Bosworth found himself shivering all over under his bearskin. "I wish to God the dark wasn't coming on," he muttered. He tethered his own horse near Brand's, and without a word he and the Deacon ploughed through the snow, in the track of Brand's huge feet. They had only a few yards to walk to overtake him. He did not hear them following him, and when Bosworth spoke his name, and he stopped short and turned, his heavy face was dim and confused, like a darker blot on the dusk. He looked at them dully, but without surprise.

"I wanted to see the place," he merely said.

The Deacon cleared his throat. "Just take a look . . . yes . . . we thought so. . . . But I guess there won't be anything to *see*. . . ." He attempted a chuckle.

The other did not seem to hear him, but labored on ahead through the pines. The three men came out together in the cleared space before the house. As they emerged from beneath the trees they seemed to have left night behind. The evening star shed a luster on the speckless snow, and Brand, in that lucid circle, stopped with a jerk, and pointed to the same light footprints turned toward the house—the track of a woman in the snow. He stood still, his face working. "Bare feet. . . ." he said.

The Deacon piped up in a quavering voice: "The feet of the dead."

Brand remained motionless. "The feet of the dead," he echoed.

Deacon Hibben laid a frightened hand on his arm. "Come away now, Brand; for the love of God come away."

The father hung there, gazing down at those light tracks on the snow—light as fox or squirrel trails they seemed, on the white immensity. Bosworth thought to himself: "The living couldn't walk so light —not even Ora Brand couldn't have, when she lived. . . ." The cold seemed to have entered into his very marrow. His teeth were chattering.

Brand swung about on them abruptly. *"Now!"* he said, moving on as if to an assault, his head bowed forward on his bull neck.

"Now—now? Not in there?" gasped the Deacon. "What's the use? It was tomorrow he said—" He shook like a leaf.

"It's now," said Brand. He went up to the door of the crazy house, pushed it inward, and meeting with an unexpected resistance, thrust his heavy shoulder against the panel. The door collapsed like a playing card, and Brand stumbled after it into the darkness of the hut. The others, after a moment's hesitation, followed.

Bosworth was never quite sure in what order the events that succeeded took place. Coming in out of the snow dazzle, he seemed to be plunging into total blackness. He groped his way across the threshold, caught a sharp splinter of the fallen door in his palm, seemed to see something white and wraithlike surge up out of the darkest corner of the hut, and then heard a revolver shot at his elbow, and a cry—

Brand had turned back, and was staggering past him out into the lingering daylight. The sunset, suddenly flushing through the trees, crimsoned his face like blood. He held a revolver in his hand and looked about him in his stupid way.

"They *do* walk, then," he said and began to laugh. He bent his head to examine his weapon. "Better here than in the churchyard. They shan't dig her up *now*," he shouted out. The two men caught him by the arms, and Bosworth got the revolver away from him.

IV

The next day Bosworth's sister Loretta, who kept house for him, asked him, when he came in for his midday dinner, if he had heard the news.

Bosworth had been sawing wood all the morning, and in spite of the cold and the driving snow, which had begun again in the night, he was covered with an icy sweat, like a man getting over a fever.

"What news?"

"Venny Brand's down sick with pneumonia. The Deacon's been there. I guess she's dying."

Bosworth looked at her with listless eyes. She seemed far off from him, miles away. "Venny Brand?" he echoed.

"You never liked her, Orrin."

"She's a child. I never knew much about her."

"Well," repeated his sister, with the guileless relish of the un-imaginative for bad news, "I guess she's dying." After a pause she added: "It'll kill Sylvester Brand, all alone up there."

Bosworth got up and said: "I've got to see to poulticing the gray's fetlock." He walked out into the steadily falling snow.

Venny Brand was buried three days later. The Deacon read the service; Bosworth was one of the pallbearers. The whole countryside turned out, for the snow had stopped falling, and at any season a funeral offered an opportunity for an outing that was not to be missed. Besides, Venny Brand was young and handsome—at least some people thought her handsome, though she was so swarthy—and her dying like that, so suddenly, had the fascination of tragedy.

"They say her lungs filled right up. . . . Seems she'd had bronchial troubles before . . . I always said both them girls was frail. . . . Look at Ora, how she took and wasted away! And it's colder'n all outdoors up there to Brand's. . . . Their mother, too, *she* pined away just the

same. They don't ever make old bones on the mother's side of the family.... There's that young Bedlow over there; they say Venny was engaged to him.... Oh, Mrs. Rutledge, excuse *me*.... Step right into the pew; there's a seat for you alongside of grandma...."

Mrs. Rutledge was advancing with deliberate step down the narrow aisle of the bleak wooden church. She had on her best bonnet, a monumental structure which no one had seen out of her trunk since old Mrs. Silsee's funeral, three years before. All the women remembered it. Under its perpendicular pile her narrow face, swaying on the long thin neck, seemed whiter than ever; but her air of fretfulness had been composed into a suitable expression of mournful immobility.

"Looks as if the stonemason had carved her to put atop of Venny's grave," Bosworth thought as she glided past him; and then shivered at his own sepulchral fancy. When she bent over her hymn book her lowered lids reminded him again of marble eyeballs; the bony hands clasping the book were bloodless. Bosworth had never seen such hands since he had seen old Aunt Cressidora Cheney strangle the canary bird because it fluttered.

The service was over, the coffin of Venny Brand had been lowered into her sister's grave, and the neighbors were slowly dispersing. Bosworth, as pallbearer, felt obliged to linger and say a word to the stricken father. He waited till Brand had turned from the grave with the Deacon at his side. The three men stood together for a moment; but not one of them spoke. Brand's face was the closed door of a vault, barred with wrinkles like bands of iron.

Finally the Deacon took his hand and said: "The Lord gave—"

Brand nodded and turned away toward the shed where the horses were hitched. Bosworth followed him. "Let me drive along home with you," he suggested.

Brand did not so much as turn his head. "Home? What home?" he said; and the other fell back.

Loretta Bosworth was talking with the other women while the men unblanketed their horses and backed the cutters out into the heavy snow. As Bosworth waited for her, a few feet off, he saw Mrs. Rutledge's tall bonnet lording it above the group. Andy Pond, the Rutledge farm hand, was backing out the sleigh.

"Saul ain't here today, Mrs. Rutledge, is he?" one of the village elders piped, turning a benevolent old tortoise head about on a loose neck, and blinking up into Mrs. Rutledge's marble face.

Bosworth heard her measure out her answer in slow incisive words. "No. Mr. Rutledge he ain't here. He would 'a' come for certain, but his aunt Minorca Cummins is being buried down to Stotesbury this very day and he had to go down there. Don't it sometimes seem zif we was all walking right in the Shadow of Death?"

As she walked toward the cutter, in which Andy Pond was already seated, the Deacon went up to her with visible hesitation. Involuntarily Bosworth also moved nearer. He heard the Deacon say: "I'm glad to hear that Saul is able to be up and around."

She turned her small head on her rigid neck, and lifted the lids of marble.

"Yes, I guess he'll sleep quieter now. And *her* too, maybe, now she don't lay there alone any longer," she added in a low voice, with a sudden twist of her chin toward the fresh black stain in the graveyard snow. She got into the cutter, and said in a clear tone to Andy Pond: " 'S long as we're down here I don't know but what I'll just call round and get a box of soap at Hiram Pringle's."

Mr. Jones

$\mathcal{L}$ady Jane Lynke was unlike other people: when she heard that she had inherited Bells, the beautiful old place which had belonged to the Lynkes of Thudeney for something like six hundred years, the fancy took her to go and see it unannounced. She was staying at a friend's nearby, in Kent, and the next morning she borrowed a motor and slipped away alone to Thudeney-Blazes, the adjacent village.

It was a lustrous motionless day. Autumn bloom lay on the Sussex downs, on the heavy trees of the weald, on streams moving indolently, far off across the marshes. Farther still, Dungeness, a fitful streak, floated on an immaterial sea which was perhaps, after all, only sky.

In the softness Thudeney-Blazes slept: a few aged houses bowed about a duck pond, a silvery spire, orchards thick with dew. Did Thudeney-Blazes ever wake?

Lady Jane left the motor to the care of the geese on a miniature common, pushed open a white gate into a field (the griffoned portals being padlocked), and struck across the park toward a group of carved chimney stacks. No one seemed aware of her.

In a dip of the land, the long low house, its ripe brick masonry overhanging a moat deeply sunk about its roots, resembled an aged cedar spreading immemorial red branches. Lady Jane held her breath and gazed.

A silence distilled from years of solitude lay on lawns and gardens. No one had lived at Bells since the last Lord Thudeney, then a penniless younger son, had forsaken it sixty years before to seek his fortune in Canada. And before that, he and his widowed mother, distant poor relations, were housed in one of the lodges, and the great place, even in their day, had been as mute and solitary as the family vault.

Lady Jane, daughter of another branch, to which an earldom and considerable possessions had accrued, had never seen Bells, hardly heard its name. A succession of deaths, and the whim of an old man she had never known, now made her heir to all this beauty; and as she stood and looked she was glad she had come to it from so far, from impressions so remote and different. "It would be dreadful to be used to it—to be thinking already about the state of the roof, or the cost of a heating system."

Till this, her thirty-fifth year, Lady Jane had led an active, independent and decided life. One of several daughters, moderately but sufficiently provided for, she had gone early from home, lived in London lodgings, traveled in tropic lands, spent studious summers in Spain and Italy, and written two or three brisk business-like little books about cities usually dealt with sentimentally. And now, just back from a summer in the south of France, she stood ankle-deep in wet bracken, and gazed at Bells lying there under a September sun that looked like moonlight.

"I shall never leave it!" she ejaculated, her heart swelling as if she had taken the vow to a lover.

She ran down the last slope of the park and entered the faded formality of gardens with clipped yews as ornate as architecture, and holly hedges as solid as walls. Adjoining the house rose a low deep-buttressed chapel. Its door was ajar, and she thought this of good augury: her forebears were waiting for her. In the porch she remarked fly-blown notices of services, an umbrella stand, a disheveled door mat: no doubt the chapel served as the village church. The thought gave her a sense of warmth and neighborliness. Across the damp flags of the chancel, monuments and brasses showed through a traceried screen. She examined them curiously. Some hailed her with vocal memories, others whispered out of the remote and the unknown: it was a shame to know so little about her own family. But neither Crofts nor Lynkes had ever greatly distinguished themselves; they had gathered substance simply by holding on to what they had, and slowly accumulating privileges and acres. "Mostly by clever marriages," Lady Jane thought with a faint contempt.

At that moment her eyes lit on one of the less ornate monuments: a plain sarcophagus of gray marble niched in the wall and surmounted by the bust of a young man with a fine arrogant head, a Byronic throat and tossed-back curls.

"Peregrine Vincent Theobald Lynke, Baron Clouds, fifteenth Viscount Thudeney of Bells, Lord of the Manors of Thudeney, Thudeney-Blazes, Upper Lynke, Lynke-Linnet—" so it ran, with the usual tedious enumeration of honors, titles, court and county offices, ending with: "Born on May 1st, 1790, perished of the plague at Aleppo in 1828." And underneath, in small cramped characters, as if crowded as an afterthought into an insufficient space: "Also His Wife."

That was all. No names, dates, honors, epithets, for the Viscountess Thudeney. Did she too die of the plague at Aleppo? Or did the "also" imply her actual presence in the sarcophagus which her husband's pride had no doubt prepared for his own last sleep, little guessing that some Syrian drain was to receive him? Lady Jane racked her memory in vain. All she knew was that the death without issue of this Lord Thudeney had caused the property to revert to the Croft-Lynkes, and so, in the end, brought her to the chancel step where, shyly, she knelt a moment, vowing to the dead to carry on their trust.

She passed on to the entrance court, and stood at last at the door of her new home, a blunt tweed figure in heavy mud-stained shoes. She felt as intrusive as a tripper, and her hand hesitated on the doorbell. "I ought to have brought someone with me," she thought; an odd admission on the part of a young woman who, when she was doing her books of travel, had prided herself on forcing single-handed the most closely guarded doors. But those other places, as she looked back, seemed easy and accessible compared to Bells.

She rang, and a tinkle answered, carried on by a flurried echo which seemed to ask what in the world was happening. Lady Jane, through the nearest window, caught the spectral vista of a long room with shrouded furniture. She could not see its farther end, but she had the feeling that someone stationed there might very well be seeing her.

"Just at first," she thought, "I shall have to invite people here—to take the chill off."

She rang again, and the tinkle again prolonged itself; but no one came.

At last she reflected that the caretakers probably lived at the back of the house, and pushing open a door in the courtyard wall she worked her way around to what seemed a stable yard. Against the purple brick sprawled a neglected magnolia, bearing one late flower as big as a planet. Lady Jane rang at a door marked "Service." This bell, though also languid, had a wakefuller sound, as if it were more used to being rung, and still knew what was likely to follow; and after a delay during which Lady Jane again had the sense of being peered at —from above, through a lowered blind—a bolt shot, and a woman looked out. She was youngish, unhealthy, respectable and frightened; and she blinked at Lady Jane like someone waking out of sleep.

"Oh," said Lady Jane—"do you think I might visit the house?"

"The house?"

"I'm staying near here—I'm interested in old houses. Mightn't I take a look?"

The young woman drew back. "The house isn't shown."

"Oh, but not to—not to—" Jane weighed the case. "You see," she explained, "I know some of the family: the Northumberland branch."

"You're related, madam?"

"Well—distantly, yes." It was exactly what she had not meant to say; but there seemed no other way.

The woman twisted her apron strings in perplexity.

"Come, you know," Lady Jane urged, producing half-a-crown. The woman turned pale.

"I couldn't, madam; not without asking." It was clear that she was sorely tempted.

"Well, ask, won't you?" Lady Jane pressed the tip into a hesitating hand. The young woman shut the door and vanished. She was away so long that the visitor concluded her half-crown had been pocketed, and there was an end; and she began to be angry with herself, which was more often her habit than to be so with others.

"Well, for a fool, Jane, you're a complete one," she grumbled.

A returning footstep, listless, reluctant—the tread of one who was not going to let her in. It began to be rather comic.

The door opened, and the young woman said in her dull singsong: "Mr. Jones says that no one is allowed to visit the house."

She and Lady Jane looked at each other for a moment, and Lady Jane read the apprehension in the other's eyes.

"Mr. Jones? Oh?—Yes; of course, keep it. . . ." She waved away the woman's hand.

"Thank you, madam." The door closed again, and Lady Jane stood and gazed up at the inexorable face of her own home.

II

"But you didn't get in? You actually came back without so much as a peep?"

Her story was received, that evening at dinner, with mingled mirth and incredulity.

"But, my dear! You mean to say you asked to see the house, and they wouldn't let you? *Who* wouldn't?" Lady Jane's hostess insisted.

"Mr. Jones."

"Mr. Jones?"

"He said no one was allowed to visit it."

"Who on earth is Mr. Jones?"

"The caretaker, I suppose. I didn't see him."

"Didn't see him either? But I never heard such nonsense! Why in the world didn't you insist?"

"Yes; why didn't you?" they all chorused; and she could only answer, a little lamely: "I think I was afraid."

"Afraid? *You*, darling?" There was fresh hilarity. "Of Mr. Jones?"

"I suppose so." She joined in the laugh, yet she knew it was true: she had been afraid.

Edward Stramer, the novelist, an old friend of her family, had been listening with an air of abstraction, his eyes on his empty coffee cup. Suddenly, as the mistress of the house pushed back her chair, he looked across the table at Lady Jane. "It's odd: I've just remembered something. Once, when I was a youngster, I tried to see Bells; over thirty years ago it must have been." He glanced at his host. "Your mother drove me over. And we were not let in."

There was a certain flatness in this conclusion, and someone remarked that Bells had always been known as harder to get into than any other house thereabouts.

"Yes," said Stramer; "but the point is that we were refused in exactly the same words. Mr. Jones said no one was allowed to visit the house."

"Ah—he was in possession already? Thirty years ago? Unsociable fellow, Jones. Well, Jane, you've got a good watchdog."

They moved to the drawing room, and the talk drifted to other topics. But Stramer came and sat down beside Lady Jane. "It is queer, though, that at such a distance of time we should have been given exactly the same answer."

She glanced up at him curiously. "Yes; and you didn't try to force your way in either?"

"Oh, no: it was not possible."

"So I felt," she agreed.

"Well, next week, my dear, I hope we shall see it all, in spite of

Mr. Jones," their hostess intervened, catching their last words as she moved toward the piano.

"I wonder if we shall see Mr. Jones," said Stramer.

III

Bells was not nearly as large as it looked; like many old houses it was very narrow, and but one story high, with servants' rooms in the low attics, and much space wasted in crooked passages and superfluous stairs. If she closed the great salon, Jane thought, she might live there comfortably with the small staff which was the most she could afford. It was a relief to find the place less important than she had feared.

For already, in that first hour of arrival, she had decided to give up everything else for Bells. Her previous plans and ambitions—except such as might fit in with living there—had fallen from her like a discarded garment, and things she had hardly thought about, or had shrugged away with the hasty subversiveness of youth, were already laying quiet hands on her; all the lives from which her life had issued, with what they bore of example or admonishment. The very shabbiness of the house moved her more than splendors, made it, after its long abandonment, seem full of the careless daily coming and going of people long dead, people to whom it had not been a museum, or a page of history, but cradle, nursery, home, and sometimes, no doubt, a prison. If those marble lips in the chapel could speak! If she could hear some of their comments on the old house which had spread its silent shelter over their sins and sorrows, their follies and submissions! A long tale, to which she was about to add another chapter, subdued and humdrum beside some of those earlier annals, yet probably freer and more varied than the unchronicled lives of the great-aunts and great-grandmothers buried there so completely that they must hardly have known when they passed from their beds to their graves. "Piled up like dead leaves," Jane thought, "layers and layers of them, to preserve something forever budding underneath."

Well, all these piled-up lives had at least preserved the old house in its integrity; and that was worth-while. She was satisfied to carry on such a trust.

She sat in the garden looking up at those rosy walls, iridescent with damp and age. She decided which windows should be hers, which rooms given to the friends from Kent who were motoring over, Stramer among them, for a modest housewarming; then she got up and went in.

The hour had come for domestic questions; for she had arrived alone, unsupported even by the old family housemaid her mother had offered her. She preferred to start afresh, convinced that her small household could be staffed from the neighborhood. Mrs. Clemm, the rosy-cheeked old person who had curtsied her across the threshold, would doubtless know.

Mrs. Clemm, summoned to the library, curtsied again. She wore black silk, gathered and spreading as to skirt, flat and perpendicular as to bodice. On her glossy false front was a black lace cap with ribbons which had faded from violet to ash-color, and a heavy watch chain descended from the lava brooch under her crochet collar. Her small round face rested on the collar like a red apple on a white plate: neat, smooth, circular, with a pursed-up mouth, eyes like black seeds, and round ruddy cheeks with the skin so taut that one had to look close to see that it was as wrinkled as a piece of old crackly.

Mrs. Clemm was sure there would be no trouble about servants. She herself could do a little cooking: though her hand might be a bit out. But there was her niece to help; and she was quite of her ladyship's opinion, that there was no need to get in strangers. They were mostly a poor lot; and besides, they might not take to Bells. There were persons who didn't. Mrs. Clemm smiled a sharp little smile, like the scratch of a pin, as she added that she hoped her ladyship wouldn't be one of them.

As for under-servants . . . well, a boy, perhaps? She had a great-nephew she might send for. But about women—under-housemaids—if her ladyship thought they couldn't manage as they were; well, she really didn't know. Thudeney-Blazes? Oh, she didn't think so. . . . There was more dead than living at Thudeney-Blazes . . . everyone was leaving there . . . or in the church yard . . . one house after another being shut . . . death was everywhere, wasn't it, my lady? Mrs. Clemm said it with another of her short sharp smiles, which provoked the appearance of a frosty dimple.

"But my niece Georgiana is a hard worker, my lady; her that let you in the other day. . . ."

"That didn't," Lady Jane corrected.

"Oh, my lady, it was too unfortunate. If only your ladyship had have said . . . poor Georgiana had ought to have seen; but she never *did* have her wits about her, not for answering the door."

"But she was only obeying orders. She went to ask Mr. Jones."

Mrs. Clemm was silent. Her small hands, wrinkled and resolute, fumbled with the folds of her apron, and her quick eyes made the circuit of the room and then came back to Lady Jane's.

"Just so, my lady; but, as I told her, she'd ought to have known—"

"And who is Mr. Jones?"

Mrs. Clemm's smile snapped out again, deprecating, respectful. "Well, my lady, he's more dead than living, too . . . if I may say so," was her surprising answer.

"Is he? I'm sorry to hear that; but who is he?"

"Well, my lady, he's . . . he's my great-uncle, as it were . . . my grandmother's own brother, as you might say."

"Ah; I see." Lady Jane considered her with growing curiosity. "He must have reached a great age, then."

"Yes, my lady; he has that. Though I'm not," Mrs. Clemm added, the dimple showing, "as old myself as your ladyship might suppose. Living at Bells all these years has been ageing to me; it would be to anybody."

"I suppose so. And yet," Lady Jane continued, "Mr. Jones has survived; has stood it well—as you certainly have?"

"Oh, not as well as I have," Mrs. Clemm interjected, as if resentful of the comparison.

"At any rate, he still mounts guard; mounts it as well as he did thirty years ago."

"Thirty years ago?" Mrs. Clemm echoed, her hands dropping from her apron to her sides.

"Wasn't he here thirty years ago?"

"Oh, yes, my lady, certainly; he's never once been away that I know of."

"What a wonderful record! And what exactly are his duties?"

Mrs. Clemm paused again, her hands still motionless in the folds of her skirt. Lady Jane noticed that the fingers were tightly clenched, as if to check an involuntary gesture.

"He began as pantry boy; then footman; then butler, my lady; but it's hard to say, isn't it, what an old servant's duties are, when he's stayed on in the same house so many years?"

"Yes; and that house always empty."

"Just so, my lady. Everything came to depend on him; one thing after another. His late lordship thought the world of him."

"His late lordship? But he was never here! He spent all his life in Canada."

Mrs. Clemm seemed slightly disconcerted. "Certainly, my lady." (Her voice said: "Who are you, to set me right as to the chronicles of Bells?") "But by letter, my lady; I can show you the letters. And there was his lordship before, the sixteenth Viscount. He *did* come here once."

"Ah, did he?" Lady Jane was embarrassed to find how little she knew of them all. She rose from her seat. "They were lucky, all these absentees, to have some one to watch over their interests so faithfully. I should like to see Mr. Jones—to thank him. Will you take me to him now?"

"Now?" Mrs. Clemm moved back a step or two; Lady Jane fancied her cheeks paled a little under their ruddy varnish. "Oh, not today, my lady."

"Why? Isn't he well enough?"

"Not nearly. He's between life and death, as it were," Mrs. Clemm repeated, as if the phrase were the nearest approach she could find to a definition of Mr. Jones's state.

"He wouldn't even know who I was?"

Mrs. Clemm considered a moment. "I don't say *that*, my lady;" her tone implied that to do so might appear disrespectful. "He'd know you, my lady; but you wouldn't know *him*." She broke off and added hastily: "I mean, for what he is: he's in no state for you to see him."

"He's so very ill? Poor man! And is everything possible being done?"

"Oh, everything; and more too, my lady. But perhaps," Mrs. Clemm suggested, with a clink of keys, "this would be a good time for your ladyship to take a look about the house. If your ladyship has no objection, I should like to begin with the linen."

IV

"And Mr. Jones?" Stramer queried, a few days later, as they sat, Lady Jane and the party from Kent, about an improvised tea table in a recess of one of the great holly hedges.

The day was as hushed and warm as that on which she had first come to Bells, and Lady Jane looked up with a smile of ownership at the old walls which seemed to smile back, the windows which now looked at her with friendly eyes.

"Mr. Jones? Who's Mr. Jones?" the others asked; only Stramer recalled their former talk.

Lady Jane hesitated. "Mr. Jones is my invisible guardian; or rather, the guardian of Bells."

They remembered then. "Invisible? You don't mean to say you haven't seen him yet?"

"Not yet; perhaps I never shall. He's very old—and very ill, I'm afraid."

"And he still rules here?"

"Oh, absolutely. The fact is," Lady Jane added, "I believe he's the only person left who really knows all about Bells."

"Jane, my *dear!* That big shrub over there against the wall! I verily believe it's *Templetonia retusa.* It *is!* Did any one ever hear of its standing an English winter?" Gardeners all, they dashed off towards the shrub in its sheltered angle. "I shall certainly try it on a south wall at Dipway," cried the hostess from Kent.

Tea over, they moved on to inspect the house. The short autumn day was drawing to a close; but the party had been able to come only for an afternoon, instead of staying over the weekend, and having lingered so long in the gardens they had only time, indoors, to puzzle out what they could through the shadows. Perhaps, Lady Jane thought, it was the best hour to see a house like Bells, so long abandoned, and not yet warmed into new life.

The fire she had had lit in the salon sent its radiance to meet them, giving the great room an air of expectancy and welcome. The portraits, the Italian cabinets, the shabby armchairs and rugs, all looked as if life had but lately left them; and Lady Jane said to herself: "Perhaps Mrs. Clemm is right in advising me to live here and close the blue parlor."

"My dear, what a fine room! Pity it faces north. Of course you'll have to shut it in winter. It would cost a fortune to heat."

Lady Jane hesitated. "I don't know: I *had* meant to. But there seems to be no other. . . ."

"No other? In all this house?" They laughed; and one of the visitors, going ahead and crossing a paneled anteroom, cried out: "But here! A delicious room; windows south—yes, and west. The warmest of the house. This is perfect."

They followed, and the blue room echoed with exclamations. "Those charming curtains with the parrots . . . and the blue of that petit point fire screen! But, Jane, of course you must live here. Look at this citron wood desk!"

Lady Jane stood on the threshold. "It seems that the chimney smokes hopelessly."

"Hopelessly? Nonsense! Have you consulted anybody? I'll send you a wonderful man. . . ."

"Besides, if you put in one of those one-pipe heaters. . . . At Dipway. . . ."

Stramer was looking over Lady Jane's shoulder. "What does Mr. Jones say about it?"

"He says no one has ever been able to use this room; not for ages. It was the housekeeper who told me. She's his great-niece, and seems simply to transmit his oracles."

Stramer shrugged. "Well, he's lived at Bells longer than you have. Perhaps he's right."

"How absurd!" one of the ladies cried. "The housekeeper and Mr. Jones probably spend their evenings here, and don't want to be disturbed. Look—ashes on the hearth! What did I tell you?"

Lady Jane echoed the laugh as they turned away. They had still to see the library, damp and dilapidated, the paneled dining room, the breakfast parlor, and such bedrooms as had any old furniture left; not many, for the late lords of Bells, at one time or another, had evidently sold most of its removable treasures.

When the visitors came down their motors were waiting. A lamp had been placed in the hall, but the rooms beyond were lit only by the broad clear band of western sky showing through uncurtained casements. On the doorstep one of the ladies exclaimed that she had lost her handbag—no, she remembered; she had laid it on the desk in the blue room. Which way was the blue room?

"I'll get it," Jane said, turning back. She heard Stramer following. He asked if he should bring the lamp.

"Oh, no; I can see."

She crossed the threshold of the blue room, guided by the light from its western window; then she stopped. Some one was in the room already; she felt rather than saw another presence. Stramer, behind her, paused also; he did not speak or move. What she saw, or thought she saw, was simply an old man with bent shoulders turning away from the citron wood desk. Almost before she had received the impression there was no one there; only the slightest stir of the needlework curtain over the farther door. She heard no step or other sound.

"There's the bag," she said, as if the act of speaking, and saying something obvious, were a relief.

In the hall her glance crossed Stramer's, but failed to find there the reflection of what her own had registered.

He shook hands, smiling. "Well, good-bye. I commit you to Mr. Jones's care; only don't let him say that *you're* not shown to visitors."

She smiled: "Come back and try," and then shivered a little as the lights of the last motor vanished beyond the great black hedges.

V

Lady Jane had exulted in her resolve to keep Bells to herself till she and the old house should have had time to make friends. But after a few days she recalled the uneasy feeling which had come over her as she stood on the threshold after her first tentative ring. Yes; she had been right in thinking she would have to have people about her to take the chill off. The house was too old, too mysterious, too much withdrawn into its own secret past, for her poor little present to fit into it without uneasiness.

But it was not a time of year when, among Lady Jane's friends, it was easy to find people free. Her own family were all in the north, and impossible to dislodge. One of her sisters, when invited, simply sent her back a list of shooting dates; and her mother wrote: "Why not come to us? What can you have to do all alone in that empty house at this time of year? Next summer we're all coming."

Having tried one or two friends with the same result, Lady Jane bethought her of Stramer. He was finishing a novel, she knew, and at such times he liked to settle down somewhere in the country where he could be sure of not being disturbed. Bells was a perfect asylum, and though it was probable that some other friend had anticipated her, and provided the requisite seclusion, Lady Jane decided to invite him. "Do bring your work and stay till it's finished—and don't be in a hurry to finish. I promise that no one shall bother you—" and she added, half-nervously: "Not even Mr. Jones." As she wrote she felt an absurd impulse to blot the words out. "He might not like it," she thought; and the "he" did not refer to Stramer.

Was the solitude already making her superstitious? She thrust the letter into an envelope, and carried it herself to the post office at Thudeney-Blazes. Two days later a wire from Stramer announced his arrival.

He came on a cold stormy afternoon, just before dinner, and as they went up to dress Lady Jane called after him: "We shall sit in the blue parlor this evening." The housemaid Georgiana was crossing the passage with hot water for the visitor. She stopped and cast a vacant glance at Lady Jane. The latter met it, and said carelessly: "You hear, Georgiana? The fire in the blue parlor."

While Lady Jane was dressing she heard a knock, and saw Mrs. Clemm's round face just inside the door, like a red apple on a garden wall.

"Is there anything wrong about the salon, my lady? Georgiana understood—"

"That I want the fire in the blue parlor. Yes. What's wrong with the salon is that one freezes there."

"But the chimney smokes in the blue parlor."

"Well, we'll give it a trial, and if it does I'll send for someone to arrange it."

"Nothing can be done, my lady. Everything has been tried, and—"

Lady Jane swung about suddenly. She had heard Stramer singing a cheerful hunting song in a cracked voice, in his dressing room at the other end of the corridor.

"That will do, Mrs. Clemm. I want the fire in the blue parlor."

"Yes, my lady." The door closed on the housekeeper.

"So you decided on the salon after all?" Stramer said, as Lady Jane led the way there after their brief repast.

"Yes: I hope you won't be frozen. Mr. Jones swears that the chimney in the blue parlor isn't safe; so, until I can fetch the mason over from Strawbridge—"

"Oh, I see." Stramer drew up to the blaze in the great fireplace. "We're very well off here; though heating this room is going to be ruinous. Meanwhile, I note that Mr. Jones still rules."

Lady Jane gave a slight laugh.

"Tell me," Stramer continued, as she bent over the mixing of the Turkish coffee, "what is there about him? I'm getting curious."

Lady Jane laughed again, and heard the embarrassment in her laugh. "So am I."

"Why—you don't mean to say you haven't seen him yet?"

"No. He's still too ill."

"What's the matter with him? What does the doctor say?"

"He won't see the doctor."

"But look here—if things take a worse turn—I don't know; but mightn't you be held to have been negligent?"

"What can I do? Mrs. Clemm says he has a doctor who treats him by correspondence. I don't see that I can interfere."

"Isn't there someone beside Mrs. Clemm whom you can consult?"

She considered: certainly, as yet, she had not made much effort to get into relation with her neighbors. "I expected the vicar to call. But I've inquired: there's no vicar any longer at Thudeney-Blazes. A curate comes from Strawbridge every other Sunday. And the one who comes now is new: nobody about the place seems to know him."

"But I thought the chapel here was in use? It looked so when you showed it to us the other day."

"I thought so too. It used to be the parish church of Lynke-Linnet and Lower-Lynke; but it seems that was years ago. The parishioners objected to coming so far; and there weren't enough of them. Mrs.

Clemm says that nearly everybody has died off or left. It's the same at Thudeney-Blazes."

Stramer glanced about the great room, with its circle of warmth and light by the hearth, and the sullen shadows huddled at its farther end, as if hungrily listening. "With this emptiness at the center, life was bound to cease gradually on the outskirts."

Lady Jane followed his glance. "Yes; it's all wrong. I must try to wake the place up."

"Why not open it to the public? Have a visitors' day?"

She thought a moment. In itself the suggestion was distasteful; she could imagine few things that would bore her more. Yet to do so might be a duty, a first step toward re-establishing relations between the lifeless house and its neighborhood. Secretly, she felt that even the coming and going of indifferent unknown people would help to take the chill from those rooms, to brush from their walls the dust of too-heavy memories.

"Who's that?" asked Stramer. Lady Jane started in spite of herself, and glanced over her shoulder; but he was only looking past her at a portrait which a dart of flame from the hearth had momentarily called from its obscurity.

"That's a Lady Thudeney." She got up and went toward the picture with a lamp. "Might be an Opie, don't you think? It's a strange face, under the smirk of the period."

Stramer took the lamp and held it up. The portrait was that of a young woman in a short-waisted muslin gown caught beneath the breast by a cameo. Between clusters of beribboned curls a long fair oval looked out dumbly, inexpressively, in a stare of frozen beauty. "It's as if the house had been too empty even then," Lady Jane murmured. "I wonder which she was? Oh, I know: it must be '*Also His Wife.*'"

Stramer stared.

"It's the only name on her monument. The wife of Peregrine Vincent Theobald, who perished of the plague at Aleppo in 1828. Perhaps she was very fond of him, and this was painted when she was an inconsolable widow."

"They didn't dress like that as late as 1828." Stramer holding the lamp closer, deciphered the inscription on the border of the lady's

India scarf; *Juliana, Viscountess Thudeney, 1818.* "She must have been inconsolable before his death, then."

Lady Jane smiled. "Let's hope she grew less so after it."

Stramer passed the lamp across the canvas. "Do you see where she was painted? In the blue parlor. Look: the old paneling; and she's leaning on the citron wood desk. They evidently used the room in winter then." The lamp paused on the background of the picture: a window framing snow-laden paths and hedges in icy perspective.

"Curious," Stramer said—"and rather melancholy: to be painted against that wintry desolation. I wish you could find out more about her. Have you dipped into your archives?"

"No. Mr. Jones—"

"He won't allow that either?"

"Yes; but he's lost the key of the muniment room. Mrs. Clemm has been trying to get a locksmith."

"Surely the neighborhood can still produce one?"

"There *was* one at Thudeney-Blazes; but he died the week before I came."

"Of course!"

"Of course?"

"Well, in Mrs. Clemm's hands keys get lost, chimneys smoke, locksmiths die. . . ." Stramer stood, light in hand, looking down the shadowy length of the salon. "I say, let's go and see what's happening now in the blue parlor."

Lady Jane laughed: a laugh seemed easy with another voice near by to echo it. "Let's—"

She followed him out of the salon, across the hall in which a single candle burned on a far-off table, and past the stairway yawning like a black funnel above them. In the doorway of the blue parlor Stramer paused. "Now, then, Mr. Jones!"

It was stupid, but Lady Jane's heart gave a jerk: she hoped the challenge would not evoke the shadowy figure she had half seen that other day.

"Lord, it's cold!" Stramer stood looking about him. "Those ashes are still on the hearth. Well, it's all very queer." He crossed over to the citron wood desk. "There's where she sat for her picture—and in this very armchair—look!"

"Oh, don't!" Lady Jane exclaimed. The words slipped out unawares.

"Don't—what?"

"Try those drawers—" she wanted to reply; for his hand was stretched toward the desk.

"I'm frozen; I think I'm starting a cold. Do come away," she grumbled, backing toward the door.

Stramer lighted her out without comment. As the lamplight slid along the walls Lady Jane fancied that the needlework curtain over the farther door stirred as it had that other day. But it may have been the wind rising outside. . . .

The salon seemed like home when they got back to it.

"There *is* no Mr. Jones!"

Stramer proclaimed it triumphantly when they met the next morning. Lady Jane had motored off early to Strawbridge in quest of a mason and a locksmith. The quest had taken longer than she had expected, for everybody in Strawbridge was busy on jobs nearer by, and unaccustomed to the idea of going to Bells, with which the town seemed to have had no communication within living memory. The younger workmen did not even know where the place was, and the best Lady Jane could do was to coax a locksmith's apprentice to come with her, on the understanding that he would be driven back to the nearest station as soon as his job was over. As for the mason, he had merely taken note of her request, and promised half-heartedly to send somebody when he could. "Rather off our beat, though."

She returned, discouraged and somewhat weary, as Stramer was coming downstairs after his morning's work.

"No Mr. Jones?" she echoed.

"Not a trace! I've been trying the old Glamis experiment—situating his room by its window. Luckily the house is smaller. . . ."

Lady Jane smiled. "Is this what you call locking yourself up with your work?"

"I can't work: that's the trouble. Not till this is settled. Bells is a fidgety place."

"Yes," she agreed.

"Well, I wasn't going to be beaten; so I went to try to find the head gardener."

"But there isn't—"

"No. Mrs. Clemm told me. The head gardener died last year. That woman positively glows with life whenever she announces a death. Have you noticed?"

Yes: Lady Jane had.

"Well—I said to myself that if there wasn't a head gardener there must be an underling; at least one. I'd seen somebody in the distance, raking leaves, and I ran him down. Of course he'd never seen Mr. Jones."

"You mean that poor old half-blind Jacob? He couldn't see anybody."

"Perhaps not. At any rate, he told me that Mr. Jones wouldn't let the leaves be buried for leaf mold—I forget why. Mr. Jones's authority extends even to the gardens."

"Yet you say he doesn't exist!"

"Wait. Jacob is half blind, but he's been here for years, and knows more about the place than you'd think. I got him talking about the house, and I pointed to one window after another, and he told me each time whose the room was, or had been. But he couldn't situate Mr.— Jones."

"I beg your ladyship's pardon—" Mrs. Clemm was on the threshold, cheeks shining, skirt rustling, her eyes like drills. "The locksmith your ladyship brought back; I understand it was for the lock of the muniment room—"

"Well?"

"He's lost one of his tools, and can't do anything without it. So he's gone. The butcher's boy gave him a lift back."

Lady Jane caught Stramer's faint chuckle. She stood and stared at Mrs. Clemm, and Mrs. Clemm stared back, deferential but unflinching.

"Gone? Very well; I'll motor after him."

"Oh, my lady, it's too late. The butcher's boy had his motorcycle. . . . Besides, what could he do?"

"Break the lock," exclaimed Lady Jane, exasperated.

"Oh, my lady—" Mrs. Clemm's intonation marked the most respectful incredulity. She waited another moment, and then withdrew, while Lady Jane and Stramer considered each other.

"But this is absurd," Lady Jane declared when they had lunched, waited on, as usual, by the flustered Georgiana. "I'll break in that door myself, if I have to.—Be careful please, Georgiana," she added; "I was speaking of doors, not dishes." For Georgiana had let fall with a crash the dish she was removing from the table. She gathered up the pieces in her tremulous fingers, and vanished. Jane and Stramer returned to the salon.

"Queer!" the novelist commented.

"Yes." Lady Jane, facing the door, started slightly. Mrs. Clemm was there again; but this time subdued, unrustling, bathed in that odd pallor which enclosed but seemed unable to penetrate the solid crimson of her cheeks.

"I beg pardon, my lady. The key is found." Her hand, as she held it out, trembled like Georgiana's.

VII

"It's not here," Stramer announced, a couple of hours later.

"What isn't?" Lady Jane queried, looking up from a heap of disordered papers. Her eyes blinked at him through the fog of yellow dust raised by her manipulations.

"The clue.— I've got all the 1800 to 1840 papers here; and there's a gap."

She moved over to the table above which he was bending. "A gap?"

"A big one. Nothing between 1815 and 1835. No mention of Peregrine or of Juliana."

They looked at each other across the tossed papers, and suddenly Stramer exclaimed: "Someone has been here before us—just lately."

Lady Jane stared, incredulous, and then followed the direction of his downward pointing hand.

"Do you wear flat heelless shoes?" he questioned. "And of that size? Even my feet are too small to fit into those footprints. Luckily there wasn't time to sweep the floor!"

Lady Jane felt a slight chill, a chill of a different and more inward quality than the shock of stuffy coldness which had met them as they entered the unaired attic set apart for the storing of the Thudeney archives.

"But how absurd! Of course when Mrs. Clemm found we were coming up she came—or sent someone—to open the shutters."

"That's not Mrs. Clemm's foot, or the other woman's. She must have sent a man—an old man with a shaky uncertain step. Look how it wanders."

"Mr. Jones, then!" said Lady Jane, half impatiently.

"Mr. Jones. And he got what he wanted, and put it—where?"

"Ah, *that*—! I'm freezing, you know; let's give this up for the present." She rose, and Stramer followed her without protest; the muniment room was really untenable.

"I must catalogue all this stuff someday, I suppose," Lady Jane continued, as they went down the stairs. "But meanwhile, what do you say to a good tramp, to get the dust out of our lungs?"

He agreed, and turned back to his room to get some letters he wanted to post at Thudeney-Blazes.

Lady Jane went down alone. It was a fine afternoon, and the sun, which had made the dust clouds of the muniment room so dazzling, sent a long shaft through the west window of the blue parlor, and across the floor of the hall.

Certainly Georgiana kept the oak floors remarkably well; considering how much else she had to do, it was surp—

Lady Jane stopped as if an unseen hand had jerked her violently back. On the smooth parquet before her she had caught the trace of dusty footprints—the prints of broad-soled heelless shoes—making for the blue parlor and crossing its threshold. She stood still with the same inward shiver that she had felt upstairs; then, avoiding the footprints, she too stole very softly toward the blue parlor, pushed the door wider, and saw, in the long dazzle of autumn light, as if translucid, edged with the glitter, an old man at the desk.

"Mr. Jones!"

A step came up behind her: Mrs. Clemm with the post bag. "You called, my lady?"

"I . . . yes. . . ."

When she turned back to the desk there was no one there.

She faced about on the housekeeper. "Who was that?"

"Where, my lady?"

Lady Jane, without answering, moved toward the needlework

curtain, in which she had detected the same faint tremor as before. "Where does that door go to—behind the curtain?"

"Nowhere, my lady. I mean; there is no door."

Mrs. Clemm had followed; her step sounded quick and assured. She lifted up the curtain with a firm hand. Behind it was a rectangle of roughly plastered wall, where an opening had visibly been bricked up.

"When was that done?"

"The wall built up? I couldn't say. I've never known it otherwise," replied the housekeeper.

The two women stood for an instant measuring each other with level eyes; then the housekeeper's were slowly lowered, and she let the curtain fall from her hand. "There are a great many things in old houses that nobody knows about," she said.

"There shall be as few as possible in mine," said Lady Jane.

"My lady!" The housekeeper stepped quickly in front of her. "My lady, what are you doing?" she gasped.

Lady Jane had turned back to the desk at which she had just seen —or fancied she had seen—the bending figure of Mr. Jones.

"I am going to look through these drawers," she said.

The housekeeper still stood in pale immobility between her and the desk. "No, my lady—no. You won't do that."

"Because—?"

Mrs. Clemm crumpled up her black silk apron with a despairing gesture. "Because—if you *will* have it—that's where Mr. Jones keeps his private papers. I know he'd oughtn't to. . . ."

"Ah—then it was Mr. Jones I saw here?"

The housekeeper's arms sank to her sides and her mouth hung open on an unspoken word. "You *saw* him?" The question came out in a confused whisper; and before Lady Jane could answer, Mrs. Clemm's arms rose again, stretched before her face as if to fend off a blaze of intolerable light, or some forbidden sight she had long since disciplined herself not to see. Thus screening her eyes she hurried across the hall to the door of the servants' wing.

Lady Jane stood for a moment looking after her; then, with a slightly shaking hand, she opened the desk and hurriedly took out from it all the papers—a small bundle—that it contained. With them she passed back into the salon.

As she entered it her eye was caught by the portrait of the melancholy lady in the short-waisted gown whom she and Stramer had christened "Also His Wife." The lady's eyes, usually so empty of all awareness save of her own frozen beauty, seemed suddenly waking to an anguished participation in the scene.

"Fudge!" muttered Lady Jane, shaking off the spectral suggestion as she turned to meet Stramer on the threshold.

VIII

The missing papers were all there. Stramer and she spread them out hurriedly on a table and at once proceeded to gloat over their find. Not a particularly important one, indeed; in the long history of the Lynkes and Crofts it took up hardly more space than the little handful of documents did, in actual bulk, among the stacks of the muniment room. But the fact that these papers filled a gap in the chronicles of the house, and situated the sad-faced beauty as veritably the wife of the Peregrine Vincent Theobald Lynke who had "perished of the plague at Aleppo in 1828"—this was a discovery sufficiently exciting to whet amateur appetites, and to put out of Lady Jane's mind the strange incident which had attended the opening of the cabinet.

For a while she and Stramer sat silently and methodically going through their respective piles of correspondence; but presently Lady Jane, after glancing over one of the yellowing pages, uttered a startled exclamation.

"How strange! Mr. Jones again—always Mr. Jones!"

Stramer looked up from the papers he was sorting. "You too? I've got a lot of letters here addressed to a Mr. Jones by Peregrine Vincent, who seems to have been always disporting himself abroad, and chronically in want of money. Gambling debts, apparently . . . ah and women . . . a dirty record altogether. . . ."

"Yes? My letter is not written to a Mr. Jones; but it's about one. Listen." Lady Jane began to read. " 'Bells, February 20th, 1826. . . .' (It's from poor 'Also His Wife' to her husband.) 'My dear Lord, Acknowledging as I ever do the burden of the sad impediment which denies me the happiness of being more frequently in your company, I yet fail to conceive how anything in my state obliges that close seclusion in

which Mr. Jones persists—and by your express orders, so he declares
—in confining me. Surely, my lord, had you found it possible to spend
more time with me since the day of our marriage, you would yourself
have seen it to be unnecessary to put this restraint upon me. It is true,
alas, that my unhappy infirmity denies me the happiness to speak with
you, or to hear the accents of the voice I should love above all others
could it but reach me; but, my dear husband, I would have you consider that my mind is in no way affected by this obstacle, but goes out
to you, as my heart does, in a perpetual eagerness of attention, and that
to sit in this great house alone, day after day, month after month,
deprived of your company, and debarred also from any intercourse but
that of the servants you have chosen to put about me, is a fate more
cruel than I deserve and more painful than I can bear. I have entreated
Mr. Jones, since he seems all-powerful with you, to represent this to
you, and to transmit this my last request—for should I fail I am resolved to make no other—that you should consent to my making the
acquaintance of a few of your friends and neighbors, among whom I
cannot but think there must be some kind hearts that would take pity
on my unhappy situation, and afford me such companionship as would
give me more courage to bear your continual absence. . . .'"

Lady Jane folded up the letter. "Deaf and dumb—ah, poor creature! That explains the look—"

"And this explains the marriage," Stramer continued, unfolding
a stiff parchment document. "Here are the Viscountess Thudeney's
marriage settlements. She appears to have been a Miss Portallo, daughter of Obadiah Portallo Esqre, of Purflew Castle, Caermarthenshire,
and Bombay House, Twickenham, East India merchant, senior member of the banking house of Portallo and Prest—and so on and so on.
And the figures run up into hundreds of thousands."

"It's rather ghastly—putting the two things together. All the
millions and—imprisonment in the blue parlor. I suppose her Viscount had to have the money, and was ashamed to have it known
how he had got it. . . ." Lady Jane shivered. "Think of it—day after
day, winter after winter, year after year . . . speechless, soundless,
alone . . . under Mr. Jones's guardianship. Let me see: what year
were they married?"

"In 1817."

"And only a year later that portrait was painted. And she had the frozen look already."

Stramer mused: "Yes, it's grim enough. But the strangest figure in the whole case is still—Mr. Jones."

"Mr. Jones—yes. Her keeper," Lady Jane mused. "I suppose he must have been this one's ancestor. The office seems to have been hereditary at Bells."

"Well—I don't know."

Stramer's voice was so odd that Lady Jane looked up at him with a stare of surprise. "What if it were the same one?" suggested Stramer with a queer smile.

"The same?" Lady Jane laughed. "You're not good at figures are you? If poor Lady Thudeney's Mr. Jones were alive now he'd be—"

"I didn't say ours was alive now," said Stramer.

"Oh—why, what . . . ?" she faltered.

But Stramer did not answer; his eyes had been arrested by the precipitate opening of the door behind his hostess, and the entry of Georgiana, a livid, dishevelled Georgiana, more than usually bereft of her faculties, and gasping out something inarticulate.

"Oh, my lady—it's my aunt—she won't answer me," Georgiana stammered in a voice of terror.

Lady Jane uttered an impatient exclamation. "Answer you? Why —what do you want her to answer?"

"Only whether she's alive, my lady," said Georgiana with streaming eyes.

Lady Jane continued to look at her severely. "Alive? Alive? Why on earth shouldn't she be?"

"She might as well be dead—by the way she just lies there."

"Your aunt dead? I saw her alive enough in the blue parlor half an hour ago," Lady Jane returned. She was growing rather blasé with regard to Georgiana's panics; but suddenly she felt this to be of a different nature from any of the others. "Where is it your aunt's lying?"

"In her own bedroom, on her bed," the other wailed, "and won't say why."

Lady Jane got to her feet, pushing aside the heaped-up papers, and hastening to the door with Stramer in her wake.

As they went up the stairs she realized that she had seen the housekeeper's bedroom only once, on the day of her first obligatory round of inspection, when she had taken possession of Bells. She did not even remember very clearly where it was, but followed Georgiana down the passage and through a door which communicated, rather surprisingly, with a narrow walled-in staircase that was unfamiliar to her. At its top she and Stramer found themselves on a small landing upon which two doors opened. Through the confusion of her mind Lady Jane noticed that these rooms, with their special staircase leading down to what had always been called his lordship's suite, must obviously have been occupied by his lordship's confidential servants. In one of them, presumably, had been lodged the original Mr. Jones, the Mr. Jones of the yellow letters, the letters purloined by Lady Jane. As she crossed the threshold, Lady Jane remembered the housekeeper's attempt to prevent her touching the contents of the desk.

Mrs. Clemm's room, like herself, was neat, glossy and extremely cold. Only Mrs. Clemm herself was no longer like Mrs. Clemm. The red-apple glaze had barely faded from her cheeks, and not a lock was disarranged in the unnatural luster of her false front; even her cap ribbons hung symmetrically along either cheek. But death had happened to her, and had made her into someone else. At first glance it was impossible to say if the unspeakable horror in her wide open eyes were only the reflection of that change, or of the agent by whom it had come. Lady Jane, shuddering, paused a moment while Stramer went up to the bed.

"Her hand is warm still—but no pulse." He glanced about the room. "A glass anywhere?" The cowering Georgiana took a hand glass from the neat chest of drawers, and Stramer held it over the housekeeper's drawn-back lip. . . .

"She's dead," he pronounced.

"Oh, poor thing! But how—?" Lady Jane drew near, and was kneeling down, taking the inanimate hand in hers, when Stramer touched her on the arm, and then silently raised a finger of warning. Georgiana was crouching in the farther corner of the room, her face buried in her lifted arms.

"Look here," Stramer whispered. He pointed to Mrs. Clemm's throat, and Lady Jane, bending over, distinctly saw a circle of red marks on it—the marks of recent bruises. She looked again into the awful eyes.

"She's been strangled," Stramer whispered.

Lady Jane, with a shiver of fear, drew down the housekeeper's lids. Georgiana, her face hidden, was still sobbing convulsively in the corner. There seemed, in the air of the cold orderly room, something that forbade wonderment and silenced conjecture. Lady Jane and Stramer stood and looked at each other without speaking. At length Stramer crossed over to Georgiana, and touched her on the shoulder. She appeared unaware of the touch, and he grasped her shoulder and shook it. "Where is Mr. Jones?" he asked.

The girl looked up, her face blurred and distorted with weeping, her eyes dilated as if with the vision of some latent terror. "Oh, sir, she's not really dead, is she?"

Stramer repeated his question in a loud authoritative tone; and slowly she echoed it in a scarce-heard whisper. "Mr. Jones—?"

"Get up, my girl, and send him here to us at once, or tell us where to find him."

Georgiana, moved by the old habit of obedience, struggled to her feet and stood unsteadily, her heaving shoulders braced against the wall. Stramer asked her sharply if she had not heard what he had said.

"Oh, poor thing, she's so upset—" Lady Jane intervened compassionately. "Tell me, Georgiana: where shall we find Mr. Jones?"

The girl turned to her with eyes as fixed as the dead woman's. "You won't find him anywhere," she slowly said.

"Why not?"

"Because he's not here."

"Not here? Where is he, then?" Stramer broke in.

Georgiana did not seem to notice the interruption. She continued to stare at Lady Jane with Mrs. Clemm's awful eyes. "He's in his grave in the churchyard—these years and years he is. Long before ever I was born . . . my aunt hadn't ever seen him herself, not since she was a tiny child. . . . That's the terror of it . . . that's why she always had to do what he told her to . . . because you couldn't ever answer him back. . . ." Her horrified gaze turned from Lady Jane to the stony face and fast-glazing pupils of the dead woman. "You hadn't ought to have meddled with his papers, my lady. . . . That's what he's punished her for. . . . When it came to those papers he wouldn't ever listen to human reason . . . he wouldn't. . . ." Then, flinging her arms above her head, Georgiana straightened herself to her full height before falling in a swoon at Stramer's feet.

Pomegranate Seed*

*C*harlotte Ashby paused on her doorstep. Dark had descended on the brilliancy of the March afternoon, and the grinding, rasping street life of the city was at its highest. She turned her back on it, standing for a moment in the old-fashioned, marble-flagged vestibule before she inserted her key in the lock. The sash curtains drawn across the panes of the inner door softened the light within to a warm blur through which no details showed. It was the hour when, in the first months of her marriage to Kenneth Ashby, she had most liked to return to that quiet house in a street long since deserted by business and fashion. The contrast between the soulless roar of New York, its devouring blaze of lights, the oppression of its congested traffic, congested houses, lives, minds and this veiled sanctuary she called home, always stirred her profoundly. In the very heart of the hurricane she had found her tiny islet—or thought she had. And now, in the last months, everything was changed, and she always wavered on the doorstep and had to force herself to enter.

While she stood there she called up the scene within: the hall hung with old prints, the ladder-like stairs, and on the left her husband's long shabby library, full of books and pipes and worn armchairs inviting to meditation. How she had loved that room! Then, upstairs, her own drawing room, in which, since the death of Kenneth's first wife, neither furniture nor hangings had been changed, because there had never been money enough, but which Charlotte had made her own by moving furniture about and adding more books, another lamp, a table for the new reviews. Even on the occasion of her only visit to the first Mrs. Ashby—a distant, self-centered woman, whom she had known very slightly—she had looked about her with an innocent envy, feeling it to be exactly the drawing room she would have liked for herself; and now for more than a year it had been hers to deal with as she chose —the room to which she hastened back at dusk on winter days, where she sat reading by the fire, or answering notes at the pleasant roomy

*Persephone, daughter of Demeter, goddess of fertility, was abducted and taken to Hades by Pluto, the god of the underworld. Her mother begged Jupiter to intercede, and he did so. But Persephone had broken her vow of abstinence in Hades by eating some pomegranate seeds. She was therefore required to spend a certain number of months each year—essentially the winter months—with Pluto.

desk, or going over her stepchildren's copybooks, till she heard her husband's step.

Sometimes friends dropped in; sometimes—oftener—she was alone; and she liked that best, since it was another way of being with Kenneth, thinking over what he had said when they parted in the morning, imagining what he would say when he sprang up the stairs, found her by herself and caught her to him.

Now, instead of this, she thought of one thing only—the letter she might or might not find on the hall table. Until she had made sure whether or not it was there, her mind had no room for anything else. The letter was always the same—a square grayish envelope with "Kenneth Ashby, Esquire," written on it in bold but faint characters. From the first it had struck Charlotte as peculiar that anyone who wrote such a firm hand should trace the letters so lightly; the address was always written as though there were not enough ink in the pen, or the writer's wrist were too weak to bear upon it. Another curious thing was that, in spite of its masculine curves, the writing was so visibly feminine. Some hands are sexless, some masculine, at first glance; the writing on the gray envelope, for all its strength and assurance, was without doubt a woman's. The envelope never bore anything but the recipient's name; no stamp, no address. The letter was presumably delivered by hand—but by whose? No doubt it was slipped into the letter box, whence the parlormaid, when she closed the shutters and lit the lights, probably extracted it. At any rate, it was always in the evening, after dark, that Charlotte saw it lying there. She thought of the letter in the singular, as "it," because, though there had been several since her marriage—seven, to be exact—they were so alike in appearance that they had become merged in one another in her mind, become one letter, become "it."

The first had come the day after their return from their honeymoon—a journey prolonged to the West Indies, from which they had returned to New York after an absence of more than two months. Re-entering the house with her husband, late on that first evening—they had dined at his mother's—she had seen, alone on the hall table, the gray envelope. Her eye fell on it before Kenneth's, and her first thought was: "Why, I've seen that writing before"; but where she could not recall. The memory was just definite enough for her to identify the script whenever it looked up at her faintly from the same pale envelope; but on that first day she would have thought no more of the letter if, when her husband's glance lit on it, she had not chanced to be looking at him. It all happened in a flash—his seeing the letter, putting out his hand for it, raising it to his shortsighted eyes to decipher the faint writing, and then abruptly withdrawing the arm he had slipped through Charlotte's, and moving away to the hanging light, his back turned to her. She had waited—waited for a sound, an exclamation; waited for him to open the letter; but he had slipped it into his pocket without a word and followed her into the library. And there they had sat down by the fire and lit their cigarettes, and he had remained silent, his head thrown back broodingly against the armchair, his eyes fixed on the hearth, and presently had passed his hand over his forehead and said: "Wasn't it unusually hot at my mother's tonight? I've got a splitting head. Mind if I take myself off to bed?"

That was the first time. Since then Charlotte had never been present when he had received the letter. It usually came before he got home from his office, and she had to go upstairs and leave it lying there. But even if she had not seen it, she would have known it had come by the change in his face when he joined her—which, on those evenings, he seldom did before they met for dinner. Evidently, whatever the letter contained, he wanted to be by himself to deal with it; and when he reappeared he looked years older, looked emptied of life and courage, and hardly conscious of her presence. Sometimes he was silent for the rest of the evening; and if he spoke, it was usually to hint some criticism of her household arrangements, suggest some change in the domestic administration, to ask, a little nervously, if she didn't think Joyce's nursery governess was rather young and flighty, or if she herself always saw to it that Peter—whose throat was delicate—was properly wrapped up when he went to school. At such times Charlotte would remember the friendly warnings she had received when she became engaged to Kenneth Ashby: "Marrying a heartbroken widower! Isn't that rather risky? You know Elsie Ashby absolutely dominated him"; and how she had jokingly replied: "He may be glad of a little liberty for a change." And in this respect she had been right. She had needed no one to tell her, during the first months, that her husband was perfectly happy with her. When they came back from their protracted honeymoon the same friends said: "What have you done to

Kenneth? He looks twenty years younger"; and this time she answered with careless joy: "I suppose I've got him out of his groove."

But what she noticed after the gray letters began to come was not so much his nervous tentative faultfinding—which always seemed to be uttered against his will—as the look in his eyes when he joined her after receiving one of the letters. The look was not unloving, not even indifferent; it was the look of a man who had been so far away from ordinary events that when he returns to familiar things they seem strange. She minded that more than the faultfinding.

Though she had been sure from the first that the handwriting on the gray envelope was a woman's, it was long before she associated the mysterious letters with any sentimental secret. She was too sure of her husband's love, too confident of filling his life, for such an idea to occur to her. It seemed far more likely that the letters—which certainly did not appear to cause him any sentimental pleasure—were addressed to the busy lawyer than to the private person. Probably they were from some tiresome client—women, he had often told her, were nearly always tiresome as clients—who did not want her letters opened by his secretary and therefore had them carried to his house. Yes; but in that case the unknown female must be unusually troublesome, judging from the effect her letters produced. Then again, though his professional discretion was exemplary, it was odd that he had never uttered an impatient comment, never remarked to Charlotte, in a moment of expansion, that there was a nuisance of a woman who kept badgering him about a case that had gone against her. He had made more than one semiconfidence of the kind—of course without giving names or details; but concerning this mysterious correspondent his lips were sealed.

There was another possibility: what is euphemistically called an "old entanglement." Charlotte Ashby was a sophisticated woman. She had few illusions about the intricacies of the human heart; she knew that there were often old entanglements. But when she had married Kenneth Ashby, her friends, instead of hinting at such a possibility, had said: "You've got your work cut out for you. Marrying a Don Juan is a sinecure to it. Kenneth's never looked at another woman since he first saw Elsie Corder. During all the years of their marriage he was more like an unhappy lover than a comfortably contented husband.

He'll never let you move an armchair or change the place of a lamp; and whatever you venture to do, he'll mentally compare with what Elsie would have done in your place."

Except for an occasional nervous mistrust as to her ability to manage the children—a mistrust gradually dispelled by her good humor and the children's obvious fondness for her—none of these forebodings had come true. The desolate widower, of whom his nearest friends said that only his absorbing professional interests had kept him from suicide after his first wife's death, had fallen in love, two years later, with Charlotte Gorse, and after an impetuous wooing had married her and carried her off on a tropical honeymoon. And ever since he had been as tender and lover-like as during those first radiant weeks. Before asking her to marry him he had spoken to her frankly of his great love for his first wife and his despair after her sudden death; but even then he had assumed no stricken attitude, or implied that life offered no possibility of renewal. He had been perfectly simple and natural, and had confessed to Charlotte that from the beginning he had hoped the future held new gifts for him. And when, after their marriage, they returned to the house where his twelve years with his first wife had been spent, he had told Charlotte at once that he was sorry he couldn't afford to do the place over for her, but that he knew every woman had her own views about furniture and all sorts of household arrangements a man would never notice, and had begged her to make any changes she saw fit without bothering to consult him. As a result, she made as few as possible; but his way of beginning their new life in the old setting was so frank and unembarrassed that it put her immediately at her ease, and she was almost sorry to find that the portrait of Elsie Ashby, which used to hang over the desk in his library, had been transferred in their absence to the children's nursery. Knowing herself to be the indirect cause of this banishment, she spoke of it to her husband; but he answered: "Oh, I thought they ought to grow up with her looking down on them." The answer moved Charlotte, and satisfied her; and as time went by she had to confess that she felt more at home in her house, more at ease and in confidence with her husband, since that long coldly beautiful face on the library wall no longer followed her with guarded eyes. It was as if Kenneth's love had penetrated to the secret she hardly acknowledged to her own heart —her passionate need to feel herself the sovereign even of his past.

With all this stored-up happiness to sustain her, it was curious that she had lately found herself yielding to a nervous apprehension. But there the apprehension was; and on this particular afternoon—perhaps because she was more tired than usual, or because of the trouble of finding a new cook or, for some other ridiculously trivial reason, moral or physical—she found herself unable to react against the feeling. Latchkey in hand, she looked back down the silent street to the whirl and illumination of the great thoroughfare beyond, and up at the sky already aflare with the city's nocturnal life. "Outside there," she thought, "skyscrapers, advertisements, telephones, wireless, airplanes, movies, motors, and all the rest of the twentieth century; and on the other side of the door something I can't explain, can't relate to them. Something as old as the world, as mysterious as life. . . . Nonsense! What am I worrying about? There hasn't been a letter for three months now—not since the day we came back from the country after Christmas. . . . Queer that they always seem to come after our holidays! . . . Why should I imagine there's going to be one tonight!"

No reason why, but that was the worst of it—one of the worst! —that there were days when she would stand there cold and shivering with the premonition of something inexplicable, intolerable, to be faced on the other side of the curtained panes; and when she opened the door and went in, there would be nothing; and on other days when she felt the same premonitory chill, it was justified by the sight of the gray envelope. So that ever since the last had come she had taken to feeling cold and premonitory every evening, because she never opened the door without thinking the letter might be there.

Well, she'd had enough of it: that was certain. She couldn't go on like that. If her husband turned white and had a headache on the days when the letter came, he seemed to recover afterward; but she couldn't. With her the strain had become chronic, and the reason was not far to seek. Her husband knew from whom the letter came and what was in it; he was prepared beforehand for whatever he had to deal with, and master of the situation, however bad; whereas she was shut out in the dark with her conjectures.

"I can't stand it! I can't stand it another day!" she exclaimed aloud, as she put her key in the lock. She turned the key and went in; and there, on the table, lay the letter.

II

She was almost glad of the sight. It seemed to justify everything, to put a seal of definiteness on the whole blurred business. A letter for her husband; a letter from a woman—no doubt another vulgar case of "old entanglement." What a fool she had been ever to doubt it, to rack her brains for less obvious explanations! She took up the envelope with a steady contemptuous hand, looked closely at the faint letters, held it against the light and just discerned the outline of the folded sheet within. She knew that now she would have no peace till she found out what was written on that sheet.

Her husband had not come in; he seldom got back from his office before half-past six or seven, and it was not yet six. She would have time to take the letter up to the drawing room, hold it over the tea kettle which at that hour always simmered by the fire in expectation of her return, solve the mystery and replace the letter where she had found it. No one would be the wiser, and her gnawing uncertainty would be over. The alternative, of course, was to question her husband; but to do that seemed even more difficult. She weighed the letter between thumb and finger, looked at it again under the light, started up the stairs with the envelope—and came down again and laid it on the table.

"No, I evidently can't," she said, disappointed.

What should she do, then? She couldn't go up alone to that warm welcoming room, pour out her tea, look over her correspondence, glance at a book or review—not with that letter lying below and the knowledge that in a little while her husband would come in, open it and turn into the library alone, as he always did on the days when the gray envelope came.

Suddenly she decided. She would wait in the library and see for herself; see what happened between him and the letter when they thought themselves unobserved. She wondered the idea had never occurred to her before. By leaving the door ajar, and sitting in the corner behind it, she could watch him unseen. . . . Well, then, she would watch him! She drew a chair into the corner, sat down, her eyes on the crack, and waited.

As far as she could remember, it was the first time she had ever

tried to surprise another person's secret, but she was conscious of no compunction. She simply felt as if she were fighting her way through a stifling fog that she must at all costs get out of.

At length she heard Kenneth's latchkey and jumped up. The impulse to rush out and meet him had nearly made her forget why she was there; but she remembered in time and sat down again. From her post she covered the whole range of his movements—saw him enter the hall, draw the key from the door and take off his hat and overcoat. Then he turned to throw his gloves on the hall table, and at that moment he saw the envelope. The light was full on his face, and what Charlotte first noted there was a look of surprise. Evidently he had not expected the letter—had not thought of the possibility of its being there that day. But though he had not expected it, now that he saw it he knew well enough what it contained. He did not open it immediately, but stood motionless, the color slowly ebbing from his face. Apparently he could not make up his mind to touch it; but at length he put out his hand, opened the envelope, and moved with it to the light. In doing so he turned his back on Charlotte, and she saw only his bent head and slightly stooping shoulders. Apparently all the writing was on one page, for he did not turn the sheet but continued to stare at it for so long that he must have reread it a dozen times—or so it seemed to the woman breathlessly watching him. At length she saw him move; he raised the letter still closer to his eyes, as though he had not fully deciphered it. Then he lowered his head, and she saw his lips touch the sheet.

"Kenneth!" she exclaimed, and went on out into the hall.

The letter clutched in his hand, her husband turned and looked at her. "Where were you?" he said, in a low bewildered voice, like a man waked out of his sleep.

"In the library, waiting for you." She tried to steady her voice: "What's the matter! What's in that letter? You look ghastly."

Her agitation seemed to calm him, and he instantly put the envelope into his pocket with a slight laugh. "Ghastly? I'm sorry. I've had a hard day in the office—one or two complicated cases. I look dog-tired, I suppose."

"You didn't look tired when you came in. It was only when you opened that letter—"

He had followed her into the library, and they stood gazing at each other. Charlotte noticed how quickly he had regained his self-control; his profession had trained him to rapid mastery of face and voice. She saw at once that she would be at a disadvantage in any attempt to surprise his secret, but at the same moment she lost all desire to maneuver, to trick him into betraying anything he wanted to conceal. Her wish was still to penetrate the mystery, but only that she might help him to bear the burden it implied. "Even if it *is* another woman," she thought.

"Kenneth," she said, her heart beating excitedly, "I waited here on purpose to see you come in. I wanted to watch you while you opened that letter."

His face, which had paled, turned to dark red; then it paled again. "That letter? Why especially that letter?"

"Because I've noticed that whenever one of those letters comes it seems to have such a strange effect on you."

A line of anger she had never seen before came out between his eyes, and she said to herself: "The upper part of his face is too narrow; this is the first time I ever noticed it."

She heard him continue, in the cool and faintly ironic tone of the prosecuting lawyer making a point: "Ah, so you're in the habit of watching people open their letters when they don't know you're there?"

"Not in the habit. I never did such a thing before. But I had to find out what she writes to you, at regular intervals, in those gray envelopes."

He weighed this for a moment; then: "The intervals have not been regular," he said.

"Oh, I dare say you've kept a better account of the dates than I have," she retorted, her magnanimity vanishing at his tone. "All I know is that every time that woman writes to you—"

"Why do you assume it's a woman?"

"It's a woman's writing. Do you deny it?"

He smiled. "No, I don't deny it. I asked only because the writing is generally supposed to look more like a man's."

Charlotte passed this over impatiently. "And this woman—what does she write to you about?"

Again he seemed to consider a moment. "About business."

"Legal business?"

"In a way, yes. Business in general."

"You look after her affairs for her?"

"Yes."

"You've looked after them for a long time?"

"Yes. A very long time."

"Kenneth, dearest, won't you tell me who she is?"

"No. I can't." He paused, and brought out, as if with a certain hesitation: "Professional secrecy."

The blood rushed from Charlotte's heart to her temples. "Don't say that—don't!"

"Why not?"

"Because I saw you kiss the letter."

The effect of the words was so disconcerting that she instantly repented having spoken them. Her husband, who had submitted to her cross-questioning with a sort of contemptuous composure, as though he were humoring an unreasonable child, turned on her a face of terror and distress. For a minute he seemed unable to speak; then, collecting himself, with an effort, he stammered out: "The writing is very faint; you must have seen me holding the letter close to my eyes to try to decipher it."

"No; I saw you kissing it." He was silent. "Didn't I see you kissing it?"

He sank back into indifference. "Perhaps."

"Kenneth! You stand there and say that—to me?"

"What possible difference can it make to you? The letter is on business, as I told you. Do you suppose I'd lie about it? The writer is a very old friend whom I haven't seen for a long time."

"Men don't kiss business letters, even from women who are very old friends, unless they have been their lovers, and still regret them."

He shrugged his shoulders slightly and turned away, as if he considered the discussion at an end and were faintly disgusted at the turn it had taken.

"Kenneth!" Charlotte moved toward him and caught hold of his arm.

He paused with a look of weariness and laid his hand over hers. "Won't you believe me?" he asked gently.

"How can I? I've watched these letters come to you—for months now they've been coming. Ever since we came back from the West

Indies—one of them greeted me the very day we arrived. And after each one of them I see their mysterious effect on you, I see you disturbed, unhappy, as if someone were trying to estrange you from me."

"No, dear; not that. Never!"

She drew back and looked at him with passionate entreaty. "Well, then, prove it to me, darling. It's so easy!"

He forced a smile. "It's not easy to prove anything to a woman who's once taken an idea into her head."

"You've only got to show me the letter."

His hand slipped from hers and he drew back and shook his head. "You won't?"

"I can't."

"Then the woman who wrote it is your mistress."

"No, dear. No."

"Not now, perhaps. I suppose she's trying to get you back, and you're struggling, out of pity for me. My poor Kenneth!"

"I swear to you she never was my mistress."

Charlotte felt the tears rushing to her eyes. "Ah, that's worse, then —that's hopeless! The prudent ones are the kind that keep their hold on a man. We all know that." She lifted her hands and hid her face in them.

Her husband remained silent; he offered neither consolation nor denial, and at length, wiping away her tears, she raised her eyes almost timidly to his.

"Kenneth, think! We've been married such a short time. Imagine what you're making me suffer. You say you can't show me this letter. You refuse even to explain it."

"I've told you the letter is on business. I will swear to that too."

"A man will swear to anything to screen a woman. If you want me to believe you, at least tell me her name. If you'll do that, I promise you I won't ask to see the letter."

There was a long interval of suspense, during which she felt her heart beating against her ribs in quick admonitory knocks, as if warning her of the danger she was incurring.

"I can't," he said at length.

"Not even her name?"

"No."

"You can't tell me anything more?"

"No."

Again a pause; this time they seemed both to have reached the end of their arguments and to be helplessly facing each other across a baffling waste of incomprehension.

Charlotte stood breathing rapidly, her hands against her breast. She felt as if she had run a hard race and missed the goal. She had meant to move her husband and had succeeded only in irritating him; and this error of reckoning seemed to change him into a stranger, a mysterious incomprehensible being whom no argument or entreaty of hers could reach. The curious thing was that she was aware in him of no hostility or even impatience, but only of a remoteness, an inaccessibility, far more difficult to overcome. She felt herself excluded, ignored, blotted out of his life. But after a moment or two, looking at him more calmly, she saw that he was suffering as much as she was. His distant guarded face was drawn with pain; the coming of the gray envelope, though it always cast a shadow, had never marked him as deeply as this discussion with his wife.

Charlotte took heart; perhaps, after all, she had not spent her last shaft. She drew nearer and once more laid her hand on his arm. "Poor Kenneth! If you knew how sorry I am for you—"

She thought he winced slightly at this expression of sympathy, but he took her hand and pressed it.

"I can think of nothing worse than to be incapable of loving long," she continued, "to feel the beauty of a great love and to be too unstable to bear its burden."

He turned on her a look of wistful reproach. "Oh, don't say that of me. Unstable!"

She felt herself at last on the right tack, and her voice trembled with excitement as she went on: "Then what about me and this other woman? Haven't you already forgotten Elsie twice within a year?"

She seldom pronounced his first wife's name; it did not come naturally to her tongue. She flung it out now as if she were flinging some dangerous explosive into the open space between them, and drew back a step, waiting to hear the mine go off.

Her husband did not move; his expression grew sadder, but showed no resentment. "I have never forgotten Elsie," he said.

Charlotte could not repress a faint laugh. "Then, you poor dear, between the three of us—"

"There are not—" he began; and then broke off and put his hand to his forehead.

"Not what?"

"I'm sorry; I don't believe I know what I'm saying. I've got a blinding headache." He looked wan and furrowed enough for the statement to be true, but she was exasperated by his evasion.

"Ah, yes; the gray envelope headache!"

She saw the surprise in his eyes. "I'd forgotten how closely I've been watched," he said coldly. "If you'll excuse me, I think I'll go up and try an hour in the dark, to see if I can get rid of this neuralgia."

She wavered; then she said, with desperate resolution: "I'm sorry your head aches. But before you go I want to say that sooner or later this question must be settled between us. Someone is trying to separate us, and I don't care what it costs me to find out who it is." She looked him steadily in the eyes. "If it costs me your love, I don't care! If I can't have your confidence I don't want anything from you."

He still looked at her wistfully. "Give me time."

"Time for what? It's only a word to say."

"Time to show you that you haven't lost my love or my confidence."

"Well, I'm waiting."

He turned toward the door, and then glanced back hesitatingly. "Oh, do wait, my love," he said, and went out of the room.

She heard his tired step on the stairs and the closing of his bedroom door above. Then she dropped into a chair and buried her face in her folded arms. Her first movement was one of compunction; she seemed to herself to have been hard, unhuman, unimaginative. "Think of telling him that I didn't care if my insistence cost me his love! The lying rubbish!" She started up to follow him and unsay the meaningless words. But she was checked by a reflection. He had had his way, after all; he had eluded all attacks on his secret, and now he was shut up alone in his room, reading that other woman's letter.

III

She was still reflecting on this when the surprised parlormaid came in and found her. No, Charlotte said, she wasn't going to dress for dinner;

Mr. Ashby didn't want to dine. He was very tired and had gone up to his room to rest; later she would have something brought on a tray to the drawing room. She mounted the stairs to her bedroom. Her dinner dress was lying on the bed, and at the sight the quiet routine of her daily life took hold of her and she began to feel as if the strange talk she had just had with her husband must have taken place in another world, between two beings who were not Charlotte Gorse and Kenneth Ashby, but phantoms projected by her fevered imagination. She recalled the year since her marriage—her husband's constant devotion; his persistent, almost too insistent tenderness; the feeling he had given her at times of being too eagerly dependent on her, too searchingly close to her, as if there were not air enough between her soul and his. It seemed preposterous, as she recalled all this, that a few moments ago she should have been accusing him of an intrigue with another woman! But, then, what—

Again she was moved by the impulse to go up to him, beg his pardon and try to laugh away the misunderstanding. But she was restrained by the fear of forcing herself upon his privacy. He was troubled and unhappy, oppressed by some grief or fear; and he had shown her that he wanted to fight out his battle alone. It would be wiser, as well as more generous, to respect his wish. Only, how strange, how unbearable, to be there, in the next room to his, and feel herself at the other end of the world! In her nervous agitation she almost regretted not having had the courage to open the letter and put it back on the hall table before he came in. At least she would have known what his secret was, and the bogy might have been laid. For she was beginning now to think of the mystery as something conscious, malevolent: a secret persecution before which he quailed, yet from which he could not free himself. Once or twice in his evasive eyes she thought she had detected a desire for help, an impulse of confession, instantly restrained and suppressed. It was as if he felt she could have helped him if she had known, and yet had been unable to tell her!

There flashed through her mind the idea of going to his mother. She was very fond of old Mrs. Ashby, a firm-fleshed clear-eyed old lady, with an astringent bluntness of speech which responded to the forthright and simple in Charlotte's own nature. There had been a tacit bond between them ever since the day when Mrs. Ashby Senior, coming to lunch for the first time with her new daughter-in-law, had been received by Charlotte downstairs in the library, and glancing up at the empty wall above her son's desk, had remarked laconically: "Elsie gone, eh?" adding, at Charlotte's murmured explanation: "Nonsense. Don't have her back. Two's company." Charlotte, at this reading of her thoughts, could hardly refrain from exchanging a smile of complicity with her mother-in-law; and it seemed to her now that Mrs. Ashby's almost uncanny directness might pierce to the core of this new mystery. But here again she hesitated, for the idea almost suggested a betrayal. What right had she to call in anyone, even so close a relation, to surprise a secret which her husband was trying to keep from her? "Perhaps, by and by, he'll talk to his mother of his own accord," she thought, and then ended: "But what does it matter? He and I must settle it between us."

She was still brooding over the problem when there was a knock on the door and her husband came in. He was dressed for dinner and seemed surprised to see her sitting there, with her evening dress lying unheeded on the bed.

"Aren't you coming down?"

"I thought you were not well and had gone to bed," she faltered.

He forced a smile. "I'm not particularly well, but we'd better go down." His face, though still drawn, looked calmer than when he had fled upstairs an hour earlier.

"There it is; he knows what's in the letter and has fought his battle out again, whatever it is," she reflected, "while I'm still in darkness." She rang and gave a hurried order that dinner should be served as soon as possible—just a short meal, whatever could be got ready quickly, as both she and Mr. Ashby were rather tired and not very hungry.

Dinner was announced, and they sat down to it. At first neither seemed able to find a word to say; then Ashby began to make conversation with an assumption of ease that was more oppressive than his silence. "How tired he is! How terribly overtired!" Charlotte said to herself, pursuing her own thoughts while he rambled on about municipal politics, aviation, an exhibition of modern French painting, the health of an old aunt and the installing of the automatic telephone. "Good heavens, how tired he is!"

When they dined alone they usually went into the library after dinner, and Charlotte curled herself up on the divan with her knitting while he settled down in his armchair under the lamp and lit a pipe.

But this evening, by tacit agreement, they avoided the room in which their strange talk had taken place, and went up to Charlotte's drawing room.

They sat down near the fire, and Charlotte said: "Your pipe?" after he had put down his hardly tasted coffee.

He shook his head. "No, not tonight."

"You must go to bed early; you look terribly tired. I'm sure they overwork you at the office."

"I suppose we all overwork at times."

She rose and stood before him with sudden resolution. "Well, I'm not going to have you use up your strength slaving in that way. It's absurd. I can see you're ill." She bent over him and laid her hand on his forehead. "My poor old Kenneth. Prepare to be taken away soon on a long holiday."

He looked up at her, startled. "A holiday?"

"Certainly. Didn't you know I was going to carry you off at Easter? We're going to start in a fortnight on a month's voyage to somewhere or other. On any one of the big cruising steamers." She paused and bent closer, touching his forehead with her lips. "I'm tired, too, Kenneth."

He seemed to pay no heed to her last words, but sat, his hands on his knees, his head drawn back a little from her caress, and looked up at her with a stare of apprehension. "Again? My dear, we can't; I can't possibly go away."

"I don't know why you say 'again,' Kenneth; we haven't taken a real holiday this year."

"At Christmas we spent a week with the children in the country."

"Yes, but this time I mean away from the children, from servants, from the house. From everything that's familiar and fatiguing. Your mother will love to have Joyce and Peter with her."

He frowned and slowly shook his head. "No, dear; I can't leave them with my mother."

"Why, Kenneth, how absurd! She adores them. You didn't hesitate to leave them with her for over two months when we went to the West Indies."

He drew a deep breath and stood up uneasily. "That was different."

"Different? Why?"

"I mean, at that time I didn't realize—" He broke off as if to choose his words and then went on: "My mother adores the children, as you say. But she isn't always very judicious. Grandmothers always spoil children. And sometimes she talks before them without thinking." He turned to his wife with an almost pitiful gesture of entreaty. "Don't ask me to, dear."

Charlotte mused. It was true that the elder Mrs. Ashby had a fearless tongue, but she was the last woman in the world to say or hint anything before her grandchildren at which the most scrupulous parent could take offense. Charlotte looked at her husband in perplexity.

"I don't understand."

He continued to turn on her the same troubled and entreating gaze. "Don't try to," he muttered.

"Not try to?"

"Not now—not yet." He put up his hands and pressed them against his temples. "Can't you see that there's no use in insisting? I can't go away, no matter how much I might want to."

Charlotte still scrutinized him gravely. "The question is, *do* you want to?"

He returned her gaze for a moment; then his lips began to tremble, and he said, hardly above his breath: "I want—anything you want."

"And yet—"

"Don't ask me. I can't leave—I can't!"

"You mean that you can't go away out of reach of those letters!"

Her husband had been standing before her in an uneasy half-hesitating attitude; now he turned abruptly away and walked once or twice up and down the length of the room, his head bent, his eyes fixed on the carpet.

Charlotte felt her resentfulness rising with her fears. "It's that," she persisted. "Why not admit it? You can't live without them."

He continued his troubled pacing of the room; then he stopped short, dropped into a chair and covered his face with his hands. From the shaking of his shoulders, Charlotte saw that he was weeping. She had never seen a man cry, except her father after her mother's death, when she was a little girl; and she remembered still how the sight had frightened her. She was frightened now; she felt that her husband was being dragged away from her into some mysterious bondage, and that she must use up her last atom of strength in the struggle for his freedom, and for hers.

"Kenneth—Kenneth!" she pleaded, kneeling down beside him. "Won't you listen to me? Won't you try to see what I'm suffering? I'm not unreasonable, darling, really not. I don't suppose I should ever have noticed the letters if it hadn't been for their effect on you. It's not my way to pry into other people's affairs; and even if the effect had been different—yes, yes, listen to me—if I'd seen that the letters made you happy, that you were watching eagerly for them, counting the days between their coming, that you wanted them, that they gave you something I haven't known how to give—why, Kenneth, I don't say I shouldn't have suffered from that, too; but it would have been in a different way, and I should have had the courage to hide what I felt, and the hope that someday you'd come to feel about me as you did about the writer of the letters. But what I can't bear is to see how you dread them, how they make you suffer, and yet how you can't live without them and won't go away lest you should miss one during your absence. Or perhaps," she added, her voice breaking into a cry of accusation—"perhaps it's because she's actually forbidden you to leave. Kenneth, you must answer me! Is that the reason? Is it because she's forbidden you that you won't go away with me?"

She continued to kneel at his side, and raising her hands, she drew his gently down. She was ashamed of her persistence, ashamed of uncovering that baffled disordered face, yet resolved that no such scruples should arrest her. His eyes were lowered, the muscles of his face quivered; she was making him suffer even more than she suffered herself. Yet this no longer restrained her.

"Kenneth, is it that? She won't let us go away together?"

Still he did not speak or turn his eyes to her; and a sense of defeat swept over her. After all, she thought, the struggle was a losing one. "You needn't answer. I see I'm right," she said.

Suddenly, as she rose, he turned and drew her down again. His hands caught hers and pressed them so tightly that she felt her rings cutting into her flesh. There was something frightened, convulsive in his hold; it was the clutch of a man who felt himself slipping over a precipice. He was staring up at her now as if salvation lay in the face she bent above him. "Of course we'll go away together. We'll go wherever you want," he said in a low confused voice; and putting his arm about her, he drew her close and pressed his lips on hers.

IV

Charlotte had said to herself: "I shall sleep tonight," but instead she sat before her fire into the small hours, listening for any sound that came from her husband's room. But he, at any rate, seemed to be resting after the tumult of the evening. Once or twice she stole to the door and in the faint light that came in from the street through his open window she saw him stretched out in heavy sleep—the sleep of weakness and exhaustion. "He's ill," she thought—"he's undoubtedly ill. And it's not overwork; it's this mysterious persecution."

She drew a breath of relief. She had fought through the weary fight and the victory was hers—at least for the moment. If only they could have started at once—started for anywhere! She knew it would be useless to ask him to leave before the holidays; and meanwhile the secret influence—as to which she was still so completely in the dark —would continue to work against her, and she would have to renew the struggle day after day till they started on their journey. But after that everything would be different. If once she could get her husband away under other skies, and all to herself, she never doubted her power to release him from the evil spell he was under. Lulled to quiet by the thought, she too slept at last.

When she woke, it was long past her usual hour, and she sat up in bed surprised and vexed at having overslept herself. She always liked to be down to share her husband's breakfast by the library fire; but a glance at the clock made it clear that he must have started long since for his office. To make sure, she jumped out of bed and went into his room, but it was empty. No doubt he had looked in on her before leaving, seen that she still slept, and gone downstairs without disturbing her; and their relations were sufficiently lover-like for her to regret having missed their morning hour.

She rang and asked if Mr. Ashby had already gone. Yes, nearly an hour ago, the maid said. He had given orders that Mrs. Ashby should not be waked and that the children should not come to her till she sent for them. . . . Yes, he had gone up to the nursery himself to give the order. All this sounded usual enough, and Charlotte hardly knew why she asked: "And did Mr. Ashby leave no other message?"

Yes, the maid said, he did; she was so sorry she'd forgotten. He'd told her, just as he was leaving, to say to Mrs. Ashby that he was going to see about their passages, and would she please be ready to sail tomorrow?

Charlotte echoed the woman's "Tomorrow," and sat staring at her incredulously. "Tomorrow—you're sure he said to sail tomorrow?"

"Oh, ever so sure, ma'am. I don't know how I could have forgotten to mention it."

"Well, it doesn't matter. Draw my bath, please." Charlotte sprang up, dashed through her dressing, and caught herself singing at her image in the glass as she sat brushing her hair. It made her feel young again to have scored such a victory. The other woman vanished to a speck on the horizon, as this one, who ruled the foreground, smiled back at the reflection of her lips and eyes. He loved her, then—he loved her as passionately as ever. He had divined what she had suffered, had understood that their happiness depended on their getting away at once, and finding each other again after yesterday's desperate groping in the fog. The nature of the influence that had come between them did not much matter to Charlotte now; she had faced the phantom and dispelled it. "Courage—that's the secret! If only people who are in love weren't always so afraid of risking their happiness by looking it in the eyes." As she brushed back her light abundant hair it waved electrically above her head, like the palms of victory. Ah, well, some women knew how to manage men, and some didn't—and only the fair—she gaily paraphrased—deserve the brave! Certainly she was looking very pretty.

The morning danced along like a cockleshell on a bright sea—such a sea as they would soon be speeding over. She ordered a particularly good dinner, saw the children off to their classes, had her trunks brought down, consulted with the maid about getting out summer clothes—for of course they would be heading for heat and sunshine—and wondered if she oughtn't to take Kenneth's flannel suits out of camphor. "But how absurd," she reflected, "that I don't yet know where we're going!" She looked at the clock, saw that it was close on noon, and decided to call him up at his office. There was a slight delay;

then she heard his secretary's voice saying that Mr. Ashby had looked in for a moment early, and left again almost immediately. . . . Oh, very well; Charlotte would ring up later. How soon was he likely to be back? The secretary answered that she couldn't tell; all they knew in the office was that when he left he had said he was in a hurry because he had to go out of town.

Out of town! Charlotte hung up the receiver and sat blankly gazing into new darkness. Why had he gone out of town? And where had he gone? And of all days, why should he have chosen the eve of their suddenly planned departure? She felt a faint shiver of apprehension. Of course he had gone to see that woman—no doubt to get her permission to leave. He was as completely in bondage as that; and Charlotte had been fatuous enough to see the palms of victory on her forehead. She burst into a laugh and, walking across the room, sat down again before her mirror. What a different face she saw! The smile on her pale lips seemed to mock the rosy vision of the other Charlotte. But gradually her color crept back. After all, she had a right to claim the victory, since her husband was doing what she wanted, not what the other woman exacted of him. It was natural enough, in view of his abrupt decision to leave the next day, that he should have arrangements to make, business matters to wind up; it was not even necessary to suppose that his mysterious trip was a visit to the writer of the letters. He might simply have gone to see a client who lived out of town. Of course they would not tell Charlotte at the office; the secretary had hesitated before imparting even such meager information as the fact of Mr. Ashby's absence. Meanwhile she would go on with her joyful preparations, content to learn later in the day to what particular island of the blest she was to be carried.

The hours wore on, or rather were swept forward on a rush of eager preparations. At last the entrance of the maid who came to draw the curtains roused Charlotte from her labors, and she saw to her surprise that the clock marked five. And she did not yet know where they were going the next day! She rang up her husband's office and was told that Mr. Ashby had not been there since the early morning. She asked for his partner, but the partner could add nothing to her information, for he himself, his suburban train having been behind time, had reached the office after Ashby had come and gone. Charlotte stood perplexed; then she decided to telephone to her mother-in-law. Of course Kenneth, on the eve of a month's absence, must have gone to see his mother. The mere fact that the children—in spite of his vague objections—would certainly have to be left with old Mrs. Ashby, made it obvious that he would have all sorts of matters to decide with her. At another time Charlotte might have felt a little hurt at being excluded from their conference, but nothing mattered now but that she had won the day, that her husband was still hers and not another woman's. Gaily she called up Mrs. Ashby, heard her friendly voice, and began: "Well, did Kenneth's news surprise you? What do you think of our elopement?"

Almost instantly, before Mrs. Ashby could answer, Charlotte knew what her reply would be. Mrs. Ashby had not seen her son, she had had no word from him and did not know what her daughter-in-law meant. Charlotte stood silent in the intensity of her surprise. "But then, where *has* he been?" she thought. Then, recovering herself, she explained their sudden decision to Mrs. Ashby, and in doing so, gradually regained her own self-confidence, her conviction that nothing could ever again come between Kenneth and herself. Mrs. Ashby took the news calmly and approvingly. She, too, had thought that Kenneth looked worried and overtired, and she agreed with her daughter-in-law that in such cases change was the surest remedy. "I'm always so glad when he gets away. Elsie hated traveling; she was always finding pretexts to prevent his going anywhere. With you, thank goodness, it's different." Nor was Mrs. Ashby surprised at his not having had time to let her know of his departure. He must have been in a rush from the moment the decision was taken; but no doubt he'd drop in before dinner. Five minutes' talk was really all they needed. "I hope you'll gradually cure Kenneth of his mania for going over and over a question that could be settled in a dozen words. He never used to be like that, and if he carried the habit into his professional work he'd soon lose all his clients. . . . Yes, do come in for a minute, dear, if you have time; no doubt he'll turn up while you're here." The tonic ring of Mrs. Ashby's voice echoed on reassuringly in the silent room while Charlotte continued her preparations.

Toward seven the telephone rang, and she darted to it. Now she would know! But it was only from the conscientious secretary, to say that Mr. Ashby hadn't been back, or sent any word, and before the office closed she thought she ought to let Mrs. Ashby know. "Oh, that's all right. Thanks a lot!" Charlotte called out cheerfully, and hung up the receiver with a trembling hand. But perhaps by this time, she reflected, he was at his mother's. She shut her drawers and cupboards, put on her hat and coat and called up to the nursery that she was going out for a minute to see the children's grandmother.

Mrs. Ashby lived nearby, and during her brief walk through the cold spring dusk Charlotte imagined that every advancing figure was her husband's. But she did not meet him on the way, and when she entered the house she found her mother-in-law alone. Kenneth had neither telephoned nor come. Old Mrs. Ashby sat by her bright fire, her knitting needles flashing steadily through her active old hands, and her mere bodily presence gave reassurance to Charlotte. Yes, it was certainly odd that Kenneth had gone off for the whole day without letting any of them know; but, after all, it was to be expected. A busy lawyer held so many threads in his hands that any sudden change of plan would oblige him to make all sorts of unforeseen arrangements and adjustments. He might have gone to see some client in the suburbs and been detained there; his mother remembered his telling her that he had charge of the legal business of a queer old recluse somewhere in New Jersey, who was immensely rich but too mean to have a telephone. Very likely Kenneth had been stranded there.

But Charlotte felt her nervousness gaining on her. When Mrs. Ashby asked her at what hour they were sailing the next day and she had to say she didn't know—that Kenneth had simply sent her word he was going to take their passages—the uttering of the words again brought home to her the strangeness of the situation. Even Mrs. Ashby conceded that it was odd; but she immediately added that it only showed what a rush he was in.

"But, mother, it's nearly eight o'clock! He must realize that I've got to know when we're starting tomorrow."

"Oh, the boat probably doesn't sail till evening. Sometimes they have to wait till midnight for the tide. Kenneth's probably counting on that. After all, he has a level head."

Charlotte stood up. "It's not that. Something has happened to him."

Mrs. Ashby took off her spectacles and rolled up her knitting. "If you begin to let yourself imagine things—"

"Aren't you in the least anxious?"

"I never am till I have to be. I wish you'd ring for dinner, my dear. You'll stay and dine? He's sure to drop in here on his way home."

Charlotte called up her own house. No, the maid said, Mr. Ashby hadn't come in and hadn't telephoned. She would tell him as soon as he came that Mrs. Ashby was dining at his mother's. Charlotte followed her mother-in-law into the dining room and sat with parched throat before her empty plate, while Mrs. Ashby dealt calmly and efficiently with a short but carefully prepared repast. "You'd better eat something, child, or you'll be as bad as Kenneth. . . . Yes, a little more asparagus, please, Jane."

She insisted on Charlotte's drinking a glass of sherry and nibbling a bit of toast; then they returned to the drawing room, where the fire had been made up, and the cushions in Mrs. Ashby's armchair shaken out and smoothed. How safe and familiar it all looked; and out there, somewhere in the uncertainty and mystery of the night, lurked the answer to the two women's conjectures, like an indistinguishable figure prowling on the threshold.

At last Charlotte got up and said: "I'd better go back. At this hour Kenneth will certainly go straight home."

Mrs. Ashby smiled indulgently. "It's not very late, my dear. It doesn't take two sparrows long to dine."

"It's after nine." Charlotte bent down to kiss her. "The fact is, I can't keep still."

Mrs. Ashby pushed aside her work and rested her two hands on the arms of her chair. "I'm going with you," she said, helping herself up.

Charlotte protested that it was too late, that it was not necessary, that she would call up as soon as Kenneth came in, but Mrs. Ashby had already rung for her maid. She was slightly lame, and stood resting on her stick while her wraps were brought. "If Mr. Kenneth turns up, tell him he'll find me at his own house," she instructed the maid as the two women got into the taxi which had been summoned. During the short drive Charlotte gave thanks that she was not returning home alone. There was something warm and substantial in the mere fact of Mrs. Ashby's nearness, something that corresponded with the clearness of her eyes and the texture of her fresh firm complexion. As the taxi drew up she laid her hand encouragingly on Charlotte's. "You'll see; there'll be a message."

The door opened at Charlotte's ring and the two entered. Charlotte's heart beat excitedly; the stimulus of her mother-in-law's confidence was beginning to flow through her veins.

"You'll see—you'll see," Mrs. Ashby repeated.

The maid who opened the door said no, Mr. Ashby had not come in, and there had been no message from him.

"You're sure the telephone's not out of order?" his mother suggested; and the maid said, well, it certainly wasn't half an hour ago; but she'd just go and ring up to make sure. She disappeared, and Charlotte turned to take off her hat and cloak. As she did so her eyes lit on the hall table, and there lay a gray envelope, her husband's name faintly traced on it. "Oh!" she cried out, suddenly aware that for the first time in months she had entered her house without wondering if one of the gray letters would be there.

"What is it, my dear?" Mrs. Ashby asked with a glance of surprise.

Charlotte did not answer. She took up the envelope and stood staring at it as if she could force her gaze to penetrate to what was within. Then an idea occurred to her. She turned and held out the envelope to her mother-in-law.

"Do you know that writing?" she asked.

Mrs. Ashby took the letter. She had to feel with her other hand for her eyeglasses, and when she had adjusted them she lifted the envelope to the light. "Why!" she exclaimed; and then stopped. Charlotte noticed that the letter shook in her usually firm hand. "But this is addressed to Kenneth," Mrs. Ashby said at length, in a low voice. Her tone seemed to imply that she felt her daughter-in-law's question to be slightly indiscreet.

"Yes, but no matter," Charlotte spoke with sudden decision. "I want to know—do you know the writing?"

Mrs. Ashby handed back the letter. "No," she said distinctly.

The two women had turned into the library. Charlotte switched on the electric light and shut the door. She still held the envelope in her hand.

"I'm going to open it," she announced.

She caught her mother-in-law's startled glance. "But, dearest—a letter not addressed to you? My dear, you can't!"

"As if I cared about that—now!" She continued to look intently at Mrs. Ashby. "This letter may tell me where Kenneth is."

Mrs. Ashby's glossy bloom was effaced by a quick pallor; her firm cheeks seemed to shrink and wither. "Why should it? What makes you believe—It can't possibly—"

Charlotte held her eyes steadily on that altered face. "Ah, then you *do* know the writing?" she flashed back.

"Know the writing? How should I? With all my son's correspondents. . . . What I do know is—" Mrs. Ashby broke off and looked at her daughter-in-law entreatingly, almost timidly.

Charlotte caught her by the wrist. "Mother! What do you know? Tell me! You must!"

"That I don't believe any good ever came of a woman's opening her husband's letters behind his back."

The words sounded to Charlotte's irritated ears as flat as a phrase culled from a book of moral axioms. She laughed impatiently and dropped her mother-in-law's wrist. "Is that all? No good can come of this letter, opened or unopened. I know that well enough. But whatever ill comes, I mean to find out what's in it." Her hands had been trembling as they held the envelope, but now they grew firm, and her voice also. She still gazed intently at Mrs. Ashby. "This is the ninth letter addressed in the same hand that has come for Kenneth since we've been married. Always these same gray envelopes. I've kept count of them because after each one he has been like a man who has had some dreadful shock. It takes him hours to shake off their effect. I've told him so. I've told him I must know from whom they come, because I can see they're killing him. He won't answer my questions; he says he can't tell me anything about the letters; but last night he promised to go away with me—to get away from them."

Mrs. Ashby, with shaking steps, had gone to one of the armchairs and sat down in it, her head drooping forward on her breast. "Ah," she murmured.

"So now you understand—"

"Did he tell you it was to get away from them?"

"He said, to get away—to get away. He was sobbing so that he could hardly speak. But I told him I knew that was why."

"And what did he say?"

"He took me in his arms and said he'd go wherever I wanted."

"Ah, thank God!" said Mrs. Ashby. There was a silence, during which she continued to sit with bowed head, and eyes averted from her daughter-in-law. At last she looked up and spoke. "Are you sure there have been as many as nine?"

"Perfectly. This is the ninth. I've kept count."

"And he has absolutely refused to explain?"

"Absolutely."

Mrs. Ashby spoke through pale contracted lips. "When did they begin to come? Do you remember?"

Charlotte laughed again. "Remember? The first one came the night we got back from our honeymoon."

"All that time?" Mrs. Ashby lifted her head and spoke with sudden energy. "Then—yes, open it."

The words were so unexpected that Charlotte felt the blood in her temples, and her hands began to tremble again. She tried to slip her finger under the flap of the envelope, but it was so tightly stuck that she had to hunt on her husband's writing table for his ivory letter opener. As she pushed about the familiar objects his own hands had so lately touched, they sent through her the icy chill emanating from the little personal effects of someone newly dead. In the deep silence of the room the tearing of the paper as she slit the envelope sounded like a human cry. She drew out the sheet and carried it to the lamp.

"Well?" Mrs. Ashby asked below her breath.

Charlotte did not move or answer. She was bending over the page with wrinkled brows, holding it nearer and nearer to the light. Her sight must be blurred, or else dazzled by the reflection of the lamplight on the smooth surface of the paper, for, strain her eyes as she would, she could discern only a few faint strokes, so faint and faltering as to be nearly undecipherable.

"I can't make it out," she said.

"What do you mean, dear?"

"The writing's too indistinct. . . . Wait."

She went back to the table and, sitting down close to Kenneth's reading lamp, slipped the letter under a magnifying glass. All this time she was aware that her mother-in-law was watching her intently.

"Well?" Mrs. Ashby breathed.

"Well, it's no clearer. I can't read it."

"You mean the paper is an absolute blank?"

"No, not quite. There is writing on it. I can make out something like 'mine'—oh, and 'come.' It might be 'come.' "

Mrs. Ashby stood up abruptly. Her face was even paler than before. She advanced to the table and, resting her two hands on it, drew a deep breath. "Let me see," she said, as if forcing herself to a hateful effort.

Charlotte felt the contagion of her whiteness. "She knows," she thought. She pushed the letter across the table. Her mother-in-law lowered her head over it in silence, but without touching it with her pale wrinkled hands.

Charlotte stood watching her as she herself, when she had tried to read the letter, had been watched by Mrs. Ashby. The latter fumbled for her glasses, held them to her eyes, and bent still closer to the outspread page, in order, as it seemed, to avoid touching it. The light of the lamp fell directly on her old face, and Charlotte reflected what depths of the unknown may lurk under the clearest and most candid lineaments. She had never seen her mother-in-law's features express any but simple and sound emotions—cordiality, amusement, a kindly sympathy; now and again a flash of wholesome anger. Now they seemed to wear a look of fear and hatred, of incredulous dismay and almost cringing defiance. It was as if the spirits warring within her had distorted her face to their own likeness. At length she raised her head. "I can't—I can't," she said in a voice of childish distress.

"You can't make it out either?"

She shook her head, and Charlotte saw two tears roll down her cheeks.

"Familiar as the writing is to you?" Charlotte insisted with twitching lips.

Mrs. Ashby did not take up the challenge. "I can make out nothing —nothing."

"But you do know the writing?"

Mrs. Ashby lifted her head timidly; her anxious eyes stole with a glance of apprehension around the quiet familiar room. "How can I tell? I was startled at first. . . ."

"Startled by the resemblance?"

"Well, I thought—"

"You'd better say it out, mother! You knew at once it was *her* writing?"

"Oh, wait, my dear—wait."

"Wait for what?"

Mrs. Ashby looked up; her eyes, traveling slowly past Charlotte, were lifted to the blank wall behind her son's writing table.

Charlotte, following the glance, burst into a shrill laugh of accusation. "I needn't wait any longer! You've answered me now! You're looking straight at the wall where her picture used to hang!"

Mrs. Ashby lifted her hand with a murmur of warning. "Sh-h."

"Oh, you needn't imagine that anything can ever frighten me again!" Charlotte cried.

Her mother-in-law still leaned against the table. Her lips moved plaintively. "But we're going mad—we're both going mad. We both know such things are impossible."

Her daughter-in-law looked at her with a pitying stare. "I've known for a long time now that everything was possible."

"Even this?"

"Yes, exactly this."

"But this letter—after all, there's nothing in this letter—"

"Perhaps there would be to him. How can I tell? I remember his saying to me once that if you were used to a handwriting the faintest stroke of it became legible. Now I see what he meant. He *was* used to it."

"But the few strokes that I can make out are so pale. No one could possibly read that letter."

Charlotte laughed again. "I suppose everything's pale about a ghost," she said stridently.

"Oh, my child—my child—don't say it!"

"Why shouldn't I say it, when even the bare walls cry it out? What difference does it make if her letters are illegible to you and me? If even you can see her face on that blank wall, why shouldn't he read her writing on this blank paper? Don't you see that she's everywhere in this house, and the closer to him because to everyone else she's become invisible?" Charlotte dropped into a chair and covered her face with her hands. A turmoil of sobbing shook her from head to foot. At length a touch on her shoulder made her look up, and she saw her mother-in-law bending over her. Mrs. Ashby's face seemed to have grown still smaller and more wasted, but it had resumed its usual quiet look. Through all her tossing anguish, Charlotte felt the impact of that resolute spirit.

"Tomorrow—tomorrow. You'll see. There'll be some explanation tomorrow."

Charlotte cut her short. "An explanation? Who's going to give it, I wonder?"

Mrs. Ashby drew back and straightened herself heroically. "Kenneth himself will," she cried out in a strong voice. Charlotte said nothing, and the old woman went on: "But meanwhile we must act; we must notify the police. Now, without a moment's delay. We must do everything—everything."

Charlotte stood up slowly and stiffly; her joints felt as cramped as an old woman's. "Exactly as if we thought it could do any good to do anything?"

Resolutely Mrs. Ashby cried: "Yes!" and Charlotte went up to the telephone and unhooked the receiver.

The Looking Glass

*M*rs. Attlee had never been able to understand why there was any harm in giving people a little encouragement when they needed it.

Sitting back in her comfortable armchair by the fire, her working days over, and her muscular masseuse's hands lying swollen and powerless on her knee, she was at leisure to turn the problem over, and ponder it as there had never been time to do before.

Mrs. Attlee was so infirm now that, when her widowed daughter-in-law was away for the day, her granddaughter Moyra Attlee had to stay with her until the kitchen girl had prepared the cold supper, and could come in and sit in the parlor.

"You'd be surprised, you know, my dear, to find how discouraged the grand people get, in those big houses with all the help, and the silver dinner plates, and a bell always handy if the fire wants poking, or the pet dog asks for a drink. . . . And what'd a masseuse be good for, if she didn't jolly up their minds a little along with their muscles?— as Dr. Welbridge used to say to me many a time, when he'd given me a difficult patient. And he always gave me the most difficult," she added proudly.

She paused, aware (for even now little escaped her) that Moyra had ceased to listen, but accepting the fact resignedly, as she did most things in the slow decline of her days.

"It's a fine afternoon," she reflected, "and likely she's fidgety because there's a new movie on; or that young fellow's fixed it up to get back earlier from New York. . . ."

She relapsed into silence, following her thoughts; but presently, as happens with old people, they came to the surface again.

"And I hope I'm a good Catholic, as I said to Father Divott the other day, and at peace with heaven, if ever I was took suddenly—but no matter what happens I've got to risk my punishment for the wrong I did to Mrs. Clingsland, because as long as I've never repented it there's no use telling Father Divott about it. Is there?"

Mrs. Attlee heaved an introspective sigh. Like many humble persons of her kind and creed, she had a vague idea that a sin unrevealed was, as far as the consequences went, a sin uncommitted; and this conviction had often helped her in the difficult task of reconciling doctrine and practice.

II

Moyra Attlee interrupted her listless stare down the empty Sunday street of the New Jersey suburb, and turned an astonished glance on her grandmother.

"Mrs. Clingsland? A wrong you did to Mrs. Clingsland?"

Hitherto she had lent an inattentive ear to her grandmother's ramblings; the talk of old people seemed to be a language hardly worth learning. But it was not always so with Mrs. Attlee's. Her activities among the rich had ceased before the first symptoms of the financial depression; but her tenacious memory was stored with pictures of the luxurious days of which her granddaughter's generation, even in a wider world, knew only by hearsay. Mrs. Attlee had a gift for evoking in a few words scenes of half-understood opulence and leisure, like a guide leading a stranger through the gallery of a palace in the twilight, and now and then lifting a lamp to a shimmering Rembrandt or a jeweled Rubens; and it was particularly when she mentioned Mrs. Clingsland that Moyra caught these dazzling glimpses. Mrs. Clingsland had always been something more than a name to the Attlee family. They knew (though they did not know why) that it was through her help that Grandmother Attlee had been able, years ago, to buy the little house at Montclair, with a patch of garden behind it, where, all through the depression, she had held out, thanks to fortunate investments made on the advice of Mrs. Clingsland's great friend, the banker.

"She had so many friends, and they were all high-up people, you understand. Many's the time she'd say to me: 'Cora' (think of the loveliness of her calling me Cora), 'Cora, I'm going to buy some Golden Flyer shares on Mr. Stoner's advice; Mr. Stoner of the National Union Bank, you know. He's getting me in on the ground floor, as they say, and if you want to step in with me, why come along. There's nothing too good for you, in my opinion,' she used to say. And, as it turned out, those shares have kept their head above water all through the bad years, and now I think they'll see me through, and be there when I'm gone, to help out you children."

Today Moyra Attlee heard the revered name with a new interest. The phrase: "The wrong I did to Mrs. Clingsland," had struck through her listlessness, rousing her to sudden curiosity. What could her grandmother mean by saying she had done a wrong to the benefactress whose bounties she was never tired of recording? Moyra believed her grandmother to be a very good woman—certainly she had been wonderfully generous in all her dealings with her children and grandchildren; and it seemed incredible that, if there had been one grave lapse in her life, it should have taken the form of an injury to Mrs. Clingsland. True, whatever the lapse was, she seemed to have made peace with herself about it; yet it was clear that its being unconfessed lurked disquietingly in the back of her mind.

"How can you say you ever did harm to a friend like Mrs. Clingsland, Gran?"

Mrs. Attlee's eyes grew sharp behind her spectacles, and she fixed them half distrustfully on the girl's face. But in a moment she seemed to recover herself. "Not harm, I don't say; I'll never think I harmed her. Bless you, it wasn't to harm her I'd ever have lifted a finger. All I wanted was to help. But when you try to help too many people at once, the devil sometimes takes note of it. You see, there's quotas nowadays for everything, doing good included, my darling."

Moyra made an impatient movement. She did not care to hear her grandmother philosophize. "Well—but you said you did a wrong to Mrs. Clingsland."

Mrs. Attlee's sharp eyes seemed to draw back behind a mist of age. She sat silent, her hands lying heavily over one another in their tragic uselessness.

"What would *you* have done, I wonder," she began suddenly, "if you'd ha' come in on her that morning, and seen her laying in her lovely great bed, with the lace a yard deep on the sheets, and her face buried in the pillows, so I knew she was crying? Would you have opened your bag same as usual, and got out your cocoanut cream and talcum powder, and the nail polishers, and all the rest of it, and waited there like a statue till she turned over to you; or'd you have gone up to her, and turned her softly round, like you would a baby, and said to her: 'Now, my dear, I guess you can tell Cora Attlee what's the trouble'? Well, that's what I did, anyhow; and there she was, with her face streaming with tears, and looking like a martyred saint on an altar, and when I said to her: 'Come, now, you tell me, and it'll help you,' she just sobbed out: 'Nothing can ever help me, now I've lost it.' "

" 'Lost what?' I said, thinking first of her boy, the Lord help me, though I'd heard him whistling on the stairs as I went up; but she said: 'My beauty, Cora—I saw it suddenly slipping out of the door from me this morning'. . . . Well, at that I had to laugh, and half angrily too. 'Your beauty,' I said to her, 'and is that all? And me that thought it was your husband, or your son—or your fortune even. If it's only your beauty, can't I give it back to you with these hands of mine? But what are you saying to me about beauty, with that seraph's face looking up at me this minute?' I said to her, for she angered me as if she'd been blaspheming."

"Well, was it true?" Moyra broke in, impatient and yet curious.

"True that she'd lost her beauty?" Mrs. Attlee paused to consider. "Do you know how it is, sometimes when you're doing a bit of fine darning, sitting by the window in the afternoon; and one minute it's full daylight, and your needle seems to find the way of itself; and the next minute you say: 'Is it my eyes?' because the work seems blurred; and presently you see it's the daylight going, stealing away, softlike, from your corner, though there's plenty left overhead. Well—it was that way with her. . . ."

But Moyra had never done fine darning, or strained her eyes in fading light, and she intervened again, more impatiently: "Well, what did she do?"

Mrs. Attlee once more reflected. "Why, she made me tell her every morning that it wasn't true; and every morning she believed me a little less. And she asked everybody in the house, beginning with her husband, poor man—him so bewildered when you asked him anything outside of his business, or his club or his horses, and never noticing any difference in her looks since the day he'd led her home as his bride, twenty years before, maybe. . . .

"But there—nothing he could have said, if he'd had the wit to say it, would have made any difference. From the day she saw the first little line around her eyes she thought of herself as an old woman, and the thought never left her for more than a few minutes at a time. Oh, when she was dressed up, and laughing, and receiving company, then I don't say the faith in her beauty wouldn't come back to her, and go to her head like champagne; but it wore off quicker than champagne, and I've seen her run upstairs with the foot of a girl, and then, before she'd tossed off her finery, sit down in a heap in front of one of her big looking glasses—it was looking glasses everywhere in her room—and stare and stare till the tears ran down over her powder."

"Oh, well, I suppose it's always hateful growing old," said Moyra, her indifference returning.

Mrs. Attlee smiled retrospectively. "How can I say that, when my own old age has been made so peaceful by all her goodness to me?"

Moyra stood up with a shrug. "And yet you tell me you acted wrong to her. How am I to know what you mean?"

Her grandmother made no answer. She closed her eyes, and leaned her head against the little cushion behind her neck. Her lips seemed to murmur, but no words came. Moyra reflected that she was probably falling asleep, and that when she woke she would not remember what she had been about to reveal.

"It's not much fun sitting here all this time, if you can't even keep awake long enough to tell me what you mean about Mrs. Clingsland," she grumbled.

Mrs. Attlee roused herself with a start.

III

Well (she began) you know what happened in the war—I mean, the way all the fine ladies, and the poor shabby ones too, took to running to the mediums and the clairvoyants, or whatever the stylish folk call 'em. The women had to have news of their men; and they were made to pay high enough for it. . . . Oh, the stories I used to hear—and the price paid wasn't only money, either! There was a fair lot of swindlers and blackmailers in the business, there was. I'd sooner have trusted a gypsy at a fair . . . but the women just *had* to go to them.

Well, my dear, I'd always had a way of seeing things; from the cradle, even. I don't mean reading the tea leaves, or dealing the cards; that's for the kitchen. No, no; I mean, feeling there's things about you, behind you, whispering over your shoulder. . . . Once my mother, on the Connemara hills, saw the leprechauns at dusk; and she said they smelt fine and high, too. . . . Well, when I used to go from one grand house to another, to give my massage and face treatment, I got more and more sorry for those poor wretches that the soothsaying swindlers were dragging the money out of for a pack of lies; and one day I couldn't stand it any longer, and though I knew the Church was against it, when I saw one lady nearly crazy, because for months she'd had no news of her boy at the front, I said to her: "If you'll come over to my place tomorrow, I might have a word for you." And the wonder of it was that I *had!* For that night I dreamt a message came saying there was good news for her, and the next day, sure enough, she had a cable, telling her her son had escaped from a German camp. . . .

After that the ladies came in flocks—in flocks fairly . . . you're too young to remember, child; but your mother could tell you. Only she wouldn't, because after a bit the priest got wind of it, and then it had to stop . . . so she won't even talk of it any more. But I always said: how could I help it? For I *did* see things, and hear things, at that time. . . . And of course the ladies were supposed to come just for the face treatment . . . and was I to blame if I kept hearing those messages for them, poor souls, or seeing things they wanted me to see?

It's no matter now, for I made it all straight with Father Divott years ago; and now nobody comes after me any more, as you can see for yourself. And all I ask is to be left alone in my chair. . . .

But with Mrs. Clingsland—well, that was different. To begin with, she was the patient I liked best. There was nothing she wouldn't do for you, if ever for a minute you could get her to stop thinking of herself . . . and that's saying a good deal, for a rich lady. Money's an armor, you see; and there's few cracks in it. But Mrs. Clingsland was a loving nature, if only anybody'd shown her how to love. . . . Oh, dear, and wouldn't she have been surprised if you'd told her that! Her that thought she was living up to her chin in love and love-making. But as soon as the lines began to come about her eyes, she didn't believe in it any more. And she had to be always hunting for new people to tell her she was as beautiful as ever; because she wore the others out, forever asking them: "Don't you think I'm beginning to go off a little?" —till finally fewer and fewer came to the house, and as far as a poor masseuse like me can judge, I didn't much fancy the looks of those that did; and I saw Mr. Clingsland didn't either.

But there was the children, you'll say. I know, I know! And she did love her children in a way; only it wasn't their way. The girl, who was a good bit the eldest, took after her father: a plain face and plain words. Dogs and horses and athletics. With her mother she was cold and scared; so her mother was cold and scared with her. The boy was delicate when he was little, so she could curl him up, and put him into black velvet pants, like that boy in the book—little Lord Something. But when his long legs grew out of the pants, and they sent him to school, she said he wasn't her own little cuddly baby any more; and it riles a growing boy to hear himself talked about like that.

She had good friends left, of course; mostly elderly ladies they were, of her own age (for she *was* elderly now; the change had come), who used to drop in often for a gossip; but, bless your heart, they weren't much help, for what she wanted, and couldn't do without, was the gaze of men struck dumb by her beauty. And that was what she couldn't get any longer, except she paid for it. And even so—!

For, you see, she was too quick and clever to be humbugged long by the kind that tried to get things out of her. How she used to laugh at the old double-chinners trotting round to the nightclubs with their boy friends! She laughed at old ladies in love; and yet she couldn't bear to be out of love, though she knew she was getting to be an old lady herself.

Well, I remember one day another patient of mine, who'd never had much looks beyond what you can buy in Fifth Avenue, laughing at me about Mrs. Clingsland, about her dread of old age, and her craze for admiration—and as I listened, I suddenly thought: "Why, we don't either of us know anything about what a beautiful woman suffers when she loses her beauty. For you and me, and thousands like us, beginning to grow old is like going from a bright warm room to one a little less warm and bright; but to a beauty like Mrs. Clingsland it's like being pushed out of an illuminated ballroom, all flowers and chandeliers, into the winter night and the snow." And I had to bite the words back, not to say them to my patient. . . .

IV

Mrs. Clingsland brightened up a little when her own son grew up and went to college. She used to go over and see him now and again; or he'd come home for the holidays. And he used to take her out for lunch, or to dance at those cabaret places; and when the headwaiters took her for his sweetheart she'd talk about it for a week. But one day a hall porter said: "Better hurry up, mister. There's your mother waiting for you over there, looking clean fagged out"; and after that she didn't go round with him so much.

For a time she used to get some comfort out of telling me about her early triumphs; and I used to listen patiently, because I knew it was safer for her to talk to me than to the flatterers who were beginning to get round her.

You mustn't think of her, though, as an unkind woman. She was friendly to her husband, and friendly to her children; but they meant less and less to her. What she wanted was a looking glass to stare into; and when her own people took enough notice of her to serve as looking glasses, which wasn't often, she didn't much fancy what she saw there. I think this was about the worst time of her life. She lost a tooth; she began to dye her hair; she went into retirement to have her face lifted, and then got frightened, and came out again looking like a ghost, with a pouch under one eye, where they'd begun the treatment. . . .

I began to be really worried about her then. She got sour and bitter toward everybody, and I seemed to be the only person she could talk out to. She used to keep me by for hours, always paying for the appointments she made me miss, and going over the same thing again and again; how when she was young and came into a ballroom, or a restaurant or a theatre, everybody stopped what they were doing to turn and look at her—even the actors on the stage did, she said; and it was the truth, I dare say. But that was over. . . .

Well, what could I say to her? She'd heard it all often enough. But there were people prowling about in the background that I didn't like the look of; people, you understand, who live on weak women that can't grow old. One day she showed me a love letter. She said she didn't know the man who'd sent it; but she knew about him. He was a Count Somebody; a foreigner. He'd had adventures. Trouble in his own country, I guess. . . . She laughed and tore the letter up. Another came from him, and I saw that too—but I didn't see her tear it up.

"Oh, I know what he's after," she said. "Those kind of men are always looking out for silly old women with money. . . . Ah," says she, "it was different in old times. I remember one day I'd gone into a florist's to buy some violets, and I saw a young fellow there; well, maybe he was a little younger than me—but I looked like a girl still. And when he saw me he just stopped short with what he was saying to the florist, and his face turned so white I thought he was going to faint. I bought my violets; and as I went out a violet dropped from the bunch, and I saw him stoop and pick it up, and hide it away as if it had been money he'd stolen. . . . Well," she says, "a few days after that I met him at a dinner, and it turned out he was the son of a friend of mine, a woman older than myself, who'd married abroad. He'd been brought up in England, and had just come to New York to take up a job there. . . ."

She lay back with her eyes closed, and a quiet smile on her poor tormented face. "I didn't know it then, but I suppose that was the only time I've ever been in love. . . ." For a while she didn't say anything more, and I noticed the tears beginning to roll down her cheeks. "Tell me about it, now do, you poor soul," I says; for I thought, this is better for her than fandangoing with that oily count whose letter she hasn't torn up.

"There's so little to tell," she said. "We met only four or five times —and then Harry went down on the 'Titanic.'"

"Mercy," says I, "and was it all those years ago?"

"The years don't make any difference, Cora," she says. "The way he looked at me I know no one ever worshiped me as he did."

"And did he tell you so?" I went on, humoring her; though I felt kind of guilty toward her husband.

"Some things don't have to be told," says she, with the smile of a bride. "If only he hadn't died, Cora. . . . It's the sorrowing for him that's made me old before my time." (Before her time! And her well over fifty.)

Well, a day or two after that I got a shock. Coming out of Mrs. Clingsland's front door as I was going into it I met a woman I'd know among a million if I was to meet her again in hell—where I will, I know, if I don't mind my steps. . . . You see, Moyra, though I broke years ago with all that crystal-reading, and table-rapping, and what the Church forbids, I was mixed up in it for a time (till Father Divott ordered me to stop), and I knew, by sight at any rate, most of the big mediums and their touts. And this woman on the doorstep was a tout, one of the worst and most notorious in New York; I knew cases where she'd sucked people dry selling them the news they wanted, like she was selling them a forbidden drug. And all of a sudden it came to me that I'd heard it said that she kept a foreign count, who was sucking *her* dry—and I gave one jump home to my own place, and sat down there to think it over.

I saw well enough what was going to happen. Either she'd persuade my poor lady that the count was mad over her beauty, and get a hold over her that way; or else—and this was worse—she'd make Mrs. Clingsland talk, and get at the story of the poor young man called Harry, who was drowned, and bring her messages from him; and that might go on forever, and bring in more money than the count. . . .

Well, Moyra, could I help it? I was so sorry for her, you see. I could see she was sick and fading away, and her will weaker than it used to be; and if I was to save her from those gangsters I had to do it right away, and make it straight with my conscience afterward—if I could. . . .

V

I don't believe I ever did such hard thinking as I did that night. For what was I after doing? Something that was against my Church and against my own principles; and if ever I got found out, it was all up with me—me, with my thirty years' name of being the best masseuse in New York, and none honester, nor more respectable!

Well, then, I says to myself, what'll happen if that woman gets hold of Mrs. Clingsland? Why, one way or another, she'll bleed her white, and then leave her without help or comfort. I'd seen households where that had happened, and I wasn't going to let it happen to my poor lady. What I was after was to make her believe in herself again, so that she'd be in a kindlier mind toward others . . . and by the next day I'd thought my plan out, and set it going.

It wasn't so easy, neither; and I sometimes wonder at my nerve. I'd figured it out that the other woman would have to work the stunt of the young man who was drowned, because I was pretty sure Mrs. Clingsland, at the last minute, would shy away from the count. Well, then, thinks I, I'll work the same stunt myself—but how?

You see, dearie, those big people, when they talk and write to each

other, they use lovely words we ain't used to; and I was afraid if I began to bring messages to her, I'd word them wrong, and she'd suspect something. I knew I could work it the first day or the second; but after that I wasn't so sure. But there was no time to lose, and when I went back to her next morning I said: "A queer thing happened to me last night. I guess it was the way you spoke to me about that gentleman —the one on the 'Titanic.' Making me see him as clear as if he was in the room with us—" and at that I had her sitting up in bed with her great eyes burning into me like gimlets. "Oh, Cora, perhaps he *is!* Oh, tell me quickly what happened!"

"Well, when I was laying in my bed last night something came to me from him. I knew at once it was from him; it was a word he was telling me to bring you. . . ."

I had to wait then, she was crying so hard, before she could listen to me again; and when I went on she hung on to me, saving the word, as if I'd been her Saviour. The poor woman!

The message I'd hit on for that first day was easy enough. I said he'd told me to tell her he'd always loved her. It went down her throat like honey, and she just lay there and tasted it. But after a while she lifted up her head. "Then why didn't he tell me so?" says she.

"Ah," says I, "I'll have to try to reach him again, and ask him that." And that day she fairly drove me off on my other jobs, for fear I'd be late getting home, and too tired to hear him if he came again. "And he *will* come, Cora; I know he will! And you must be ready for him, and write down everything. I want every word written down the minute he says it, for fear you'll forget a single one."

Well, that was a new difficulty. Writing wasn't ever my strong point; and when it came to finding the words for a young gentleman in love who'd gone down on the "Titanic," you might as well have asked me to write a Chinese dictionary. Not that I couldn't imagine how he'd have felt; but I didn't for Mary's grace know how to say it for him.

But it's wonderful, as Father Divott says, how Providence sometimes seems to be listening behind the door. That night when I got home I found a message from a patient, asking me to go to see a poor young fellow she'd befriended when she was better off—he'd been her children's tutor, I believe—who was down and out, and dying in a miserable rooming house down here at Montclair. Well, I went; and

I saw at once why he hadn't kept this job, or any other job. Poor fellow, it was the drink; and now he was dying of it. It was a pretty bad story, but there's only a bit of it belongs to what I'm telling you.

He was a highly educated gentleman, and as quick as a flash; and before I'd half explained, he told me what to say, and wrote out the message for me. I remember it now. "He was so blinded by your beauty that he couldn't speak—and when he saw you the next time, at that dinner, in your bare shoulders and your pearls, he felt farther away from you than ever. And he walked the streets till morning, and then went home, and wrote you a letter; but he didn't dare to send it after all."

This time Mrs. Clingsland swallowed it down like champagne. Blinded by her beauty; struck dumb by love of her! Oh, but that's what she'd been thirsting and hungering for all these years. Only, once it had begun, she had to have more of it, and always more . . . and my job didn't get any easier.

Luckily, though, I had that young fellow to help me; and after a while, when I'd given him a hint of what it was all about, he got as much interested as I was, and began to fret for me the days I didn't come.

But, my, what questions she asked. "Tell him, if it's true that I took his breath away that first evening at dinner, to describe to you how I was dressed. They must remember things like that even in the other world, don't you think so? And you say he noticed my pearls?"

Luckily she'd described that dress to me so often that I had no difficulty about telling the young man what to say—and so it went on, and it went on, and one way or another I managed each time to have an answer that satisfied her. But one day, after Harry'd sent her a particularly lovely message from the Over There (as those people call it) she burst into tears and cried out: "Oh, why did he never say things like that to me when we were together?"

That was a poser, as they say; I couldn't imagine why he hadn't. Of course I knew it was all wrong and immoral, anyway; but, poor thing, I don't see who it can hurt to help the love-making between a sick woman and a ghost. And I'd taken care to say a Novena against Father Divott finding me out.

Well, I told the poor young man what she wanted to know, and he said: "Oh, you can tell her an evil influence came between them.

Someone who was jealous, and worked against him—here, give me a pencil, and I'll write it out. . . . " and he pushed out his hot twitching hand for the paper.

That message fairly made her face burn with joy. "I knew it—I always knew it!" She flung her thin arms about me, and kissed me. "Tell me again, Cora, how he said I looked the first day he saw me. . . . "

"Why, you must have looked as you look now," says I to her, "for there's twenty years fallen from your face." And so there was.

What helped me to keep on was that she'd grown so much gentler and quieter. Less impatient with the people who waited on her, more understanding with the daughter and Mr. Clingsland. There was a different atmosphere in the house. And sometimes she'd say: "Cora, there must be poor souls in trouble, with nobody to hold out a hand to them; and I want you to come to me when you run across anybody like that." So I used to keep that poor young fellow well looked after, and cheered up with little dainties. And you'll never make me believe there was anything wrong in that—or in letting Mrs. Clingsland help me out with the new roof on this house, either.

But there was a day when I found her sitting up in bed when I came in, with two red spots on her thin cheeks. And all the peace had gone out of her poor face. "Why, Mrs. Clingsland, my dear, what's the matter?" But I could see well enough what it was. Somebody'd been undermining her belief in spirit communications, or whatever they call them, and she'd been crying herself into a fever, thinking I'd made up all I'd told her. "How do I know you're a medium, anyhow," she flung out at me with pitiful furious eyes, "and not taking advantage of me with all this stuff every morning?"

Well, the queer thing was that I took offense at that, not because I was afraid of being found out, but because—heaven help us!—I'd somehow come to believe in that young man Harry and his love-making, and it made me angry to be treated as a fraud. But I kept my temper and my tongue, and went on with the message as if I hadn't heard her; and she was ashamed to say any more to me. The quarrel between us lasted a week; and then one day, poor soul, she said, whimpering like a drug taker: "Cora, I can't get on without the messages you bring me. The ones I get through other people don't sound like Harry —and yours do."

I was so sorry for her then that I had hard work not to cry with her; but I kept my head, and answered quietly: "Mrs. Clingsland, I've been going against my Church, and risking my immortal soul, to get those messages through to you; and if you've found others that can help you, so much the better for me, and I'll go and make my peace with Heaven this very evening," I said.

"But the other messages don't help me, and I don't want to disbelieve in you," she sobbed out. "Only lying awake all night and turning things over, I get so miserable. I shall die if you can't prove to me that it's really Harry speaking to you."

I began to pack up my things. "I can't prove that, I'm afraid," I says in a cold voice, turning away my head so she wouldn't see the tears running down my cheeks.

"Oh, but you must, Cora, or I shall die!" she entreated me; and she looked as if she would, the poor soul.

"How can I prove it to you?" I answered. For all my pity for her, I still resented the way she'd spoken; and I thought how glad I'd be to get the whole business off my soul that very night in the confessional.

She opened her great eyes and looked up at me; and I seemed to see the wraith of her young beauty looking out of them. "There's only one way," she whispered.

"Well," I said, still offended, "what's the way?"

"You must ask him to repeat to you that letter he wrote, and didn't dare send to me. I'll know instantly then if you're in communication with him, and if you are I'll never doubt you any more."

Well, I sat down and gave a laugh. "You think it's as easy as that to talk with the dead, do you?"

"I think he'll know I'm dying too, and have pity on me, and do as I ask." I said nothing more, but packed up my things and went away.

VI

That letter seemed to me a mountain in my path; and the poor young man, when I told him, thought so too. "Ah, that's too difficult," he said. But he told me he'd think it over, and do his best—and I was to come back the next day if I could. "If only I knew more about her—or about *him*. It's damn difficult, making love for a dead man to a woman you've never seen," says he with his little cracked laugh. I couldn't deny that it was; but I knew he'd do what he could, and I could see that the difficulty of it somehow spurred him on, while me it only cast down.

So I went back to his room the next evening; and as I climbed the stairs I felt one of those sudden warnings that sometimes used to take me by the throat.

"It's as cold as ice on these stairs," I thought, "and I'll wager there's no one made up the fire in his room since morning." But it wasn't really the cold I was afraid of; I could tell there was worse than that waiting for me.

I pushed open the door and went in. "Well," says I, as cheerful as I could, "I've got a pint of champagne and a thermos of hot soup for you; but before you get them you've got to tell me—"

He laid there in his bed as if he didn't see me, though his eyes were open; and when I spoke to him he didn't answer. I tried to laugh. "Mercy!" I says, "are you so sleepy you can't even look round to see the champagne? Hasn't that slut of a woman been in to 'tend to the stove for you? The room's as cold as death—" I says, and at the word I stopped short. He neither moved nor spoke; and I felt that the cold came from him, and not from the empty stove. I took hold of his hand, and held the cracked looking glass to his lips; and I knew he was gone to his Maker. I drew his lids down, and fell on my knees beside the bed. "You shan't go without a prayer, you poor fellow," I whispered to him, pulling out my beads.

But though my heart was full of mourning I dursn't pray for long, for I knew I ought to call the people of the house. So I just muttered a prayer for the dead, and then got to my feet again. But before calling in anybody I took a quick look around; for I said to myself it would be better not to leave about any of those bits he'd written down for me. In the shock of finding the poor young man gone I'd clean forgotten all about the letter; but I looked among his few books and papers for anything about the spirit messages, and found nothing. After that I turned back for a last look at him, and a last blessing; and then it was, fallen on the floor and half under the bed, I saw a sheet of paper scribbled over in pencil in his weak writing. I picked it up, and, holy Mother, it was the letter! I hid it away quick in my bag, and I stooped down and kissed him. And then I called the people in.

Well, I mourned the poor young man like a son, and I had a busy day arranging things, and settling about the funeral with the lady that used to befriend him. And with all there was to do I never went near Mrs. Clingsland nor so much as thought of her, that day or the next; and the day after that there was a frantic message, asking what had happened, and saying she was very ill, and I was to come quick, no matter how much else I had to do.

I didn't more than half believe in the illness; I've been about too long among the rich not to be pretty well used to their scares and fusses. But I knew Mrs. Clingsland was just pining to find out if I'd got the letter, and that my only chance of keeping my hold over her was to have it ready in my bag when I went back. And if I didn't keep my hold over her, I knew what slimy hands were waiting in the dark to pull her down.

Well, the labor I had copying out that letter was so great that I didn't hardly notice what was in it; and if I thought about it at all, it was only to wonder if it wasn't worded too plainlike, and if there oughtn't to have been more long words in it, coming from a gentleman to his lady. So with one thing and another I wasn't any too easy in my mind when I appeared again at Mrs. Clingsland's; and if ever I wished myself out of a dangerous job, my dear, I can tell you that was the day. . . .

I went up to her room, the poor lady, and found her in bed, and tossing about, her eyes blazing, and her face full of all the wrinkles I'd worked so hard to rub out of it; and the sight of her softened my heart. After all, I thought, these people don't know what real trouble is; but they've manufactured something so like it that it's about as bad as the genuine thing.

"Well," she said in a fever, "well, Cora—the letter? Have you brought me the letter?"

I pulled it out of my bag, and handed it to her; and then I sat down and waited, my heart in my boots. I waited a long time, looking away from her; you couldn't stare at a lady who was reading a message from her sweetheart, could you?

I waited a long time; she must have read the letter very slowly, and then reread it. Once she sighed, ever so softly; and once she said: "Oh, Harry, no, no—how foolish" . . . and laughed a little under her breath. Then she was still again for so long that at last I turned my head and took a stealthy look at her. And there she lay on her pillows, the hair waving over them, the letter clasped tight in her hands, and her face smoothed out the way it was years before, when I first knew her. Yes—those few words had done more for her than all my labor.

"Well—?" said I, smiling a little at her.

"Oh, Cora—now at last he's spoken to me, really spoken." And the tears were running down her young cheeks.

I couldn't hardly keep back my own, the heart was so light in me. "And now you'll believe in me, I hope, ma'am, won't you?"

"I was mad ever to doubt you, Cora. . . ." She lifted the letter to her breast, and slipped it in among her laces. "How did you manage to get it, you darling, you?"

Dear me, thinks I, and what if she asks me to get her another one like it, and then another? I waited a moment, and then I spoke very gravely. "It's not an easy thing, ma'am, coaxing a letter like that from the dead." And suddenly, with a start, I saw that I'd spoken the truth. It *was* from the dead that I'd got it.

"No, Cora; I can well believe it. But this is a treasure I can live on for years. Only you must tell me how I can repay you. . . . In a hundred years I could never do enough for you," she says.

Well, that word went to my heart; but for a minute I didn't know how to answer. For it was true I'd risked my soul, and that was something she couldn't pay me for; but then maybe I'd saved hers, in getting her away from those foul people, so the whole business was more of a puzzle to me than ever. But then I had a thought that made me easier.

"Well, ma'am, the day before yesterday I was with a young man about the age of—of your Harry; a poor young man, without health or hope, lying sick in a mean rooming house. I used to go there and see him sometimes—"

Mrs. Clingsland sat up in bed in a flutter of pity. "Oh, Cora, how dreadful! Why did you never tell me? You must hire a better room for him at once. Has he a doctor? Has he a nurse? Quick—give me my checkbook!"

"Thank you, ma'am. But he don't need no nurse nor no doctor; and he's in a room underground by now. All I wanted to ask you for," said I at length, though I knew I might have got a king's ransom from her, "is money enough to have a few masses said for his soul—because maybe there's no one else to do it."

I had hard work making her believe there was no end to the masses you could say for a hundred dollars; but somehow it's comforted me ever since that I took no more from her that day. I saw to it that Father Divott said the masses and got a good bit of the money; so he was a sort of accomplice too, though he never knew it.

All Souls'

*Q*ueer and inexplicable as the business was, on the surface it appeared fairly simple—at the time, at least; but with the passing of years, and owing to there not having been a single witness of what happened except Sara Clayburn herself, the stories about it have become so exaggerated, and often so ridiculously inaccurate, that it seems necessary that someone connected with the affair, though not actually present—I repeat that when it happened my cousin was (or thought she was) quite alone in her house—should record the few facts actually known.

In those days I was often at Whitegates (as the place had always been called)—I was there, in fact, not long before, and almost immediately after, the strange happenings of those thirty-six hours. Jim Clayburn and his widow were both my cousins, and because of that, and of my intimacy with them, both families think I am more likely than anybody else to be able to get at the facts, as far as they can be called facts, and as anybody can get at them. So I have written down, as clearly as I could, the gist of the various talks I had with cousin Sara, when she could be got to talk—it wasn't often—about what occurred during that mysterious weekend.

I read the other day in a book by a fashionable essayist that ghosts went out when electric light came in. What nonsense! The writer, though he is fond of dabbling, in a literary way, in the supernatural, hasn't even reached the threshold of his subject. As between turreted castles patrolled by headless victims with clanking chains, and the comfortable suburban house with a refrigerator and central heating where you feel, as soon as you're in it, *that there's something wrong*, give me the latter for sending a chill down the spine! And, by the way, haven't you noticed that it's generally not the high-strung and imaginative who see ghosts, but the calm matter-of-fact people who don't believe in them, and are sure they wouldn't mind if they did see one? Well, that was the case with Sara Clayburn and her house. The house, in spite of its age—it was built, I believe, about 1780—was open, airy, high-ceilinged, with electricity, central heating and all the modern appliances: and its mistress was—well, very much like her house. And, anyhow, this isn't exactly a ghost story and I've dragged in the analogy only as a way of showing you what kind of woman my cousin was, and how unlikely it would have seemed that what happened at Whitegates should have happened just there—or to her.

When Jim Clayburn died the family all thought that, as the couple had no children, his widow would give up Whitegates and move either to New York or Boston—for being of good Colonial stock, with many relatives and friends, she would have found a place ready for her in either. But Sara Clayburn seldom did what other people expected, and in this case she did exactly the contrary; she stayed at Whitegates.

"What, turn my back on the old house—tear up all the family roots, and go and hang myself up in a bird-cage flat in one of those new skyscrapers in Lexington Avenue, with a bunch of chickweed and a cuttlefish to replace my good Connecticut mutton? No, thank you. Here I belong, and here I stay till my executors hand the place over to Jim's next-of-kin—that stupid fat Presley boy. . . . Well, don't let's talk about him. But I tell you what—I'll keep him out of here as long as I can." And she did—for being still in the early fifties when her husband died, and a muscular, resolute figure of a woman, she was more than a match for the fat Presley boy, and attended his funeral a few years ago, in correct mourning, with a faint smile under her veil.

Whitegates was a pleasant hospitable-looking house, on a height overlooking the stately windings of the Connecticut River; but it was five or six miles from Norrington, the nearest town, and its situation would certainly have seemed remote and lonely to modern servants. Luckily, however, Sara Clayburn had inherited from her mother-in-law two or three old stand-bys who seemed as much a part of the family tradition as the roof they lived under; and I never heard of her having any trouble in her domestic arrangements.

The house, in Colonial days, had been foursquare, with four spacious rooms on the ground floor, an oak-floored hall dividing them, the usual kitchen extension at the back, and a good attic under the roof. But Jim's grandparents, when interest in the "Colonial" began to revive, in the early eighties, had added two wings, at right angles to the south front, so that the old "circle" before the front door became a grassy court, enclosed on three sides, with a big elm in the middle. Thus the house was turned into a roomy dwelling, in which the last three generations of Clayburns had exercised a large hospitality; but the architect had respected the character of the old house, and the enlargement made it more comfortable without lessening its simplicity. There was a lot of land about it, and Jim Clayburn, like his fathers before him, farmed it, not without profit, and played a considerable and respected part in state politics. The Clayburns were always spoken of as a "good influence" in the county, and the townspeople were glad when they learned that Sara did not mean to desert the place —"though it must be lonesome, winters, living all alone up there atop of that hill"—they remarked as the days shortened, and the first snow began to pile up under the quadruple row of elms along the common.

Well, if I've given you a sufficiently clear idea of Whitegates and the Clayburns—who shared with their old house a sort of reassuring orderliness and dignity—I'll efface myself, and tell the tale, not in my cousin's words, for they were too confused and fragmentary, but as I built it up gradually out of her half-avowals and nervous reticences. If the thing happened at all—and I must leave you to judge of that— I think it must have happened in this way. . . .

I

The morning had been bitter, with a driving sleet—though it was only the last day of October—but after lunch a watery sun showed for a while through banked-up woolly clouds, and tempted Sara Clayburn out. She was an energetic walker, and given, at that season, to tramping three or four miles along the valley road, and coming back by way of Shaker's wood. She had made her usual round, and was following the main drive to the house when she overtook a plainly-dressed woman walking in the same direction. If the scene had not been so lonely—the way to Whitegates at the end of an autumn day was not a frequented one—Mrs. Clayburn might not have paid any attention to the woman, for she was in no way noticeable; but when she caught up with the intruder my cousin was surprised to find that she was a stranger—for the mistress of Whitegates prided herself on knowing, at least by sight, most of her country neighbors. It was almost dark, and the woman's face was hardly visible, but Mrs. Clayburn told me she recalled her as middle-aged, plain and rather pale.

Mrs. Clayburn greeted her, and then added: "You're going to the house?"

"Yes, ma'am," the woman answered, in a voice that the Connecticut Valley in old days would have called "foreign," but that would have been unnoticed by ears used to the modern multiplicity of tongues. "No, I couldn't say where she came from," Sara always said. "What struck me as queer was that I didn't know her."

She asked the woman, politely, what she wanted, and the woman answered: "Only to see one of the girls." The answer was natural enough, and Mrs. Clayburn nodded and turned off from the drive to the lower part of the gardens, so that she saw no more of the visitor then or afterward. And, in fact, a half hour later something happened which put the stranger entirely out of her mind. The brisk and light-footed Mrs. Clayburn, as she approached the house, slipped on a frozen puddle, turned her ankle and lay suddenly helpless.

Price, the butler, and Agnes, the dour old Scottish maid whom Sara had inherited from her mother-in-law, of course knew exactly what to do. In no time they had their mistress stretched out on a lounge, and Dr. Selgrove had been called up from Norrington. When he arrived, he ordered Mrs. Clayburn to bed, did the necessary examining and bandaging, and shook his head over her ankle, which he feared was fractured. He thought, however, that if she would swear not to get up, or even shift the position of her leg, he could spare her the discomfort of putting it in plaster. Mrs. Clayburn agreed, the more promptly as the doctor warned her that any rash movement would prolong her immobility. Her quick imperious nature made the prospect trying, and she was annoyed with herself for having been so clumsy. But the mischief was done, and she immediately thought what an opportunity she would have for going over her accounts and catching up with her correspondence. So she settled down resignedly in her bed.

"And you won't miss much, you know, if you have to stay there a few days. It's beginning to snow, and it looks as if we were in for a good spell of it," the doctor remarked, glancing through the window as he gathered up his implements. "Well, we don't often get snow here as early as this; but winter's got to begin sometime," he concluded philosophically. At the door he stopped to add: "You don't want me to send up a nurse from Norrington? Not to nurse you, you know; there's nothing much to do till I see you again. But this is a pretty lonely place when the snow begins, and I thought maybe—"

Sara Clayburn laughed. "Lonely? With my old servants? You forget how many winters I've spent here alone with them. Two of them were with me in my mother-in-law's time."

"That's so," Dr. Selgrove agreed. "You're a good deal luckier than most people, that way. Well, let me see; this is Saturday. We'll have to let the inflammation go down before we can X-ray you. Monday morning, first thing, I'll be here with the X-ray man. If you want me sooner, call me up." And he was gone.

II

The foot at first, had not been very painful; but toward the small hours Mrs. Clayburn began to suffer. She was a bad patient, like most healthy and active people. Not being used to pain she did not know how to bear it, and the hours of wakefulness and immobility seemed endless. Agnes, before leaving her, had made everything as comfortable as possible. She had put a jug of lemonade within reach, and had even (Mrs. Clayburn thought it odd afterward) insisted on bringing in a tray with sandwiches and a thermos of tea. "In case you're hungry in the night, madam."

"Thank you; but I'm never hungry in the night. And I certainly shan't be tonight—only thirsty. I think I'm feverish."

"Well, there's the lemonade, madam."

"That will do. Take the other things away, please." (Sara had always hated the sight of unwanted food "messing about" in her room.)

"Very well, madam. Only you might—"

"Please take it away," Mrs. Clayburn repeated irritably.

"Very good, madam." But as Agnes went out, her mistress heard her set the tray down softly on a table behind the screen which shut off the door.

"Obstinate old goose!" she thought, rather touched by the old woman's insistence.

Sleep, once it had gone, would not return, and the long black hours moved more and more slowly. How late the dawn came in November! "If only I could move my leg," she grumbled.

She lay still and strained her ears for the first steps of the servants.

Whitegates was an early house, its mistress setting the example; it would surely not be long now before one of the women came. She was tempted to ring for Agnes, but refrained. The woman had been up late, and this was Sunday morning, when the household was always allowed a little extra time. Mrs. Clayburn reflected restlessly: "I was a fool not to let her leave the tea beside the bed, as she wanted to. I wonder if I could get up and get it?" But she remembered the doctor's warning, and dared not move. Anything rather than risk prolonging her imprisonment. . . .

Ah, there was the stable clock striking. How loud it sounded in the snowy stillness! One—two—three—four—five. . . .

What? Only five? Three hours and a quarter more before she could hope to hear the door handle turned. . . . After a while she dozed off again, uncomfortably.

Another sound aroused her. Again the stable clock. She listened. But the room was still in deep darkness, and only six strokes fell. . . . She thought of reciting something to put her to sleep; but she seldom read poetry, and being naturally a good sleeper, she could not remember any of the usual devices against insomnia. The whole of her leg felt like lead now. The bandages had grown terribly tight—her ankle must have swollen. . . . She lay staring at the dark windows, watching for the first glimmer of dawn. At last she saw a pale filter of daylight through the shutters. One by one the objects between the bed and the window recovered first their outline, then their bulk, and seemed to be stealthily regrouping themselves, after goodness knows what secret displacements during the night. Who that has lived in an old house could possibly believe that the furniture in it stays still all night? Mrs. Clayburn almost fancied she saw one little slender-legged table slipping hastily back into its place.

"It knows Agnes is coming, and it's afraid," she thought whimsically. Her bad night must have made her imaginative for such nonsense as that about the furniture had never occurred to her before. . . .

At length, after hours more, as it seemed, the stable clock struck eight. Only another quarter of an hour. She watched the hand moving slowly across the face of the little clock beside her bed . . . ten minutes . . . five . . . only five! Agnes was as punctual as destiny . . . in two minutes now she would come. The two minutes passed, and she did not come. Poor Agnes—she had looked pale and tired the night before. She had overslept herself, no doubt—or perhaps she felt ill, and would send the housemaid to replace her. Mrs. Clayburn waited.

She waited half an hour; then she reached up to the bell at the head of the bed. Poor old Agnes—her mistress felt guilty about waking her. But Agnes did not appear—and after a considerable interval Mrs. Clayburn, now with a certain impatience, rang again. She rang once; twice; three times—but still no one came.

Once more she waited; then she said to herself: "There must be something wrong with the electricity." Well—she could find out by switching on the bed lamp at her elbow (how admirably the room was equipped with every practical appliance!). She switched it on—but no light came. Electric current cut off; and it was Sunday, and nothing could be done about it till the next morning. Unless it turned out to be just a burnt-out fuse, which Price could remedy. Well, in a moment now some one would surely come to her door.

It was nine o'clock before she admitted to herself that something uncommonly strange must have happened in the house. She began to feel a nervous apprehension; but she was not the woman to encourage it. If only she had had the telephone put in her room, instead of out on the landing! She measured mentally the distance to be traveled, remembered Dr. Selgrove's admonition, and wondered if her broken ankle would carry her there. She dreaded the prospect of being put in plaster, but she had to get to the telephone, whatever happened.

She wrapped herself in her dressing gown, found a walking stick, and, resting heavily on it, dragged herself to the door. In her bedroom the careful Agnes had closed and fastened the shutters, so that it was not much lighter there than at dawn; but outside in the corridor the cold whiteness of the snowy morning seemed almost reassuring. Mysterious things—dreadful things—were associated with darkness; and here was the wholesome prosaic daylight come again to banish them. Mrs. Clayburn looked about her and listened. Silence. A deep nocturnal silence in that day-lit house, in which five people were presumably coming and going about their work. It was certainly strange. . . . She looked out of the window, hoping to see someone crossing the court or coming along the drive. But no one was in sight, and the snow seemed to have the place to itself: a quiet steady snow. It was still falling, with a business-like regularity, muffling the outer world in layers on layers of thick white velvet, and intensifying the silence within. A noiseless world—were people so sure that absence of noise was what they wanted? Let them first try a lonely country house in a November snowstorm!

She dragged herself along the passage to the telephone. When she unhooked the receiver she noticed that her hand trembled.

She rang up the pantry—no answer. She rang again. Silence—more silence! It seemed to be piling itself up like the snow on the roof and in the gutters. Silence. How many people that she knew had any idea what silence was—and how loud it sounded when you really listened to it?

Again she waited: then she rang up "Central." No answer. She tried three times. After that she tried the pantry again. . . . The telephone was cut off, then; like the electric current. Who was at work downstairs, isolating her thus from the world? Her heart began to hammer. Luckily there was a chair near the telephone, and she sat down to recover her strength—or was it her courage?

Agnes and the housemaid slept in the nearest wing. She would certainly get as far as that when she had pulled herself together. Had she the courage—? Yes, of course she had. She had always been regarded as a plucky woman; and had so regarded herself. But this silence—

It occurred to her that by looking from the window of a neighboring bathroom she could see the kitchen chimney. There ought to be smoke coming from it at that hour; and if there were she thought she would be less afraid to go on. She got as far as the bathroom and looking through the window saw that no smoke came from the chimney. Her sense of loneliness grew more acute. Whatever had happened belowstairs must have happened before the morning's work had begun. The cook had not had time to light the fire, the other servants had not yet begun their round. She sank down on the nearest chair, struggling against her fears. What next would she discover if she carried on her investigations?

The pain in her ankle made progress difficult; but she was aware of it now only as an obstacle to haste. No matter what it cost her in physical suffering, she must find out what was happening belowstairs —or had happened. But first she would go to the maid's room. And if that were empty—well, somehow she would have to get herself downstairs.

She limped along the passage, and on the way steadied herself by resting her hand on a radiator. It was stone-cold. Yet in that well-ordered house in winter the central heating, though damped down at night, was never allowed to go out, and by eight in the morning a mellow warmth pervaded the rooms. The icy chill of the pipes startled her. It was the chauffeur who looked after the heating—so he too was involved in the mystery, whatever it was, as well as the house servants. But this only deepened the problem.

III

At Agnes's door Mrs. Clayburn paused and knocked. She expected no answer, and there was none. She opened the door and went in. The room was dark and very cold. She went to the window and flung back the shutters; then she looked slowly around, vaguely apprehensive of what she might see. The room was empty but what frightened her was not so much its emptiness as its air of scrupulous and undisturbed order. There was no sign of anyone having lately dressed in it—or undressed the night before. And the bed had not been slept in.

Mrs. Clayburn leaned against the wall for a moment; then she crossed the floor and opened the cupboard. That was where Agnes kept her dresses; and the dresses were there, neatly hanging in a row. On the shelf above were Agnes's few and unfashionable hats, rearrangements of her mistress's old ones. Mrs. Clayburn, who knew them all, looked at the shelf, and saw that one was missing. And so was also the warm winter coat she had given to Agnes the previous winter.

The woman was out, then; had gone out, no doubt, the night before, since the bed was unslept in, the dressing and washing appliances untouched. Agnes, who never set foot out of the house after dark, who despised the movies as much as she did the wireless, and could never be persuaded that a little innocent amusement was a necessary element in life, had deserted the house on a snowy winter night, while her mistress lay upstairs, suffering and helpless! Why had she gone, and where had she gone? When she was undressing Mrs. Clayburn the night before, taking her orders, trying to make her more comfortable, was she already planning this mysterious nocturnal escape? Or had something—the mysterious and dreadful Something for the clue of which Mrs. Clayburn was still groping—occurred later in the evening, sending the maid downstairs and out of doors into the bitter night? Perhaps one of the men at the garage—where the chauffeur and gardener lived—had been suddenly taken ill, and someone had run up to the house for Agnes. Yes—that must be the explanation. . . . Yet how much it left unexplained.

Next to Agnes's room was the linen room; beyond that was the housemaid's door. Mrs. Clayburn went to it and knocked. "Mary!" No one answered, and she went in. The room was in the same immaculate order as her maid's, and here too the bed was unslept in, and there were no signs of dressing or undressing. The two women had no doubt gone out together—gone where?

More and more the cold unanswering silence of the house weighed down on Mrs. Clayburn. She had never thought of it as a big house, but now, in this snowy winter light, it seemed immense, and full of ominous corners around which one dared not look.

Beyond the housemaid's room were the back stairs. It was the nearest way down, and every step that Mrs. Clayburn took was increasingly painful; but she decided to walk slowly back, the whole length of the passage, and go down by the front stairs. She did not know why she did this; but she felt that at the moment she was past reasoning, and had better obey her instinct.

More than once she had explored the ground floor alone in the small hours, in search of unwonted midnight noises; but now it was not the idea of noises that frightened her, but that inexorable and hostile silence, the sense that the house had retained in full daylight its nocturnal mystery, and was watching her as she was watching it; that in entering those empty orderly rooms she might be disturbing some unseen confabulation on which beings of flesh-and-blood had better not intrude.

The broad oak stairs were beautifully polished, and so slippery that she had to cling to the rail and let herself down tread by tread. And as she descended, the silence descended with her—heavier, denser, more absolute. She seemed to feel its steps just behind her, softly keeping time with hers. It had a quality she had never been aware of in any other silence, as though it were not merely an absence of sound, a thin barrier between the ear and the surging murmur of life just beyond, but an impenetrable substance made out of the world-wide cessation of all life and all movement.

Yes, that was what laid a chill on her: the feeling that there was no limit to this silence, no outer margin, nothing beyond it. By this time she had reached the foot of the stairs and was limping across the hall to the drawing room. Whatever she found there, she was sure, would be mute and lifeless; but what would it be? The bodies of her dead servants, mown down by some homicidal maniac? And what if it were her turn next—if he were waiting for her behind the heavy curtains of the room she was about to enter? Well, she must find out —she must face whatever lay in wait. Not impelled by bravery—the last drop of courage had oozed out of her—but because anything, anything was better than to remain shut up in that snowbound house without knowing whether she was alone in it or not, "I must find that out, I must find that out," she repeated to herself in a sort of meaning-less sing-song.

The cold outer light flooded the drawing room. The shutters had not been closed, nor the curtains drawn. She looked about her. The room was empty, and every chair in its usual place. Her armchair was pushed up by the chimney, and the cold hearth was piled with the ashes of the fire at which she had warmed herself before starting on her ill-fated walk. Even her empty coffee cup stood on a table near the armchair. It was evident that the servants had not been in the room since she had left it the day before after luncheon. And suddenly the conviction entered into her that, as she found the drawing room, so she would find the rest of the house; cold, orderly—and empty. She would find nothing, she would find no one. She no longer felt any dread of ordinary human dangers lurking in those dumb spaces ahead of her. She knew she was utterly alone under her own roof. She sat down to rest her aching ankle, and looked slowly about her.

There were the other rooms to be visited, and she was determined to go through them all—but she knew in advance that they would give no answer to her question. She knew it, seemingly, from the quality of the silence which enveloped her. There was no break, no thinnest crack in it anywhere. It had the cold continuity of the snow which was still falling steadily outside.

She had no idea how long she waited before nerving herself to continue her inspection. She no longer felt the pain in her ankle, but was only conscious that she must not bear her weight on it, and therefore moved very slowly, supporting herself on each piece of furniture in her path. On the ground floor no shutter had been closed, no curtain drawn, and she progressed without difficulty from room to room: the library, her morning room, the dining room. In each of them, every piece of furniture was in its usual place. In the dining room, the table had been laid for her dinner of the previous evening, and the candelabra, with candles unlit, stood reflected in the dark mahogany. She was not the kind of woman to nibble a poached egg on a tray when she was alone, but always came down to the dining room, and had what she called a civilized meal.

The back premises remained to be visited. From the dining room she entered the pantry, and there too everything was in irreproachable order. She opened the door and looked down the back passage with its neat linoleum floor covering. The deep silence accompanied her; she still felt it moving watchfully at her side, as though she were its prisoner and it might throw itself upon her if she attempted to escape. She limped on toward the kitchen. That of course would be empty too, and immaculate. But she must see it.

She leaned a minute in the embrasure of a window in the passage. "It's like the 'Mary Celeste'—a 'Mary Celeste' on *terra firma*," she thought, recalling the unsolved sea mystery of her childhood. "No one ever knew what happened on board the 'Mary Celeste.' And perhaps no one will ever know what has happened here. Even I shan't know."

At the thought her latent fear seemed to take on a new quality. It was like an icy liquid running through every vein, and lying in a pool about her heart. She understood now that she had never before known what fear was, and that most of the people she had met had probably never known either. For this sensation was something quite different. . . .

It absorbed her so completely that she was not aware how long she remained leaning there. But suddenly a new impulse pushed her forward, and she walked on toward the scullery. She went there first because there was a service slide in the wall, through which she might peep into the kitchen without being seen; and some indefinable instinct told her that the kitchen held the clue to the mystery. She still felt strongly that whatever had happened in the house must have its source and center in the kitchen.

In the scullery, as she had expected, everything was clean and tidy. Whatever had happened, no one in the house appeared to have been taken by surprise; there was nowhere any sign of confusion or disorder. "It looks as if they'd known beforehand, and put everything straight," she thought. She glanced at the wall facing the door, and saw that the slide was open. And then, as she was approaching it, the silence was broken. A voice was speaking in the kitchen—a man's voice, low but emphatic, and which she had never heard before.

She stood still, cold with fear. But this fear was again a different one. Her previous terrors had been speculative, conjectural, a ghostly emanation of the surrounding silence. This was a plain everyday dread of evildoers. Oh, God, why had she not remembered her husband's revolver, which ever since his death had lain in a drawer in her room?

She turned to retreat across the smooth slippery floor but half-way her stick slipped from her, and crashed down on the tiles. The noise seemed to echo on and on through the emptiness, and she stood still, aghast. Now that she had betrayed her presence, flight was useless. Whoever was beyond the kitchen door would be upon her in a second. . . .

But to her astonishment the voice went on speaking. It was as though neither the speaker nor his listeners had heard her. The invisible stranger spoke so low that she could not make out what he was saying, but the tone was passionately earnest, almost threatening. The next moment she realized that he was speaking in a foreign language, a language unknown to her. Once more her terror was surmounted by the urgent desire to know what was going on, so close to her yet unseen. She crept to the slide, peered cautiously through into the kitchen, and saw that it was as orderly and empty as the other rooms. But in the middle of the carefully scoured table stood a portable wireless, and the voice she heard came out of it. . . .

She must have fainted then, she supposed; at any rate she felt so weak and dizzy that her memory of what next happened remained indistinct. But in the course of time she groped her way back to the pantry, and there found a bottle of spirits—brandy or whisky, she could not remember which. She found a glass, poured herself a stiff drink, and while it was flushing through her veins, managed, she never knew with how many shuddering delays, to drag herself through the deserted ground floor, up the stairs, and down the corridor to her own room. There, apparently, she fell across the threshold, again unconscious. . . .

When she came to, she remembered, her first care had been to lock herself in; then to recover her husband's revolver. It was not loaded, but she found some cartridges, and succeeded in loading it. Then she remembered that Agnes, on leaving her the evening before, had refused to carry away the tray with the tea and sandwiches, and she fell on them with a sudden hunger. She recalled also noticing that a flask of brandy had been put beside the thermos, and being vaguely surprised. Agnes's departure, then, had been deliberately planned, and she had known that her mistress, who never touched spirits, might have need of a stimulant before she returned. Mrs. Clayburn poured some of the brandy into her tea, and swallowed it greedily.

After that (she told me later) she remembered that she had managed to start a fire in her grate, and after warming herself, had got back into her bed, piling on it all the coverings she could find. The afternoon passed in a haze of pain, out of which there emerged now and then a dim shape of fear—the fear that she might lie there alone and untended till she died of cold, and of the terror of her solitude. For she was sure by this time that the house was empty—completely empty, from garret to cellar. She knew it was so, she could not tell why; but again she felt that it must be because of the peculiar quality of the silence—the silence which had dogged her steps wherever she went, and was now folded down on her like a pall. She was sure that the nearness of any other human being, however dumb and secret, would have made a faint crack in the texture of that silence, flawed it as a sheet of glass is flawed by a pebble thrown against it. . . .

IV

"Is that easier?" the doctor asked, lifting himself from bending over her ankle. He shook his head disapprovingly. "Looks to me as if you'd disobeyed orders—eh? Been moving about, haven't you? And I guess Dr. Selgrove told you to keep quiet till he saw you again, didn't he?"

The speaker was a stranger, whom Mrs. Clayburn knew only by

name. Her own doctor had been called away that morning to the bedside of an old patient in Baltimore, and had asked this young man, who was beginning to be known at Norrington, to replace him. The newcomer was shy, and somewhat familiar, as the shy often are, and Mrs. Clayburn decided that she did not much like him. But before she could convey this by the tone of her reply (and she was past mistress of the shades of disapproval) she heard Agnes speaking—yes, Agnes, the same, the usual Agnes, standing behind the doctor, neat and stern-looking as ever. "Mrs. Clayburn must have got up and walked about in the night instead of ringing for me, as she'd ought to," Agnes intervened severely.

This was too much! In spite of the pain, which was now exquisite, Mrs. Clayburn laughed. "Ringing for you? How could I, with the electricity cut off?"

"The electricity cut off?" Agnes's surprise was masterly. "Why, when was it cut off?" She pressed her finger on the bell beside the bed, and the call tinkled through the quiet room. "I tried that bell before I left you last night, madam, because if there'd been anything wrong with it I'd have come and slept in the dressing room sooner than leave you here alone."

Mrs. Clayburn lay speechless, staring up at her. "Last night? But last night I was all alone in the house."

Agnes's firm features did not alter. She folded her hands resignedly across her trim apron. "Perhaps the pain's made you a little confused, madam." She looked at the doctor, who nodded.

"The pain in your foot must have been pretty bad," he said.

"It was," Mrs. Clayburn replied. "But it was nothing to the horror of being left alone in this empty house since the day before yesterday, with the heat and the electricity cut off, and the telephone not working."

The doctor was looking at her in evident wonder. Agnes's sallow face flushed slightly, but only as if in indignation at an unjust charge. "But, madam, I made up your fire with my own hands last night—and look, it's smoldering still. I was getting ready to start it again just now, when the doctor came."

"That's so. She was down on her knees before it," the doctor corroborated.

Again Mrs. Clayburn laughed. Ingeniously as the tissue of lies was being woven about her, she felt she could still break through it. "I made up the fire myself yesterday—there was no one else to do it," she said, addressing the doctor, but keeping her eyes on her maid. "I got up twice to put on more coal, because the house was like a sepulcher. The central heating must have been out since Saturday afternoon."

At this incredible statement Agnes's face expressed only a polite distress; but the new doctor was evidently embarrassed at being drawn into an unintelligible controversy with which he had no time to deal. He said he had brought the X-ray photographer with him, but that the ankle was too much swollen to be photographed at present. He asked Mrs. Clayburn to excuse his haste, as he had all Dr. Selgrove's patients to visit besides his own, and promised to come back that evening to decide whether she could be X-rayed then, and whether, as he evidently feared, the ankle would have to be put in plaster. Then, handing his prescriptions to Agnes, he departed.

Mrs. Clayburn spent a feverish and suffering day. She did not feel well enough to carry on the discussion with Agnes; she did not ask to see the other servants. She grew drowsy, and understood that her mind was confused with fever. Agnes and the housemaid waited on her as attentively as usual, and by the time the doctor returned in the evening her temperature had fallen; but she decided not to speak of what was on her mind until Dr. Selgrove reappeared. He was to be back the following evening; and the new doctor preferred to wait for him before deciding to put the ankle in plaster—though he feared this was now inevitable.

V

That afternoon Mrs. Clayburn had me summoned by telephone, and I arrived at Whitegates the following day. My cousin, who looked pale and nervous, merely pointed to her foot, which had been put in plaster, and thanked me for coming to keep her company. She explained that Dr. Selgrove had been taken suddenly ill in Baltimore, and would not be back for several days, but that the young man who replaced him seemed fairly competent. She made no allusion to the strange incidents I have set down, but I felt at once that she had received a shock which her accident, however painful, could not explain.

Finally, one evening, she told me the story of her strange week-end, as it had presented itself to her unusually clear and accurate mind, and as I have recorded it above. She did not tell me this till several weeks after my arrival; but she was still upstairs at the time, and obliged to divide her days between her bed and a lounge. During those endless intervening weeks, she told me, she had thought the whole matter over: and though the events of the mysterious thirty-six hours were still vivid to her, they had already lost something of their haunting terror, and she had finally decided not to reopen the question with Agnes, or to touch on it in speaking to the other servants. Dr. Selgrove's illness had been not only serious but prolonged. He had not yet returned, and it was reported that as soon as he was well enough he would go on a West Indian cruise, and not resume his practice at Norrington till the spring. Dr. Selgrove, as my cousin was perfectly aware, was the only person who could prove that thirty-six hours had elapsed between his visit and that of his successor; and the latter, a shy young man, burdened by the heavy additional practice suddenly thrown on his shoulders, told me (when I risked a little private talk with him) that in the haste of Dr. Selgrove's departure the only instructions he had given about Mrs. Clayburn were summed up in the brief memorandum: "Broken ankle. Have X-rayed."

Knowing my cousin's authoritative character, I was surprised at her decision not to speak to the servants of what had happened; but on thinking it over I concluded she was right. They were all exactly as they had been before that unexplained episode: efficient, devoted, respectful and respectable. She was dependent on them and felt at home with them, and she evidently preferred to put the whole matter out of her mind, as far as she could. She was absolutely certain that something strange had happened in her house, and I was more than ever convinced that she had received a shock which the accident of a broken ankle was not sufficient to account for; but in the end I agreed that nothing was to be gained by cross-questioning the servants or the new doctor.

I was at Whitegates off and on that winter and during the following summer, and when I went home to New York for good early in October I left my cousin in her old health and spirits. Dr. Selgrove had been ordered to Switzerland for the summer, and this further postponement of his return to his practice seemed to have put the happenings of the strange weekend out of her mind. Her life was going on as peacefully and normally as usual, and I left her without anxiety, and indeed without a thought of the mystery, which was now nearly a year old.

I was living then in a small flat in New York by myself, and I had hardly settled into it when, very late one evening—on the last day of October—I heard my bell ring. As it was my maid's evening out, and I was alone, I went to the door myself, and on the threshold, to my amazement, I saw Sara Clayburn. She was wrapped in a fur cloak, with a hat drawn down over her forehead, and a face so pale and haggard that I saw something dreadful must have happened to her. "Sara," I gasped, not knowing what I was saying, "where in the world have you come from at this hour?"

"From Whitegates. I missed the last train and came by car." She came in and sat down on the bench near the door. I saw that she could hardly stand, and sat down beside her, putting my arm about her. "For heaven's sake, tell me what's happened."

She looked at me without seeming to see me. "I telephoned to Nixon's and hired a car. It took me five hours and a quarter to get here." She looked about her. "Can you take me in for the night? I've left my luggage downstairs."

"For as many nights as you like. But you look so ill—"

She shook her head. "No; I'm not ill. I'm only frightened—deathly frightened," she repeated in a whisper.

Her voice was so strange, and the hands I was pressing between mine were so cold, that I drew her to her feet and led her straight to my little guest room. My flat was in an old-fashioned building, not many stories high, and I was on more human terms with the staff than is possible in one of the modern Babels. I telephoned down to have my cousin's bags brought up, and meanwhile I filled a hot water bottle, warmed the bed, and got her into it as quickly as I could. I had never seen her as unquestioning and submissive, and that alarmed me even more than her pallor. She was not the woman to let herself be undressed and put to bed like a baby; but she submitted without a word, as though aware that she had reached the end of her tether.

"It's good to be here," she said in a quieter tone, as I tucked her up and smoothed the pillows. "Don't leave me yet, will you—not just yet."

"I'm not going to leave you for more than a minute—just to get you a cup of tea," I reassured her; and she lay still. I left the door open, so that she could hear me stirring about in the little pantry across the passage, and when I brought her the tea she swallowed it gratefully, and a little color came into her face. I sat with her in silence for some time; but at last she began: "You see it's exactly a year—"

I should have preferred to have her put off till the next morning whatever she had to tell me; but I saw from her burning eyes that she was determined to rid her mind of what was burdening it, and that until she had done so it would be useless to proffer the sleeping draft I had ready.

"A year since what?" I asked stupidly, not yet associating her precipitate arrival with the mysterious occurrences of the previous year at Whitegates.

She looked at me in surprise. "A year since I met that woman. Don't you remember—the strange woman who was coming up the drive the afternoon when I broke my ankle? I didn't think of it at the time, but it was on All Souls' eve that I met her."

Yes, I said, I remembered that it was.

"Well—and this is All Souls' eve, isn't it? I'm not as good as you are on Church dates, but I thought it was."

"Yes. This is All Souls' eve."

"I thought so. . . . Well, this afternoon I went out for my usual walk. I'd been writing letters, and paying bills, and didn't start till late; not till it was nearly dusk. But it was a lovely clear evening. And as I got near the gate, there was the woman coming in—the same woman . . . going toward the house. . . . "

I pressed my cousin's hand, which was hot and feverish now. "If it was dusk, could you be perfectly sure it was the same woman?" I asked.

"Oh, perfectly sure, the evening was so clear. I knew her and she knew me; and I could see she was angry at meeting me. I stopped her and asked: 'Where are you going?' just as I had asked her last year. And she said, in the same queer half-foreign voice: 'Only to see one of the girls,' as she had before. Then I felt angry all of a sudden, and I said: 'You shan't set foot in my house again. Do you hear me? I order you to leave.' And she laughed; yes, she laughed—very low, but distinctly. By that time it had got quite dark, as if a sudden storm was sweeping up over the sky, so that though she was so near me I could hardly see her. We were standing by the clump of hemlocks at the turn of the drive, and as I went up to her, furious at her impertinence, she passed behind the hemlocks, and when I followed her she wasn't there. . . . No; I swear to you she wasn't there. . . . And in the darkness I hurried back to the house, afraid that she would slip by me and get there first. And the queer thing was that as I reached the door the black cloud vanished, and there was the transparent twilight again. In the house everything seemed as usual, and the servants were busy about their work; but I couldn't get it out of my head that the woman, under the shadow of that cloud, had somehow got there before me." She paused for breath, and began again. "In the hall I stopped at the telephone and rang up Nixon, and told him to send me a car at once to go to New York, with a man he knew to drive me. And Nixon came with the car himself. . . . "

Her head sank back on the pillow and she looked at me like a frightened child. "It was good of Nixon," she said.

"Yes; it was very good of him. But when they saw you leaving— the servants, I mean. . . . "

"Yes. Well, when I got upstairs to my room I rang for Agnes. She came, looking just as cool and quiet as usual. And when I told her I was starting for New York in half an hour—I said it was on account of a sudden business call—well, then her presence of mind failed her for the first time. She forgot to look surprised, she even forgot to make an objection—and you know what an objector Agnes is. And as I watched her I could see a little secret spark of relief in her eyes, though she was so on her guard. And she just said: 'Very well, madam,' and asked me what I wanted to take with me. Just as if I were in the habit of dashing off to New York after dark on an autumn night to meet a business engagement! No, she made a mistake not to show any surprise —and not even to ask me why I didn't take my own car. And her losing her head in that way frightened me more than anything else. For I saw she was so thankful I was going that she hardly dared speak, for fear she should betray herself, or I should change my mind."

After that Mrs. Clayburn lay a long while silent, breathing less unrestfully; and at last she closed her eyes, as though she felt more at ease now that she had spoken, and wanted to sleep. As I got up quietly to leave her, she turned her head a little and murmured: "I shall never

go back to Whitegates again." Then she shut her eyes and I saw that she was falling asleep.

I have set down above, I hope without omitting anything essential, the record of my cousin's strange experience as she told it to me. Of what happened at Whitegates that is all I can personally vouch for. The rest—and of course there is a rest—is pure conjecture; and I give it only as such.

My cousin's maid, Agnes, was from the isle of Skye, and the Hebrides, as everyone knows, are full of the supernatural—whether in the shape of ghostly presences, or the almost ghostlier sense of unseen watchers peopling the long nights of those stormy solitudes. My cousin, at any rate, always regarded Agnes as the—perhaps unconscious, at any rate irresponsible—channel through which communications from the other side of the veil reached the submissive household at Whitegates. Though Agnes had been with Mrs. Clayburn for a long time without any peculiar incident revealing this affinity with the unknown forces, the power to communicate with them may all the while have been latent in the woman, only awaiting a kindred touch; and that touch may have been given by the unknown visitor whom my cousin, two years in succession, had met coming up the drive at Whitegates on the eve of All Souls'. Certainly the date bears out my hypothesis; for I suppose that, even in this unimaginative age, a few people still remember that All Souls' eve is the night when the dead can walk—and when, by the same token, other spirits, piteous or malevolent, are also freed from the restrictions which secure the earth to the living on the other days of the year.

If the recurrence of this date is more than a coincidence—and for my part I think it is—then I take it that the strange woman who twice came up the drive at Whitegates on All Souls' eve was either a "fetch," or else, more probably, and more alarmingly, a living woman inhabited by a witch. The history of witchcraft, as is well known, abounds in such cases, and such a messenger might well have been delegated by the powers who rule in these matters to summon Agnes and her fellow servants to a midnight "Coven" in some neighboring solitude. To learn what happens at Covens, and the reason of the irresistible fascination they exercise over the timorous and superstitious, one need only address oneself to the immense body of literature dealing with these mysterious rites. Anyone who has once felt the faintest curiosity to assist at a Coven apparently soon finds the curiosity increase to desire, the desire to an uncontrollable longing, which, when the opportunity presents itself, breaks down all inhibitions; for those who have once taken part in a Coven will move heaven and earth to take part again.

Such is my—conjectural—explanation of the strange happenings at Whitegates. My cousin always said she could not believe that incidents which might fit into the desolate landscape of the Hebrides could occur in the cheerful and populous Connecticut Valley; but if she did not believe, she at least feared—such moral paradoxes are not uncommon—and though she insisted that there must be some natural explanation of the mystery, she never returned to investigate it.

"No, no," she said with a little shiver, whenever I touched on the subject of her going back to Whitegates, "I don't want ever to risk seeing that woman again. . . . " And she never went back.

An Autobiographical Postscript

The following paragraphs were part of the original
manuscript of Edith Wharton's autobiography, *A Backward Glance*,
and are published here for the first time.

When I was nine years old I fell ill of typhoid fever, and lay for weeks at the point of death. We were at Mildbad in the Black Forest, then a small unfashionable "Bad," where my mother was taking the cure. The leading physician of the place (the only one, perhaps) had never seen a case of typhoid, and was obliged to write daily for advice to his son, also a physician, who was with the German army (it was just before the close of the Franco-Prussian war).

This method of "absent treatment" was not successful, and at last the Doctor told my parents that I was dying. That very day they happened to hear that the physician of the Czar of Russia was passing through Mildbad. In their despair they appealed to him, and on his way to the train he stopped at our hotel for five minutes, looked at me, changed the treatment—and saved my life.

This illness formed the dividing line between my little-childhood and the next stage. It obliterated—as far as I can recall—the torturing moral scruples which had darkened my life hitherto, but left me the prey to an internal and unreasoning physical timidity. During my convalescence, my one prayer was to be allowed to read, and among the books given me was one of the detestable "children's books" which poison the youthful mind when they do not hopelessly weaken it. I must do my mother the justice to say that, though wholly indifferent to literature, she had a wholesome horror of what she called "silly books," and always kept them from me; but the volume in question was lent by two little playmates, a brother and sister, who were very "nicely" brought up, and of whom it was to be assumed that they would have only "nice" stories in their possession. To an unimaginative child the tale would no doubt have been harmless; but it was a "robber-story," and with my intense Celtic sense of the super-natural, tales of robbers and ghosts were perilous reading. This one brought on a serious relapse, and again my life was in danger; and when I came to myself, it was to enter a world haunted by formless horrors. I had been naturally a fearless child; now I lived in a state of chronic fear. Fear of *what*? I cannot say—and even at the time, I was never able to formulate my terror. It was like some dark undefinable menace, forever dogging my steps, lurking, and threatening; I was conscious of it wherever I went by day, and at night it made sleep impossible, unless a light and a nurse-maid were in the room. But, whatever it was, it was most formidable and pressing when I was returning from my daily walk (which I always took with a maid or governess, or with my father). During the last few yards, and while I waited on the door-step for the door to be opened, I could feel it behind me, upon me; and if there was any delay in the opening of the door I was seized by a choking agony of terror. It did not matter who was with me, for no one could protect me; but, oh, the rapture of relief if my companion had a latch-key, and we could get in at once, before It caught me!

This species of hallucination lasted seven or eight years, and I was a "young lady" with long skirts and my hair up before my heart ceased to beat with fear if I had to stand for half a minute on a door-step! I am often inclined—like most people—to think my parents might have brought me up in a manner more suited to my tastes and disposition; but I owe them the deepest gratitude for their treatment of me during this difficult phase. They made as light of my fears as they could, without hurting my feelings; but they never scolded or ridiculed me for them, or tried to "harden" me by making me sleep in the dark, or doing any of the things which are supposed to give courage to timid children. I believe it is owing to this kindness and forbearance that my terror gradually wore off, and that I became what I am now—a woman hardly conscious of physical fear. But how long the traces of my illness lasted may be judged from the fact that, till I was twenty-seven or eight, I could not sleep in the room with a book containing a ghost-story, and that I have frequently had to burn books of this kind, because it frightened me to know that they were downstairs in the library!

RENÉ DUBOS	Beast or Angel · $7.95
	So Human an Animal · $7.95
	The Wooing of Earth · $5.95
LOREN EISELEY	All the Strange Hours · $6.95
	The Innocent Assassins · $3.95
	The Invisible Pyramid · $5.95
	The Man Who Saw Through Time · $4.95
	The Night Country · $6.95
	Notes of an Alchemist · $5.95
F. SCOTT FITZGERALD	Afternoon of an Author · $2.95
	Babylon Revisited and Other Stories · $5.95
	The Beautiful and Damned · $7.95
	Flappers and Philosophers · $2.95
	The Great Gatsby · $4.95
	The Last Tycoon · $5.95
	Six Tales of the Jazz Age and Other Stories · $4.95
	Stories of F. Scott Fitzgerald · $8.95
	Tender Is the Night · $5.95
	This Side of Paradise · $5.95
	The Vegetable, or From President to Postman · $2.95
JOHN GALSWORTHY	The Forsyte Saga · $12.95
KENNETH GRAHAME	The Wind in the Willows · $6.95
ERNEST HEMINGWAY	Across the River and Into the Trees · $6.95
	By-Line: Ernest Hemingway · $11.95
	Death in the Afternoon · $9.95
	A Farewell to Arms · $6.95
	The Fifth Column and Four Stories of the Spanish Civil War · $4.95
	For Whom the Bell Tolls · $8.95
	Green Hills of Africa · $6.95
	In Our Time · $4.50
	Islands in the Stream · $7.95
	Men Without Women · $5.95
	A Moveable Feast · $6.95
	The Nick Adams Stories · $6.95
	The Old Man and the Sea · $3.95
	Selected Letters, edited by Carlos Baker · $12.95
	The Short Stories of Ernest Hemingway · $8.95
	The Snows of Kilimanjaro and Other Stories · $4.95

ERNEST HEMINGWAY	The Sun Also Rises · $5.95
	To Have and Have Not · $6.95
	Winner Take Nothing · $4.95
WILL JAMES	Smoky the Cow Horse · $5.95
RING LARDNER	Best Short Stories of Ring Lardner · $7.95
	Some Champions · $3.95
REINHOLD NIEBUHR	Moral Man and Immoral Society · $7.95
ALAN PATON	Cry, the Beloved Country · $5.95
	Too Late the Phalarope · $6.95
JANE PORTER	The Scottish Chiefs,
	illustrated by N. C. Wyeth · $15.95
MARJORIE KINNAN RAWLINGS	The Yearling · $7.95
C. P. SNOW	A Coat of Varnish · $7.95
	Death Under Sail · $5.95
	The Masters · $6.95
JESSE STUART	The Thread that Runs So True · $6.95
PAUL TILLICH	The Eternal Now · $5.95
	The New Being · $5.95
	The Shaking of the Foundations · $4.95
EDITH WHARTON	The Age of Innocence · $6.95
	Ethan Frome · $4.95
	The House of Mirth · $6.95
	Madame de Treymes and Others · $5.95
	Roman Fever and Other Stories · $5.95
THOMAS WOLFE	From Death to Morning · $4.95
	Look Homeward, Angel · $7.95
	Of Time and the River, one vol. · $14.95

All books listed are trade paperbacks, which are the same size as the original hardcover editions. If any of these titles are not available at your local bookstore, you can order them directly from Charles Scribner's Sons, 597 Fifth Avenue, New York, NY 10017. Enclose a check or money order for the price of the books ordered plus $1.50 for postage for the first book, 75¢ for each additional book. Prices are subject to change.